A Tangled Ruse

A Tangled Ruse

Laura Beers

MORE ROMANCE BY LAURA BEERS

ENGLAND, 1813

DO NOT SHOW ANY HINT OF WEAKNESS, LADY RACHEL THOUGHT as she stared at her formidable opponent. *Do not let him intimidate you.* He sat across from her in the coach, appearing oblivious to her internal struggle. Her eyes narrowed, and her lips tightened. The swaying of the coach was doing little to distract her from her objective: to engage Mr. Larson in a conversation. Not even a witty, informative discussion; a dull chat would suffice.

To the world, Mr. Larson was a stoic, dangerous man, but Rachel had witnessed on more than one occasion a softer, more vulnerable side of him. She needed to find a way to break through his defenses but was unsure how to accomplish that. *Perhaps her assessment of him was wrong?* No, she had to be right.

For the past three days, Rachel had done very little but dwell on why Mr. Larson was the way he was. At one point, she had concluded that he was secretly a lord concealing his identity, because his evil younger brother was trying to kill him. Eventually, she had given up on that theory, but she had an immense desire to crack the code that was Mr. Larson.

The coach lurched to one side then rocked back into place, causing her heart to race. She closed her eyes and took a shuddering breath, hoping to banish the memory that threatened to engulf her. Four days ago, someone had attempted to abduct her in front of Gunter's Tea Shop in London. Fortunately, her good friend, Lady Eliza Lansdowne, had interceded on her behalf by shooting her assailant in the leg. Even though her friend was a marchioness, she was also an agent for the Crown, known only as *Shadow*. As a notorious spy, she always kept a pistol in her reticule, and a dagger strapped to her thigh.

Within hours of the attempted abduction, Rachel was riding in the Lansdowne's crested coach, traveling to her uncle's estate near Rockcliffe, Scotland. By sending her in the Lansdowne's coach, they hoped her abductors would be fooled into believing that she was in London and still within reach. To ease Lord Exeter's discomfort about sending his daughter so far away, Eliza sent along her most trusted protector, Mr. Larson. His job was to ensure she arrived safely in Scotland, but apparently, he did not intend to engage in any nonessential communication with her.

The man in question let out a low, disapproving sigh. "Lady Rachel, may I ask why you have been staring at me for the past hour?"

"Have I?" she asked innocently.

"You have."

She maintained her steady gaze. Even though Mr. Larson had just spoken more words than he had in the past two days, Rachel was not ready to give up her advantage. "I am curious, how much longer till we arrive at my uncle's estate?"

With a soft, almost nonexistent huff, Mr. Larson replied, "In a few hours or so, assuming we do not stop unnecessarily."

Rachel's eyes darted towards the roof of the coach and thought about her poor lady's maid, Savannah, sitting next to the driver. Her stomach did not appreciate extended travel in a stuffy, jerky coach for days on end. After stopping for the tenth time today, Mr. Larson graciously gave up his seat to Savannah, allowing her to enjoy the fresh air.

Turning her attention back to her protector, she eyed his wrinkled white shirt and knew her dark blue traveling dress did not fare much better. A flowered straw hat sat next to her on the bench, practically begging to be tossed out the window. Her mother insisted that she always wear a hat in public, but she abhorred the long pins necessary to secure it to her head.

"What is truly bothering you?" Mr. Larson asked gently, quieting her desire to fling her hat from the coach.

This is a trick, she thought, as her eyes grew wary of his kind tone. What game is he playing? Instead of answering him, she asked a question of her own. "Why would you believe something is bothering me?"

One side of Mr. Larson's lips curled so slightly that it was barely discernable. "To start with, I fear that you intend to do harm to your hat," he revealed knowingly, before pausing, "and you cannot seem to sit still."

"I am dreadfully bored," she confessed, dropping her hands into her lap. "For the past three days, I was in a coach with Savannah fanning her face. Now I am with you, and you don't seem to think polite conversation is necessary."

He shrugged unapologetically. "I admit, I do think polite conversation is pointless."

"Believe me, I know," Rachel huffed, amused. "However, I do not believe you are a lost cause… yet."

"No?"

Feeling bold, she prodded, "I think you want to tell me about your life as a spy."

Mr. Larson stared at her for a long moment. "And why would I want to do that?"

"It would only be fair, since I plan to share my own stories about being a spy," Rachel replied with a twinkle in her eye.

He shook his head. "You are not a spy."

"No?" Rachel smirked. "I seem to recall helping *Shadow* bring down an entire slavery ring."

He gave her an exasperated look. "I will concede that you saved Eliza's life, but Lord Beckett did not hire you as an agent of the Crown."

Her smile grew more mischievous. "True, but Eliza made me a spy."

Mr. Larson emitted a noise that suspiciously sounded like a laugh, covering it with a cough. "Eliza cannot assign agents on a whim."

Taking a long moment to smooth out her skirt, she asserted, "Oh, I can assure you that it was not on a whim. Eliza is training me to decipher codes and even showed me how to detect invisible ink."

"Why would you wish to know how to decrypt codes?" he asked, obviously not pleased by her confession.

Leaning forward, Rachel lowered her voice. "Can you keep a secret?"

"I keep secrets for a living."

"I am planning to write a book about a female spy and her adventures."

With narrowed eyes, Mr. Larson growled, "Unacceptable. You could expose Eliza."

Frowning, she leaned back against the bench. Rachel was used to disapproval whenever she told people about her plans to write a book, but his rejection stung. "I would never do that to her. I am writing about an agent that goes to America and helps bring down the rebels' government, restoring English reign." Giving him a disapproving look, she asked, "Or did you forget that England is at war with the American colonies again?"

"Does *this* spy shoot the longbow?"

"No, her weapon of choice is a pistol." She smiled smugly.

"And yes, I happen to be quite the marksman. I can shoot a pistol accurately up to twenty meters away."

Mr. Larson frowned, clearly not believing her. "That is quite the feat for a lady."

She ignored his skepticism. "Thank you. I also became proficient with a musket by joining my father's fox hunts."

"Your father, the Earl of Exeter, allowed you to ride along on a fox hunt?" Mr. Larson drawled.

"In a way," Rachel admitted, giving a little one-sided shrug. "I *may* have dressed in men's clothing and joined the hunt a few times before my father discovered me."

"Did he let you continue?"

She shook her head in response. "No. He claimed it would cause a scandal and demanded that I stop." She huffed, frustrated. "My parents fear that I am too much of a hoyden and are determined to make me a proper lady."

"And do you wish to be a proper lady?"

Turning her head to glance out the window, Rachel winced at his words. "I know what Society expects from me, but I want more from life. I want to write a book. I want to fall in love, on my own terms. I want more…" Her voice trailed off, along with her thoughts. Then, in a tone far more confident than she felt, she continued, "I want adventure."

Mr. Larson lifted his brow in apparent disbelief. "A little over two months ago, you were abducted by the vile Mr. Wade, placed aboard a rat-infested brig with the intent of being sold to a brothel, and you single-handedly saved Eliza's life by tripping Wade as he prepared to stab her. That was not adventurous enough?"

Her fingers trailed along the bridge of her nose. It was slightly crooked since Mr. Wade had kicked her in the face. That had been his response to being tripped, which had caused him to lose his dagger and his advantage against *Shadow*. The force of the booted blow had momentarily rendered her unconscious, but she awoke in time to witness Eliza throwing a knife into Wade's blackened heart.

That experience caused her to hate being in dark, confined spaces. Her fear was so palpable she insisted her drapes remain open at night, allowing the moonlight to illuminate her bedchamber, and demanded all her windows to be nailed shut. The unshakable fear that accompanied the memory of being taken from her home at knife-point had caused many sleepless nights.

Knowing that Mr. Larson was still waiting for her response, Rachel tried to find a way to explain her thoughts. "If I marry," she began, giving him a pointed look, "I will be expected to behave as a proper lady, but until then, I want to experience what life has to offer. I want to help people and discover what I am truly capable of."

Mr. Larson nodded approvingly. "Now you sound like Eliza."

"I take that as a compliment."

"You should. It was meant as one."

Rachel tucked a piece of her unruly blonde hair behind her ear. No matter how many pins Savannah used to secure her hair, it refused to behave. It was ironic that her hair was almost identical to her personality. "Now, back to my original question. What is it like being a spy?"

A flash of anguish passed through Mr. Larson's eyes as he solemnly answered, "Lonely." He cleared his throat. "Being a spy requires you to lose yourself in pursuit of a greater good."

"And have you lost yourself?" she asked curiously.

For a long moment, he was silent, his face conveying mixed emotions. "I lost everything, including myself." He hesitated, looking pained by his own admission. "That was until I was assigned to protect Eliza. She gave me a renewed purpose."

Giving him an understanding nod, Rachel prodded gently, "Have you always been an agent?"

"No, I was in the British infantry before I was recruited by the home office." His eyes focused on the passing green countryside. "My father died unexpectedly, and my mother needed me to go to work."

"How old were you?"

"I was fifteen. My father was a blacksmith, but we had to sell off all his tools after he died. There was an accident in his shop, and he perished in the fire," he revealed. "I couldn't find employment anywhere in our small village, so I lied about my age and joined the army."

She couldn't help but notice that Mr. Larson avoided making eye contact. There was a light sheen of moisture in his eyes before he blinked it away. "Your mother must have been very proud of you for taking on so much responsibility so young," she said, attempting to comfort him.

He looked at her, not bothering to disguise his anguish. "I joined the British army, and less than a month later, disease swept through our small village. She was one of the first to die. I wasn't informed of her death for two years."

"I am sorry," she sighed, softly.

He acknowledged her comment with a nod. "Many years later, I came home between assignments from the home office and courted the daughter of a merchant. She was beautiful and kind," he added wistfully, "but we were not meant to be."

"Why not?"

He shifted in his seat, hesitantly. "I was assigned to assume an alias of Marcus Guilbault, the owner of a profitable inn alongside a well-traveled road near Paris. The French Army officers would routinely be guests of the inn, because our tavern did not water down the ale."

With a small smile, Rachel surmised, "If I had to guess, I bet the intoxicated officers divulged too much of their plans without realizing they were even doing so."

Mr. Larson's face broke into a broad, approving smile, something she had never witnessed before. "The French are unbearable, but drunk French officers are comical." He chuckled softly.

"I once convinced a French captain that I was taking his map out to be laundered. By the time he woke up the next morning, his military map, showing the placement of troops, had been returned to his bag and the copied version was on its way to England."

"How long were you in France?"

The smile faded from his face. "Too long."

"And the girl?"

"Married my best friend." Turning to glance out the window, his voice was resigned. "I was gone for so long that everyone assumed I was dead, including my fiancée."

With a surge of compassion rushing through her, Rachel saw not a hardened spy, but a man who had served his country fiercely, sacrificing everything in the process. "Mr. Larson," she spoke softly, waiting for him to turn to face her, "you are a good man. I am grateful there are men like you willing to fight for king and country."

Her words had the intended effect, and the tension in his eyes dimmed. "Thank you, Lady Rachel."

"Although, you did threaten to kill me," she pointed out with a teasing tone. "And, if I remember correctly, you threatened to kill my family and friends if I ever revealed who *Shadow* was."

"I did." Appearing unrepentant, he crossed his arms over his chest. "If it helps, I have no desire to kill you now."

Surprised by his response, Rachel laughed. "Well, I thank you for that admission."

Mr. Larson nodded his response as the coach dipped to one side. Looking out the window, she saw they were nearing the rolling hills that eventually would lead to her destination.

Her uncle's estate was a twenty-minute ride from a small village called Rockcliffe, which lies on the eastern side of where the Urr Water and sea meet, creating an estuary. Not much happened in this quiet, sleepy village, but as darkened clouds loomed ahead, she hoped that it was not a sign of things to come.

TWO HOURS LATER, RACHEL KEPT HER GAZE FIXED ON THE scenery as the coach slowly wound up a long, curving dirt path. Beautiful, overflowing woodland trees lined both sides of the road, allowing only a small glimpse of the green fields that lay beyond. Playful red squirrels running up and down the birch trees simultaneously froze to watch the coach pass by.

At the top of the hill sat a large, dignified estate, but it wasn't the imposing size of the structure that gave her pause, it was the color. The walls were bright red. As they drew closer, she realized it wasn't painted red but constructed with small red bricks. The coach jerked to a stop as she frowned. This was not the same estate she had visited as a girl. She would have remembered visiting a red home. She wondered what else had changed.

Exiting the coach first, Mr. Larson turned back to assist her. As she placed her gloved hand into his, she hesitated. Her arrival was unexpected, and she hadn't seen her aunt and uncle in years. How would they react to her impromptu visit? Would they welcome her with open arms or be furious at the imposition? Would they send her back to London?

The apprehension must have shown on her face because Mr.

Larson gently squeezed her fingers. "I will stay with you until I deem it is safe to depart."

Giving him a faint smile, Rachel replied, "I wanted adventure, right?"

Mr. Larson nodded his response. "A journey of a thousand miles begins with a single step."

She chuckled softly. "Are you a philosopher, Mr. Larson?"

"No, far from it," he responded with a twinkle in his eye. "I am quoting a Chinese proverb."

"Well, I believe you sound wise."

He smiled. "Never fear, if your aunt and uncle aren't overjoyed by your unexpected visit, then I can persuade them to change their minds."

As she stepped out of the coach, she couldn't help but tease her new-found friend. "Dear me, did you just attempt to make a joke?"

Wiping away all traces of humor, his face turned stoic again. This was the face she was familiar with, but now it appeared softer somehow. "I did, but it must stay between us." His voice was stern, but he winked at her, letting her know he was teasing.

"Understood." She tried to stifle her smile, but her lips refused to cooperate as she gazed at Mr. Larson. She found him to be a perplexing puzzle. She felt safe and protected around him, knowing he would defend her from any threat. However, he was immensely private and not one to cross. Either way, it felt wonderful to have him as a friend.

Withdrawing her hand from his, Rachel attempted to smooth out her horribly wrinkled traveling dress. She had intentionally left that hideous flowered hat in Lady Lansdowne's coach and hoped it would disappear on the journey back to London.

Before she took another step, the door flew open and her Aunt Jessamine rushed out to greet her. "Rachel, I can't believe it is you!" she exclaimed with a welcoming smile.

Within a few moments, she found herself being warmly

embraced by her aunt. Dropping her arms, but staying close, her aunt's eyes roamed her face as she declared, "You have become such a beautiful young woman. We are so happy that you have come for a visit."

Relieved that her presence wouldn't be considered too irksome, Rachel returned her aunt's smile. "I was fearful that my unexpected arrival would be burdensome to you."

"Nonsense," her aunt admonished with a flick of her wrist. "You are family and are always welcome in our home."

Aunt Jessamine was a beautiful woman with a thin face that drew attention to her full lips. Her tawny hair was neatly coiffed, and she was smartly dressed in a high-waisted green dress with embroidered yellow flowers. Even though her aunt looked the epitome of high fashion, it was her genuine smile that drew people in.

Turning her gaze towards the red bricks, Rachel acknowledged, "I don't remember this estate being red."

"Three years back, there was a fire, and we were forced to rebuild," her aunt explained.

"Where did you find red bricks?"

Her aunt smiled with pride as she gazed upon her home. "The red sandstone is locally quarried. Isn't it marvelous?"

"It is," Rachel admitted. "It is beautiful."

Her aunt glanced curiously at Mr. Larson, and her eyes grew wide at the pistol sticking out of his trousers. Her eyes then darted over Rachel's shoulder at the other guards that had accompanied her on the trip. Addressing her niece, she asked in a hushed voice, "Rachel, why are you traveling with guards?"

As Rachel opened her mouth to explain, Mr. Larson interjected, "Mrs. Maddix, may we discuss this with you in private?"

"Of course. Where are my manners? Please follow me, and we will order some tea." Linking arms with Rachel, her aunt led her towards the door. "Your Uncle Edwin is in his office and will be pleased to learn of your arrival. Also, your cousin Emmett is here."

"Isn't he a surgeon in the navy?" Rachel inquired.

With a shake of her head, her aunt replied, "He was shot in the leg and is recovering at home."

"Oh dear! I hope he is recovering quickly."

"His leg is healing nicely," her aunt hedged.

Oblivious to the undercurrent in her aunt's tone, Rachel smiled. She loved her cousin and only wanted the best for him. He was a few years older, but they had been inseparable when their families were together. "I am excited to spend time with Emmett. After all, he is my favorite cousin."

Her aunt chuckled. "He is your only cousin."

The red brick also dominated the interior of the estate but mixed well with beautiful wood paneling. The ornate gold sconces were placed strategically in front of small mirrors, projecting light throughout the hall. The main entry was circular, and to the left was a large hall with exquisite furniture and a massive fireplace. Being ushered towards the right wing, Rachel admired the landscape portraits that were prominently displayed on the papered walls.

One particular portrait caught her eye, and she stopped to study it. The painting was from the vantage point of a cliff that overlooked the estuary where a whaler was anchored. The ship had incredible detail, and Rachel took a step closer to admire the painting. Tilting her head towards her aunt, she asked, "Who painted this?"

"I did," her aunt admitted.

"It is exquisite."

Her aunt's eyes roamed the painting with immense pride. "That is Edwin's favorite whaling ship, *Jessamine*."

Rachel smiled. "Your husband named his ship after you?"

"He did." Tearing her gaze away from the portrait, Aunt Jessamine continued down the hall as she explained, "Even though hunting whales in the Arctic is dangerous, we have been blessed to have never lost a whaler or a seaman on their voyages."

Rachel knew that her Uncle Edwin had amassed a fortune by hunting whales, but she had never thought about the dangers associated with this challenging profession. Quickening her steps, she caught up to her aunt as Mr. Larson and another agent trailed closely behind.

Her aunt stopped before a closed door, and all expression left her face. She took a deep breath, her anxious eyes dim with pain. "Before we go in, I feel that I should warn you about Emmett."

"What do you mean?"

"Emmett is struggling right now. He refuses to discuss what is bothering him, but something is most assuredly wrong," she said softly, sadness shading her voice.

"How so?" Rachel pressed quietly.

She frowned sadly, placing her hand on the door handle. "You shall see." In one swift motion, she opened the door.

"I DO NOT SEE WHY THIS IS ANY OF YOUR BUSINESS. I HAVE NO desire to go to London…" A man's voice tapered off as they walked into the room.

Looking at the man who spoke, Rachel recognized her cousin, but he appeared different. Physically, Emmett was as she remembered. He was tall, with broad shoulders and brown hair, but his eyes were unfamiliar to her. They reflected an intense sorrow, appearing as if he was barely surviving rather than living.

Emmett met her gaze, tilting his head to acknowledge her. "Cousin." His voice sounded as haunted as his eyes appeared.

"Emmett," Rachel replied as she debated about embracing him. His curt tone surprised... no, shocked her. Where was the fun-loving cousin that she grew up with?

"Rachel, my dear, what a pleasant surprise," her Uncle Edwin proclaimed as he came around his desk and embraced her warmly. "It is good to see you." Stepping back, he glanced warily at the two men standing behind her. "And you brought guests."

Turning towards the men, Rachel provided the introductions. "May I introduce Mr. George Larson, who is my protector, and..." Her voice trailed off as she realized she didn't know the other guard's name.

The burly man stepped forward and introduced himself. "Mr. and Mrs. Maddix, my name is David... er... Mr. David Pearson," he stumbled.

Mr. Maddix tilted his head in acknowledgment. "You are most welcome in our home. Thank you for escorting my niece all the way to Scotland."

Mr. Larson stepped forward. "Sir, I was tasked by the Crown and Lord Exeter to ensure that Lady Rachel was safely delivered to your estate. Now that my assignment is complete, I'm afraid I must depart immediately." He nodded respectfully at David. "However, I have assigned Mr. Pearson to stay and protect Lady Rachel until the threat has passed."

"You are leaving so soon?" Rachel asked him in surprise.

Giving her an understanding smile, Mr. Larson replied, "I am needed back in London to stop the French spies from passing the bill."

Her uncle's eyes narrowed, growing impatient. "Can someone explain to me why my niece is in danger?"

"Someone attempted to abduct me in London, but was unsuccessful," Rachel rushed to explain.

Her aunt gasped. "How did you escape?"

"A bystander interceded on my behalf," Rachel stated as she watched Emmett's eyes flash with anger.

With a commanding voice, Mr. Larson took control of the conversation. "French spies have managed to infiltrate Parliament and are attempting to push through a bill to end the war against France. By abducting the women and children of influential lords, they hope to force these lords to support the bill."

"That is rubbish," Emmett asserted gruffly. "If we ended the war with France, nothing would stop Napoleon from conquering Europe and then England. Why would anyone vote to support that bill?"

Mr. Larson nodded in response. "Unfortunately, the Whigs and a few Tories do support the bill and are rallying support in the rookeries." Turning his focus back to Mr. Maddix, he continued. "Lord Exeter is a leader among the Tories and is a staunch opponent of the bill, making his wife and Lady Rachel ideal targets."

"Where is your mother? Did she not make the journey with you?" her aunt asked Rachel.

"No, my mother is at our country home in Bath," she explained. "Father thought it was best if I came straight here."

Uncle Edwin placed his arm around her shoulder. "We will keep Lady Rachel safe. It is not necessary for Mr. Pearson to stay. We have plenty of footmen that can guard her anytime she leaves the estate."

Mr. Larson's gaze grew determined. "I have a direct order from the Crown to leave Mr. Pearson here to protect Lady Rachel." His clipped tone brooked no argument. "Her life could still be at risk."

At Mr. Larson's last words, her uncle's face softened as understanding dawned. "In that case, we welcome Mr. Pearson to stay here as our guest."

Mr. Pearson cleared his throat and spoke loudly, "Sir, I am perfectly content sleeping in the servant's quarters."

"Nonsense," her aunt stated. "If you are protecting my niece then you will be our guest; end of discussion." She turned towards Mr. Larson. "I will set up a guest room for you as well. It is much too dangerous to start your return journey tonight."

With a polite bow, Mr. Larson conceded, "Thank you, ma'am."

It was apparent to all that Mr. Larson was comfortable around gentry, but Rachel could tell that Mr. Pearson was not. He awkwardly bowed after he saw Mr. Larson bow to Mrs. Maddix, which caused her to stifle a laugh. Usually, Rachel would never laugh at another's discomfort, but it seemed incongruous that a man of Mr. Pearson's size would be uneasy around others.

With a side glance at Mr. Pearson, she studied him carefully. He was a brawny man, standing almost a head taller than everyone else in the room, and appeared to be only a few years older than she was. His white shirt and trousers were snug, and she could see the outline of his muscular physique. Even without the pistol sticking out of his waistband, this was not a man to trifle with.

A servant arrived, interrupting her thoughts, to inform Mrs. Maddix that Lady Rachel's trunks had been placed in a guest bedchamber and a bath was prepared for her. She was so giddy with excitement at the prospect of a warm bath that she practically ran towards her guest room.

THE FOLLOWING MORNING, RACHEL WATCHED AS MR. LARSON walked out of her uncle's estate wearing a blue tailcoat, buff trousers, and tall, black boots. Any hint of fatigue had been wiped from his face, and he appeared eager to start the journey back to London. When Mr. Larson caught sight of her, he offered her a minimal smile, which was a great compliment to her. "Good morning. I did not think you would be up so early," he said.

From an early age, Rachel had discovered morning rides were the most invigorating, because she was free to ride as fast and long as she wanted through the fields near her country home. Ladies were discouraged from riding at high speeds, but the feel of the crisp morning air hitting her cheeks was worth the risk. It made her feel alive.

"I plan to go riding," she informed him as she rubbed the sleeves of her riding habit. Even though it was June, sunrise tended to be quite chilly along the cliffs of Scotland, so she was enjoying the warmth her jacket provided.

"Without Mr. Pearson?" Mr. Larson asked with a disapproving look.

Brushing aside his question, she grinned. "I have never seen you in a coat before."

He tugged at the front of his coat, looking decisively uncomfortable. "They are blasted things, are they not?"

"Then why are you wearing it?" Rachel attempted to hide her growing smile by covering her mouth with her fingers.

Giving up on the coat, Mr. Larson removed it and tossed it into the coach. "I need to wear it when I request an audience with Lord Downshire."

She nodded her understanding. "Eliza informed me that my uncle's estate borders his property." Glancing towards the edge of the cliff, she felt a twinge of sadness that Mr. Larson was leaving. He had become her friend, her ally.

Taking a step closer, Mr. Larson placed his hand on her shoulder. He waited till she turned her gaze back to him. "Mr. Pearson is a good man, and we spoke at great lengths last night about your protection. Between your uncle and Mr. Pearson, I have no doubt you will be safe here. You need not fear."

"Thank you," Rachel replied, giving him a faint smile. "At least this will give me time to become reacquainted with my cousin."

Dropping his hand, Mr. Larson took a step back. "Lady Lansdowne asked me to stop at her brother's estate and tell him of your arrival. She was insistent that Lord Downshire would assist you if a need arises."

Four beautiful Cleveland Bays drew the Lansdowne's coach. Approaching the horses, Rachel gently ran her hand down the brown horse's neck. She huffed, "Eliza informed me her brother is a recluse. I highly doubt that Lord Downshire will be excited at the prospect of watching out for the daughter of the Earl of Exeter."

In a dry tone, he stated, "I will ensure his cooperation."

Knowing she had no intention of ever seeking out Lord

Downshire, Rachel smiled. "I have no doubt. But try not to scare him too much."

"I won't," Mr. Larson smirked, "assuming he behaves." His eyes flickered back to the estate, all humor stripped from his face. "Mr. Pearson is an excellent agent and will protect you with his life, assuming you allow him to do his job."

She stepped back from the coach, ignoring his censure. "I do not need a nursemaid in Rockcliffe. No harm could possibly befall me in this sleepy village."

He chuckled. "I daresay Mr. Pearson has never been described as a nursemaid before."

"Regardless, I have been riding on my uncle's property since I was a little girl. I assure you that I am completely safe."

Mr. Larson grinned as his eyes rested on the trees behind her. She turned around to see what grabbed his attention and saw a red squirrel charging up the birch tree. Before he stepped into the coach, he said, "Take care of yourself, Lady Rachel." The door shut, and the coach jerked forward.

Rachel watched the coach until it was out of sight before she turned and walked towards the stable. As she waited for a groomsman to saddle a horse, she reached for a few apples from a bucket and tucked them into her saddlebags. Before long, she was racing her horse alongside the cliffs, feeling free from all her constraints. It was just her, her horse, and to her left, the beautiful, calm water of the estuary, stretching as far as the eye could see. As the sunlight reflected off the glassy water, bright, sparkling lights twinkled on the horizon.

Aware that she had pushed her horse hard, she reined him in near broad-leaved woodlands and rested her gloved hands on the saddle's pommel. The trees were situated around a meadow with purple wildflowers swaying in the light breeze. Bold, colorful butterflies fluttered around playfully. This meadow provided so many pleasant memories of playing with her cousin during the summers. They would climb trees, play hide-and-seek amongst the tall grass, and laugh until their sides ached.

The sound of horses whinnying could be heard over a songbird's enchanting tune, and Rachel decided to investigate. After securing her horse, she placed her hands out and ran them along the purple wildflowers. Walking out of the security of the trees, she saw a wide-open pasture filled with magnificent thoroughbred horses. A few old, open-grown trees remained in the fenced area as the horses grazed next to them.

Remembering the apples, she quickly ran back to her saddlebag and retrieved them. Walking slowly so the horses wouldn't spook, she stepped onto the bottom beam of the fence. Placing one apple in the palm of her hand, she waited calmly as a chestnut horse with a shiny black mane approached cautiously. Taking a moment to admire him, she noted the ears were erect and slender, his neck was gracefully arched, and intelligence radiated from his warm, brown eyes.

The horse stopped a few feet from her hand and started pawing at the ground, almost as if protesting that he had to walk to her to accept the apple. Seeing the desire in his eyes, Rachel knew that the horse wanted this delicious treat but seemed to be assessing her. In response, she waited patiently for him to deem her worthy. With a flip of his head, the horse walked over to her and accepted the apple. He chewed it down quickly and then nudged his nose up against her, shamelessly begging for another.

Placing the other apple in her pocket, she informed him, "If you want this apple, you will need to work for it." The horse pawed at the ground as if accepting her terms. Feeling brave, she climbed onto the top beam of the fence and reached out to grip the black mane. Encouraging him to shift towards her, she made a small leap and straddled him. After the horse adjusted to her weight, she kicked in her heels and laughed as he broke into a run.

Luke Beckett, the Marquess of Downshire, slammed his fist on the desk. How the blazes did they steal another horse? Guards were posted around the clock, and he had personally ensured that all the fences were secure.

Last night it was reported that another two of his thoroughbred mares had been stolen, upping the total to ten horses. The new constable was as useless as the last one had been. They assumed the horses wandered off and would be recovered soon enough. But Luke was not a fool. These horses had been stolen.

Thieves were invading his sanctuary, and they would not get away with this. He would see that his horses were found, and the perpetrators would be hung for their crimes. It was no less than they deserved.

"M'lord," his middle-aged butler, Mr. Kelly, said in a thick Scottish accent. "A Mr. George Larson is 'ere tae see ye."

Without even bothering to look up, Luke grumbled, "I do not know a Mr. Larson. Do not grant him entry."

Not moving from his location in the doorway, Mr. Kelly explained, "He claims he works with yer brother, Lord Jonathon."

Raising his gaze to meet his butler's, Luke begrudgingly nodded his acceptance. He was aware that his brother worked for the Crown. There must be a good reason this Mr. Larson had traveled all the way to Scotland to meet with him.

"Wait," Luke demanded, calling back his butler. "Send for the constable. I need to speak to him, again."

Mr. Kelly frowned. "It appears that Mr. Briggs has gone missing."

"What?" Luke roared in frustration. "That is the fourth constable to go missing in the past six months."

"Aye, m'lord."

Stifling a groan, Luke dismissed him with a wave of his hand. It was rumored that the constables were murdered, but no bodies had ever been retrieved. Most likely, these men became bored with the lack of excitement in Rockcliffe and returned to Dumfries. He had lived here for seven years, and this was the first time he had ever needed to seek out the constable.

He would send a missive to John Stenhouse, the Master of Police in the City of Glasgow, to request an inspector, knowing it would cost him an additional fee. Dumfries and the surrounding villages still relied on constables and citizen volunteers to police the streets. Rockcliffe was only given one lone, utterly incompetent constable at a time. Unfortunately, the last few had run off, and these thieves continued to get away with stealing his horses.

Expecting to see a man similar in age to his brother, Luke was surprised to see an older gentleman with black hair, mingled with white, walk into the room. Even though this man was not young, he held himself with confidence, his eyes were alert, sharp, and a pistol was tucked into the waistband of his trousers. He had no doubt that this Mr. Larson was who he claimed to be.

Walking further into the room, Mr. Larson stopped and bowed politely. "Thank you for seeing me at such an early hour, Lord Downshire."

Luke pointed towards an armless chair, indicating Mr. Larson should sit. He waited till Mr. Larson was comfortable before saying, "I was informed you work with my brother."

"I do," he confirmed.

Rising from his chair, Luke walked over to the drink tray and poured two glasses of brandy. After handing one to Mr. Larson, he leaned back against the edge of his desk. "And how may I help you today?"

Mr. Larson frowned at the glass in his hand and lowered it to his lap. "Have you seen anything suspicious or unusual in the past few weeks?"

Luke gulped back his drink. "I have. Some thieves have been stealing my horses."

With a disapproving glance at Luke's empty glass, Mr. Larson said, "Stealing horses is a terrible offense, but the Crown is more concerned about any rumors regarding the French military."

He shook his head. "I have not heard of any such rumors. Normally, I would encourage you to seek out the constable. However, they keep turning up missing."

"Missing?"

"I can only imagine they grew tired of resolving civil disputes between land-owning farmers. Besides, they have been no help in retrieving my stolen horses."

Mr. Larson furrowed his brow. "How frequently do these constables go missing?"

Placing his glass on the table, he replied, "Four in the past six months."

"And does no one find that suspicious?"

Luke huffed, "You have to understand that nothing of consequence happens in Rockcliffe. The closest town is Dumfries, and that is a two-hour ride. These constables most likely grew bored and requested to be transferred to another village."

"Without notifying anyone in Rockcliffe?" Mr. Larson asked with an uplifted brow.

Shaking his head in frustration, Luke responded, "I wouldn't know. I don't go into Rockcliffe unless it is absolutely necessary. I plan to contact the city of Glasgow's master of police to request assistance in retrieving my stolen horses. I will mention that constables have been going missing as well, but I fear you are too quick to pass judgment."

"And I contend that you are not taking this matter seriously enough."

Luke scoffed dismissively. "I will continue to keep my guards and footmen on high alert, and I will send word to

Jonathon if anything should arise." He crossed his arms over his chest. He was becoming increasingly annoyed by this useless interruption. "Did you travel all this way to inform me of a frivolous concern when a letter from my brother would have sufficed? After all, I do so love to be lectured in my own home about matters that are none of your business," he drawled.

Luke realized he might have gone too far when Mr. Larson's demeanor suddenly changed, all traces of politeness gone from his face. After a few tense moments, he reached over and placed his untouched glass on the desk. "No, there is more. Lady Lansdowne asked me personally to escort Lady Rachel, daughter of Lord Exeter, to her uncle's estate near here. You may know your neighbors, Mr. and Mrs. Maddix?"

"I am aware of them," Luke replied, attempting to keep the irritation out of his tone. "However, I do not have time to socialize with my neighbors or their guests."

Mr. Larson clenched his jaw before continuing, "French spies attempted to abduct Lady Rachel on the streets of London, but another agent interceded on her behalf. Your uncle, Lord Beckett, decided that she should be brought to the Maddix's estate until the threat has passed. You must understand that this is part of a much larger conspiracy…"

Luke placed his hand up in front of him to stop Mr. Larson's explanation. "What is it that you want, Mr. Larson? I am a busy man, and I do not have time to entertain the pampered, entitled daughter of an earl."

Mr. Larson's eyes hardened, and his blinks seemed to become calculated. "Your sister, Lady Lansdowne, was under the impression that you were a gentleman," he growled, paused, and then added, "but I conclude that to be false."

"I beg your pardon?" Luke roared, straightening up from the desk.

Keeping his gaze firmly on him, Mr. Larson rose from his seat and tugged at the end of his coat. "I will make this very clear." His voice took on a deadly edge that gave little doubt about the validity of his words. "If Lady Rachel comes to you for anything, you will assist her. If you displease Lady Rachel in any way, I will travel back to Scotland and kill you."

"Mr. Larson, you have tried my patience…" Luke was interrupted by the roar of a pistol and a bullet whizzing past his head.

Tucking the smoking pistol back into the waistband of his trousers, Mr. Larson bowed in contempt. "You have been warned."

Fearing any words would anger Mr. Larson even more, Luke waited till he left the room and then turned to see where the bullet had embedded. A small portrait of him hung on the wall, and there was a hole right between the eyes that had not been there before.

Shuddering at the accuracy of the bullet, Luke walked to his window and watched as the crested coach pulled away, taking Mr. Larson with it. How dare that man come into his home and make demands of him?

If he had witnessed any signs of a French presence, he would have sent word to his brother, Jonathon, or his uncle, Lord Beckett. He knew they both worked for the Crown, and he would be a fool not to alert them of an impending threat.

However, Luke had no desire to meet this spoiled, pompous, and most likely brainless Lady Rachel. Women could not be trusted, since they only cared about themselves. The moment the girl found out there was an unattached, titled lord in her proximity, he had no doubt that she would attempt to seek him out, with the intention of entrapping him with her feminine wiles.

No, he would go to great lengths to ensure he avoided this Lady Rachel at all costs.

4

ONCE MR. LARSON WAS FAR AWAY, LUKE MADE HIS WAY DOWN
the muddy footpath towards the stables. It wasn't long before his
boots were coated with mud. It was a beautiful day, but earlier, a
sudden downpour of rain had drenched his lands.

He took a moment to admire the three buildings surrounding
a curved, cobblestone yard. The main stable sat between two
smaller stables and was the length of a large estate. This allowed
him plenty of room to house his prized horses during the brutally
frigid winter months.

Walking through the open stable door, he was met with the
familiar sounds of whinnying and his men talking calmly to the
horses. As he passed by the stalls, he took time to acknowledge
each horse that vied for his attention, calling them by name.

For the past seven years, he had painstakingly transformed an
ailing estate into Downshire Farms, a highly prosperous stud
farm. He was known for thoroughbred horses that were well-
trained, incredibly fast, and with superior intellect.

Across the stable, Luke could see his stable master, Hugh,
brushing down his horse, Magnus. He was dressed in his plaid
great kilt, a white, long-sleeved linen shirt, and his brogans,

which were heavy, ankle-high boots. At first, the belted, plaid fabric, which wrapped around the waist and was thrown over the shoulder, did not seem practical on a stud farm, but his highlander workers preferred it over breeks, their word for trousers.

Walking closer, he picked up a brush and focused on brushing down the other side of Magnus, nodding at his stable master. Hugh was older than him by a few years and had been raised around horses. He had a firm, but tender approach when it came to horse training.

"Lord Downshire," Hugh greeted him, in a thick Scottish accent. "I hud th' gumption that ye would want tae tour th' pastures on th' eastern side."

"You assumed correctly." Luke dropped the brush and came around the other side.

Hugh placed his brush on the straw-covered ground and reached for the saddle. After securing it on Magnus, he asked, "Would ye lik' me tae accompany ye?"

"No," he said. "I doubt I will find anything, but I wanted to re-examine the fences. I don't know how the thieves are absconding with the horses right from under us." He shook his head. "Where are these thieves even securing them?"

Grabbing Magnus's reins, Hugh led him out of the stable. "It is nae just horses, m'lord. People in th' village are complaining aboot chickens and goats gaun missing. A few wummin even swear that clothing off their drying lines have bin stolen."

Luke shook his head in frustration. "Who would be bold enough to steal from under their neighbor's noses?"

"Desperate people," Hugh replied. "*Scunnered* people that cannae feed their families fur they cannae fin' wirk."

Putting on his riding gloves, Luke quickly mounted his horse. "I will be back in a few hours. Let's hope I do not meet any of those desperate people."

Stepping back, Hugh asked, "Do ye have yer pistol?"

"In my bag." Lightly patting Magnus on the neck, he nudged

him into a slow trot as they left the stable yard. His horse started chomping at the bit, eager to start running. Loosening the reins, he gave him the freedom to break into a hard run.

The rhythmic ride through his property and passing pastures of his prized horses almost made Luke forget the reason he was out here. He needed to look for any signs of weakness in the fences or any easy access by the thieves.

Hearing a lovely feminine laugh in the wind, he turned his head, attempting to determine which direction the sound originated from. He couldn't mistake the pure joy in that voice. He didn't remember ever hearing laughter like that. He must find the source!

Determining the direction, Luke turned towards the far corner of his property. After a few moments, he slowed Magnus into a slow gait and stared at the sight in front of him. A young woman, wearing a blue riding habit, was straddling one of his horses, using only the horse's mane for reins. Her laughter was carefree, and her blonde hair flowed most scandalously behind her. The horse she was riding gave no indication of distress. In fact, he appeared almost boastful about having a beautiful lady on his back.

More curious than angry, Luke watched the scene unfold. This had to be one of the thieves that had been stealing his horses. Odd that she would do so in the middle of the day, but it made sense, he supposed. Who would suspect a lady of quality to steal a horse? Then again, who would suspect a lady of quality to be riding astride? Well, he was about to find out.

The lady led the horse over to the fence, using it to dismount. Reaching into a pocket, she pulled out a large apple and held it out. She giggled as the horse's mouth hovered over her hand. Once he stepped back, she raised her hand and began to stroke his neck.

She didn't appear to be a thief, he thought, but who else could she be?

Removing her hand, the horse nudged her, urging her to continue, and she chuckled.

With one more longing glance, she turned and started towards a cluster of trees that separated his property from the Maddix's.

"You there, lass," Luke shouted as he trotted his horse closer.

Turning, she watched him approach. He was awestruck by the beauty of this woman. Even though her skin was creamy white, her cheeks were bright pink from the morning chill, highlighting her high cheekbones, slender nose, and strong jawline. The blue riding habit complimented her wide blue eyes, and her hair hung well below the middle of her back.

The lady quickly scooped her hair to the side, and in a fast motion, tied it into a braid. Her lips were pressed into a straight line as her eyes glanced at the birch trees along the edge of his property. He feared she would run from him, so he repositioned his horse to block her retreat. He was not going to let her get away from him so easily.

RACHEL'S EYES DARTED NERVOUSLY TOWARDS THE BROAD-leafed woodlands where she'd left her horse. Did she dare run from this man? She had not determined his intent. He was dressed in a white shirt, tan trousers, and wore mud-encased black boots. His hair was dark brown, cut fashionably short, and he had a strong, square jaw. Not only was he ruggedly handsome, but he looked exactly like the hero she had always imagined in all her stories.

Squaring her shoulders, she put on a brave face. At least, she hoped it was a brave face. Cautiously, she watched the man move his horse, so he was between her and the trees. Leaning forward, he placed his arms on the horn of his saddle. "You are trespassing, lass," he accused in a deep, baritone voice.

She shrugged one shoulder. "I did no harm."

"You are English," he observed, eyeing her suspiciously.

"As are you," she replied flippantly.

His brown eyes grew hard. "I caught you trying to steal a horse."

Gasping, she argued, "I did no such thing."

He tilted his head towards the gated pasture. "I saw you riding a horse that did not belong to you."

"And to *whom* do those horses belong?" she responded haughtily. She knew Society expected her to be polite, docile even, but there was something about this man that irked her.

"Downshire Farms," he informed her.

Relief washed over her, and a smile came to her lips. "This is just a big misunderstanding. I am friends with Lord Downshire's sister, Lady Lansdowne."

"I was not aware that Lady Lansdowne was in town," the infuriating man said.

Rachel shook her head. "She is not. Lady Lansdowne is residing in London."

"Did Lady Lansdowne give you permission to ride her brother's horses?"

Startled by his direct question, her gaze turned defiant. She didn't have to answer to this man. "No, but I was doing Lord Downshire a favor by exercising his horse."

"Pray tell, does Lord Downshire know you are doing him this grand favor?"

"No," she acknowledged as her gaze turned back towards the trees. In her mind, she was calculating the distance between her and the tree line. "But I have no doubt he would see the validity of my claim."

The man reached up and ran his hand along his jawline. "No, I believe he would see this for what it is."

Taking a step back to provide herself with greater distance, she asked, "And that would be?" She now regretted her choice not to allow Mr. Pearson to escort her on her morning ride.

"You are a horse thief," he accused.

Rachel laughed loudly. "I assure you that I am no horse thief."

"Why don't we take a trip to the magistrate and work this out?"

"No."

In response, the man frowned before deliberately repeating, "No?"

"I said no," she stated curtly. "I plan to approach Lord Downshire about buying the horse I rode anyway."

Turning to look at the horses again, the man's frustrated gaze slowly turned to hers. "That horse is not for sale."

"And why not?" She really did want that horse. It was the perfect horse for her.

"That is a breeding horse," the man informed her.

"I am afraid we are at an impasse then. Good day, sir." With a flick of her hand, Rachel spun around and started walking swiftly towards the safety of the woodlands.

Hearing the man dismount, Rachel picked up her skirts and began running through the clearing.

"I won't hurt you," he yelled from behind her. Well, she was not going to bloody well sit around and see if he was telling the truth.

Racing through the woods, she approached her horse and unwound the reins from the tree limb she'd tied him to. In one smooth motion, she stepped, turned, and placed her foot in the stirrup. Using the momentum of her turn, she attempted to leap from the ground to mount her horse without assistance.

She failed, lost her balance, and nearly fell backwards. Now the man was getting closer. She could hear his boots stomping through the trees. After another failed attempt, she started to turn around to confront him but found herself being hoisted into the air and placed onto her side saddle.

Surprised, she looked down at the man who was now standing next to her. "I told you that I was not going to hurt you," he said, frowning.

"I'm sure you understand why I failed to believe you." She gripped the reins tightly in case she needed to distance herself from the man.

"Someone has been stealing horses off this land, and I had every right to question you. You were trespassing."

"Things are done differently where I am from," she admonished. In all her days, she had never been accused of being a thief. After all, she was the daughter of an earl. However, he didn't know that. She couldn't fault him for being diligent at his job.

"And where exactly is that?"

Opening her mouth to say London, she quickly closed it. She was not going to reveal any more information about herself than absolutely necessary. "I am afraid I must be off, or my uncle will send someone in search of me."

The man looked at her curiously, as if he was trying to sort out a puzzle. "And your uncle would be?"

"Sir, you are much too bold," she declared in a haughty tone. There was something about this man that made her anxious, but not afraid.

Stepping forward, the man reached up and grabbed her horse's bridle. "And your behavior is meek?"

"A gentleman does not discuss a woman's endearing behaviors." As she said the words, Rachel found herself staring into the man's brown eyes, becoming distracted by his intense gaze.

"I never said I was a gentleman," he responded with a half-smile, "or that your behavior was endearing."

"Then what would you call it?"

His eyes roamed her face but stopped when he landed on her lips. Clearing his throat, he brought his gaze back up to meet hers. "Irritating." His words were so smooth that at first Rachel did not realize he'd insulted her.

She rolled her eyes dramatically. "Here we go again."

A loud, demanding voice broke through the trees causing birds to take flight. "Step away from the lady's horse." Rachel shifted her body and saw a very serious Mr. Pearson walking out of the trees with a pistol pointed directly at the man holding her horse's bridle.

He dropped the bridle, raised his hands in the air, and slowly took a few steps back. "This lady was trespassing."

Mr. Pearson kept his lethal gaze on the man as he walked closer, each step purposeful. "And now you are trespassing on the Maddix's land," he responded, his tone authoritative.

If her protector hadn't been there to protect her, she knew she would have been the one shrinking back in fear.

"I will go," the man sighed. He continued to back up, keeping his hands in view. "But be warned that a horse thief still roams these lands."

Rachel watched as the man disappeared through the cover of the trees. Surprisingly, a part of her was sad to see him go. As she turned to thank Mr. Pearson for his assistance, she was surprised to see the anger in his eyes.

"French spies are attempting to abduct you, and you thought it was a clever idea to gallivant around Scotland without the agent assigned to protect you?" His voice was firm yet controlled.

Even though his words were formed as a question, Rachel stopped herself from replying with a teasing comment. Typically, when things got too intense for her, she resorted to humor to alleviate the tension. This, however, would not be one of those times.

Opening her mouth, she started to apologize, but he put his hand up to stop her. "We must have an understanding, Lady Rachel. I will protect you, but only if you are smart enough to protect yourself."

"I did not want to wake you this morning. I left right after Mr. Larson departed," she hesitated, "and I prefer to ride alone."

"Not anymore," Mr. Pearson stated in a tone that left no room for negotiation. "You do not leave the Maddix's estate without notifying me." He tucked the pistol into his trousers. "Do you understand?"

She smiled apologetically. "Then riding partners we shall be." He nodded, and she added, "Mr. Pearson, I am sorry."

Mr. Pearson rocked back on his heels, appearing uncomfortable; almost as uncomfortable as she had seen him in her uncle's study. "I prefer that you call me David."

With a tilt of her head, Rachel replied, "David it is, then."

Stepping closer to her horse, he looked up at her with a smile on his face. "Do all ladies ride astride when they trespass on others' property?"

Rachel's eyes grew wide at his question. "You... saw that?" she stammered.

He lifted his brow, amusement in his eyes. "I did, and so did that man you were conversing with."

Her mouth gaped. It had not occurred to her that the man had seen her riding astride. He hadn't mentioned it at all. For the first time in her life, she was stunned into silence.

RAPIDLY DESCENDING THE MAIN STAIRS, RACHEL WAS PLEASED to see her Uncle Edwin at the bottom. He had just turned away from conversing with their butler, Mr. Wallice.

"Good morning," Rachel said with a wide smile. "How is my favorite uncle today?"

Chuckling, he replied, "I am doing well. You have arrived at the perfect time to allow me to escort you to breakfast." Offering his arm, they started walking down the hall. "What are your plans for today?"

She kept her voice low, so no one could overhear. "I am hoping to convince Emmett to go on a morning ride with me. Do you think he will go?"

Stopping outside the dining room, Uncle Edwin shrugged dejectedly. "Most likely not. I don't know which is worse; worrying about Emmett when he was out at sea or watching him fight his demons right in front of me."

Hearing the pain in his voice, she asked curiously, "Does he talk about the war?"

"Never," came his simple reply.

Contriving a smile, Rachel said, "He will come around." She

desperately wanted to believe her own words, but there was no denying Emmett's haunted eyes.

With a reassuring pat on her hand, Uncle Edwin led her into the dining room. Her aunt was sitting down at the table reading the newspaper. Lowering the paper, her aunt smiled at her. "Good morning."

"Morning," Rachel replied as she walked over to the buffet table. After filling her plate with food, she sat next to her aunt. "Anything interesting in the newspaper?"

"You would know more than we do," her uncle said as he wiped his mouth with a cloth. "It takes almost a week to get the news from London, and by then it is old news."

Her aunt nodded her head in agreement. "That is usually the case. The bill to end the war with France is on the front pages, and the war with the colonies is on the back page." She folded the newspaper and rested it on the table.

"Speaking of war," Rachel started, "where is Emmett this morning?"

"You might want to work on your segues," her uncle suggested with an amused expression. "That was not the smoothest transition."

"Leave the poor girl alone," her aunt admonished with a smile. Picking up her teacup, she pointed towards the gardens. "He is walking the grounds."

Reaching for her linen cloth, Rachel placed it on the table. "I believe I will go see if Emmett is amenable to a morning ride."

"By all means, ask him," Aunt Jessamine encouraged as Rachel rose from her seat. Turning to leave, her aunt's voice stopped her. "Tonight, we are hosting a dinner party with Viscount Melville. Please say that you will come."

A refusal sprang to her lips. Then she saw her aunt's hopeful expression. She didn't want to disappoint her aunt, but she hated dinner parties with boring, pretentious lords that were only looking for marriages of convenience. Even worse, she had grown tired of entitled lords and their silly games. Swallowing her trepidation, she responded through clenched teeth, "I wouldn't miss it."

Exiting the rear of the estate, she saw her cousin sitting on a bench looking out towards the cliffs. Keeping her steps intentionally quiet, she sat down on the edge of the bench. It was a few moments before he glanced in her direction. "Cousin," he said flatly.

She scooted closer to him. "I was hoping you would go riding with me."

"No, thank you," he replied dismissively.

"Take a walk on the beach?" she asked, nudging him with her shoulder.

"No."

"Go shopping in the village?"

"No."

Grinning at his half-hearted responses, she pressed, "Tour the hillfort ruins on the Mote of Mark?"

"No."

Rachel leaned forward in her seat and rested her arms on her legs to match her cousin's position. "I am writing a book about a female spy," she informed him, waiting for him to look at her, but he kept his gaze straight ahead.

Shifting in her seat, she angled her body, so she could face him as she continued. "This woman travels to the colonies working as a spy. She eventually tricks the rebels into returning America to English rule."

He huffed, "That premise is flawed; not everyone we fight is our enemy."

"But the rebels..."

Emmett jumped up from his seat and stood above her. "They are not rebels. They are good, honest men who fought for their freedom against oppression, our oppression," he stated adamantly, "and won. They won their freedom, and we are now the tormentors."

Storming off a few paces, he put his hands on the back of his head, keeping his stiffened back to her. She hesitantly rose and walked closer. "Do you wish to go to America? Is that what you desire?"

Turning around, Emmett dropped his hands in defeat. "Maybe."

Not understanding his logic, Rachel reminded him, "But if something happens to my uncle, you would be my father's heir." She gave him a sympathetic smile. "If money is a problem, then I can give…"

His dry laugh cut her off. "No, money is not the problem. I daresay my father is richer than yours. Although, I suppose your new-found wealth is more than theirs combined."

Unsure how to proceed, she ventured, "My grandmother did leave me an inheritance, but I would gladly give you half, if only you would tell me what is wrong." It pained her heart to see her cousin in such agony and not know the reason.

He threw his hands up in the air. "Why? So you can fix it?" he exclaimed, his eyes blazing with regret. "No one can undo what I have seen." Emmett pointed to his head. "Every time I close my eyes, I see her lifeless body; every time I see someone smile, I remember her smile…" His voice dropped to a hoarse whisper as he hesitated and then finished, "… before she was killed."

Not caring about his possible rejection, Rachel quickly closed the distance between them and threw her arms around her cousin. At first, he stiffened, but slowly he brought his arms around her, holding her tight. It was a long time before he relaxed his hold and took a step back. His eyes were red-lined, and his jaw was clenched.

"Thank you, Rachel," he acknowledged before he strode towards the estate.

Taking a step forward to see if Emmett was all right, she was startled by a deep voice behind her. "Let him go."

Gasping, her hand flew up to her heart. Turning to see David next to her, Rachel admonished, "Good heavens, you scared me."

Clasping his hands behind his back, David tilted his head towards Emmett's retreating figure. "He is right though. You can't fix this. Only your cousin can heal himself."

Turning in a full circle, her eyes roamed the well-manicured gardens, not seeing one place to disguise oneself. "Pray tell, where did you come from?" she asked, her eyes wide in awe.

David chuckled under his breath. "I am a spy."

As they started walking towards the stable, Rachel said, "Did you know I occasionally work as a spy?"

"Do you now?" came his amused reply.

With a playful smile, she informed him, "Yes, *Shadow* made me one."

"Ah, so it is official." He tilted his head towards her, studying her. "Am I expected to believe that *Shadow*, the most notorious spy in England, possibly the world, made *you* an agent of the Crown?"

"An *occasional* agent," she clarified with a teasing arch of her brow. "Now you'd better be on your best behavior."

"Yes, my lady," he teased as they arrived at the stable, "the very best."

As David helped her mount her horse, she asked, "How long have you been an agent?"

"Six years," came his quick reply.

She took a moment to adjust her skirts while he mounted. "And before that?"

"Boarding school." He nudged his horse forward.

Rachel smiled at his direct answers, noting that he was careful not to divulge anything beyond what she asked. "And where are you from, David?"

"Just outside of Kent."

As their horses walked side by side up a dirt road, she inquired, "Do you have any family, or were you raised in an orphanage?"

David gave her a baffled look. "Why would you think I was born in an orphanage?"

"I was just curious where you learned your conversational skills." She smiled innocently.

He chuckled under his breath. "It is my turn to apologize. I don't normally converse with the people I am assigned to guard and never with someone from the ton."

Taking a moment to listen to the cheerful melody of the birds dancing merrily in the woodland trees, she tilted her head up to feel the rays of the sun on her face. "Well, perhaps you could treat me as a normal person and lengthen your answers."

"No, I cannot," he huffed. "You are the daughter of an earl. My sole responsibility is to protect you and keep you safe from any harm."

She arched an eyebrow, challenging him. "And this requires you to avoid polite conversation?"

"Fair enough, Lady Rachel," he conceded, grinning. "What do you wish to know?"

Her smile grew victorious as they trotted along a footpath lined with trees. "Tell me about your family."

David cleared his throat, his eyes scanning the woods. "My father was a constable, but my mother passed away almost a year ago." He cleared his throat again as if reigning in his emotions. "I have a lively sister named Emma, who is sixteen. She was at boarding school before our mother's death. Now she takes care of my dad."

Rachel did not fail to notice the look of regret in his eyes. "My condolences," she said softly.

"Thank you," he acknowledged, glancing at her. "My wages are sent home to support my family. My poor sister has had to endure enough. Her burden would only increase if she had to work outside the home."

"That is very admirable."

"I believe I have answered a sufficient number of questions." His eyes met hers, and they were soft, but guarded. "Now, for one of mine. Where are we riding to?"

She smiled mischievously. "You'll see," she teased as she urged her horse into a run.

LUKE'S PATIENCE HAD VANISHED OVER AN HOUR AGO. LEANING his forearms against the fence, he watched as one of his new workers walked a colt through training exercises. The first lesson included having the colt learn to walk quietly beside the horse trainer. It sounded simple, but the colt was more interested in attempting to nibble the trainer's shirt.

"This is not playtime," he growled. "Give him a firm but quick reprimand."

"Aye, m'lord," came the quick reply.

If the new worker did not obey his orders precisely, then he would take over the training session. He loved his horses. They provided him with much-needed solace and direction in his life. Furthermore, he understood that if he was consistent in his teaching, the horses would respond with predictable behavior. It was refreshing to know the outcome of the training depended on him and his proven techniques.

This morning, he had received good news when Hugh reported that no horses had gone missing through the night. That alone should have elated him. However, he was exhausted and quick-tempered this morning, even more than usual. Last night, he had tossed and turned as he kept replaying the conversation with that mysterious girl in his head. Who was she? Was she the Maddix's daughter? A friend, perhaps? Maybe she lived beyond the Maddix's property? For the first time, Luke regretted not being acquainted with his neighbors.

It mattered not, he kept telling himself. He never wanted to see that vexing young woman again. It did not matter that she rode astride better than most men, or that she had the most interesting green flecks in her blue eyes.

Shaking his head, he returned his focus to the lesson in front of him. "M'lord," Hugh said, drawing his attention. "Riders are approaching."

Placing his hand over his eyes to shield the glare from the sun, he saw a woman riding high in the saddle and a man riding next to her. There was something familiar about them. Then it hit him. He knew exactly who these two visitors were. Hugh moved to greet the riders, but Luke placed a hand on his shoulder stopping him. "I will greet them myself," he told him.

Approaching the riders, he saw the woman's eyes widen in recognition, and she quickly diverted her eyes to avoid his gaze. He stifled his own smile at her reaction. Placing his hand up to say hello, he waited till their horses stopped in front of him. He reached for her horse's bridle. "Good morning."

"Morning," she replied quickly, her face expressionless.

"We meet again."

Careful not to meet his gaze, the woman nodded politely. "Yes." Her eyes started roaming the pastures and stables. His chest puffed with pride at the awe reflected in her eyes. "Lord Downshire has magnificent horses," she murmured in an approving tone.

"That he does." For some reason, Luke felt it was important to conceal his identity, allowing her to believe he was just a worker. He wanted to see what her intentions were before giving away his advantage. "How may I help you?"

Keeping herself rigid in the saddle, the woman's lips tightened into a flat line. Glancing over at her companion, he nodded at her reassuringly. She turned back towards him and smiled cordially, but not amiably. "I was wondering…" Her voice was barely a whisper, and he couldn't hear her over the noise of the stables.

Without saying a word, he reached up, grabbed her waist, and lowered her down to the ground. He smiled at her gasp of outrage. "Now, what can I do for you?" he asked.

She frowned and crossed her arms over her chest. "I would prefer someone else to assist me."

"May I ask why?" he pressed, mirroring her stance.

She huffed. "Why must you be so difficult?"

"I could ask you the same question."

In response, the woman grabbed his upper arm and dragged him a few feet away. Dropping her gloved hand, which for some reason disappointed him immensely, she tried again. "I was wondering… er… that is…" She took a deep breath. "Is Lord Downshire at home?"

Narrowing his eyes, he found himself disappointed by her words. She was just like every other debutante that wanted him only because of his title. This woman was vain, pompous…

She cut off his line of thought, saying, "I was hoping to break into his library."

"I beg your pardon?" Now he was confused.

"Lord Downshire's sister told me that his estate boasted a library greater than the palace."

Trying to understand her intention, he asked, "Do you want to steal a book?"

She furrowed her brow in apparent frustration. "Good heavens, no. I was just hoping to borrow a few. I was unable to take any with me on my journey."

"And keep them?" He felt it was important to clarify.

Rolling her eyes towards the sky, she replied, "No, I plan to return them. Are you not familiar with the concept of borrowing something?"

"Why not just go ask to see the library?"

The woman shook her head, causing his attention to focus on the blonde curls that framed her face. "Can you keep a secret?" He nodded, only because his curiosity won out. Frowning, she admitted, "I have no desire to meet Lord Downshire."

"None?"

"None," she repeated back. "I just want to sneak into his library and borrow a book or two."

"Why?" he found himself asking.

"I have heard he is a recluse and is known to be abrasive, brash, and downright rude," she responded unapologetically.

"I daresay you are too quick to past judgement for a man you have never met," he argued.

She frowned at him. "I would have met him at his sister's wedding luncheon, but the audacious man returned to Scotland immediately after the ceremony, without so much as saying goodbye." She shifted her gaze towards his castle. "Besides, why would I want to meet a man who lived in that ostentatious castle?"

Offended by her disdainful comments, Luke replied, his tone snide, "Don't all women want to marry a rich lord?"

It seemed that was the wrong thing to say. Rachel's eyes flashed with a fiery temper. She brushed past him without saying a word and moved to retrieve her horse.

Recovering quickly, he reached for her forearm, stopping her before she reached her horse and that overly-protective burly man. He dropped his hand when she glared down at his hold on her arm. "I apologize for that comment. It was wrong of me." Waiting for her to say something, he became increasingly annoyed that he could only hear the tapping of her boot impatiently on the ground.

The sound of the tapping slowed, followed by a weak smile.

"Thank you for your apology, but it was wrong of me to ask you to betray your lord." Walking around him, she reached for the reins from her protector.

Luke was stunned. He had apologized, and she was still leaving. She couldn't go yet. He didn't even know her name. "Wait," he found himself shouting. He stepped closer to her, shocked by the words that were coming out of his mouth. "Lord Downshire is out of town for a fortnight and would have no issue with you visiting his library, assuming I escort you."

The woman's weak smile turned into a wide one, transforming her into the most beautiful creature he had ever seen. Her eyes twinkled with excitement, and he found himself transfixed.

"Thank you," she said gratefully. "Are you available now?"

Blazes! They couldn't go now. If they walked towards his castle, his identity as lord of the manor would be exposed. "No." He rushed to amend his refusal when the light in her eyes dimmed. "Would tomorrow work? Same time?"

"Oh, yes," she breathed.

He smiled because the light was back.

She continued, gushing, "I cannot wait to look at the library. Eliza will be so jealous because she has only heard rumors of its magnitude."

"Eliza?" Luke asked. He was trying to focus on her words but was fascinated by a small dimple on the right side of her mouth that only appeared when she smiled broadly.

"Eliza is Lord Downshire's sister," she explained. "She is also known as Lady Lansdowne."

Where was his head today? He had forgotten his own sister's name as he spoke to this mysterious woman. He needed to focus on what she was saying. But first, he needed to discover her name.

He stepped closer. "And what shall I call you?"

Glancing over her shoulder at her protector, she lowered her voice. "You may call me Miss Rachel."

Suddenly, realization dawned on him. This was Lady Rachel. The daughter of the Earl of Exeter, niece of the Maddix family. What a fool he was! He should walk away and not look back.

Instead, he bowed and said the one thing that sealed his fate, "I will see you tomorrow, Miss Rachel."

LUKE WATCHED AS LADY RACHEL AND HER PROTECTOR RODE OFF into the distance. What was he thinking? It was apparent that she believed him to be a lowly worker on Lord Downshire's estate… his estate.

He cast his gaze towards his castle. He knew it was massive and intimidating to most, but it had been in his family for centuries. It had been designed to withstand an attack, with the lower story structure holding few windows and a large interior courtyard. Finely sculpted turrets and elaborately high corbelling work softened the idyllic dwelling. He'd had the exterior harled to withstand the weather, but he still wasn't sure why he'd chosen pink for the lime-based mortar.

Before he arrived in Scotland, the castle had fallen into disrepair, taking a small fortune to restore it to its former glory. To the world, it had outlived its usefulness, but to him, it was worth the work.

What does the world think of me, Luke wondered. Not of Lord Downshire, but of me as a person? If he asked any of his workers, they would tell him exactly what he wanted to hear. But Lady Rachel didn't know he was the Marquess of Downshire, heir to his father's title, the Duke of Remington. To her, he was an ordinary worker at Downshire Farms. This was his chance for someone to get to know him before discovering his title and connections. Besides, she was lying to him as well. An eye for an eye, he thought.

Making his decision, he shouted, "Hugh!"

Hugh appeared out of the main stable and walked over to him. He was wiping his hands with a towel as he said, "Aye, m'lord."

"I want everyone under my employ to meet me in the main hall in ten minutes," Luke ordered.

"Everyone?" Hugh stared back with wide, disbelieving eyes.

Not understanding his hesitancy, Luke made his way towards the castle. "In ten minutes," he barked over his shoulder. As he rushed up the few steps towards the main door, it opened, and Mr. Kelly stepped aside to allow him entry. Before his butler opened his mouth, Luke commanded, "I want all of my household staff to meet in the main hall in eight minutes."

Luke brushed by Mr. Kelly but stopped at his words. "M'lord, could ye clarify yer order?"

Swiveling around, he gave his butler an exasperated look. "Anyone who works for me is to assemble in the main hall. I wish to address them," he explained deliberately.

Surprise flashed on Mr. Kelly's face. "Ye wish tae address them?"

"Yes." Luke was starting to become irritated by his staff's insubordination.

With a small frown, his butler continued with his line of questions. "And ye wish for me tae assemble th' maids, cooks, gardeners, delivery boys, and groomsmen in eight minutes?" When Luke nodded his response, he replied, "Ye have over one hundred people in yer employ, not including yer workers of Downshire Farms. I daresay it will take longer than eight minutes tae round everyone up."

Feeling exasperated, Luke started walking towards his study. Over his shoulder, he stated, "I will be in my study. Alert me when everyone is assembled." Just how long could it take to assemble his staff?

Forty-five minutes later, Luke walked up the broad staircase that dominated one side of the main hall with Mr. Kelly trailing close behind. Turning to address his servants, he could see some of the men and women glancing nervously at each other. Luke had never called a meeting before. He preferred to let his butler handle the staff. However, he needed to explain his unusual situation.

Except for the sound of a cough here or there, the hall was silent. With a booming voice, Luke announced, "Tomorrow a *Miss* Rachel will be visiting us. Do not be fooled by her name because she is no mere country miss. Her true name is Lady Rachel, and she is the daughter of one of the most powerful men in the Tory party."

Luke was met with expressionless stares as he pressed forward. "I have not discovered why she is concealing her identity, but I intend to find out. Lady Rachel assumed incorrectly that I was employed at Downshire Farms and does not know my name or title. I want to keep it that way." He clasped his hands behind his back. "When Lady Rachel is present, you will keep up the pretext of calling her Miss Rachel and," he paused, dramatically, "you will refer to me as John."

Mr. Kelly cleared his throat. "John? But your given name is Luke."

"I am aware of my given name, Mr. Kelly," he replied dryly, "but I have reason to believe that Lady Rachel is aware that Luke is my Christian name. She is good friends with my sister, Lady Lansdowne, after all."

Pacing back and forth along the full tread, he continued with his tirade. "If I am with Lady Rachel, you do not bow or address me formally. You will treat me as a fellow servant and show me no favoritism. Do I make myself clear?" His voice was firm, uncompromising.

Stopping, he glared down at the large group. With a swipe of his hand, he declared harshly, "If anyone slips up or makes a mistake, you will be fired immediately, with no references." A few of the maids in the front row started whimpering at his threats, but he cared not. He would ensure that Mr. Kelly would remind every member of his staff of their role to play tomorrow. Before he turned to leave, he added, "Lastly, be on your guard, because there is still a horse thief in the woods."

Mr. Kelly followed him up the stairs and down the hall before he said, "Sir, if I may."

Keeping his back rigid, Luke turned to face his butler. "Yes."

He walked closer, keeping his voice discreet. "I find that bonnie lasses do not like tae be lied tae. Have ye considered asking her why she introduced herself as Miss Rachel and not Lady Rachel?" He had a concerned look on his brow. "Ye might discover that she has a good reason tae conceal her identity."

Luke clenched his jaw tightly. "You are wrong," he argued. "Based on my experience, it is ingrained in all women to lie and deceive."

Mr. Kelly's eyes softened, reflecting pity. "Yer experience is narrow-minded, m'lord. Ye are wrong tae believe that aboot all wummin." Taking one more step closer, he tilted his head towards him. "If Lady Rachel is a friend of yer sister's, should ye not give her th' benefit of th' doubt?"

Hardening his resolve, he refused to re-evaluate his judgment of Lady Rachel. "To answer your question, no, I am not familiar enough with my sister to trust her when it comes to the selection of her friends." Frowning, he continued to explain, "You must understand, except for attending her wedding, I haven't seen my sister in more than seven years."

"Perhaps ye don't know Lady Rachel well enough tae judge her so harshly then?"

"No," Luke said sharply. "It is wrong of *her* to try to deceive me." With a huff, he retreated into the quiet solitude of his bedchamber. For so long he had been alone. Maybe his actions were deplorable? No, Lady Rachel was up to something.

SAVANNAH JABBED ANOTHER PIN INTO HER HAIR. "ALMOST there, my lady."

"Ouch," Rachel mumbled under her breath. She had learned a long time ago that pins were uncooperative when it came to her hair and complaining did no good. Her lady's maid always did the best she could, with the least amount of pain possible.

Stepping back, Savannah smiled at her mistress. "You look beautiful."

Staring at her reflection, Rachel saw her hair was piled high on top of her head, and small ringlets framed her face. "I am dreading this dinner party," she shared as she rose from her dressing table.

"And why is that?" her lady's maid inquired as she assisted Rachel into an azure dress with jeweled, embroidered flowers.

Diligently, Savannah began fastening the dozens of small buttons along the back. Rachel sighed, "I tire of the marriage mart. To be honest, I was relieved to have been sent to Scotland during the Season, or at least part of it."

"You are only twenty-three," Savannah reminded her. "Besides, the downstairs maids have told me that Lord Melville is very handsome and charming."

"Perhaps a summer flirtation would be a fun distraction," Rachel mused. "If not, I will sequester myself in the library and read to my heart's content."

"I have never known you to play with another's affections," Savannah stated, stepping back after finishing the last button.

She walked to the dressing table, picked up her matching long kid gloves, and pulled them on. "I need to do some research. A female spy must flirt with men to keep them engaged."

Reorganizing the dressing table, her lady's maid gave her head a shake of disapproval. "There are other ways to entertain a man, my lady."

"The last few Seasons, I attempted to engage men in intellectually stimulating conversations about books, but that approach has never proved successful," Rachel admitted sadly. "I've had many suitors simply because of my father's title. Now that the ton has learned of my grandmother's inheritance, I can't count the number of gentlemen who come calling."

Savannah picked up a red shawl and handed it to Rachel. "It could be that the gentlemen are now seeing you for what you truly are... a beautiful lady with a keen intellect."

Wrapping the shawl around her shoulders, Rachel corrected her. "Rather an heiress with hoydenish tendencies."

"Yes, what a burden your life must be," Savannah teased as she drifted out of the room with a pair of Rachel's shoes to be polished.

A few minutes later, she found herself outside the drawing room. She could hear merry voices floating out into the hall. Forcing a polite smile on her lips, she walked into the room and saw her aunt and uncle talking to a very handsome man. He was tall, with broad shoulders, and in full dress attire. His black hair had the most unusual wave to it, but it was his strong nose that was his most handsome feature.

She was vaguely aware of her aunt introducing her to Lord Melville, but she became distracted when his piercing blue eyes landed on her. He reached for her gloved hand, gently bringing it up to his lips. "It is a pleasure to meet you, Lady Rachel."

Finally finding her voice, she replied, "The pleasure is mine, Lord Melville."

He smiled at her compliment and released her hand. "Your aunt has told me much about you."

She raised her eyebrows in surprise.

With no hesitation, he continued, "All good things, I assure you."

With a small laugh, her aunt added, "I informed Lord Melville that you have joined us on holiday and how pleased we are that you could visit."

Remaining close to her, Lord Melville stated, "I am surprised that your mother and father allowed you to leave during the Season."

With a smile to soften her words, she went on the defensive, mindful that he was her aunt's guest. "I am a grown woman, Lord Melville, and my parents have raised me to have my own mind."

"Point taken, my lady," he said, his tone holding amusement.

Dressed in a black dinner jacket, Emmett walked into the room and stopped when he saw Lord Melville. Rachel was positive she heard him mumble an expletive under his breath. Before her cousin could retreat, Aunt Jessamine cheerfully announced that dinner was ready.

Lord Melville offered his arm, which she politely accepted, and he escorted her into the dining room. After they were seated, her aunt shared, "Lord Melville has graciously come to take care of his ailing aunt, who is our dear neighbor."

Picking up his glass, Emmett interjected, "I believe he is more interested in assuring his aunt's will lists him as the beneficiary."

Leaning back in his chair, Lord Melville maintained a polite, but tense smile on his face. "Sadly, our society places great emphasis on wealth and position, but I value more the connections I make with friends and family." His eyes met hers. "Family is what is truly important."

Picking up his glass, Emmett twirled it as he appeared to ponder Lord Melville's words with skepticism on his face. After a moment, he placed the glass down on the table. "I find it interesting that you preach of family when the first you ever visited your aunt was seven months ago."

"It's such a shame that all those years were wasted." A sad smile formed on Lord Melville's lips. "How I wish I could go back in time and convince my father to allow us to visit his sister." He sighed. "My father and aunt had a falling out, and we were forbidden to see her."

"That is horrible," Rachel said, reaching for her glass.

"It truly was," he stated. "However, my father passed away last year, and I immediately set out to right his wrongs."

Leaning forward, Emmett rested his forearms on the table, causing Aunt Jessamine to cast a disapproving glance his way. "It is rumored that your aunt lies in a coma, but you are attending dinner parties with your neighbors," her cousin mocked.

Nodding, Lord Melville admitted, "It is true. My aunt is in a coma, but she would want me to go out and enjoy the world."

Rachel couldn't help but notice that the handsome viscount always managed to say the right words. They were smooth, sounding sincere, but his speech almost sounded rehearsed. And for some unknown reason, Emmett seemed to loathe the man. Interesting, she thought as she took a sip, feeling the tension between the two men.

Her cousin scoffed. "Aye, and does that include leaving more than a dozen women with child?"

Aunt Jessamine gasped as Uncle Edwin declared, "That is quite enough! Lord Melville is our guest."

Shoving back his chair, Emmett rose and glared at Lord Melville. "I agree, Father. That is enough."

Without another word he exited the dining room, leaving everyone looking awkwardly at each other.

Graciously, Lord Melville broke the silence. "I do not hold Emmett's words against him. He has served king and country admirably, and I fear he hasn't fully left the horrors of the war behind."

Her uncle nodded tensely. "I agree with your sentiment. Thank you for your understanding."

As the next course came out, Aunt Jessamine said, "I do apologize for my son's behavior, and I hope that you will join us again for dinner."

Shifting his gaze to her, Lord Melville gave her a roguish smile. "I would be honored to join you for dinner again, assuming the lovely Lady Rachel will also be in attendance."

With blushing cheeks, Rachel lowered her gaze towards her lap. Could Lord Melville be as dashing as he appeared, or was he as despicable as Emmett implied? She would have to investigate this further.

❧ 7 ❧

RACING OUT THE MAIN DOOR, RACHEL HEADED TOWARDS THE stable. She was eager to see Lord Downshire's library, regardless of whether that stubborn, brooding man had to accompany her. This morning, as she lay in bed, she realized that he never mentioned his name or his position.

The man was undoubtedly handsome, but his eyes held distrust. She sensed that he was more than he let on. However, she did not have time to unravel that mystery, nor did she want to. He just made her angry. The man would say something pleasant, only to follow it with an insult. He was a walking contradiction.

Despite everything, her taking extra care with her person this morning had nothing to do with Lord Downshire's employee. Since it was only a short ride to Downshire Farms, she opted to wear a primrose dress with a rich blue spencer in lieu of her riding habit. To complete her look, Savanah had twisted her hair into a simple but elegant style.

Secretly, Rachel was hoping she would run into Lord Melville. Was he truly a rogue? His smooth, rehearsed words indicated he most likely was, but perhaps he was genuine.

Maybe he really was a loving nephew that came only to care for his ailing aunt.

Lost in thought, she entered the stable and almost ran into her cousin as he led his horse out. Taking a step back, she took a moment to really look at Emmett. He was dressed in riding clothes, his hair groomed, and his Hessian boots were polished to perfection, but he seemed hollow, defeated. What was causing Emmett to hurt so deeply?

With a furrowed brow, she ventured to ask her cousin about his pain. "What happened?" Rachel didn't think she needed to clarify her question. She was sure they both knew what she was asking.

With a huff, Emmett ignored her and continued to lead his horse out of the stable. He is not going to get away that easily, she thought, as she started walking next to him.

In silence, they walked side-by-side until Emmett started to mount the horse. Reaching over, Rachel placed her hand on the sleeve of his riding coat, repeating her question. "What happened?"

Removing his foot from the stirrup, he turned to face her, his jaw tight. "It does not matter."

"How can you say that to me?" she asked. "Of course, it matters. I want to understand why you are in pain."

Emmett shook his head in response. "What makes you think I am in pain?"

She widened her eyes in disbelief. "I haven't seen you smile since I arrived in Scotland, and not once have you teased me by calling me a wee lass." She gave him a knowing look, dreading the truthfulness of her next few words. "My fun-loving cousin is gone and is replaced with a shell of a man."

Expecting anger in response, she was disappointed when Emmett just sighed. "I can't change what I have done, but I can atone for it."

"What have you done?"

Turning his head to look out towards the cliff, Emmett's eyes roamed the horizon. It was as if he was searching for something to help him find what he had lost. At last, he said, "Let it go, Rachel."

Fighting a strong urge to roll her eyes at his dismissive words, she decided to change tactics. "Where are you riding this morning?"

Grabbing the horn of the saddle, Emmett placed his foot into the stirrup and mounted the horse. Looking down at her, he replied, "I have some business in the village."

"But it is so early," she stated in confusion.

Emmett frowned. "The village does not have a doctor, and the closest village that does is a five-hour walk away."

"That is admirable of you," she admitted as she watched the sun rise high over the cliffs.

Maneuvering the horse away from her, Emmett warned, "Stay away from Lord Melville. He is a wolf in sheep's clothing."

"How do you know this?"

Emmett glanced over her shoulder. "Keep my cousin away from Lord Melville."

Turning her head to see who he was speaking to, Rachel saw David standing behind her with two saddled horses. He answered quickly, "Yes, sir."

She pursed her lips toward her protector. How dare he take orders from her cousin? Rachel would do as she pleased, and if she wanted to see Lord Melville, then she would. Focusing back on her cousin, she said, "You do not get to dictate whom I spend my time with. I will do as you ask only if you tell me why Lord Melville is so horrible."

"I am afraid I cannot, but you must trust me," Emmett responded dismissively.

The wind whipped around her, causing her skirts to billow around her legs. "You ask me to trust you, but you do not trust me," she challenged. "You refuse to talk to me even though I see the anguish in your eyes."

Emmett sighed deeply. "I will not burden you with my troubles. How could you possibly understand the horrors I have seen?"

Fisting her hands against her sides, the frustration that had been festering inside her exploded. "How could I understand?" she shouted. "I was abducted from my bedroom at knifepoint and kept in the cargo hold of a merchant ship for two days." Her voice rattled with emotion. "I had rats climb on top of me, and I could not stop them." She shuddered at the memory. "My hands were chained to the floor."

Rachel stepped closer to Emmett's horse and pointed a finger at him. "Yet, when *Shadow* came to free us, I had to be strong. I had to help save myself and the other women." She shook her head adamantly. "You do not get to sit there and say that I wouldn't understand the horrors you saw. I've lived through hell, and my nightmares won't let me forget."

Emmett stared at her with shock on his face. He took a hand and wiped it over his chin before saying, "I had no idea. When did this happen?"

Dropping her hands to her side, she admitted, "Over two months ago. A man named Mr. Wade had created an elaborate trap to ensnare *Shadow*, but in the end, *Shadow* saved all of us and killed Wade."

His face grew solemn. "I heard about that, but I had no idea you were one of the women abducted."

Shifting her eyes away from her cousin's sympathetic gaze, Rachel stifled a sigh. "No one knows except my parents," she paused, "and the other women."

Emmett dismounted and reached for her, pulling her tight against him. Immediately, her arms slid around his waist, and she clung to him. He spoke into her hair, "I am so sorry, cousin. Were you hurt?"

"Mr. Wade broke my nose when he kicked me, but everything else was superficial."

He asked, his voice hesitant, "Were you abused?"

Understanding what he referred to, she answered, "No, I was not."

"Thank goodness." His arms tightened around her, the relief in his voice evident.

She dropped her arms and stepped back. "*Shadow* saved us in time."

Even though his eyes held compassion, his voice was hard, cynical. "Men are despicable and are capable of vile actions. You must stay away from them."

"Surely not all men are like that. Your father isn't like that; you aren't like that," she insisted.

"You are wrong," he stated firmly. "You must stay away from me, too." Without saying another word, Emmett mounted his horse and kicked it into a run.

She watched him flee from her presence. How was she going to help him if he didn't confide in her? David moved to stand next to her, giving her sidelong glances, before he finally asked, "Were you really one of those ladies abducted?"

"I was," she confirmed.

"I'm sorry."

She nodded to acknowledge his words. However, she did not wish to continue discussing her abduction. Watching Emmett till he was out of view, she tilted her head towards David. "What do you think happened to him?"

David shrugged. "During war, people can change to ensure they survive the battle, but when they finally come home, they can't cope with what they had to do to live another day."

Swiftly turning to face her protector, her next words sounded confident. "I am going to help my cousin."

He chuckled. "I distinctly remember Emmett asking you to stay away from him."

"You heard him," she said, a mischievous smile growing on her face, "men can't be trusted. Which means I will do the opposite of what Emmett told me to do."

LORD DOWNSHIRE PACED OUTSIDE THE MAIN STABLE. LADY Rachel should have been here by now. How dare she keep him waiting! Glancing towards the sky, he recalled that they hadn't set a specific time, but he assumed she would have come around the same time as yesterday. He had a stud farm to run, and he did not have time to entertain a bluestocking.

His face became grim, knowing he would have to watch her carefully in the library. If she did attempt to steal from him, she would regret it.

"M'lord," a voice said close to him, breaking through his thoughts.

He looked over and saw Hugh standing next to him. "What is it?"

"Urr ye a' richt?"

"English, if you don't mind," he grumbled.

"Are ye a' right?" Hugh questioned, blending the two dialects together.

Skimming a hand over the surface of his impeccably groomed hair, he answered, "Perfectly content." He wore the white work shirt that he used when training his horses, tan trousers, and black Hessian boots to continue the ruse that he was an employee of Downshire Farms.

Leaning over, Hugh picked up a bucket as he stated, "That lassie got tae yer head."

"You are wrong. Lady Rachel is not in my head," he denied

adamantly. "She was the woman I told you about, the one who tried to steal a horse."

"She does nae look lik' a horse thief."

"That is the point. No one would suspect her."

Hugh smiled knowingly. "Thare is a Scot saying, 'Yer bum's oot the windae'." He lifted his brow in amusement. "Loosely translated, it means 'ye'r speaking rubbish'."

Luke frowned. "I beg your pardon?"

"That lassie is no more a horse thief then ye are."

"I still don't trust her."

"Regardless, I think it's good that ye'r taking th' mornin' off tae show her th' library. Ye have not taken one day off since ye hired me seven years ago."

He smiled at his loyal stable master, acknowledging that hiring Hugh was one of the best decisions he'd made after he started Downshire Farms.

Before he could respond, Hugh pointed over his shoulder. "Yer lassie approaches."

Turning around, Luke could not help but admire Rachel's posture on her horse. Her blonde hair glowed in the sun, and a brilliant smile was on her face as she spoke to her guard. "She is not my lady," he mumbled under his breath.

"My apologies, m'lord," Hugh teased.

He furrowed his brow in annoyance. "You must remember to call her Miss Rachel and refer to me as John."

His stable master laughed loudly, much to his frustration. "Ye will not be able tae pull off this farce. Just tell her th' truth and attempt tae woo her correctly."

"I am not trying to woo her," Luke asserted. "I am attempting to understand why she is concealing her identity."

"So yer plan is tae deceive her in th' identical manner she is deceiving ye."

"It is entirely different."

"Is it now?" Hugh asked, amused.

Watching Lady Rachel's horse meander towards the stable yard, he decided not to justify Hugh's comment with a response.

"Guid mornin', Miss Rachel." Hugh's booming voice filled the stable yard.

Lady Rachel smiled kindly down at the stable master. "Guid mornin' tae ye. How are ye faring this bonny day?"

Hugh smiled approvingly at her. "Why, ye sound lik' ye were born here, Miss Rachel."

"Dae nae be impressed. I hae only picked up a few wurds," she admitted.

"It's guid enough fur me," he said, his smile still intact.

Looking around, Luke saw that his workers had stopped performing their tasks and were all watching Lady Rachel with admiring grins on their faces. He felt his stomach muscles clench as an unfamiliar surge of jealousy came over him. This woman had already beguiled his men, and she'd only spoken a few words in their dialect. Unbelievable!

As Lady Rachel's guard dismounted, Luke walked over without saying a word and placed his hands on her waist, lifting her off the horse. When her feet were on the ground, he took a step back and pointed towards his castle. "Follow me, and I will show you the library." He barked his order and headed towards the castle.

After a few moments, Luke realized that Rachel was not behind him. He turned back to see what delayed her. Instead of following his orders, she had engaged in a conversation with Hugh and was laughing.

Huffing, he walked back to the group. As he joined them, they all turned towards him with big, expectant smiles. "May I ask what is so funny?" he asked in a stern voice.

Hugh had the decency to look embarrassed, but Lady Rachel stood her ground. "You," she answered, unabashed.

Taken aback by her rudeness, he replied, "I beg your pardon?"

She took a small step towards him, her eyes holding mischief. "We took bets on when you would notice that I failed to follow you. I bet that you wouldn't notice until you reached the castle, but David said you wouldn't notice till the library."

Lifting his brows, Luke shifted his gaze towards Rachel's guard. "I assume you are David?"

Rachel's protector was a large, intimidating man who appeared to hold no respect for him. He confirmed boldly, "I am."

"And what did Hugh say?" he asked, giving him an annoyed glance.

Sharing a smile with Hugh, Rachel said, "You must be good friends with Hugh, because he bet you would figure it out right away."

He nodded in approval. "Which I did, I would like to point out."

Crossing her arms over her chest, Rachel appeared to be mulling over a few thoughts in her head. After a moment, she asked, "Before we go into the library, I would like to know what I should call you?"

He attempted a smile, but it fell flat. "Call me John."

She eyed him suspiciously. "Do you not have a last name, John?"

He panicked as he tried to come up with an answer. His eyes darted around the stable yard in a frenzy until his horse, Magnus, whinnied, causing a spark of genius. "Magnus," he blurted out. He cleared his throat. "My name is Mr. John Magnus, but I prefer to be called John."

"All right, John," she repeated slowly. "Would you like to escort me to the library, or may I ask Hugh to be so kind?" Rachel shifted her gaze towards Hugh and gave him a sweet smile. Luke had a sudden urge to hit his stable master.

"I will escort you," Luke growled, extending his arm towards her.

Rachel huffed. "Is John always so pleasant to be around?" she asked Hugh, completely ignoring his outstretched arm.

"He is not th' most social person, Miss Rachel," Hugh replied, clearly enjoying himself.

Dropping his arm, Luke stepped back and gave her a haughty glare. "I was doing *you* a favor by taking you to see Lord Downshire's library, but you stand here insulting me." His voice held an aristocratic tone. "I am in the right mind *not* to show you the library now."

Expecting her to apologize, he was surprised to see Rachel's fiery eyes challenge him. She didn't say anything as her eyes roamed his face, narrowing more on each pass. Finally, she spoke, "I appreciate your kind offer, but I will read books from my uncle's library until I go home. Good day, Mr. Magnus." Tilting her head towards Hugh, she smiled as she wished him a good day.

Her words should have brought him relief, but instead, they stung deeply. Why should he care? After all, he was sacrificing his time to escort her today. She should be thanking him for his kindness, not insulting him. He stifled a groan. In all honesty, he had been looking forward to showing her the library. It had been so long since he had gone into that room, mainly because he didn't have time to read.

He frowned, unsure how to proceed. If Lady Rachel left, he doubted she would ever come back, and he wanted her to return. He found her fascinating yet vexing at the same time. Besides, he hadn't figured out why she lied to him.

As David moved to help Lady Rachel mount her horse, Luke decided to appeal to her love of books. "I thought you wanted to glimpse Lord Downshire's library. Didn't you say it was perhaps the largest private library in all of Scotland?"

He saw the indecision in her gaze, but stubbornness still laced her features. "I did, but…" Her voice trailed off.

Taking advantage of the silence, he revealed, "And I have it on authority that the library boasts many first editions, including some that date back to the 1400s."

Rachel's eyes gravitated towards his castle, her emotions playing across her beautiful face. He knew she was mulling over her conflicting thoughts quietly, but he wasn't at all sure the outcome would be in his favor. Deciding he needed to make a bolder gesture, he bowed and offered a polite smile. "It would be my honor to escort you to the library," he said respectfully.

Her face softened immediately. "Thank you, John." She stepped closer and accepted his offered arm. "You do not fight fair. You have discovered my love of books and are using it against me," she chastised lightly even as she smiled.

Feeling victorious, Luke found himself smiling at Rachel as they walked towards his castle. Suddenly, it occurred to him that he hadn't genuinely smiled in years.

8

STEPPING INTO LORD DOWNSHIRE'S CASTLE, THE SHEER magnificence of the entry hall awed Rachel. The exterior held the appearance of a medieval castle, but the interior had been completely redone. Royal purple-striped papered walls mingled with beautiful wood paneling, allowing the rooms to radiate character and distinction. Bright, bold-colored carpets laid on the marble floor and elaborate jeweled chandeliers hung low from the ceiling.

As John led her down the expansive hall, Rachel turned her head to admire the décor and stated, "Lord Downshire's estate is beautiful. The exterior is so rustic, but the interior reflects a softer, more distinguished touch."

John nodded as his eyes roamed the hall as well. "Lord Downshire remodeled the castle when he first arrived in Scotland."

A young, brunette maid, carrying a bundle of linens, walked out of a room and squeaked as she saw them. Clumsily, she attempted a curtsy but stopped short. A look of sheer panic came over her face as she gazed at John.

Not understanding the maid's anxious reaction, Rachel stepped closer to reassure her. "Are you all right?"

Nodding at a fast pace, she answered, "Aye, Miss. Thank ye for asking."

Glancing over her shoulder, she could see John's eyes held irritation, which was nothing new to her. He always seemed to be in a state of agitation. Turning her attention back to the maid, she spoke softly, "My name is Rachel. What's yours?"

"Angelica," she responded as she shifted the bundle of linens in her arms.

Rachel smiled. "Well, Angelica, it is nice to meet you. If you don't mind, John is going to show me the library." Leaning closer, she put a hand next to her mouth. "Lord Downshire doesn't know I'm here."

Angelica's eyes shifted towards John and back to Rachel. "No?"

"Do you think Lord Downshire would have let me visit his library if he was here?" she asked curiously.

"Oh yes, Miss Rachel," Angelica said in a rush. "Lord Downshire is most generous, and I am grateful to be in his employ." With a quick curtsy, she walked swiftly down the hall.

Rachel watched the maid as she walked away. "That was odd," she muttered.

John gave her a puzzled look. "I didn't notice anything unusual." He offered his arm. "Shall we?"

All suspicious thoughts disappeared as she entered Lord Downshire's library. One side of the room had floor-to-ceiling windows, and the drapes were pulled open, allowing light to bathe the books and furnishings. The other three walls held countless shelves with books stacked pristinely next to each other. Ladders propped up next to the walls provided access to the higher shelves.

Releasing John's arm, she ran towards the shelves and gently slid her hands along the spines of the books. Every so often, she pulled out a book and added it to the collection already growing in her arms.

After pulling out ten books, Rachel brought them over to the table near a burgundy sofa. She placed the books on the table and sat down in a most unladylike fashion. She felt too excited to worry about decorum at this moment. Reaching for a book titled *Don Quixote*, she started reading the first few pages but stopped when she remembered that she was not alone. Raising her head, her eyes sought out John, who was leaning against the wall, watching her.

She decided she should attempt to be social. "Would you like for me to read aloud?"

John nodded as he walked over and sat down next to her, leaving proper distance between them. "What book do you have?"

"*Don Quixote*."

"I am not familiar with that one."

"Nor I." Starting from the beginning, Rachel read the first few chapters before she finally stopped to take a break. Closing the book, she placed it next to her and shifted slightly to face him. "What did you think?"

To her surprise, he gave her a gracious smile, his face appearing more relaxed. "Thank you. I can't remember the last time I was read to."

"No?" she asked. "Don't you remember your mother reading to you?"

John huffed, "No, my mother never had time to read to us." His words sounded harsh, but an underlying sadness tinged with regret lingered in his voice as well.

"Never?" Rachel pressed. Some of her favorite memories were of her parents tucking her in at night and reading to her.

"Truthfully, I don't ever remember my mother reading to us," he responded in a resigned voice.

Her heart stirred with compassion. "I am sorry. Did your

mother have to work?" She was aware that many lower-class families required the wife to work alongside the man, so the family could survive.

With a shocked glance, he looked bewildered by her words before he blinked it away. He scoffed, "No, my mother did not work. She willingly chose to ignore her children, because we were nuisances to her."

Rachel's eyes widened at his strong words, unsure of what she could say to provide comfort.

His jaw clenched so tightly she could see a muscle ticking just under his ear. "I can count on my hand how often I saw my mother in my youth, and it was always accompanied by criticism and cruelty."

"I am..."

Cutting her off, he snapped, "Do not apologize for her."

Not knowing how to respond, she lowered her eyes, and her fingers trailed along the edges of *Don Quixote*. His declaration didn't make her uncomfortable, but she yearned to know more about his situation. She wanted to help ease his pain. She attempted to formulate her thoughts, but she couldn't seem to find the right words.

She glanced at him, and he was watching her... no, studying her. "Why do you love books so much?" he asked.

Oh, that was an easy question. Rachel's hands became animated as she started to explain, "When I read a book, I am transported into another time, another life, and I can go anywhere in the world." She pointed to the walls of books with a smile on her face. "Every one of these books represents a life-time of learning. They allow you to ponder all the concepts, theories, and formulas from the greatest minds."

Rachel stopped her passionate speech to see John grinning at her. "I have never met someone so enthusiastic about books," he stated.

Picking up a book from the table, she grasped it to her chest as she tried to explain what she felt. "I have always loved reading. That is how I met Lady Lansdowne." She smiled at the vivid memory. "I was at a house party and had snuck into the library to read. When I discovered her there, we struck up a conversation, and now she is one of my greatest friends."

"I thought the purpose of a house party was for women to try to seduce titled men into marrying them," John remarked dryly.

Her mouth gaped in surprise as she stared into his unrepentant eyes. After a moment, she composed herself enough to say, "How dare you presume that all women have to seduce men into marrying them."

Straightforwardly returning her gaze, it appeared that he was not backing down. "Women of the ton are all similar, are they not? They marry for titles, power, and money. They care little about integrity or honor," he spat out.

Fully knowing that he had insulted her, Rachel decided to divert the conversation and address something that she was curious about. "How do you know so much about women of the ton?"

John shrugged. "I have not always been a horse trainer."

Rachel placed the book on the table. With a tight frown, she turned her gaze back towards him. "I do not contest that. You are obviously a man that is educated, but you are also a cantankerous fool." Ignoring his reaction, she continued, "You assume that all noble women are the same, but you are wrong. Some women have no choice but to marry well. It could mean the difference between living a life of ease and one of economic hardship. You should not judge those women so harshly."

"Pray tell, why not?" John asked severely.

She tilted her chin defiantly, refusing to back down. If he wanted to engage in a war of words, she was prepared for battle. "You talk as if women are the ones at fault. Men will marry women for their dowries, using those funds to support their mistresses' household. Where is their honor, their integrity? I say they have none."

His eyes sparked with contempt. "You speak as if aristocratic women have honor, but they do not. They will lie, deceive, and accuse to entrap a husband; a husband that they no more want than the children that they conceive."

Before she could respond, a small knock came at the library door. John barked, "Enter."

Angelica walked in carrying a tray stacked with tea and pastries. She placed it on a table near a group of chairs. Turning her gaze to Rachel, her eyes were puffy and red. "My apologies. I had assumed that your companion had joined you."

Glancing around the room, Rachel noticed for the first time that David had not followed them into the library. She had been too distracted by the books to notice he wasn't with them. Smiling at the maid, she said, "I have no doubt that Mr. Pearson will reappear shortly."

Reaching for a teacup, the maid asked, "May I offer you some tea?"

Rachel moved to sit at the edge of her seat. "Heavens, no. I am not a guest here, so you do not have to serve me." She pointed at the chair behind Angelica. "Please sit down."

Angelica's eyes landed on John, as if seeking permission, before she awkwardly sat down where Rachel directed. "As you wish," she mumbled softly.

Pouring three cups of tea, Rachel offered one to Angelica and one to John. For a few uncomfortable moments, no one spoke as they drank in absolute silence. Over the rim of her teacup, she asked, "You are English, are you not?"

"Yes, ma'am, but I have been attempting to use more Scottish words," she replied, averting her eyes.

Placing her cup on the table, Rachel offered Angelica a faint smile before asking, "Why were you crying?"

Raising the teacup in her hand, Angelica's hand started shaking. Immediately, she lowered the cup to the saucer and placed it on the table. "May I be excused?"

With a surge of compassion, Rachel wanted to help Angelica but knew she could not force her to accept. "If you desire, you may go." Angelica started to rise as she continued, "But is there a way I can help you?"

Angelica shook her head. "No," she responded dejectedly. "My mama is real sick, and there is no doctor in Rockcliffe."

Leaning back in her seat, Rachel felt somewhat elated to share her news. "I know a doctor who lives in Rockcliffe."

With defeated shoulders, Angelica admitted, "Even if you know a doctor, we don't have funds to pay." Her eyes darted towards John in panic, but they relaxed as they focused back on her. "Lord Downshire is generous in his wages, but we don't have money for extra." Her added words seemed forced.

Rachel was watching this poor young maid as she struggled with her emotions. It was apparent she was overcome with anxiety about her mother. Emmett would undoubtedly attend to this girl's mother, but he would need to know more about her condition. "What ails your mother?"

Angelica wrung her hands in front of her. "About two months ago, my mama got real sick and started coughing. One morning, my mama said she couldn't go to work and sent me in her place. Luckily, the housekeeper agreed, but I was to be paid a lower wage. It barely covers the rent and food for my mama."

"Food for your mama?" she repeated in concern. "Do you not have funds to eat, Angelica?"

"No," she confirmed, offering a sad smile, "but I am granted two small meals on the days I work."

Knowing she must act to help ease this girl's suffering, Rachel glanced at John who was listening intently to the conversation but wasn't saying anything. "How long did your mother work for Lord Downshire?" she asked.

"Six years," came her reply.

"And how old are you?"

"Sixteen, miss."

Finally, John spoke up, "Where is your father?"

Angelica's eyes grew sorrowful. "He was in the Royal Navy, but he died seven years ago."

Rachel began to understand the heartache this young woman was feeling. "Your mother is a brave woman, indeed," she said as Angelica lifted her eyes and watched her intently. "Your mother set out to find employment after your father died serving his country. Now, she is sick, and you are heartbroken that you can't repay her for everything she has done for you."

Tears welled in the maid's eyes. "You are right. We moved away from our home in Durham, so my mama could accept a position here." One tear fell down her cheek, and she hastily wiped it away. "My mama is my only relation. I can't lose her."

Hoping her words were not in vain, Rachel promised, "You won't. My cousin is a doctor, and he will visit your mother. Furthermore, I will pay for any medication that she requires. Next time I am in town, I will set up an account with the apothecary and instruct the owner to cover anything that you charge to the account, including food for you."

The maid rose and started shaking her hands in front of her, attempting to refuse her offer. "No, I cannot accept. I could never even attempt to repay you."

Rising, Rachel smoothed out her dress. "I never asked for any payment in return. I am helping you because I'm in a position to do so." She gave her an understanding smile. "You are a strong young woman, stronger than you give yourself credit for."

Sniffing, Angelica managed to say, "Thank you."

"Can you write?" Rachel asked her, and she nodded. "Please write down where you live so my cousin, Dr. Emmett Maddix, can administer to your mother. I will instruct him to bring some medicine with him when he goes."

Without warning, Angelica threw her arms around Rachel

and pulled her tight against her. "Thank you," she said softly. Those simple words held an intense sense of gratitude. Dropping her arms, she quickly curtsied to John and walked out of the room.

Feeling pleased that she was able to do something so little to help another's burden, she was not prepared for John's ire. He cast her a frustrated look. "I do not know why you offered to help that maid, but you will grow tired of helping her, and then where will she be?"

Placing a hand on her hip, Rachel did not feel the need to justify her actions. "First of all, that *maid* is named Angelica, and I offered to help her because I can. My cousin is a doctor, and the cost of medicine is of little consequence to me."

John waved his hand dismissively. "You come in and give Angelica hope, but women always have an ulterior motive. I have not yet figured out what you hope to gain from this."

Fisting her hands tightly against her sides, Rachel let her rage brew inside of her before she snapped. "I do not know what happened in your life to cause you to be so bitter and suspicious of women, but you have been deceived. I am helping Angelica, and if I have to leave before her mother is well, then I will ensure provisions are in place."

He scoffed condescendingly, "Your dowry is not your money. It will belong to your husband."

Taking two powerful steps forward, Rachel stood in front of John and stared down at him. She leaned down and poked him in the chest. "I have my own money. I do not need a husband, or even desire one, especially if you are an example of what men are. You may be handsome on the outside, but I find you to be grotesque on the inside."

His eyes narrowed, but she continued, "You have lectured me, accused me of stealing a horse, and blatantly insulted me, but I thought I saw glimpses of a decent, kind human being." She paused to emphasize her next words. "I was wrong."

Glancing around the extraordinary library one more time, Rachel knew it would be the last time she would see it. Without waiting for his reply, she added, "I thought we could be friends, but I was wrong about that, too."

With those words, Rachel marched out of the library, leaving the books behind, and refusing to feel bad about her bold, unconstrained words. Shaking her head, she wondered how such a handsome horse trainer could be such a bloody fool about life.

9

Grunting loudly, Luke put on his own clothing and stormed out of his bedchamber. He'd had a fitful night of sleep, and he was furious. How dare Lady Rachel speak to him in that manner? He was a marquess! Besides, she was the one deceiving herself. Not him.

Women lie and exploit others in their games; his own mother taught him that. Diana was a despicable mother and a worse human being. If he could not trust his own mother, how could he trust any woman?

Walking down the hall, he was so preoccupied with his own thoughts that he crashed into someone, causing her to fall. Looking down, he realized he had knocked over his maid. It was the one he'd met yesterday in the library with Lady Rachel. What was her name again? Oh yes... Angelica. Reaching his hand out, he offered to help her up. Hesitantly, and with a fearful expression, she accepted his outstretched hand.

When she was on her feet, Angelica immediately withdrew her hand and dropped into a curtsy. "Thank you, my lord."

As she started to walk past him, Luke surprised himself by asking, "How is your mother faring?"

A grateful smile lit her face. "Dr. Maddix came by and saw my mama last night. He gave her medicine, and she is already feeling better."

Inexplicably annoyed that Lady Rachel had followed through with her promise, Luke pressed, "Did Lady Rachel set up an account at the apothecary?"

She nodded enthusiastically. "Not only did she set up an account for us at the apothecary, but one at the mercantile as well. Dr. Maddix instructed us to eat more and told us we needed to gain weight."

He forced a smile. "I am glad that Lady Rachel's money fixed the problem."

"Oh, Lady Rachel did more than just give us money. She visited with her cousin and brought us a basket of food. She even helped clean our tiny cottage," Angelica revealed.

Luke couldn't believe what he was hearing. "Lady Rachel helped clean your cottage?"

"She did."

"Lovely," he mumbled sarcastically as he went in search of his irritating butler.

Even though he found Mr. Kelly's cheerful personality to be quite irksome, he had grown to respect his butler over these years. He found he needed an unbiased opinion, and he was confident Mr. Kelly would answer honestly.

Seeing his butler at the base of the stairs, he jogged down. "Mr. Kelly, a word please," he grumbled loudly.

Predictably, Mr. Kelly acknowledged him with a smile. "Aye, m'lord."

Blast that man! Why did he always have to be so pleasant?

Glancing around the hall to ensure no one could overhear them, Luke took a step closer to Mr. Kelly. In a hushed voice, he said, "It has recently come to my attention that I may be a tad cynical."

"Was that a question or a statement?" Mr. Kelly asked, amused.

Ignoring his butler's sarcasm, he inquired, "Do you think I am cynical?"

Clasping his hands behind his back, Mr. Kelly rocked on the heels of his feet as he appeared to contemplate Luke's question. "May I ask where this is comin' from?"

He ran his hand through his hair in frustration. "Lady Rachel may have said a few words about my behavior."

"A few?"

Throwing his head back, he covered his face with his hands for a moment, then he sighed and dropped them. "She told me that I was handsome, but on the inside, I was grotesque." Mr. Kelly lifted his brows in response but didn't say anything, so Luke mumbled, "And she doesn't want to be my friend."

Mr. Kelly started laughing but turned it into a cough when Luke glared at him. With a subdued grin, he joked, "I tak' it that ye want her as a playmate?"

"Be serious, Mr. Kelly," Luke complained as he crossed his arms over his chest. "Do you find me cynical?"

Mr. Kelly eyed him carefully. "Aye, ye'r extremely cynical, but if it helps, Lady Rachel said ye were handsome."

Resisting the urge to roll his eyes, Luke replied, "No, that does not help." Even as he said the words, he knew he was lying. Of course it was flattering that Lady Rachel found him attractive, but he hadn't wanted to think about that. Actually, if he acknowledged the truthfulness of those words, then the rest of her words might be accurate as well.

Mr. Kelly smirked knowingly. "Why do ye care what Lady Rachel thinks aboot ye?"

"I don't care what *she* thinks," Luke stated adamantly, "but I am concerned about whether she is right."

With a concerned brow, Mr. Kelly sighed. "Tae be frank, since ye arrived in Scotland seven years ago, ye restored yer estate and established a thriving stud farm, but ye failed tae host one house party, or even attend one, for that matter."

Luke frowned at his butler's words. "Why would I want to host a house party?"

Mr. Kelly shrugged. "Tae have fun?"

"I have plenty of fun managing my stud farm," Luke informed him.

"Ye refuse all callers and have only left th' estate for yer sisters' weddings." He gave him a pointed look. "And if I recall correctly, ye didn't even stay long enough to be properly introduced at th' wedding luncheons."

"Why would I stay longer than required?" he huffed. "I had no desire to be introduced to unattached females with match-making schemes."

"By chance, do ye consider all wummin tae be thieves and liars?"

He nodded. "It is in women's natures to lie and deceive."

Mr. Kelly gave him an exasperated look. "And where did ye learn that?"

"From my own mother," he admitted bitterly.

Stepping back, Mr. Kelly kept his lips in a tight line before saying, "If ye look closely, ye will find yer mother and Lady Rachel are nothing alike."

Luke gave him a quick nod and started walking away. After a few steps, he stopped and spun back around. "Were you aware that one of the maids has a mother that is very sick?"

"Aye. Mrs. Walker became sick about two months ago."

"Why was I not notified?"

Mr. Kelly lifted his brow, albeit slightly. "Ye specifically requested not tae be bothered by th' tedious private affairs of yer staff."

He winced at the reminder of his harsh words, almost seven years ago. "I have changed my mind. I would like to be updated on the staff's health or any other concerns that should arise."

"As ye wish, m'lord."

He took his hand and rubbed the back of his neck. "I accused Lady Rachel of having ulterior motives when she offered to send her cousin, Dr. Maddix, to attend to Angelica's mother."

"And did she?"

"I cannot think of one." He sighed. "Do you truly believe that Lady Rachel wants nothing in return for helping Angelica?"

"I wholeheartedly believe that."

He frowned. "Do you think I should apologize to Lady Rachel?"

"Generally, wummin like apologies, sir."

Looking down at his white shirt, he asked, "And how exactly does one go about apologizing to a lady?"

"Now that is a very difficult question," Mr. Kelly remarked with a smile. "Let's get ye dressed properly and call for yer carriage, while I explain th' basics of apologies."

"Ouch," Lady Rachel yelped as she pricked her finger with her needle, reinforcing in her mind that needles were torture devices. Tossing the handkerchief and needle onto the table, she could not fathom how ladies enjoyed embroidery. Her eyes wandered to the window, and she debated going on another ride.

Briefly glancing up from her embroidery, her aunt had a smile on her lips as she prodded, "After John accused you of evil intent, what did you say?"

"I told him he was wrong in his assessment, and I didn't want to be his friend."

"I see," her aunt teased as she pulled the needle through the handkerchief. "Was this before or after you called him handsome?"

"After, but that was a mishap." She smoothed out her skirts. "Almost everything out of his mouth infuriates me so. We would never suit as friends."

Lowering the handkerchief, Aunt Jessamine smiled knowingly. "And if I had to guess, you told him that in the politest way possible."

Leaning forward, Rachel decided to share her new theory with her aunt. "I suspect that John is no mere horse trainer," she began in a dramatic tone, "I believe he is an assassin for the Crown." In a hushed voice, she continued to jest, "And only our beloved Prinny can assign him tasks."

Aunt Jessamine raised an eyebrow, and one corner of her mouth quirked up just a bit. "Do you have proof of this?"

Rachel sat back in the grey wingback chair with a playful smile on her lips. "No, but that is the only theory that makes sense."

"You could always ask Lord Downshire when he returns home from his holiday. He may tell you whether he's hired an assassin as a horse trainer."

With mirth in her eyes, Rachel responded, "No, I will demand that Lord Downshire tell me the truth."

"That sounds like a flawless plan, my dear." Her aunt chuckled. "I do so love your 'theories'."

"Thank you." Rachel's eyes trailed back towards the window. "I plan to walk along the shore before dinner. Would you like to join me?"

Aunt Jessamine continued with her needlework. "I will pass on the walk, but I assume Mr. Pearson will be joining you?"

Rachel nodded as David's muffled reply came from the hall, "Yes, Mrs. Maddix."

Aunt Jessamine grinned as she raised her voice. "You are welcome to join us in the drawing room, Mr. Pearson."

"Thank you for the offer, ma'am, but I prefer to stand guard in the main hall," his reply came.

"And what is your opinion of John and my niece's feud?" Her aunt's eyes twinkled as she kept her gaze on Rachel.

David chuckled softly. "It isn't much of a feud since Lady Rachel put John in his place, but her theory about John being an assassin is rubbish."

Feigning outrage, Rachel started to challenge David when a loud pounding came from the main door, echoing throughout the entry hall. Setting her embroidery aside, Aunt Jessamine smoothed out her dress and murmured, "I wonder who that could be."

A moment later, Mr. Wallice came into the room and announced, "A Mr. John Magnus is here to see Lady Rachel." He turned his gaze towards her. "Are you available for callers, my lady?"

Groaning inwardly, Rachel was wondering how she could decline his visit. She kept telling herself that she never wanted to see John again. As she opened her mouth to ask Mr. Wallice to send him away, her aunt answered for her. "Please show Mr. Magnus in."

Rachel cast Aunt Jessamine a disapproving look as they waited for the world's most contrary man to join them in the drawing room. However, she was rendered speechless by his sudden transformation from horse trainer to gentleman. Wearing an indigo tailcoat, white waistcoat and cravat, buff trousers, and black Hessian boots, his attire highlighted his broad shoulders and muscular physique. His strong jaw held no hint of stubble, and his thick, solemn brows were offset by a boyish grin. As his piercing eyes latched onto her, she slowly rose, unable to formulate any words that were appropriate to say in front of her aunt.

Luckily, her aunt came to her rescue by rising as well. "Welcome, Mr. Magnus. May I offer you some refreshment?"

John shifted his gaze towards Aunt Jessamine which gave

Rachel time to recover. "No, thank you," he declined in a deep, smooth voice.

Pointing to a floral chair near Rachel, her aunt indicated he should sit. Once they were all situated, she asked, "Mr. John Magnus, is it?"

"Just John, ma'am."

Aunt Jessamine smiled. "I understand you are a horse trainer at Lord Downshire's farms."

"I am," came his response. His eyes flitted between Aunt Jessamine and Rachel, appearing to be nervous.

Crossing her ankles, her aunt rested her arms on her chair before saying, "I had the opportunity to visit with Lord Downshire when he first arrived. I called upon him, and we had a pleasant conversation. He told me of his vision of Downshire Farms, and I am pleased it has come to fruition."

John's eyes fixed on her aunt. "Did you now?"

"Most likely my visit failed to make an impression on him, but I found him to be an honorable young man," her aunt asserted. "Which is why I would assume any workers he employed would be equally as honorable. Am I right to assume that, John?"

"Yes, ma'am."

She nodded approvingly. "Now, what is it that you hope to accomplish with this visit?"

He cleared his throat, a half-smile on his face. "I was hoping to convince Miss Rachel to go on a carriage ride with me."

"Miss Rachel, is it?" Her aunt cast her an amused smile. "If Rachel agrees, I certainly have no objections."

Returning his gaze to her, his eyes held uncertainty, something she'd never seen there before. If she didn't know any better, she might assume he was nervous about extending his invitation. Before she agreed to spend more time with him, she needed to ask one question. "Why would you seek me out when you already made your low opinion of me known?"

"I have come to acknowledge that I was wrong in my assessment of you."

"How gracious of you," she responded, sarcastically.

He winced. "I know now that your offering to help Angelica was an act of kindness, and I was wrong to accuse you otherwise."

Rachel's lips curled into an ever-so-slight smile. "That must have been hard for you to admit."

"And I apologize for my behavior," he blurted out, looking pained by his own admission.

Stifling the urge to giggle, she tipped her head graciously. "Thank you for that, John."

His gaze never left her face, imploring a familiarity she had never known before. "Please," he paused, "say that you will join me on a carriage ride."

She decided to take pity on the man. He did apologize for his behavior, even though it appeared he was unaccustomed to showing any type of remorse. She rose from her seat. John rose, as well. "I believe I will join you. Please give me a moment to collect my shawl."

10

Lord Downshire smiled as he watched Rachel swiftly walk out of the room. She could not seem to walk at a demure, ladylike pace.

Earlier, when he walked into the drawing room, his rehearsed apology had dissipated when he saw Rachel. Her hair was piled high upon her head, practically begging to be released from the confines of her pins, and her puce-colored dress highlighted her brilliant blue eyes. She was a remarkable, beautiful lady, but it was her personality that intrigued him. He had never met anyone like her, and he found it disconcerting.

"Lord Downshire," Mrs. Maddix said in a hushed voice, drawing his attention back to her. She rose and walked closer. "If you insist on masquerading as a horse trainer, then you need to know a few things."

He expected censure in Mrs. Maddix's tone, but to his surprise, he could detect none. "Such as?"

She perused his elegant garments, before saying, "Servants do not enter through the main door nor do they wear such fine clothing."

Tugging at his coat sleeves, he had no objection to losing the stuffy clothes. "I see your point."

Mrs. Maddix smiled. "Lastly, and most importantly, servants do not call upon titled ladies, especially the daughter of an earl." Noting the surprise on his face, she added, "I am not a simpleton, Lord Downshire. It is obvious you saw through her ruse, but I am shocked that Rachel has not seen through yours. Especially since you called on 'Lady Rachel' rather than asking for 'Miss Rachel' at the servants' door."

Her expression turned serious as she pressed her lips together. "For what purpose are you trying to deceive my niece?"

He had a feeling that his answer would determine if Mrs. Maddix would play along or inform her niece of his deceit. "When I first met Lady Rachel, I thought she was a horse thief." He stopped, knowing that was not the answer she was looking for.

Mrs. Maddix's hand shot up to her mouth to cover a bark of laughter. "A horse thief?"

He chuckled. "She was riding one of my horses astride and without a saddle."

"Lord Exeter would be horrified by his daughter's actions," Mrs. Maddix murmured in a concerned voice.

He grinned sheepishly. "I did say some contrary words, and she incorrectly assumed I work for Lord Downshire. Later, when she rode up to the stables, I was there helping the men train a foal, and I may have mentioned that Lord Downshire was on holiday."

"May have?"

Walking towards the window, he placed a hand on the wall and leaned in. "For the first time, someone saw me as a person and not just my title. When Lady Rachel introduced herself as Miss Rachel, I thought perhaps I could disguise my identity as well."

Mrs. Maddix moved closer to him, gently placing her hand on his sleeve. "But for what purpose?"

Tilting his head towards Mrs. Maddix, he was surprised to see compassion in her eyes, setting him at ease. Slowly, he admitted, "I wanted to see if Lady Rachel saw a man worth knowing without revealing my lineage as the future Duke of Remington."

An understanding smile formed on the matron's face. "You are playing a dangerous game, my lord. Rachel is clever, and will no doubt figure out your deception." She removed her hand from his sleeve as her smile grew. "But my niece lives for adventure, so I will not reveal who you truly are, assuming you have honorable intentions."

Pushing off from the wall, Luke replied in earnest, "All I seek is friendship with Lady Rachel."

"We shall see," she said with amusement in her eyes.

Before he could respond, Rachel walked into the room with a slate shawl wrapped around her body. She stopped and smiled at him, causing him to focus on her red, full lips.

Shaking off inappropriate thoughts, he offered his arm. "May I escort you to the carriage?"

As she climbed into the carriage, he saw David mounting his horse near the gate. He certainly takes his protector role seriously, he thought. Protector and chaperone all rolled into one. Convenient.

A little while later, she and Luke sat in silence as they rode along the cart path below the Maddix's estate. Rachel kept her gaze on the horizon, and he found the quiet unsettling. Clearing his throat, he ventured, "Do you take walks along the shore?"

At last, she turned to face him and nodded. "There is a narrow path at my uncle's estate that leads down to the shoreline. My cousin, Emmett, and I used to climb up and down that path whenever I was here on holiday. My mother was so afraid that I would fall and break my neck."

"Is that so?" Luke asked, eyeing her with puzzled interest. Her voice was always so full of animation.

"We used to play in the caves during low tide and pretend we were pirates. One time, I even borrowed one of my mother's coral necklaces, placed it in a small box, and pretended it was our buried treasure." She smiled. "My mother was not amused, but we had such fun." Rachel's voice turned melancholy as she seemed to drift back into her own thoughts.

Watching her from the corner of his eye, he was surprised to see a deep sadness sweeping over her face. He had yet to see her sad, and his heart constricted at the sight. He wanted her to smile again. "Why do those memories make you sad?" he prodded.

She shifted in her seat, angling her body towards him. "My cousin was injured during the war and recently ended his commission with the navy." She frowned despairingly. "Something happened that has caused him great pain, but he won't tell me why. I have pleaded for him to trust me, but he won't confide in me."

"I see," Luke huffed, his voice growing hard. It seemed Rachel wanted to discover Emmett's secrets, so she could chatter about it the next time ladies came to call. *Women are all the same!*

"You obviously don't see." She crossed her arms angrily and sat back. "You asked me what was wrong and then something happened in there," she said, pointing at his head, "that caused you to grumble and turn bitter."

"I don't grumble," he growled, "and I'm not bitter."

She humphed. "Then what caused your sudden change of mood?"

Pulling back on the reins, Luke stopped the carriage to give Rachel his full attention. "You claim you worry about your cousin, but you demand to know his secrets. What gives you the right to ask a man to divulge that which causes his greatest pain?"

Rearing back, her eyes grew wide. "What right do I have to care about another human being? That is ridiculous. Emmett is my cousin, and we used to be friends. I want to help him." A sense of urgency filled her voice. "He has become jaded about titles and is bitter about our role in the war against the American colonies."

"It sounds like he doesn't want your help, but you pester him anyway," Luke pointed out. "In my experience, women always make a situation worse."

"How dare you?" Her voice rose with each word. "You bring me on a carriage ride under the false pretense of apologizing, and then you insult me yet again." Placing her hand on the side of the carriage, she started climbing down. "I will not sit here and be insulted. Good day!"

Tossing the reins at his feet, Luke jumped off the side of the carriage and landed soundly on the ground. "Lady Rachel," he grunted at her retreating figure. Not only was she storming off, but she was heading across a wide field and towards the woodlands. "You are going the wrong way."

"I know," she shouted over her shoulder. "I don't want you to follow me, insolent fool."

How did this happen? He now had to chase an ornery female across the fields of Scotland. Tossing his coat and starched collar off, he increased his stride to catch up to her before she hurt herself.

BREATHING HARD, RACHEL HURRIED AS FAST AS SHE COULD without breaking into a run. How dare John criticize her for trying to help! Didn't he know that she loved her cousin and she

His eyes lowered to her hand on his sleeve. "I learned these things from watching my own mother."

She closed her eyes in mortification. What had his mother done to cause him to have such a critical opinion of all women? Opening her eyes, she saw him watching her with an intense look of sorrow. Usually, she would have bombarded him with questions, attempting to fix the problem, but hadn't he just criticized her for that approach with her cousin? With sincerity in her voice, she expressed, "I am sorry you have a horrible mother…"

"Had," he corrected forcefully.

"Oh. Please accept…"

With a dismissive swipe of his hand, John cut her off. "Don't." His jaw was clenched as he kept his eyes straight ahead.

Rachel watched as his mood started souring again and decided she needed to distract him. Moving to stand in front of him, she took her finger and jabbed him in the chest. "If you want to be friends, you need to stop acting like such a nincompoop."

Eyebrows raised in surprise, he mouthed, "Nincompoop?"

Pushing forward with her impulsive plan, she pointed towards the woodlands that lined the field. "I am going to race you to the trees. If I win, I get to drive the carriage back." Without waiting for his response, she lifted her skirts and started running across the field.

As she neared the trees, she worried that she had made a fool of herself, because he had not caught up. Just before she slowed down to look over her shoulder, John ran past her and touched the tree a few yards away. He placed his hands on his knees and bent over, breathing hard.

He glanced up, looking victorious. "I won."

Calming her racing heart, Rachel smiled that her ruse worked. "That you did."

"What did I win?" he asked with a grin.

"You won the privilege of escorting me home." She smirked.

He straightened up and walked closer to her. His eyes held a playful gleam. "That hardly seems like a fair prize."

She decided to play along. "No? Then what would you desire as the winner?"

Stopping when he was right in front of her, his eyes roamed her face until they landed on her lips. In response, her lips parted at the boldness of his stare, which seemed to break him of his trance. Clearing his throat, he stepped back, leaving her momentarily disappointed. Offering his arm, he started escorting her back to the carriage.

As they approached the carriage, John said, "I am glad that we reached an understanding, so you didn't have to walk all the way back to your uncle's estate."

"Who said I would have walked?" she asked lightheartedly.

Confusion was evident on his brow as he inquired, "How else would you have gotten home?"

"David would have given me a ride," she informed him, smiling.

John's eyes started perusing the field, until finally, his gaze returned to her. "I know he was following us, but I don't see him now."

Putting her hands to her mouth, Rachel shouted, "David!"

From the trees on the opposite side of the field, a reply floated to their ears. "Yes, Lady Rachel."

Chuckling, John shook his head. "That man is a very proficient protector."

"He is," she admitted as he assisted her into the carriage. Once he was situated on the bench next to her, he picked up the reins and urged the horses forward. A long, comfortable silence descended over them, interrupted only by the melody of the songbirds.

"Did you decide what you wanted your prize to be for winning the race?" she asked, breaking the quiet.

John gave her a cocky smile that caused her breath to hitch in anticipation. "I have a few ideas."

"Which are?" she prodded.

"You'll see," he said, as his eyes dropped flirtatiously to her lips.

Warmth crept into her cheeks, and she ducked her head to hide her blush. Why was the thought of kissing John so strangely compelling?

THEY CHATTED MERRILY ABOUT A WIDE RANGE OF TOPICS AS they rode to the Maddix's estate. Luke did not want to drop Rachel off just yet. He found it oddly satisfying to listen to her opinions about events around her. Everything seemed like an adventure to her, and she managed to make the most mundane tasks seem exciting.

"That is the path that leads down to the water," she informed him, pointing at a dirt footpath leading to the edge of the cliff. "I plan to take a stroll at low tide."

Before Luke could stop himself, he asked, "May I join you?"

Turning to look at him, Rachel smiled. "I would like that very much." With a teasing twinkle in her eye, she added, "Assuming you don't have nefarious plans to get me alone, so you can toss me off the side of the cliff."

He chuckled. "I have no intention of murdering you today."

Rachel sighed loudly in relief. "That is good. We might just be friends yet."

"Are we friends?" He asked the question casually, but he was eager to hear her response.

"I see no reason not to be friends, especially since you don't plan to throw me off a cliff," she bantered.

He playfully nudged her shoulder with his. "I think you need higher standards for your friends."

A sad smile came to her lips. "I have a lot of close acquaintances, but very few trusted friends. I find that the ton is fickle when it comes to friendships."

He couldn't have agreed more with her statement. Sadly, he was not surprised that high Society did not embrace Lady Rachel. She was well-read, opinionated, and prone to wild, impulsive acts. Any of those traits would be highly criticized by the ton, but to have all three would cause anyone to get the direct cut.

Suddenly, an image of dancing with Rachel at a ball floated to his mind, and he found himself preoccupied with it. They were waltzing, completely enamored with each other. His gloved hand was on her back as they swayed to the music.

"… don't you agree?" Rachel asked, her voice breaking through his musings.

Giving her a perplexed look, he questioned, "Agree to what?"

She shook her head good-naturedly. "I believe I will need to add a requirement for my friends to be better listeners."

Placing a hand over his heart, he feigned distress. "You have wounded me, my lady."

Her hand shot up as a sudden burst of wind whipped strands of blonde hair around her face. After she tucked the errant strands behind her ears, she groaned. "I hate it when my mother is right. I should have worn a hat, or at least a bonnet, to protect my hair from the wind."

Another burst of wind caused a few more strands of her hair to cover her face. Without thinking, Luke reached over and tucked them behind her ear, his fingers brushing her cheek.

She blushed and lowered her gaze.

Reluctantly, he dropped his hand. "I find I prefer you without a hat or bonnet."

As they approached the estate, they saw a beautiful, shiny black curricle with equally majestic horses standing in front. Rachel eyed it and muttered, "I wonder who has come to call."

Before Luke could respond, the main door opened, and Mrs. Maddix stepped out onto the front steps with a tall dandy. She waved at them, but the man did not appear as friendly. Luke pulled the brake, hopped down, and walked over to assist Rachel. As he lowered her from the carriage, she whispered, "That is Lord Melville."

Keeping his voice low, he responded, "Ah." Luke ground his teeth together. On the rare occasions he'd gone into the village, he heard whisperings about Lord Melville and his roguish ways. Apparently, the man had left many women with child during the seven months he'd been in town.

Offering his arm, he escorted Rachel to the door as she made the proper introductions. "Lord Melville, I would like you to meet my friend, Mr. John Magnus."

Lord Melville eyed his white shirt as he gave him a curt nod. "Mr. Magnus, I have not had the pleasure of meeting you before." His smile was strained, his voice emotionless.

Appearing oblivious to the tension between the two men, Rachel cheerfully added, "Mr. Magnus is a horse trainer at Downshire Farms."

Luke watched as Lord Melville's sharp eyes switched to disdain and contempt, narrowing at the sight of Lady Rachel's hand on his sleeve. It was clear that he did not approve of her spending time with a common horse trainer. Good! It was better for Rachel to spend time with a servant than a rogue.

As much as he wanted to reveal that he was the Marquess of Downshire, mainly to put Lord Melville in his place, Luke knew this was not the time to admit the truth. Instead, he corrected Rachel, "Lead horse trainer."

Turning her head, she smiled with approval. Taken aback, he marveled that Lady Rachel believed he was only a lowly horse trainer, and yet she befriended him. There was no judgment in her eyes for his supposed lowly position. How was it possible that a lady could mingle with nobility and commoners with such ease?

Lord Melville dismissed him, focusing solely on Lady Rachel. "It is a fine day today, and I was hoping you would join me for a carriage ride."

Glancing over at Mrs. Maddix, Rachel waited for her permission before addressing Lord Melville. "I would be honored."

Without taking his predatory eyes off Rachel, Lord Melville hurried down the stairs and offered his arm to her. As he escorted her to his carriage, Luke could hear him discussing how beautiful the weather was. Trying not to roll his eyes in annoyance, he caught Mrs. Maddix smiling at him.

Mustering up his dignity, he bowed politely to her and walked towards his carriage. It should not matter to him who Rachel spent her time with. If she wanted to spend her time with a known rake, then so be it. Eventually, Lord Melville's act would become apparent. What if she didn't realize in time? Luke stopped, taking a moment to pet one of his horses as Lord Melville's carriage lurched forward.

"Lord Downshire," a voice said from behind him.

Turning his head, he was startled to see David standing near him, and he was holding the reins to two horses. When had David approached him? The man certainly had an uncanny ability to sneak around silently. Regardless, this man had discovered his true identity, and he begged the question, "How long have you known?"

"Right from the start," David admitted nonchalantly. "But it was confirmed when Lady Rachel toured the library at your estate." He smirked. "Next time Lady Rachel comes to call, you might want to take down the painting of you in your study."

With an exasperated look, he stated, "My study was locked and was nowhere near the library."

David shrugged as if picking a lock was not an issue. "I had to ensure Lady Rachel was protected."

"From what?" Luke countered, "Dusty books?"

Looking amused, David didn't seem phased by his question and tilted his head towards the departing carriage. "Would you like to join me as I protect Lady Rachel from that fool?" When Luke didn't respond right away, he added, "Unless you would prefer to go back to your estate and take a nap?"

Feeling the need to defend himself, Luke replied gruffly, "I don't nap."

"No?" David mocked. "Prepare for a ball then?"

Luke huffed, "I run a thriving stud farm. I don't have time for social events."

Quickly, David walked to the side of one of the horses and mounted it effortlessly. "I don't have time for chit-chat. We both know what kind of reputation Lord Melville has, and I don't intend to allow Lady Rachel out of my sight."

Luke watched as the carriage rolled further away from view. He couldn't spy on Rachel. That was an invasion of her privacy. Although, Mr. Larson had strongly encouraged him to help her, assuming the occasion presented itself. As the road curved, Luke saw Lord Melville scoot closer to Lady Rachel and place his arm on the back of the bench. Swearing under his breath, Luke made a rash decision. "I'm in."

As Lord Melville scooted closer to her, Rachel politely attempted to create more distance between them but was impeded by the side of the bench. Fortunately, she had no doubt that David was trailing behind the carriage, keeping her safe. That knowledge provided her with much reassurance.

Over these past few days, David had become a loyal friend. At first, he refused to converse with her, partially because she was under his protection, but he had relaxed his stance. She had learned that David had been selected from a large group of applicants to work at the home office. His missions were mostly local, but he routinely went into the underbelly of London to meet his contacts.

With a polite smile, Rachel listened to Lord Melville ramble on about his aunt, her poor health, and her incompetent household staff. Needing a break from his drivel, she acknowledged, "It was kind of you to leave before the end of the Season to help her."

Puffing out his chest, her comment seemed to encourage him to praise himself. "As a good nephew, I feel I am duty bound to help my aunt until her body gives up her spirit." Lord Melville's gaze roamed her face and slowly lowered until it stopped at her chest.

Feeling self-conscious by his blatant perusal, Rachel wrapped the shawl across her chest. A flicker of disappointment flashed in his eyes, but he blinked it away. As he returned his gaze towards the road, he said, "I must admit, I was devastated to miss the balls and soirées that the ton host every year, but your arrival has invigorated me." He winked at her. "When your aunt informed me that her niece, the daughter of the Earl of Exeter, had arrived, I had no idea that you would be so beautiful."

"It was an impromptu holiday, but I am grateful to spend time with my relations," she shared, hoping to change the direction of the conversation.

Ignoring her subtle cue, he responded, "From the moment I

laid eyes on you, I knew we would suit. I can't help but wonder if you feel the same?"

She tried hard to keep her expression unreadable, but every fiber of her body wanted to scream no. Lord Melville was a vain, foolish lord that assumed she would fall at his feet after their first meeting. Flashing an annoyed smile, she attempted to find the right words to express her disdain for him. "I assure you that I do not feel the same."

"No?"

She could tell by the expression in his dark eyes that he didn't believe her. She decided to press her point. "I am not interested in a suitor at this time."

He smirked roguishly at her. "I believe you feel that way only because you have not met the right man." Steering the horses towards a large tree that shaded the road, the carriage came to a jerky stop, and he angled his body, allowing their knees to brush up against each other.

"I like challenges, and I prefer a woman who makes the chase interesting." His rakish eyes focused on her lips as he added, "It makes the reward that much sweeter." His tongue darted out along his bottom lip.

Rachel felt like gagging at the sight of him wetting his lips, and she wondered how she had ever found this man attractive. He was far too arrogant and much too bold for her liking.

He reached for her hand in her lap, making her grateful that her mother always demanded she wear gloves in public. Tugging her hand out of his hold, Rachel gave him a disapproving look. "Lord Melville, you are much too forward and…"

He placed a finger on her lips, stopping her words. "You may call me Colin." Rubbing his finger along her bottom lip, he leaned forward, lips pursed for a kiss. Jerking her head back, she placed her hands on his chest and shoved him, hard.

Looking startled, Lord Melville just stared at her while she chastised him. "How dare you! I am not a strumpet." Trembling with rage, she felt her chest heave as she tried to calm down. "I demand that you take me home at once."

Lord Melville sighed and lowered his gaze. After a few moments, he looked up. "I apologize for my actions. I thought you were flirting with me."

"Flirting?" She scoffed. "No, sir, I was not."

He appeared remorseful, but his next words caught her completely off guard. "I have compromised you. I will ask your uncle for permission to court you."

"No, no, no," she stammered, waving her hands in front of her, attempting to ward off his absurd plan. "I will demand that my uncle refuse your suit."

He frowned. "Then I will petition your father. Once he realizes you were compromised…"

She shouted, interrupting him, "I was not compromised, and I have no intention of ever marrying you."

Lord Melville looked pained, but Rachel did not want any confusion between them. She would rather become a spinster than marry someone like him. Feeling no need to apologize, she crossed her arms over her chest and waited for the man to come to his senses.

Pushing off the bench, he moved towards the opposite end. His eyes held sadness as he gazed at her. "I am fond of you. You are beautiful and charming, and I do believe we would suit."

Lowering her gaze, Rachel sighed. "We hardly know each other."

Lord Melville ran his hand over his groomed hair as if to place any unruly strands back into place. "I found myself beguiled by you after we had dinner, and I fantasized that you might hold me in some regard." When she didn't respond, he continued, "I thought you might want to be seduced."

Confused, Rachel furrowed her brow. "You thought I was the type of woman that wanted to be seduced?" She frowned deeply. How should one respond to that ludicrous statement?

"No," he mumbled. "Well, perhaps given the right circumstances."

Rachel started tapping her right boot as she imagined jabbing her fist into Lord Melville's face. He picked up the reins, flicked them, and maneuvered the horses back towards her uncle's estate. She was aware that he would periodically glance her way, but she kept her gaze fixed straight ahead.

Suddenly, Lord Melville yanked on the reins causing the carriage to come to a complete stop. She fell forward and placed her hand out to steady herself. As she prepared to voice her displeasure, he issued a passionate plea. "I admit that I jumbled my proposal back there, but give me a chance to woo you."

She shook her head, but he pressed on. "I am a lowly viscount, but I have no doubt, in time, we would become a love match. Furthermore, with your fortune and you on my arm," he hesitated, "we would be the envy of the ton." He smiled as if pleased by his choice of words.

Mortified, she closed her eyes. That is what this was about. Lord Melville wanted her fortune. He must have heard that she was an heiress. That would explain why he was proposing so quickly after their first meeting. At least he didn't abduct her and force a local blacksmith to marry them. In Scotland, the rules for marriage were much more relaxed.

Clasping her hands tightly in her lap, Rachel kept her back rigid. "I thank you for your offer, but I must decline."

"You would rather remain a spinster?"

Her eyes widened at his insult. "I resent that implication. I am only twenty-three years old."

Lord Melville shrugged. "Your aunt told me that you are a lover of books. I would be willing to overlook your bluestocking tendencies. You won't receive that same consideration from anyone else among the ton."

"How gracious of you," she declared, her voice dripping with sarcasm.

Choosing to ignore her tone, or oblivious to it, he continued to insult her. "I would expect you to produce an heir and a spare as a precaution. After that, you may take lovers, assuming you use precautions to avoid getting pregnant. I refuse to recognize another man's child."

"Am I to assume you would take mistresses then?" she asked.

He looked startled by her question. "Why would I not? One woman alone could not satisfy my needs."

She stared at him in shock. Did this man have no shred of decency in him? Aghast, she again asserted, "I refuse your offer. Frankly, I find the terms to be offensive."

"Which part?"

Narrowing her eyes, she stated, "Your entire proposal." She pursed her lips together. "I do not intend to marry for convenience."

His lip curled up in disbelief. "Who would offer you protection then? Until you marry, you will be at the mercy of every fortune hunter."

"My answer is no." Her voice was unyielding.

A snapping twig caught Rachel's attention. Scanning a nearby group of trees, she spotted a man crouching down behind a large bush. She rolled her eyes as she recognized him. Good heavens, was John spying on her? Were all the men in her life going mad?

John caught her gaze, froze and then ducked lower. Puzzled, she frowned. He must know that ducking wouldn't take away the fact that she'd seen him. Shaking her head in frustration, she turned back towards Lord Melville. He was saying something about courting, but she was finished with that conversation.

Reaching over, she yanked the reins out of his hands and urged the horses into a run. Lord Melville gripped the sides of the bench tightly. Approaching the estate, Rachel pulled back on the reins until the horses stopped on the gravel-lined path. She tossed the reins at her would-be suitor and hopped off the carriage, unassisted.

Racing up the stairs, she flung open the main door and slammed it behind her. She didn't know who she was more upset with, Lord Melville for his asinine proposal or John for spying on her. Either way, she was not amused.

❦ 12 ❦

RACHEL TURNED HER HEAD FROM THE BOOK SHE HAD BEEN reading as she heard a sharp tap on her bedchamber window. Staring at the large window, she frowned when the noise did not repeat itself. It must be my imagination, she thought. Her eyes drifted back to her book, and she continued reading. Then she heard the sound again, more forcefully this time. There was no mistaking it. What was causing that strange noise? Was someone attempting to break in?

The terrifying memory of being abducted from her town-house crashed into her mind. Shaking her head, she tried to banish the thought. No one was trying to kidnap her in Scotland. I am safe, she thought, reassuring herself.

Although, when she thought about approaching the window to investigate the noise, her heart started pounding rapidly. A ripple of fear passed through her, and she considered fleeing from her room to find a footman to assist her. No, that would be silly. She was safe at her uncle's estate. Maybe it was a tree branch brushing up against the glass.

Slowly, fearfully, she laid her book down and stood, keeping her eyes firmly planted on the window. As the sounds intensified, she thought that it sounded suspiciously like something small and hard being thrown against the glass. Just then, she saw a small pebble hit the window and bounce off. Then another, and another. Someone was throwing rocks at her second story window. But why?

Fears now eased, Rachel walked swiftly to the window, unlatched it and pushed it open. Looking down, she saw John, holding a handful of pebbles. One hand was pulled back as if preparing to throw another rock when he saw her. Lowering his hand, he exclaimed, "Are you deaf, woman?"

"I beg your pardon?" she asked, returning his bristly tone.

Dropping the rocks to the ground, John wiped his hands on his trousers. "I have been throwing rocks at your window for the past twenty minutes."

"You have not," she contested.

"He has, my lady," David confirmed as he walked into her line of sight. "It took him awhile to perfect his aim, but he has been throwing rocks for some time."

Rachel frowned at her protector. "I assume you told him which window was mine."

"He offered me a horse in exchange for that information," David confessed, shrugging unapologetically.

"A horse?" she questioned in disbelief. How could he afford to give a horse away? David must be teasing her.

"I had no choice," John asserted, drawing her attention back to him. "You refused to see me when I came to call."

Crossing her arms over her chest in annoyance, she huffed, "Of course I did. I caught you spying on me."

"I did no such thing," he argued. "I was merely protecting you from Lord Melville."

Dropping her arms, Rachel placed them on the window sill and leaned out. "I do not need, nor did I ask for your protection, John," she drawled emphatically.

"I know that, but..." John took his hand and raked it through his already-disheveled hair. Gruffly, he demanded, "Come down here so we can talk about this like civilized adults."

Rachel's eyes widened at his authoritative tone. As she opened her mouth to unleash her sharp tongue on him, she heard David instructing him in a hushed voice to choose his words more carefully. His tone frustrated, John growled, "But she is being difficult."

David shook his head and took a step closer to John. Rachel leaned forward to try and hear what David was saying, but his voice was too quiet. After a moment, David nodded at John and stepped back.

Returning his gaze towards her, John bowed politely, but his smile was forced. When he straightened, he asked, "Will you *please* come down, so I may apologize for my inappropriate behavior?"

Rachel stifled a laugh. She knew that admission had to have hurt John's pride, and she did appreciate his grand gesture. She tilted her head and said, "I will be right down."

As she was closing the window, she heard him grumble, "I don't know why I have to apologize. I was only trying to protect her." Before Rachel could respond, she heard David tell him that men always apologize to women, with or without justification.

Smiling, Rachel latched the window and started down the hall towards the main entry. As she passed by the drawing room, she saw her aunt working on her embroidery and her uncle reading a book. Walking into the room, she started to announce she was going for a walk when her uncle lowered his book and acknowledged, "I see John finally stopped throwing pebbles at your window."

"You knew?" she asked, bewildered.

Amusement lined her features as Aunt Jessamine lowered her handkerchief. "The whole staff knows. John was quite persistent in his attempts to get your attention."

"He ordered me to come down, so we could talk," she informed them.

"Oh dear," her aunt murmured softly. "I take it that did not go well for him."

"It did not," Rachel confirmed, "but David instructed him, and his second attempt was much better."

Her uncle laughed. "Sadly, John is not the first man who bungled his words trying to get a beautiful lady to talk to him."

"It is not like that," Rachel insisted, feeling a need to clarify her friendship with John. "He and I are just friends."

With a raised brow, her aunt asked, "Do you take issue with him being a horse trainer?"

Surprised by the question, she answered, "Why would I judge another for their job or status?" She lowered herself down into an upholstered armchair. "I am upset with John because I caught him spying on me while I was on a carriage ride with Lord Melville."

Her uncle placed his book on the table and leaned forward. "I am grateful that John did spy on you. Lord Melville has an appalling reputation." He gave a disapproving glance at his wife. "I have been telling Jessamine as much."

Her aunt frowned in response. "He is our neighbor and the nephew of our beloved friend, Mrs. Felix. It would not be appropriate to shun the young man."

"No, but we must keep him away from our niece, especially after he offered for her." Uncle Edwin shook his head. "I am still furious that Lord Melville offered for Rachel in such a despicable fashion. She deserves much more than a marriage of convenience, especially to that rake."

Aunt Jessamine nodded. "I agree. We will remain cordial, but I insist you avoid Lord Melville." She reached over and placed her hands on her husband's. "I am grateful that David is protecting you. I daresay that he could frighten most men."

"I have no problem with the idea of avoiding Lord Melville," she expressed. "His proposal almost seemed desperate."

Uncle Edwin huffed, "I disagree. Not only are you beautiful and charming, but you are an heiress. Any man would be lucky to marry you."

She pressed her lips together tightly. "Sometimes I feel that the gentlemen of the ton are looking at me as if I am a prize to be won and not seeing me as a real person."

"The right man will," her aunt advised, smiling. "Now, go see John. He is waiting for you."

"I can't believe I caught him spying on me," she muttered as she stood up.

"Be patient with him," Aunt Jessamine said as she resumed her embroidery. "He has a good heart."

"I am not contesting that but..." Her voice trailed off. How could she explain her jumbled thoughts? "John has been very secretive about his background. It is obvious he was raised to be a gentleman. What led him to become a horse trainer?"

"*Lead* horse trainer," her uncle clarified with an amused smile.

"Be off with you, child," her aunt teased. "Dinner will be at eight, and I do not want you down at the shore for long. I have heard enough rumors of men roaming the shoreline at night to give them credence."

Walking out the main door and down the stairs, Rachel saw John standing back, looking entirely unsure of himself. She stopped in front of him and waited for him to say something. Instead of an immediate apology, John looked deeply into her eyes, appearing relieved. His next words completely disarmed her. "You came."

Tingles coursed through her body at those simple words. "I did."

Taking a small step forward, John reached for her hand and

slowly brought it up until his lips hovered over her ungloved hand. "I am sorry, Rachel," he said humbly.

She gasped softly at his use of her given name. However, the way he said it made her feel special, almost precious. He kissed her hand and Rachel closed her eyes, attempting to memorize the soft caress of his lips on her skin.

Releasing her hand, John took a step back and clasped his hands behind him.

When she found her voice, she assured him, "You are forgiven."

His wide smile and the slight puffing up of his chest made him look like a small boy who was very proud of himself.

Unable to resist, she teased, "Did David tutor you on that apology?"

"He did." With an impish grin, John revealed, "Although, kissing your hand was my idea."

"That was a nice touch," she admitted.

He placed his hand out towards the cliffs. "Would you be willing to show me that path you so vividly described earlier?"

Rachel raised an inquiring eyebrow towards him. "Don't you have horses to train?"

Humor flashed in his eyes. "I do, eventually. But Lord Downshire is on holiday and left me in charge."

"I see," she said. "Well, we don't want to dally any longer for fear of losing the light."

As they walked towards the edge of the cliff, Rachel showed him the rocky trail that led from the top to the coast below. Climbing over and around large boulders, they finally found a narrow and extremely steep path. Keeping their bodies close to the cliff wall, they slowly made their way to the shoreline.

Dropping down onto the sand, Rachel started walking towards a cave set back from the water. As they approached the familiar opening, she placed her hand on the cold, uneven stone lining the cave. The opening was large enough for two people to walk through, and deep enough that no light penetrated the back of the cavern.

The dark, damp cave held so many memories of her youth. She took a deep breath of the musty odor mixed with the salty sea air. John stood next to her, placed his hand on the opposite wall, and peered deep into the cave. Turning to face her, his eyes were full of excitement. "You ready?"

LUKE WATCHED AS RACHEL'S FACE PALED. "WHAT IS WRONG?" he asked, alarmed by her sudden change of behavior.

Dropping her hand from the damp cave wall, she took a step back but continued gazing into the darkness. "I can't go in there," she replied, almost regretfully. "But you can. It is safe."

"Didn't you say you used to explore this cave with your cousin?"

"I did," she admitted with a slight shudder. "However, I find myself now afraid of dark, cramped spaces."

The fear in her voice was undeniable, causing a surge of protectiveness to shoot through him; a fierce protectiveness he'd never felt before in his life. Moving so he blocked her view of the cave, he inquired gently, "What happened to cause you to be so afraid?"

With a resigned look in her eyes, Rachel lowered her gaze towards his chest. Surprising himself, he reached out and pulled her close. At first, she stood rigid in his arms, but slowly she relaxed and finally wrapped her arms around his waist. He held her as they listened to the lapping of the water behind them. He attempted his question again. "What happened, Rachel?"

Stepping out of his arms, she swiped at her tear-stained cheeks. "Nothing of consequence."

Resisting the urge to command her to tell him the truth, Luke leaned his back against the entrance of the cave. "I find that hard to believe. You are still shaking."

"Am I?" She started rubbing her hands up and down her arms as her gaze shifted back towards the cave.

Gently, he spoke, "Rachel."

Hearing her name broke the trance that had come upon her, and she hesitantly turned away from the entrance. Taking a few steps away, Rachel said over her shoulder, "Let me show you a cave that has the most unusual markings. Rumor has it…"

Pushing off the cave wall, Luke interrupted her, "Why are you so stubborn?"

Rachel stopped and turned back towards him. Her face was expressionless, but her words held sadness. "We should head back."

Sitting down on a large rock nearby, he declared, "Not until you tell me what has unnerved you."

Turning her back to him, Rachel's dress flowed around her body as she stared out into the water. Not wanting to rush her, Luke waited till she walked over and sat down next to him. She failed to meet his gaze, and her words came slowly. "About two months ago, I was abducted from my bedchamber at knifepoint. I was taken to a ship's cargo hold and held in a dark, cold prison that reeked of paint and mildew."

Frowning, Rachel added, "I was given a thin, fishy soup to eat and was chained to the floor, along with twenty-five other women." She wrapped her arms around her waist. "Luckily, *Shadow* rescued us, and we survived."

Luke couldn't place it, but her story sounded familiar. He had read something about that recently. Suddenly, he remembered. "You were one of the women that merchant Wade abducted."

Rachel began trembling. "I was."

Those simple words caused a lump in his throat. Not knowing what to do, he quietly murmured, "I'm sorry."

Slowly Rachel's hand brushed the top of her nose. "When *Shadow* and Wade were fighting, I tripped Wade, which allowed *Shadow* time to throw a dagger into his heart. Unfortunately, before Wade was killed, he kicked me in the face and broke my nose. That is why my nose is crooked."

He hadn't noticed her crooked nose until now. Attempting to reassure her, he said, "It is barely discernable."

She huffed her disbelief. Her eyes sought out the cave again. "I know that the cave is safe, but I can't seem to convince my body to go in. Sometimes my heart is gripped with fear, and I find myself unable to move."

He thought of a perfect solution. "I will carry you into the cave."

With a shake of her head, Rachel replied, "No, that won't work. I need to do it on my own."

As the sun set, beautiful colors filled the darkening sky and shadows were cast along the cliffs and rocky shore. Standing up, Rachel walked closer to the water and pointed towards a vast stretch of the beach further down the shoreline. "At low tide, you can walk out to Hestan Island. It is almost two miles out to sea."

Straining to see the island in the dimming light, Luke shook his head. "I can't see an island."

Peering out over the water, she nodded. "The tide's too high right now. It is a hike through knee-deep water across firm, sandy mud. I have done it a few times." She turned towards him with an inquisitive glance. "How is it that you have lived in Rockcliffe for all these years, and you don't know about that island?"

"I have been busy at Downshire Farms." He shrugged, and Rachel smiled. "What is so funny?"

Her eyes twinkled, and he swore they were more beautiful than all the stars in the sky. "It just seems contradictory to what I have seen. You have escorted me into the library, taken me on a carriage ride, and now you're walking along the shoreline with me. I have seen you work very little."

He laughed. "That is the difference between a *lead* horse trainer and a regular horse trainer."

"Ah, I see." She grinned and took a step closer to him, her expression curious. "You were clearly raised as a gentleman, but what led you to become a horse trainer at Downshire Farms?"

Luke cleared his throat, stalling, giving himself a moment to think. Maybe it was time to reveal his identity? Would she reject him for lying to her, or would she understand? Their whole friendship was based on a lie, and he wasn't ready to say goodbye yet. He decided to tell her the partial truth. "I was raised outside of London. After my younger brother was born, we lived with my mother and her lover."

Rachel's brow rose, but she didn't say anything. It was scandalous that his mother openly lived with her lover, but his father, the Duke of Remington, lived with his mistress, as well. He shook his head in disgust. "When my sisters were born, my mother's lover went away. I was shipped off to Eton on the eve of my thirteenth birthday, only coming home during holidays and after I graduated from Oxford."

His eyes shifted over the calm waters; the contempt he felt for his mother needed to be set free. "I left when my mother tried to arrange a marriage between me and a woman exactly like her." He kicked the sand in frustration. "My mother never cared for me, or my siblings, and when she did visit the nursery, she acted like it was a burden to interact with us. There was no way I was going to marry a woman that was cruel, selfish…" His breathing became labored as an image of Lady Marianne came to his mind. She was undeniably beautiful, but her heart was icy cold.

Rachel's hand touched his sleeve, providing him with much-needed comfort. He opened his eyes and was rendered speechless by the compassion on her face. Her grip on his arm increased as she said, "I understand why you fled to Scotland." She smiled sweetly. "I hope you have found joy here." Her words were spoken with such tenderness that he felt valued, as if his joy truly mattered to her.

Luke noticed a movement near the cliff. He saw David pointing out towards the water. Luke and Rachel both turned their heads and saw two small boats, silently making their way closer to shore. The oars were strategically being placed at such an angle that they avoided the slapping of water which would alert others to their presence. In each one, there appeared to be a group of six men with large muskets.

Anxiety washed over him when he heard an order drifting in the wind. It was given in French. Grabbing Rachel's hand, he turned to race up the pathway, but then stopped. If they went that route, they would be exposed. Glancing towards the cave, he knew it was their only hope for remaining alive.

Rachel started dragging her feet when she realized his intent. Quickly turning around, he picked her up and raced into the cave, plunging them into the darkness. The sound of trickling water was the only sound around them. Shaking, Rachel's breathing became labored as he gently placed her down, ensuring she was stable on her feet before he put his arms around her.

She trembled harder, and he did the only thing that he could think of to comfort her. He kissed her.

❧ 13 ❧

SITTING AT HIS DESK, LUKE FOUND HE HAD LITTLE INTEREST IN the ledger that had sat unopened on his desk all morning. His mind continued reliving that momentous kiss he had shared with Rachel the night before.

When his lips had sought hers out in the dark, she had gasped, allowing him to deepen the kiss. Almost immediately, her hands slid around his neck as she returned the kiss with the same passion and urgency. It was as if they each realized how fleeting the moment was.

Lost in each other's arms, they clung to each other until David announced all was clear from outside of the cave. Releasing Rachel was the hardest thing he had ever done, but they had to leave the cave before the French soldiers returned.

The journey back up the trail was no less arduous, but they arrived at the top of the cliff completely unharmed. When he walked Rachel back to her uncle's estate, Mrs. Maddix met him at the door and invited him to stay for dinner. She claimed Emmett had been called away for a doctoring emergency, and they had an extra plate set. Rachel encouraged him to stay, but her cheeks were pink. He wondered if she was remembering their kiss, too.

A soft knock interrupted his thoughts. "Enter," he ordered.

The door opened, and a young maid walked in carrying a tray of tea and pastries. She curtsied. "Mrs. Henderson sent up yer breakfast, m'lord." Glancing at the desk, she asked, "Do ye have a preference where ye would lik' me tae place th' tray?"

He pointed at the table near her. "Right there will be fine." Placing the tray where he'd indicated, she curtsied and turned to leave, but Luke stopped her. "What is your name?"

Slowly turning around, she began wringing her hands. "Sophia, m'lord."

Sensing her discomfort, he tried to think of how Rachel would handle this. No doubt she would ask a personal question to set the other person at ease. "How long have you worked for me?"

"Three years." Her eyes stayed firmly fixed on the floor.

Smiling, Luke sat back in his chair. He wanted to do something nice for the maid. "Take the rest of the day off."

Instead of the eager reply he anticipated, he was met with tears. Sophia broke down and began sobbing. "Please, dinnae… fire me," she begged in between sobs. "I need this job."

Luke jumped up from his seat and stepped closer to her. His hands were in front of him as if trying to soothe a horse. "No, Sophia, I am not firing you. I just thought you might like a day off."

Tear soaked eyes stared up at him. "But my wages would be docked."

"No, you would be paid for the day," he assured her, now realizing why she was upset. "I wanted you to go enjoy the shoreline and watch the sunset."

Sophia watched him, her face showing her confusion. "I would rather be workin'. I am needin' all my wages tae help support my family."

"Of course. Please, go back to work," Luke encouraged. "I apologize for the intrusion."

Relief flashed across her face as she dropped into a curtsy. "Thank ye, m'lord." Before he could utter another word, she disappeared out the door.

"What in the world happened?" Luke mumbled to himself.

Mr. Kelly walked in, closing the door behind him. "Would ye know why Sophia was crying?"

Sighing, Luke walked back to his desk chair. "I told her to take the rest of the day off."

"Did she do something tae displease ye?"

"No," Luke grunted, completely exasperated. "I was attempting to be nice."

His butler's lips curled into a smile. "I tak' it that idea was not well received."

Sitting down, Luke shook his head. "No, she thought I was dismissing her." Grabbing a letter on his desk, he extended it to his butler. "Please send a messenger to deliver this letter to my brother, Lord Jonathon, posthaste. He should be residing at Lord Lansdowne's estate, Chatswich Manor."

"Aye, m'lord," Mr. Kelly said, accepting the letter. "I would assume this letter details the French soldiers ye saw last night."

"It does." Luke reached for his ledger. He might as well attempt to get his books in order. After a moment, he noticed that Mr. Kelly was still in the room. Glancing up, he asked, "Is there something else I can help you with?"

Mr. Kelly smirked. "Have ye informed Lady Rachel that ye'r Lord Downshire and not just a horse trainer?"

Closing the leger, Luke leaned back in his chair looking uncomfortable. "It has become complicated."

"Complicated, sir?" Mr. Kelly looked amused.

Stretching out his legs, Luke crossed his ankles as he attempted to delay his response. How could he find the words to explain what he was feeling? An image of Lady Rachel came to his mind. She was coyly smiling at him from across the dinner table but quickly schooled her features when her aunt glanced her way.

"Ye are smiling," his butler informed him, causing the image to disappear.

He cleared his throat. "Is there anything else you needed?" he asked, dismissively. "I am trying to work here."

All hint of humor dropped from Mr. Kelly's face. "Two of yer workers are here. They wish tae speak tae ye aboot something that happened in th' village yesterday."

"Isn't that what I pay you for?"

Not deterred by his response, his butler continued, "I think ye should hear them out first."

Luke nodded his assent and sat back in his chair.

Mr. Kelly opened the door, ushered them inside, and then closed the door behind them.

He recognized the two men as workers from the stable. Wracking his brain, he thought one was named Sean and the other Bernard. Both men wore worn kilts and faded shirts, holding their caps in their dirtied, brown hands. Their gazes were downcast, their movements hesitant.

Mr. Kelly stepped up next to them and prodded, "Go ahead. Tell Lord Downshire what transpired."

The servant he thought was named Sean stepped forward. "We wur in town getting supplies, and a bloke approached us. He invited us tae a meetin' tomorrow night at th' pub, The Fat Whaler." He awkwardly twisted the cap in his hand. "From whit I gathered, 'twas a meetin' tae call up arms against th' King."

Shocked by this news, Luke placed his arms on the desk and leaned forward. "What did the man say exactly?"

Bernard spoke up, "It wasn't what he said but what he hinted at. Th' bloke told us that France was winnin' th' war and th' King was not servin' his people."

"Did you recognize this man?" Luke asked.

Both men shook their heads. Sean replied, "Nay, I have ne'er seen him before. He wis young, well dressed, with dark hair, and he wis English." With a nervous glance at his friend, he added, "He wis very convincing."

"It seemed lik' he wis trying tae start an uprising, m'lord," Bernard expressed.

Luke jerked his eyes towards Mr. Kelly. "Inform the entire staff that if anyone is caught attending these types of meetings, or associating with anyone that does, they will be fired immediately, without references."

Nodding in acknowledgment, his butler confirmed, "As ye wish, m'lord."

Turning back to his servants, he said, "Thank you for bringing this to my attention. As a reward, please take the rest of the day off, fully paid. I will inform Hugh of my decision."

The two men smiled broadly. "Thank you," they responded in unison.

They exited the room, but Mr. Kelly stayed behind, waiting for further instructions from him. "Has a new constable arrived in Rockcliffe?" Luke asked.

"Aye, he arrived this mornin'."

"I would like to investigate this more. I will ride into the village and speak to the new constable." Glancing out the window, he saw a light, misty rain blanketing the fields around his castle. "I will depart as soon as the rain ceases."

Mr. Kelly nodded and placed his hand on the door handle. "A few men reported they saw Lady Rachel heading towards th' village not more than thirty minutes ago."

He pretended to mull over his butler's words before replying, "On second thought, ensure my horse is readied as soon as possible. I wish to investigate this matter immediately."

"I guessed as much, which is why I already ordered Hugh tae ready yer horse," Mr. Kelly informed him. "Do ye require an escort tae th' village?

"No, I know where the village is," he answered. Usually, he only went into the village if a large order of supplies was needed, mainly because he preferred his solitude. Now, however, he found himself quite motivated to make the trip.

LADY RACHEL STOPPED AT THE MERCANTILE, ADMIRING THE brightly-colored ribbons and lace handkerchiefs on display in the window. A hideous hat with an enormous flower hung nearby, but she gave it only a passing glance.

"How do men wear these contraptions?" David mumbled as he attempted to turn his neck, which was trapped in a starched collar.

Laughing softly, she turned to smile at her protector, who continued to grumble about his clothing. Her aunt had insisted David be fashionably dressed, since he insisted on escorting her niece into town. Borrowing a few articles of clothing from Emmett's wardrobe, she dressed David in a black tailcoat, green paisley waistcoat with matching cravat and pairing it with buff trousers. Unfortunately for David, he was bigger than her cousin, and the tailcoat was a bit too snug for him.

"Poor man," she teased without an ounce of sympathy. "Am I to assume that you have never worn a waistcoat before?"

"Waistcoats are unnecessary and restrictive, much like this devilish collar," David grumbled, tugging at the collar to empha-size his point. "If you are attacked, I hope you stay in my line of sight because I am physically unable to turn my head to the left or the right."

Scanning the cobblestone street, it seemed an attack was improbable. Stands were lined up along the pavement selling produce, food, and livestock. Behind them, thatched, half-timbered houses sat beside large, stone-and-slate-roofed town-houses. Nicely dressed women shopped next to women in tattered gowns, complacently focusing on their own errands. An occasional carriage drove slowly through the center, skirting the children playing in the road.

Resuming her walk along the busy street, Rachel asked David, "If you could choose, would you rather work as a constable in your home village or continue working as an agent?"

"Work as an agent," he responded without hesitation. He smiled proudly. "A constable handles drunks, petty fights, and thefts. An agent helps to ensure England remains safe, which is much more dangerous, and exciting."

"You mentioned your father is in poor health," she started, giving him a side-long glance. He nodded, and she continued, "When he dies, what will you do with your sister?"

The sounds of an approaching carriage caused David to reach for Rachel's elbow to maneuver her further from the street. After he dropped his hand, he replied, "I hadn't considered that."

"I ask only because she is sixteen. I hope you do not plan to marry her off so young."

With attentive eyes, David scanned the street as he acknowledged her words. "Honestly, I hope my father lives for many more years." He grinned at her. "After meeting you, I have come to realize that not all women eagerly anticipate marriage and a full nursery."

"Love should be the foremost requirement of marriage," she asserted unapologetically.

"As it should be, Lady Rachel," he agreed, meeting her gaze.

She opened her mouth to respond but was startled to hear her name being called from across the bustling street. "Lady Rachel," a man's voice shouted again. Turning her head, she saw Lord Melville striding towards her, impeccably dressed, as usual.

She groaned inwardly but forced herself to smile politely. "Fancy seeing you in the village," she said through gritted teeth.

She noticed that David had stepped back to allow her some privacy, but his body was tense as he watched Lord Melville. Ignoring her protector, Lord Melville smiled at her, his eyes brazenly roaming her face and trailing down to the square neckline of her pomona-green dress. He brought his approving eyes back up to meet her gaze. "I have some business I must attend to, but I would be honored if you would allow me to escort you home."

"It is kind of you to offer, but completely unnecessary." She angled her body to include David in the conversation. "David will escort me home."

Lord Melville frowned his disapproval as he maintained his gaze on her. "Perhaps I could call on you tomorrow?"

"That would be…" She stopped speaking when a weak tug came on her skirt, causing her to look down. A little boy with sunken eyes and pale cheeks had his hand gripped on the folds of her skirt. His threadbare clothing hung on him. "I'm hungry," he announced weakly.

"We can't have that, now can we?" Her words were kind and soothing.

"Be off with you, boy," Lord Melville demanded in a harsh tone. "Go beg somewhere else."

The boy's eyes grew wide in fear, and his small hand dropped from her skirt, causing her maternal instincts to flare up. "Good day, Lord Melville," she remarked firmly, dismissing him as she crouched down to speak to the boy. "Before we can go over and get you some food, you will need more appropriate clothing."

Lord Melville's shiny black boots disappeared from her view as the boy's eyes reflected his despair. Lowering his gaze, he admitted, "This is all I have."

Placing her hand on the boy's shoulder, sadness filled her

heart as she felt the bones through his shirt. "Well, it is a good thing the mercantile carries boys' clothing in your size." Extending her hand, she added, "I insist."

As Rachel rose, the boy accepted her hand, and they went inside the mercantile. Twenty minutes later, they emerged with sturdier clothes on the smiling boy. After they purchased bread and pastries from a street vendor, they were granted permission to sit on the back of his wagon.

Before she started eating, Rachel saw her cousin walking through the street. She waved, gesturing him over.

"Cousin," Emmett said politely as he approached. He tilted his head, acknowledging David before his eyes focused on the boy. "I see that little Tommy has found some new clothes."

With a toothless smile, the boy shared enthusiastically, "This nice lady bought me some clothes and food."

Turning his head towards her, Emmett's eyes shone with approval. "That was most kind of you."

"Nonsense, I was not about to let the boy starve," she admonished. "We were lucky that the mercantile had some clothes near his size." She scooted over in the wagon, creating more space. "Please, join us."

Emmett took his gloves off before he placed his hand on the boy's hair and ruffled it affectionately. Rachel handed him one of her pastries as she asked, "What were you doing in town?"

"He's a doctor," Tommy announced with a full mouth. "He helps my mama."

"Oh no, what ails your mother?" Rachel inquired, glancing between them.

The boy shrugged as Emmett informed her, "Nothing that won't be cured in six months."

"Oh," Rachel replied knowingly before placing a piece of pastry in her mouth.

"My mama has been real sick and can't work," Tommy admitted, taking another bite of his chunk of bread.

Leaning closer to Emmett, she asked in a hushed voice, "The boy's father?"

"Died last year," he stated, giving the boy a sad smile.

"What about the babe's father?" she questioned hopefully.

Emmett humphed in response. "You mean Lord Melville."

David picked that moment to interject, "It is a good thing that you rejected Lord Melville's suit."

"What!" her cousin roared, jumping up so fast that the wagon wobbled.

Rising, she leaned in and urged, "You need to calm down."

Grabbing her arm, Emmett led her down the street towards the local church. Once they were away from prying ears, he released her. "I told you to stay away from Lord Melville."

Placing her hands on her hips, she defiantly countered, "And I thought I asked you why."

He threw his hands up in the air. "You are unbelievable. Why can't you trust me?"

Dropping her hands, she gave him a look of utter disbelief. "Trust you? How can I trust *you* when you won't talk to me?"

"You don't understand men like Lord Melville, they are…"

Not letting him finish, she cut him off. "I understand men like Lord Melville perfectly well. He offered a marriage of convenience because he wants my fortune, not me."

Emmett turned around and placed his hands over his face. He lowered them, groaned loudly, then turned back to face her. "You are so incredibly naïve. He may want your money, but it is apparent he wants *you* as well."

"Well, I rejected his suit," she reassured him.

Walking closer, her cousin grabbed her shoulders. "Lord Melville doesn't take no for an answer. He will get you alone and hurt you." Fear reflected in Emmett's eyes as he pleaded with her. "I won't let him hurt you. I will die first."

Placing her hands on his sleeves, she replied, "It won't come to that."

Tightening his hold on her shoulders, he shook her. "Don't be ignorant! He will kill you and discard your body like waste. He won't even give you a proper burial."

Attempting to keep herself steady, her hands gripped his forearms tightly as her cousin kept shaking her. He was yelling at her, but his words did not apply to her situation. It appeared that he was reliving a painful memory. His eyes were haunted, withdrawn.

Knowing her cousin was not himself, she tried to find the words to snap him back into the present. "I won't go near Lord Melville again," she asserted.

Her words seemed to still her cousin. "Lord Melville?"

"Get your hands off of Lady Rachel," a man ordered next to her, stepping between them. Gripping her cousin's lapels, John threw a punch at her cousin. Staggering back in surprise, Emmett regained his bearings and came back, swinging at John's jaw.

"Stop!" Rachel demanded, watching the two men engaging in fisticuffs. Suddenly, David was by her side and took control of the situation. As Emmett swung his arm back, David grabbed it and forced it back down, slowly.

Both Emmett and John stood there breathing hard, glaring unrepentantly at each other. Stepping between them, she asked, "What is the matter with both of you?"

With his piercing eyes on her, John declared, "He was hurting you."

All residual anger dropped from Emmett's shoulders as he turned his wide, regretful eyes on her. "Cousin, did I hurt you?"

"Cousin?" Rachel heard John mumble in surprise. Attempting to reassure Emmett, she replied, "No, you did not, but I don't believe you were talking to me at the end."

"I am so sorry for scaring you. I never meant to hurt you." After she nodded in response, Emmett turned towards John. "Thank you for interceding on my cousin's behalf. I wasn't myself." He adjusted his waistcoat before saying, "I am Dr. Emmett Maddix."

"John," he replied. "John Magnus."

"How are you acquainted with my cousin?" Emmett asked him.

"We became friends after he accused me of stealing a horse," she interjected, smiling.

Emmett lifted his brow in disbelief, then he turned towards David. "I also thank you for ending the fight before I hurt John."

John scoffed. "I believe it was the other way around."

Glancing curiously at David's outfit, Emmett asked, "Are those my clothes?"

"They are," David mumbled as he started to button the tail-coat but discovered one of the buttons was missing.

Rachel felt it was her duty to reveal, "David is wearing a waistcoat for the first time."

"And a choker," David grumbled.

John corrected, "You mean collar."

"I mean what I said," David complained, tugging on the collar.

Emmett chuckled. "If you are such a fan of gentlemen's clothing, I insist you keep them."

Stretching from side to side, David protested, "Oh no, I have no desire to keep these torture devices."

Rachel turned to look for the little boy. "Where did Tommy go?"

David shrugged. "After you and Emmett left, I gave Tommy some money and told him to go home."

Emmett nodded. "I will go check on Tommy and his mother, but first," he paused, turning a heated glare back to John, "what the blazes is going on between you and my cousin?"

14

LUKE STOOD HIS GROUND CONFIDENTLY AGAINST EMMETT'S harsh glare. He huffed, "Nothing is going on between us." With a quick side-long glance to confirm his response with Rachel, he was surprised to see her eyes dimmed slightly. Was she saddened by his response?

Before he could ask, Rachel chided harshly, "Emmett, stop being such a bully. John and I are just friends."

Now it was Luke's turn to frown. Rachel was more than just a friend to him, but he couldn't define what their relationship was exactly.

Ignoring their responses, Emmett looked at David piercingly. "Are you chaperoning them at all times?" he asked, his tone skeptical.

David responded with a glare, "I hope you are not insinuating that my protection of Lady Rachel has been lacking."

Not backing down, Emmett challenged, "I am indeed." He frowned as he glanced at Rachel. "How else would my cousin be accused of horse thievery?"

Rachel smiled because that was easy to explain. "I went on a ride without David, and I came across Lord Downshire's pastures. Upon finding the most beautiful chestnut horse, I decided to go for a ride. Unfortunately, I did not realize that John witnessed me riding astride and assumed I was attempting to steal the horse." She threw Luke a smug look. "Which I clearly was not."

Listening to her explanation, Emmett grew increasingly agitated. Once she was finished, her cousin chastised, "You are not a child anymore. You can't ride astride, and certainly not on someone else's horse. What were you thinking?" He shook his head in frustration. "It is time for you to grow up, Rachel."

Instead of the witty retort that Luke had anticipated, Rachel lowered her eyes, appearing embarrassed by her cousin's rebuke. Emmett started to open his mouth again, but Luke declared, "That is enough. You have made your point."

Emmett frowned at Rachel's downcast eyes, apparently only now realizing that his words had hurt her. "I am sorry, again. I fear you don't understand the ramifications of your actions. Have you considered…" His voice trailed off, and he stepped back. "We shall talk more about this at home."

As he walked off, Luke had the craziest desire to wrap his arms around Rachel to comfort her. It was clear that Emmett's words had upset her, and he wished he could have spared her that verbal lashing. Facing her, he waited until her eyes rose to his before saying, "Don't give Emmett's words any heed. You are wild and unpredictable, but that is what makes you so perfectly unique." He smiled. "Although, I would highly recommend you stop riding horses that don't belong to you."

With a timid smile, she responded, "Thank you."

Admiring Rachel's piercing blue eyes that spoke of intelligence and wit, Luke didn't realize he was staring until he saw her blush. He turned to face David. "I came to the village in hopes of finding you here. We have a situation, and I need your expertise."

"I'm listening." David's response was vague, but his eyes were alert.

Including Rachel in the conversation, Luke explained, "A couple of my workers informed me that a man is trying to recruit men to join some type of militia. Apparently, the man stated that the French will be landing in Scotland, and he is riling men up against King George."

David's eyes grew hard. "Was a meeting place discussed?"

Luke nodded. "Yes, there will be a meeting tomorrow night at the pub, The Fat Whaler."

Clenching his jaw, Rachel's protector stated, "I will need to send a missive to my superior and notify him."

"I already sent a note to my brother," Luke informed him. "He works for the Crown."

Luke could see realization dawn on David's face. His younger brother, Lord Jonathon, was a highly valuable agent who worked closely with his uncle, Lord Charles Beckett, England's chief spymaster. "Good, good," David muttered his approval.

Joining in their discussion, Rachel added, "That is not necessary. I wrote a missive to *Shadow,* and a messenger departed this morning to deliver it."

Both men turned to look at Rachel with wide eyes. Luke was the first to break the silence. "You know *Shadow?*"

"I do," she confirmed. "Both of you were aware that *Shadow* rescued me."

Giving her an exasperated look, Luke insisted, "I remembered. However, being rescued by *Shadow* is different from knowing who *Shadow* is and where to find him."

She shrugged one shoulder. "Perhaps. But I do know *Shadow.* Is that so hard to believe?"

"Pardon me, but it is nearly impossible to believe, Lady Rachel," David contended. "I was on the brig *Brazen Hine* when *Shadow* killed over a dozen men with his longbow. Truth be told,

I never even saw him, but I heard the arrows whizzing by me, hitting the thugs with deadly accuracy. Knowing the identity of *Shadow*, and staying alive, is quite an honor."

"I suppose so, but *Shadow* and I are friends," Rachel shared, her voice adamant. "I would never reveal *Shadow's* identity."

"You are friends with a deadly assassin?" Luke asked, his voice rising. "How close are you to him?" Rachel's association with *Shadow* obviously upset him. It was as if he was jealous, which was ridiculous.

Rachel defended her position. "*Shadow* is not an assassin. Besides, aren't you glad that I have such a close association with *Shadow?* I was able to alert the Crown about a possible invasion."

"Lady Rachel does have a point," David admitted.

Crossing his arms over his chest, Luke grumbled, "We don't need *Shadow*. We can handle this situation ourselves, or at least until my brother arrives."

Rachel's lips twitched in amusement, which annoyed him even more. "Stop being so stubborn. Why wouldn't we call England's most famous spy to help with a French invasion?" She paused and smirked, "Unless you believe one agent, a horse trainer, and a lady can stop a French army?"

Dropping his arms, Luke took a firm step closer to Rachel. "Oh no, you will not be anywhere near danger."

Matching one of his steps with one of her own, she challenged, "What entitles *you* to make that decision for me?"

"Well, someone has to," Luke huffed. Didn't she realize that someone needed to protect her? Well, someone besides David. They both could keep her safe.

Rachel pursed her lips. "You are unbelievable. You think just because you kissed me that you have a right to order me around."

"That has nothing to do with this…" Luke started but was cut off by David muttering expletives under his breath, loudly at that.

David scoffed. "It was in the cave, wasn't it?" When they both averted their eyes from his judging glare, he continued, "It had to have been. That was the only time I took my eyes off Lady Rachel."

Marching up to them, David gently moved Rachel towards one direction and shoved Luke towards another. Standing between them, he growled, "You two will not be left alone again. I forbid it."

Pushing his rising irritation aside, Luke wanted to refocus the conversation back on the possible French invasion and a growing militia. "I will go to the meeting tomorrow night at The Fat Whaler and determine if the militia is a credible threat."

"I will go, as well," David stated, his tone leaving no room for argument.

Luke frowned. "Who will protect Lady Rachel?"

"I can protect myself," Rachel declared defiantly.

In unison, both David and Luke replied, "No, you can't."

Rachel smoothed out her dress, and that drew Luke's eyes towards her comely figure. Smiling to himself, he remembered wrapping his arms around her waist in the cave. However, the smile dropped when she said, "I will just have to go with you two to the meeting."

Luke pointed his finger at her, and in his most authoritative voice, he ordered, "You will not. You will stay home and not leave the Maddix's estate until David returns."

"As you wish," she conceded with a polite nod.

Finally, she was beginning to see reason, he thought. He was getting through to her.

As the moon rose high in the sky, Luke waited at the edge of town for David. Sitting on his horse, his hands on the saddle horn, he let his mind wander towards the infuriating, yet alluring, Rachel.

She was the opposite of everything that he knew about women. Even though Rachel was undeniably beautiful, that was not what captivated his attention. It was her compassionate nature and the kindness she demonstrated to others, regardless of their social standing. She used her connections to help people and did not ask for anything in return. But more importantly, Rachel made everything seem like an adventure with her unconquerable zest for life. For the first time, it made him consider his own life and priorities.

What had he been doing these past seven years since moving to Scotland, besides running his stud farm and estate? Nothing, he admitted to himself. He had done nothing with his money or connections to help the people of Rockcliffe.

Before he could dwell on his thoughts anymore, two riders broke through the trees and slowed their horses to a trot as they approached. Immediately, Luke recognized David, who wore a cream shirt, and dark trousers. The rider next to him appeared to be a boy wearing an oversized white shirt and a cap sitting low on his head.

"Who did you bring with you?" Luke asked curiously as they reined in their horses.

With an exasperated grunt, David replied, "Who do you think?"

The boy lifted his head, and the moonlight highlighted feminine features with blonde hair. Sucking in his breath, he tried to control the fury raging through his body. "Do you have a death wish, Lady Rachel?" His tone was accusatory as he glared at her.

Undeterred by his anger, she informed him, "I am curious how this meeting will play out, since…"

"You disobeyed me. I specifically ordered you to stay home," he exclaimed, cutting her off in a tone that had sent others scurrying with fear.

To his surprise, Rachel laughed at him. No one had ever laughed at him! When she was calmer, she fixed her gaze on him, all traces of humor gone. "What right do you have to order me around?"

Luke frowned at her question. He knew she was right. However, he was a marquess, son of the Duke of Remington, and everyone always followed his directions without hesitation. He threw David a glance, hoping Rachel's protector could help her see reason but was met with a helpless shrug.

Urging her horse closer to his, Rachel kept impressive control as she moved in beside him. "In case you are confused, I am a grown woman, and I dictate my own actions," she declared in a controlled voice.

Oh, he was quite aware that Rachel was a grown woman, an exquisite woman that defied his expectations, but she was being foolish with her safety. Attempting to appeal to her rational side, he asked, "Do you know what would happen to you if some of these unscrupulous men discovered that you were a lady?"

Tugging her cap lower on her face, Rachel had the nerve to say, "I will blend in."

Luke stifled a laugh at the thought of Rachel blending in, because she was born to stand out. He perused her obviously-borrowed outfit. "First of all, your cap is pulled down too low. That by itself is suspicious, but let's address the rest of your clothing." He sighed, frustrated. "Your shirt is ridiculously too large, your trousers are being held up by twine, and you're wearing ladies riding boots."

Gazing at Rachel's face, Luke knew that anyone would be a fool not to recognize her for the beauty that she was. How were they going to keep this hoyden safe? Focusing on David, he clenched his jaw before asking, "Explain to me how Lady Rachel is dressed like a boy, and why she intends to go to a militia meeting."

David gave him an amused smile. "She offered me £50 to escort her to the meeting."

Running a hand through his brown hair, Luke was trying hard not to explode with fury over the carelessness that Rachel's protector was demonstrating for her safety. As he prepared to lecture David on the inappropriateness of his actions, Rachel stated, "Do not be mad at David. I wanted to come to this meeting for research on my book."

Shaking his head, Luke started again to open his mouth, when she continued, "Besides, if you recall, you previously offered David a horse to point out my window, so it is only fair that he bent the rules for me as well."

Turning his attention towards David, Luke's glare was full of anger and intensity. "You are a bloody fool to fall for her feminine wiles. Rachel could be killed, and you don't seem very worried." In a flash of an eye, David's eyes narrowed, and his cold gaze turned palpable. Apparently, his powerful gaze did not work on Rachel or David. Neither of them cowered in fear.

Slowly, David pulled out the pistol tucked into the waistband of his trousers. "I am carrying three pistols and two daggers on my person. Plus, Lady Rachel has an overcoat pistol of her own."

Luke's disapproving eyes flickered to Rachel. "Do you even know how to use a pistol?" he questioned, frowning.

A slow, satisfied smile came to her lips. "I am an excellent shot. Do not fear."

Shoving his pistol back into his trousers, David asserted, "My job is to protect Lady Rachel, and I have no doubt that I can keep her safe." He paused, and a smug smile came to his lips.

"However, I am not duty-bound to protect you, so try not to get yourself killed."

Rachel laughed but covered her mouth with her fingers when Luke glanced her way. Finally, he conceded, "All right, I am outnumbered, and we need to hurry if we want to arrive before the meeting starts."

As they moved towards The Fat Whaler, rowdy voices could be heard from the opened windows. The half-timbered building stood near the outskirts of town. A narrow, wooden door was opened, and a rectangle of light flooded the street.

They dismounted and tied their horses to a post. Luke moved to stand in front of Rachel, ensuring that she was blocked from the view of patrons in the pub. He leaned close and warned, "You will stay behind me and don't say anything. A pub is no place for a lady, especially tonight when treasonous activities will be discussed."

Rachel smiled up at him as though it was some type of game to her. Giving her a scolding look, Luke attempted to explain his anger. "You are driving me mad."

"That was my intention all along," Rachel quipped, her smile growing more mischievous.

Luke growled, "Just do as you're told."

David cleared his throat and shook his head. "Try again."

Clenching his jaw, he said, "Just do as you're told," he hesitated, "please."

Tilting her head, Rachel's eyes roamed his face for a moment before smiling. "I will stay behind you, but only because you said 'please'."

Walking around the horses, they headed toward the pub's entrance. As they went in, the number of patrons surprised them. The long, rectangular wooden tables were filled with men sitting shoulder to shoulder with large tin cups in front of them. Along the walls, men loitered with drinks in their hands, some chatting with the men next to them, others drinking in silence. Three serving wenches were bustling around, clearing away empty tankards and replacing them with full ones.

One of the serving wenches approached them, wearing a revealing dress that accentuated her bosoms. She leaned in close to be heard above the din in the room. "Drinks are on the house. What can I get for ye lads?"

Declining the drinks, Luke and David moved to stand by the back wall, tucking Lady Rachel safely behind them. Luke's eyes scanned the men, looking for anyone familiar. Luckily, none of his workers were here. He'd been serious about firing them if they attended the meeting. He would not accept mutiny among his men.

A loud whistle swept through the pub as a tall man, with broad shoulders and a crooked nose, stood in front holding his fingers in his mouth. Lowering his fingers, he proclaimed, "My name is Thorne. I hope you are enjoying the free drinks and will continue to do so all night. However, I am eager to present an opportunity that will only come around once in a lifetime."

Everyone grew silent as Thorne hopped up onto a table and continued, "The French are outside our harbor, and they are preparing to land. They have enough men to conquer England and finally rid the world of lazy, mad King George." A few boos were heard from the men, but that did not deter him. "Napoleon will seize England, and you will be free from the clutches of a monarchy that steals your money and gives you nothing in return."

Pacing the length of the long, rectangular table, Thorne's eyes scanned the people gathered, his voice full of passion. "Your prince regent, Prinny, maintains a lavish lifestyle despite being heavily in debt. Where is he getting the money to maintain his mistresses, his bastard children, and his castles?" He pointed to the group. "He is taking your money, your hard-earned money. Prinny is not starving because of high food prices, nor does he have to watch his children suffer from an empty stomach."

LAURA BEERS

Thorne crouched down low on the table and addressed a patron. "Why can't you take *his* money and live like a king?"

"Hear, hear," a few men shouted, energetically.

Thorne continued to engage the patron as he said, "The French will invade England, and Napoleon wants to make you a rich man." He stood up and addressed the whole group. "We are recruiting men from each village to form a militia to help fight against the men who are loyal to mad King George."

Several men shifted their gazes around the group, appearing uncomfortable with Thorne's proposal. A few husky thugs stood in the room, their massive arms crossed against their chests, intimidating the men with hardened glares. Thorne's smile dimmed as he placed his hands in front of him. "I know that many of you are displaced cottiers from the lowlands, having no skills other than weaving. Some of you may have been forced from your homes by landlords more interested in profit. You may have watched as your communities were razed to the ground." He frowned deeply. "Life is hard; poverty, disease, and desperation are everyday struggles."

Again, Thorne paced up and down the long tables. "Napoleon is your ally! The French will conquer England, but he is offering the good people of Scotland a chance to become part of history. Join us, and you will be paid beyond your wildest dreams. You will be able to take back what is rightfully yours, and you can keep everything you pilfer from those rich, entitled lords' townhouses." As the crowd cheered louder, the man shouted, "It is your turn to live like kings! Come join us!"

Luke's eyes wandered over the pub full of men as they became riotous in their excitement. They were shoving each other, and it was quickly getting out of hand. A burly man walked by and knocked his shoulder hard against him, causing him to stagger back. Rachel placed her hands on his back to keep him from slamming her against the wall, but he noticed that she didn't release her hold on his shirt.

"It is time for us to depart," David informed them in a stern voice.

Slowly, they made their way towards the door, only to be stopped by a large, domineering guard. Glaring at them, the man asked in a threatening tone, "Are ye wi' us or against us?"

"We are wi' ye," David replied firmly in a Scottish accent. "We are tired o' bein' oppressed by a mad king, and his dandy son, Prinny."

The man's eyes roamed over the two of them and nodded. "In six days, we wull hae th' final meetin'. Ye wull be paid ten shillings upfront."

Rubbing his hands together greedily, David stated, "I cannot wait tae show my wummin a' those coins." He glanced at Luke. "I cannot wait tae raid th' palace."

The guard's eyes flashed with approval. "Ye wull hae yer chance." Standing aside, he added, "Dinnae forgoat, six days, same time."

As they walked out the door, the guard's voice turned menacing. "Whit's this? Ye brought a lass tae th' meeting?"

Turning around, Luke saw the guard grasping Rachel's arm tightly, and she looked up at him with sheer panic in her eyes. Before he opened his mouth, David came to stand next to Rachel as he explained, "Ye hae tae excuse my sister. She wis abused by oor English landlord and wants tae help wi' th' cause."

The guard released her arm. "I understand yer need fur revenge, bit we dinnae tak' wummin."

David grabbed Rachel's arm and pushed her towards the door. "Stupid lass. I told her tae stay home, bit she followed. Next time, I wull tie her tae a chair tae prevent her from comin'."

The guard nodded approvingly and stepped aside. They walked swiftly over to their horses and mounted quickly. Silently, they rode hard until they were far away from the pub. Luke slowed his horse to a trot and addressed David. "I will send another missive to my brother and my uncle. The Crown needs to know about this."

David bobbed his head in agreement. "With any luck, your brother is already on his way. I will send word to the constable about a rising militia in the village."

"What about the other villages?" Rachel asked. "The man said men from other villages are being recruited."

"I will inform the constable and request that he pass along the information to them as well," David replied.

Luke couldn't help but comment on David's Scottish accent. "Thank you for stepping in to protect Rachel. If I didn't know better, I would have thought you were a native of Scotland."

David shrugged. "Over the years, I have perfected my lowland Scots and Gaelic."

"Really?" Rachel questioned.

"I am educated, my lady," David said, grinning. "I was sent off to a boarding school near the English-Scottish border." He winked at her. "Why do you think Mr. Larson requested me for this assignment?"

Rachel laughed. "My apologies, my lowlander protector."

Luke's stomach churned, and he pushed down the surge of jealousy washing over him as he watched Rachel interact with David. He unconsciously clenched his fist, pressing the reins deep into his hand. How was David able to converse with Rachel so easily? It seemed so smooth.

As they neared the turn-off for the Maddix's estate, he thought about ways to get Lady Rachel alone again, without appearing too eager to spend more time with her. Why did he have to find her so intriguing?

Just before they veered off, he cleared his throat, hoping his intended ruse would be good enough. "Lord Downshire wants to send his sister a first edition book from his library as a wedding present and has tasked me with finding the perfect book." He took a deep breath, hoping she would agree to his next question.

"Would you mind helping me, since you are friends with Lady Lansdowne?"

Rachel's eyes lit up with excitement. "I would love to," she responded eagerly. "I have been dying to go back to that library since you first showed it to me."

Keeping his face expressionless, Luke confirmed, "Tomorrow, then."

"Tomorrow it is," she said in a cheery voice.

David nodded, and Rachel waved goodbye before they raced their horses back towards the Maddix's estate. Luke watched their retreating figures, knowing he needed to stop his growing attraction towards Rachel. It would only end in heartache for him. Even as a marquess, he didn't deserve someone like her. He was a reclusive lord, and Rachel was... what was she?

He smiled at the memory of Rachel riding his horse across the field. She was a strikingly beautiful woman, and her heart was pure, her mind still unblemished by the atrocities of the world. However, he was a cynic and had vowed never to get married. That institution was for fools and hypocrites, and he was neither, making it impossible to have a future with her. He knew he needed to stop seeing her before she developed any foolish ideas about the two of them.

Kicking his horse into a run, Luke decided to enjoy tomorrow, because after that, he wouldn't see Lady Rachel again.

15

Lady Rachel reached for another book, pulling it off the shelf in Lord Downshire's library. She gasped as she read the title. Turning towards John, she wanted to jump up and down with excitement. Holding out the book, she announced, "This is a first printed edition of *The Canterbury Tales*."

John looked at her blankly, apparently not recognizing the significance of her find.

"This book was written by Chaucer and was printed in 1476," she explained.

As she started to return the book to the shelf, John asked, "What are you doing?"

"Lord Downshire would never let a book this rare go to his sister," she informed him, tucking the book gently back into its original spot.

"And you would know this how?"

As she trailed her fingers along the bookends looking for another title that piqued her interest, she clarified, "*The Canterbury Tales* is worth a fortune and is coveted by the ton." She pulled out a book titled *Utopia* by Sir Thomas More and placed it on the small pile that John held for her.

John smirked. "I think you need to make a decision about what book Lord Downshire should send his sister." To emphasize his point, he lifted the pile of books in his hands. "I am carrying eight books, and that pile on the table contains more than fifty."

She sighed reluctantly as her gaze traveled towards the pile of books. How was she going to make such a monumental decision? There were so many first edition books in this library that it put her father's library to shame. She had an overwhelming desire to curl up near the fireplace and read as many books as she could before Lord Downshire returned home from holiday.

Walking to the table, John carefully laid the books in his hands next to the taller pile. "I must admit that I have never met a woman so interested in books before."

Excitement bubbled inside of her as she tried to explain why she loved books so much. "These books hold historical facts, poetry, plays, mathematical equations, and love stories that caused nations to go to war."

John lifted his brow in amusement. "War?"

Rachel smiled. "Not every love story ends happily."

"Is that what you are after?" John questioned as he sat on the sofa. "A love story with a happy ending?"

Rachel looked at him in surprise. "Of course, eventually," she admitted. "I believe every woman wants to fall in love and marry a man that is devoted to her." She sat on the other end of the sofa. "Don't you want to fall in love, marry your sweetheart, and have a house full of little children running around?"

John scoffed, "I do not intend to marry."

"I see," Rachel murmured, although she clearly did not. "I suppose you plan to be a horse trainer for the rest of your days."

John shrugged one shoulder. "I am living my dream."

Reaching for one of the books in the small pile, Rachel asked curiously, "Why not dream bigger?"

"Pardon?"

Rachel brought back a small, old book and fingered the spine. "Why not dream of owning your own stud farm?"

John brought his arms up and rested his hands on the back of his head. He pursed his lips, thinking. "One day, I hope to own my own stud farm," he declared, glancing at her, amusement in his eyes. "Is that better?"

"Yes," Rachel replied, attempting to keep a smile off her face. "And I hope that one day you will trust another woman with your heart and fall madly, deliriously in love."

"Are you applying for the position, Rachel?" John asked with a flirtatious smile.

My goodness, he looks dashingly handsome when he smiles that way, she thought. She lowered her eyes to the book in front of her. Rachel felt her cheeks grow warm as she sensed his gaze lingering on her face. After mustering up her courage, she answered, "I'm afraid not. You will have to trick another woman to fall for your gentlemanly wiles."

John laughed in response and his voice echoed throughout the rafters of the two-story library.

His laughter took her by surprise, but it also caused her heart to soar. She peeked at his face and took a moment to admire his strong jaw, which held a hint of dark stubble.

"Touché," he replied after he stopped laughing.

"You should laugh more," Rachel remarked, dropping her gaze back to the book in her lap. "It suits you."

Removing his hands from behind his head, John angled his body to face her. "I suppose I haven't had a reason to laugh in a very long while."

Rachel matched his posture. "That is a shame. If you can't find amusement in the mundane tasks, then where will you find it?"

John huffed, "It is not that easy."

"It is," she insisted.

"Not everyone is blessed with an upbringing such as yours,"

John stated, suddenly growing defensive. "You were loved, wanted even, but I was just my parent's heir."

Rachel frowned at his curt tone. Whenever he grew uncomfortable with the topic being discussed, John became defensive. Pushing her point, she said, "You blame your parents for your unhappiness. When are you going to stop and claim your own life, your own happiness?"

"You don't understand..." John started but stopped when Rachel put her hand up.

Maintaining her gaze, she lowered her hand. "It is true that my parents loved me and showered me with attention from the moment I was born. However, as I have grown up, I have tried to become a lady that my parents would be proud of, but I have failed repeatedly. I have always had a burning desire to do more in my life than what is offered to women."

Fingering the book in her lap, she hesitated, reluctant to say her next words. "I understand that my actions may cause me to become a spinster, but I will not settle for less. I can't."

John rested his elbow on the back of the sofa. "And what is it that you want to do with your life?"

"I hope to make a difference in the lives of people I associate with," Rachel shared. "Maybe open an orphanage for girls?"

"Sounds honorable."

She started flipping through the pages of the book. "Everyone we meet has their own unique story to share; some have joy, some hold regret, but I have discovered heartache transcends all levels of our society." She closed the book and placed it on her lap. "I am fascinated when I meet new people and hear their stories. I want to understand why people behave the way they do."

John smirked, amused. "And you like to help people."

"I do, especially since I'm in a position to do so," Rachel confirmed. "I believe people are inherently good, but their circumstances force them to make decisions contrary to what their conscience dictates."

"I disagree," John argued. "People are selfish and use others only for their personal gain."

Rachel's heart constricted at the pain reflected in his eyes, knowing he fully believed the validity of his statement. "Why do you believe the worst in people?" she questioned, gently.

Leaning forward in his seat, John wiped a hand over his chin as he took his time to respond. "I have always been expected to be an honorable gentleman, even though it was contrary to how my own parents behaved." He stopped, his words pained. "My father has lived with his mistress for over twenty years, and my mother paraded her lovers in regular rotations. My parents hated each other, but it was my mother that openly spewed hate about my father."

Rachel placed the book next to her and moved closer to him. "That was your parent's choice, not yours."

Casting a skeptical eye at her, John said, "Our society presses us into marriage, not for joy and happiness, but for status, wealth, and an heir. I refuse to be a part of it." He frowned. "I will not bring a child into a loveless marriage."

Placing her hands over his, she urged, "Then don't. Marry for love."

John turned his gaze towards the window and slumped his shoulders. "When I was at Eton, I fancied myself in love with the groundkeeper's daughter, Joane. She used to meet me at the stream after supper, and we would talk for hours."

Rachel nudged him with her shoulder. "You expect me to believe that you met a beautiful girl by the stream and you just talked?" she teased.

He withdrew his hand from hers and sighed. "I was lonely at Eton, and I needed a friend. Joane filled that void."

"What happened?"

He ran his hand over his chin, deliberately. "A few months

later, I declared my love, and she claimed to return my affections. She even kissed me." He smiled weakly. "However, the headmaster caught us, and I was flogged as punishment for sneaking out." His voice was filled with deep pain and remorse. "After I was beaten, I ran to her cottage, where I was going to ask her to run away with me and get married."

"How old were you?"

"Sixteen."

"You wanted to get married at sixteen?" she asked in disbelief.

"I thought I was in love," came his simple response. "As I was running through the clearing, I found Joane in an intimate position with one of my classmates." He scoffed, his voice becoming cynical. "Apparently, she wanted to raise her station in life, by any means possible."

Placing her hand over his once again, she waited till he met her gaze. "Not every girl is like Joane, you know. You need to keep your heart open and not closed up."

John grinned. "You are trying to fix this… fix me." His smile grew until it reached his eyes, pleasing Rachel immensely. "If only everything were so simple."

"It can be," she responded.

Glancing down at their adjoined hands, he teased, "You are a wise woman."

Feeling a connection with him, Rachel wanted to share her greatest wish, but she feared his reaction. His response would decide whether their friendship would progress, or if he was like all the vain, pompous men she knew. Taking a shaky breath, she revealed, "One day, I hope to write a book."

"A book?" John asked in disbelief. "Is that what your 'research' is about?"

She nodded. "It is."

He looked puzzled. "But you are a woman."

"Thank you for clearing that up," Rachel said dryly, pulling her hands back.

John pressed, "Women don't write books."

She rolled her eyes dramatically. "Two books have been published recently, both written under the name A Lady. Furthermore, other women on the continent have been writing books for years. Mary Wollstonecraft, for example. She's been published for twenty years!"

"A small handful compared to thousands of men," he pointed out.

Reaching for the book next to her, Rachel placed it on the table and rose, mumbling, "Imbecile."

"Did you just call me an imbecile?"

"I did," she admitted, standing over him. "I am not content to live a safe, boring life. Unlike you, I want to experience all aspects of life. I don't want to be limited by what high Society expects of me." She pointed towards the books. "Many of the books housed in this library alone were written by men who were forced to endure criticism at the hand of rulers, peers, and ignorant people. Their cynics cited their ideas were too radical for the day, but most proved their critics wrong." She tilted her chin. "As will I."

Spinning around to leave, Rachel was stilled by his hand on her forearm. "Don't go," he pleaded. "I have never considered that a woman might be an author because…"

"Because women have delicate constitutions?" she asked, cutting him off.

"No," he answered with a shake of his head.

"Let me guess, women should focus on getting married and should have no desire to better themselves?" Turning back to face him, her voice grew with indignation. "Or…"

John jumped up and placed his finger on her lips, silencing her immediately. "If you would stop spouting nonsense, I will tell you what I was going to say." As he lowered his finger, he kept a watchful eye on her. "I had never considered that a

woman might be an author before because I didn't realize
women wanted to write books."

"And?" she said, waiting for the real reason.

"That's it," John revealed, dropping his hold on her hand and
stepping back. "If writing a book will make you happy, then I
applaud your tenacity."

Crossing her arms over her chest, Rachel evaluated her opponent. He seemed genuine, but no man had ever encouraged her
before. Most of the time, men dismissed the notion as if it was a
passing whim. She watched him as he picked up a book from the
large pile and started flipping through the pages.

Feeling a mixture of confusion and happiness, Rachel finally
found her voice. "Thank you for that."

Handing her the book, John shared, "Even though I was
raised by a loveless mother, I never doubted her keen intellect.
Watching my mother was like watching a game of chess.
Everyone around her was a pawn, and she ensured they all
played by the rules, even when she didn't."

"Oh," Rachel mumbled, not sure what else she could add.
"I'm sorry."

"Don't be," John said, taking a step closer. "I admit I was
taken aback by your admission that you want to write a book, but
I shouldn't have been. After all, I have come to expect the unexpected from you."

She heard the amusement in his words, but all she could
think about was what an oddity she was. Rachel knew she was
different than the other ladies of the ton, but it hurt to hear it
from a new friend's mouth, especially one as handsome as John.
She flipped through the pages of the book and handed it back to
him. "Tell Lord Downshire that this book would be an excellent
choice for his sister."

Turning to leave, John grabbed her hand and drew her back
to face him. "What is wrong, Rachel?" His eyes roamed her face.
"Did I say something wrong?"

Rachel shook her head. "No, everything you said was the truth." When John's eyes hinted at confusion, she added, "You just reminded me how truly odd I am among the ton."

"Odd?" John repeated. Huffing, he admonished, "You are delightful, charming, inquisitive, and impulsive, but you are most definitely not odd."

Biting her lower lip, she ventured to voice her greatest worry and feared his reaction. Taking a breath, she asked, "Do you think it would be easier if I acted the way the ton expected me to?"

"Easier on whom?" John took another step closer. Standing in front of her, he still held her hand in his. "If you ask me, I don't think you should change to fit the ton's expectations, but the ton should change its expectations to accommodate you."

"You don't think I'm too reckless?"

"Yes, I do," John stated very quickly. "I think you are stubborn, impulsive, and you drive me mad. But," he paused, a crooked smile forming on his lips, "you are infuriatingly perfect."

He raised her hand up to his lips and tenderly kissed her knuckles. As he lowered her hand, his eyes kept glancing at her lips as if waiting for her approval. Her silence must have been enough because he slowly lowered his head. Rachel closed her eyes in anticipation of the kiss when a loud clearing of a throat could be heard.

Opening her eyes, Rachel looked towards the offending noise and saw David slowly shaking his head at them. He growled deliberately, "Never again on my watch."

Attempting to hide her pink cheeks, she put her hands up to cover them. "I should go," she murmured regretfully.

Stepping aside, John looked as if he wanted to say more but just mumbled his goodbyes. As she headed for the door, his voice unexpectedly filled the library. "I have two horses that need to be exercised tomorrow. Would you like to join me for a ride?"

With a smile, Rachel admitted, "I would, very much."

"Wonderful," John said with a bow. "I will see you tomorrow."

As Rachel left the library, she noticed a bemused expression on his face. She realized how much she wanted to kiss him again. Perhaps he wanted to kiss her, too? Maybe tomorrow she could offer David a tidy sum to linger further back on the ride? Now, that sounded like a plan.

THE NEXT MORNING, LUKE WAS WHISTLING AT HIS DESK WHEN Mr. Kelly walked in and announced, "Th' staff is assembled as ye requested, m'lord." He paused, his brow lowered in confusion. "Were ye whistling?"

"I was," Luke admitted, surprising even himself.

Mr. Kelly walked closer to the desk and crouched down next to him. His eyes roamed over Luke's face. "Are ye feeling a' right?"

Resting his arms on his desk, Luke just ignored his meddlesome butler and continued rifling through his correspondence. "Thank you for assembling the staff. I believe they should be rewarded for their service."

Not moving from his position, Mr. Kelly eyed him suspiciously. "Perhaps I should fetch a doctor?"

Pushing back his chair, Luke rose and reached for his riding coat, putting it on over his paisley waistcoat. As he adjusted his cravat, he headed for the door, not bothering to see if Mr. Kelly followed him.

At the front staircase, he took two stairs at a time before turning and facing his staff. "I appreciate you leaving your tasks, so I may address you." With a brief nod at Hugh, he said, "I am grateful for the hospitality that you have shown Lady Rachel and for keeping the ruse of me being a horse trainer. To reward each of you for your loyalty, I will ask Mr. Kelly to provide each of you with a raise. It will be reflected next time you are paid." A collective gasp echoed throughout the main hall.

Luke put his hand up to silence the noise before he continued, "More importantly, I have recently learned of health concerns among my staff and their family members. Thus, I have petitioned a hospital in Edinburgh to send a doctor to practice in Rockcliffe."

Cheering erupted, and Luke found himself smiling at their happy expressions. To provide a doctor for the people of Rockcliffe was a paltry sum to him, and he knew it would help his staff and the people of the village.

As Luke walked down the stairs, his female employees were all smiling at him, not flirtatiously, but with gratitude. Not used to such praise, he quickly rushed down the remaining stairs and out the main door. Walking towards the stables, Hugh caught up to him, matching his stride. "I hae brought th' horse ye requested from th' east pasture, and he is saddled next tae Magnus."

"Thank you," Luke responded, eagerly. He was excited to see Rachel's reaction to the horse he had selected for her. It was the same horse that she had been riding when he first laid eyes on her.

With a chuckle, Hugh remarked, "I cannae help bit believe this transformation is due tae yer bonnie Lady Rachel."

Tilting his head, Luke corrected him, "Lady Rachel is not mine. We are just friends."

"Ye'r denyin' the truth," Hugh said with a knowing smile. "Whit did Lady Rachel say whin ye told her that ye'r not a horse trainer bit th' Marquess of Downshire?"

Walking into the stable, Luke headed towards the saddled horses and grabbed the leads but was stopped when Hugh put his hand on his shoulder. "Ye haven't told her, have ye?"

Luke frowned. "It is complicated."

Hugh gave him an exasperated look. "Then uncomplicate it. Th' longer ye go on lying tae th' lassie th' less chance she will forgive ye."

One of the horses whinnied, causing Luke's eyes to focus on his horse. "What if she doesn't forgive me?"

"How could she not? Ye'r a laird, a rich marquess, and th' eldest son o' th' Duke of Remington," Hugh pointed out.

Kicking at the straw on the ground with his Hessian boot, Luke winced as he tried to avoid Hugh's sharp gaze. "It would impress any other lady of the ton, but not Rachel. Wealth, titles, and prestige mean very little to her." His gaze shifted over his stable master's shoulder. "She has given me a new perspective on life."

Hugh laughed. "That is good, because yer old perspective was suspect, at best."

Taking his hand, he rubbed the neck of Magnus, slowly. "If I tell her who I truly am, she may find me lacking." He turned to face Hugh. "And I have never lacked for anything. I have money, power, and respect, but for the first time, is it enough?"

For a moment, Hugh didn't say anything as he appeared to mull over his words. After a moment, he said, "Tae th' right lassie, th' things that ye mentioned mean very little. It sounds tae me that Lady Rachel looks at yer heart, and cares not for yer station." Picking up a brush from the ground, he placed it in a bucket. "After a', she believes that a horse trainer is befriending her. Most wummin of high Society would nae be friends wi' a servant."

Smiling, Luke admitted, "Technically, she believes I am the *lead* horse trainer."

"Lead horse trainer?" Hugh laughed. "I dinnae know we had

that position."

"We do now." He grinned as he started leading the horses out.

Hugh matched his stride as they left the stable and walked towards the pasture. Two riders approached from the distance. Immediately, he recognized Rachel's graceful riding posture and her blonde hair pulled back into a chignon.

Putting his hand up, Luke waved and was pleased to see Lady Rachel wave in response. A smile came to his lips as he watched her approach.

Hugh's voice distracted him. "I would recommend telling her sooner rather than later, m'lord," he advised in a hushed voice.

Hugh was right. It was time. He needed to hope that Rachel would forgive him for his dishonesty and accept him for who he truly was. He was a marquess and not a lowly servant. He owned Downshire Farms and amassed his own fortune. Furthermore, one day he would inherit more money than he could spend in twenty lifetimes. She would understand, wouldn't she?

Rachel's face brightened as she approached, and he returned her smile. She had come to mean so much to him. Could he risk losing her friendship?

Walking over to her, he helped her dismount, allowing his hands to linger on her waist. Her eyes widened in surprise as she saw the horse that he had selected for her. She walked over and started petting his neck. "How are you today, beautiful beast? I have missed you," she murmured to the horse. Turning to face him, her eyes sparkled with happiness. "Do you suppose Lord Downshire will sell me this horse?"

He leaned closer to her, taking in the delightful smell of rose water. "Lord Downshire will never sell this horse."

Looking disappointed, she asked, "Does this horse have a name?"

"Yes, his name is Chester," Luke informed her, enjoying their private interlude.

"Hmm, Chester," Rachel said, eyeing the horse. "I will allow it."

Luke laughed in response. "You will allow it?"

Rachel started petting Chester's nose before saying, "When I buy this horse, I will keep the name Chester. It suits him."

Hugh stepped up and collected the horse Lady Rachel had ridden in on and nodded politely at her as he led the horse away to be brushed.

"Shall we?" Luke asked Rachel as she continued to admire Chester.

A brief time later, they were riding near his south pasture and racing through the vast green field. Glancing behind him, Luke did not see David, but he had no doubt that he was keeping a constant visual on Rachel.

They slowed their horses to a trot and Luke rode next to her. "I am glad that we have a chance to talk."

Rachel turned to face him, her cheeks pink from the wind, and pieces of her hair had fallen from her chignon, cascading down her back. He was momentarily distracted as he pondered what her hair would feel like if he ran his hand through her long tresses. He hadn't realized he was staring until he saw Rachel blush.

Clearing his throat, Luke turned his gaze back towards the field. A hint of the river could be seen glimmering in the distance. He had always thought the beauty of Scotland was incomparable, but it was merely pretty compared to Rachel.

As he started to reveal his identity, Rachel's question cut him off. "Will you tell me about your siblings?"

"I have a younger brother and twin sisters," he answered, realizing this was an excellent transition into what could be an awkward conversation.

"Is that so?" Rachel asked, fascinated. "Are your sisters very alike?"

Chuckling, Luke admitted, "Not in the least. They are as

different as a horse and a cow."

She arched an eyebrow. "Did you just compare your sisters to farm animals?"

"I did," Luke said as he watched her wide, expressive eyes. He could get lost in those forever. Averting his gaze back towards the field, he took a deep breath to build his courage. "I have a confession to make, and I hope..." His voice trailed off as he heard the horses in the south pasture become increasingly agitated. Several horses were scattering, tossing their manes, and neighing anxiously.

Turning his gaze towards Rachel, Luke saw that she was also intently watching the horses. Something was wrong. Without a word, they kicked their horses into a run and ran parallel to the fence until they saw a horse, with a rope tied around its neck, trailing behind a lone rider.

The thief was directing the horse towards the woodlands at the end of his property. Rachel and Luke kept their horses running until they hit the trees and they both pulled up. Circling around his horse, Rachel asked, "Are we still on Lord Downshire's property?"

Keeping his eyes trained on the horse thief, Luke watched as the man slowed down to navigate both horses through the trees. Their best advantage would be to follow the man and see where he hid the other horses. Rachel was looking at him expectantly, so he informed her, "No, we are now on Mrs. Felix's property. The woodlands surround my lands, creating a natural barrier between all my neighbors' property."

"Why would he take the horse onto Mrs. Felix's property?"

The thief was about sixty yards ahead of them, and Luke didn't want to lose him in the woodlands. "I don't know, but I intend to find out," he asserted, kicking his horse into a run.

Without waiting for Rachel's response, Luke veered into the trees and hoped he would soon catch the thief that had been plaguing the villagers for months.

RACHEL RODE LOW ON HER HORSE AS SHE NAVIGATED BETWEEN the trees, being careful not to ride too close to John. She couldn't see the horse thief, but the trees had low-hanging branches, and she was concentrating hard, so she wouldn't fall off her horse.

Up ahead, John was about to clear the trees when he reined in his horse and put his hand up to indicate she should be silent. Rachel rode up next to him and saw a large field encircled by large, imposing, broad-leafed trees. The thief was leading the horse through the field of overgrown grass towards a large stable that sat near a modest-sized estate.

In a hushed voice, Rachel asked, "Is this Mrs. Felix's estate?"

John's eyes held disappointment as he looked at the condition of the property. "Last year I sold Mrs. Felix one of my horses and her estate was in pristine condition." Muttering under his breath, his words sounded pained, "What happened?"

Rachel adjusted the reins in her hand and sensed her horse wanted to run again. "What is the plan? Should we alert the constable?"

John frowned. "By the time we alert the constable, the horse could be relocated."

They heard rustling leaves before David's horse appeared next to her. He pointed towards the trees directly behind the stable. "I have identified at least four guards by the stables and two near the estate."

John adjusted the reins in his hands. "I want to investigate that stable. I've had ten horses, now eleven, stolen in the past few months, and I want to see if they are in the stable."

David shook his head in disagreement. "No, it is too dangerous to approach the property right now."

Frustrated, Rachel blew out a puff of air. "Mrs. Felix is in a coma. Why would her staff resort to stealing horses?"

"I don't know," John answered, sadly. "I was informed she was a wealthy woman, which is why her nephew, Lord Melville, started sniffing around months ago."

Starting to piece together past conversations, Rachel asked curiously, "When exactly did Mrs. Felix fall into a coma? Before or after Lord Melville arrived?"

John gave her a puzzled look. "I don't rightly know."

"That can't be a coincidence," David acknowledged, heavily leaning his arms on the saddle horn. "As much as I hate to say this, maybe we should go back and alert the constable. If we approach the stable without reinforcements, we risk putting Lady Rachel in harm's way."

Rachel frowned. "Lord Melville may be a rogue, but I can't believe he would kill his own aunt. When he talked about his desire to have a relationship with her, it seemed genuine."

David sighed deeply. "Regardless, we can't simply ride up and ask to speak to Lord Melville about the stolen horses."

"Why not?" Rachel asked.

Impulsively, she kicked her horse into a run and heard the pounding of hoofbeats behind her. Leading her horse onto the stone pathway, she slowed him to a walk as they approached the estate. As she reined him in, she noticed that the front draperies were opened just enough for someone to peek through, but then they were quickly closed again.

Sliding off her horse, she waited for David and John to pull up next to her. While Rachel waited, she noticed that no one came from the stable or the estate to collect her horse. Maybe her rash decision was not as wise as she had thought. Before she had time to dwell on her actions, the men jumped off their horses and stormed towards her, with matching angry expressions.

Reaching her first, John grabbed her arms and asked with fury in his eyes, "Are you mad?" Tightening his grip, he leaned closer. "We don't know what we are up against and..."

"Lady Rachel," a voice boomed from the doorway of the estate.

Releasing his hold on her, John stepped aside as Rachel turned towards the main door and saw Lord Melville standing in the doorway. He was dressed in a black tailcoat, with a blue waistcoat, and buff trousers. His hands were open, welcoming her, and he had a broad smile on his face. "Please join me for a cup of tea and my aunt's delicious biscuits."

Dropping into a polite curtsy, Rachel returned his smile. "I would be honored."

As she started walking towards Lord Melville, he glanced over her shoulder, and his smile dimmed. His next words were dripping with contempt. "Why don't your servants wait for you by the horses?"

Keeping the smile on her face, Rachel replied, "Actually, John works for Lord Downshire, and he has a few questions for you." She glanced at David, apologetically. "And David is not my servant, he is my friend."

Lord Melville bowed. "My apologies, then. Please join me in the drawing room."

Placing her foot on the first step, she felt John's hand on her elbow as he politely assisted her. Leaning closer, he muttered, "We will discuss your hoydenish behavior later."

Stifling a smile, Rachel couldn't believe that John had just used the word 'hoydenish'. He dropped her elbow as they walked into a small drawing room. The drapes were pulled back, but dust floated in the air as if they had just been opened. A light layer of dust coated the table and various vases on the mantel. Apparently, this room had not been used, or cleaned, in some time.

Ignoring the dust, Rachel sat down on a floral settee. The yellow-papered walls kept the room bright and cheery, but the mood was far from happy. Lord Melville quickly moved to sit down next to her. "I am so pleased that you came to call on me."

She clasped her hands in her lap. "I actually came to inquire about your aunt's health."

A wave of Lord Melville's hand dismissed her comment as unimportant. "I'm afraid my aunt is still in a coma." He scooted closer and asked flirtatiously, "Would you like to go on a carriage ride with me tomorrow?"

Rachel tried hard to look flattered, but her face fell flat. "I do not think that is wise. My position has not changed since we last spoke."

Not deterred by her rejection, Lord Melville's eyes kept flickering to her lips. His words were meant for her ears only as he said, "Don't be afraid my fair maiden. I will fight for you."

"Lady Rachel does not want you to fight for her," came John's gruff reply. At some point, David and John had both moved closer to them, and they were not amused by Lord Melville's blatant attempts at flirting.

Trying to keep the visit cordial, Rachel smiled at her host. "May I come by and read to your aunt?" Lord Melville's face paled slightly, but she continued. "I have heard that reading to people in comas is very beneficial to their health."

Lord Melville smiled, but it lacked any warmth. "I appreciate your generous offer, but my aunt is near death." Boldly, he extended his hand and patted her leg. "However, I will consult with my aunt's doctor and see what he recommends."

"Thank you," Rachel murmured, tipping her head graciously. Although, she knew that Emmett was not doctoring Mrs. Felix and the nearest medical help was a two-hour ride away. It was clear that Mrs. Felix was not under the care of a doctor. Ignoring Lord Melville's piercing gaze, she turned to look at John. "Since we are here, John mentioned that he hoped to get a moment of your time."

Lord Melville's smile grew hard as he angled his body to include John and David in the conversation. "Normally I do not speak to lowly servants, but I will make an exception for Lady Rachel. What did you wish to ask me?"

John's glare was full of disdain as he addressed Lord Melville. "Eleven of Lord Downshire's horses have disappeared, and we have tracked them to your aunt's property."

Lord Melville scoffed dismissively. "Have you considered that you may have been neglectful and allowed the horses to wander off? Perhaps you are trying to blame others for your mistakes?"

With clenched hands at his sides, John's eyes narrowed, and Rachel was sure that he was going to throw a punch at Lord Melville. Attempting to ease the tension in the room, she interjected, "We witnessed someone stealing a horse and leading them towards your aunt's property. Have you seen anything that could arouse suspicion?"

Lord Melville turned back to face her, frowning. "The thieves must have crossed through my aunt's property. I will send out a few footmen to see if anything can be discovered." Leaning closer, he whispered next to her ear, "Your reputation will be in tatters if you continue to spend time with servants."

Ignoring the unpleasant warmth of his breath on her skin,

Rachel responded firmly, "Whom I spend time with is none of your concern, Lord Melville."

"Isn't it?" Lord Melville challenged as he placed his hand on the back of the sofa directly behind her.

Before Rachel could respond, a young servant girl, keeping her gaze firmly on the ground, walked in with a tray of tea and biscuits. She placed it on the table, then scurried off. Lord Melville's sigh was filled with disgust. "Please excuse my aunt's staff. I intend to fire them as soon as it is feasible." Putting his hand out towards the tray, he asked, "Would you mind pouring us some tea, Lady Rachel?"

"Of course," Rachel said, rising slowly, hoping that she didn't appear too eager to move away from Lord Melville. After handing everyone a cup of tea, she sat down on a chair on the opposite side of the table, closer to David.

Leaning back against the papered walls, David questioned, "Would you mind if we searched your aunt's stable?"

"There is no need. I can assure you that no stolen horses are in the stable," Lord Melville declared arrogantly as he took a sip of tea.

"I insist," John growled. He placed his untouched cup on the table next to him. "Or we can bring back the constable if you prefer."

Lord Melville tsked rudely. "I believe a constable will take a lord's word over that of a simple servant. Why don't you go back to your master and whine to him?"

"How dare you!" John roared, causing Rachel to jump, spilling tea onto her dress. "You are a lowly viscount and I…"

Shouting over him, David ordered, "John, be quiet!" Astonishingly, John closed his mouth, but it was clear that David's demand did not please him.

Placing her cup on the tray, Rachel picked up a white linen napkin and wiped at the spots on her dress. "Oh, dear me. What a mess I made," she said, dramatically. She rose quickly. "Thank you for your time and the tea, but I need to go home and have my lady's maid clean this dress before the stain sets in."

Lord Melville's eyes held disappointment, but he nodded. "I understand." Reaching for her hand, he brought it to his lips and placed a wet, lingering kiss on her gloved hands. Once again, she was grateful that her gloves provided a barrier between her skin and his lips.

Trying not to yank her hand back too quickly, Rachel kept a forced smile on her face. As soon as Lord Melville released her hand, she moved towards the entry hall. David opened the door and stood aside as she and John exited.

Mounting their horses, they rode until they reached Lord Downshire's land. Reining in his horse, David kept his eyes trained on the trees as he asked, "Did anyone else notice the lack of servants?"

Rachel nodded. "That was unusual. Additionally, Lord Melville refused to allow me to see his aunt, so I wonder if Mrs. Felix is even still alive."

"I highly doubt it," replied John.

Turning his horse back towards the road, David remarked, "We should alert the constable as quickly as possible."

"I will go into the village tomorrow," John stated, kicking his horse into a run.

THE NEXT MORNING, LUKE PACED UP AND DOWN THE PAVEMENT in front of the constable's office. He was anxiously waiting to speak to Rachel privately before demanding that the constable mount an investigation into Lord Melville. To be taken seriously, he had to resume his identity as the Marquess of Downshire. In preparation, he wore his tailcoat, white waistcoat and cravat, buff trousers and, most importantly, his signet ring.

How would Rachel react to the truth? He had acted out every possible scenario in his head, and in each one, she refused to forgive him for his dishonesty. He was so distracted by his thoughts, that his mind barely registered the words, "Well, well, well... the horse trainer decided to play dress up with his master's clothes."

Glancing towards the offending voice, Luke clenched his jaw as he recognized Lord Melville. "Go away," he grunted.

With a huff, Lord Melville took a step closer to him. "If you are planning to see the constable, then you will be waiting a long time."

Luke narrowed his eyes in suspicion. "And why is that?"

"Oh, he's dead," Lord Melville said with a sinister smile.

Outraged, Luke shoved Lord Melville and shouted, "You killed him!"

"No," Lord Melville answered, adjusting his waistcoat. "I didn't," he paused and pointed at three dangerous-looking thugs leaning against the side of the building. "They did."

"Did you have the other four constables killed as well?"

"Only those foolish enough to refuse bribes are killed."

Luke glanced up and down the street, but no one appeared to be giving them any heed. He glared at Lord Melville. "What is it that you want?"

Reaching into his coat pocket, Lord Melville pulled out a small coin purse. He extended it towards Luke. "I need more horses."

"Do you wish to buy them?" Luke asked, even though he already knew the answer.

Laughing, Lord Melville appeared amused by his question. "No, I plan to take them, but this little fortune is for your silence."

"No," he said, slapping the coin purse out of Lord Melville's hand. "No one is going to steal my horses."

"Your horses?" Lord Melville repeated dismissively as he signaled the three men. "Then there is only one other option."

Grabbing Lord Melville's coat lapels, Luke slammed him into the stone wall and punched him in the eye before the thugs pulled him off. Dragging him deep into the alley, the two men pinned his arms back as the third hit him hard in the stomach. Trying to suck in a breath, he was not prepared for a punch in the face which caused his head to whip back. As his head came forward again, the man hit him harder, and he could feel blood trickling down his lips.

The two men dropped his arms and let him fall to his knees. The third man crouched down and pulled out a dagger, taking pleasure in showing it to him. "You should have listened to Melville, and you would have been a wealthy man." Running the tip of the blade over Luke's cheek, the man sneered. "But now, you will die."

Without warning, the sound of a pistol discharging echoed through the alley, and the man in front of him slumped to the ground. Before Luke even picked up the dagger from the dead man's hand, David came charging into the alley. He used his pistol to hit one of the men, dropping him to the ground. The last man standing pulled out a dagger and swiped it at David. He jumped back out of reach, then advanced suddenly, grabbing the man's wrist and twisting it sharply. The blade fell to the ground, and David punched the man in the face, rendering him unconscious.

David focused on Luke, and his eyes were wide with worry. "Are you all…"

The roar of another pistol being discharged caused David to spin around in time to witness a man falling face forward, dead. Luke and David turned towards the direction of the shot and saw Lady Rachel standing at the edge of the alley with a smoking pistol in her hand. Her face was pale, and she hadn't lowered her weapon yet.

Cautiously, David approached her with his hand out. "Lady Rachel," he directed in a soothing voice, "it is all right. Hand me the pistol."

With wide eyes, she instinctively handed the pistol to him. "I had to kill him. He was going to kill you and John," she whimpered.

David stepped closer and placed his hand on her shoulder. His eyes held sympathy as he reassured her, "I know. You saved our lives." He tilted his head towards Luke. "Why don't you see if John is injured?"

Rachel's eyes sought out Luke, and she hurried over to him. Standing in front of him, her eyes reflected compassion and sadness. "You are hurt." Her hand disappeared into her reticule and produced a handkerchief. Cautiously, she brought it to his bottom lip and wiped away the blood. The tenderness of the moment touched him deeply.

Luke's hand reached for her wrist, stopping her. He didn't care about his wounds. He was more concerned with what Lady Rachel must be enduring after killing a man. "Stop," he ordered gently. "Are you all right?" Tears welled in her eyes, and he pulled her into a tight embrace. As he rubbed her back, Rachel sobbed into his chest.

Luke was reluctant to let her go, but David walked up to them and reported, "The constable was murdered last night. It would be in our best interest if we disappeared right now."

With a decisive head nod, Luke reluctantly brought his hands to Rachel's forearms and took a step back. "David is right," he stated. "We need to leave, now."

Rachel's eyes were red and puffy, but she nodded her understanding. With one hand on her forearm, he led her out the back of the alley, mindfully keeping his head down as they hurried along the street. No one stopped them as they passed by men and women rushing towards the scene in the alley.

David brought their horses, and Luke assisted Rachel onto hers before mounting his. They raced along the countryside, only slowing the horses' gait as they neared the turnoff to the Maddix's estate. He gave David a grateful smile. "Thank you for saving my life."

With a lifted brow, David asked, "Do you want to explain to us what happened?"

As he shared the conversation with Lord Melville and the beating that ensued, Rachel's eyes grew more solemn, almost withdrawn. Luke's heart ached at the sight of her trembling lower lip, but she did not shed another tear. With worry, he inquired, "What is it?"

"I'm sorry," she said, stifling a sob. "I'm so sorry."

Luke had no idea what she could possibly be apologizing for, so he glanced at David for help. Unfortunately, David just shrugged helplessly at him. "Rachel," he ventured, "you did nothing wrong."

She drew a deep, shuddering breath. "This was all my fault." Her eyes betrayed the emotional turmoil playing deep within her soul. "I am so sorry," she hesitated, "to both of you."

Turning towards her uncle's estate, Rachel kicked her horse into a run and raced down the pathway. As Luke started to follow her, David ordered, "John, stop."

"Why?"

Watching the dust trail from Rachel's horse, David asked, "How would you explain your injuries to Mr. and Mrs. Maddix or their household staff?"

Scoffing in disbelief, Luke shouted, "I don't care!"

"Give me two days," David said, putting his hand up to stop his retort. "Rachel is already involved, but we don't want to pull the Maddix family into this tangled web. Besides, Lord Melville believes you are dead, and we need to keep it that way for as long as possible."

Luke frowned. "When Lord Melville's men don't return, he will know I am not dead."

"Not necessarily," David contended. "I can't imagine Lord Melville stayed around long enough to incriminate himself once he turned you over to his thugs."

"I can't…" His voice cracked in despair. "I have to help Lady Rachel."

Adjusting his reins in his hands, David's voice became stern. "Trust me. If we want to keep Lady Rachel safe, then we need to keep her away from Lord Melville."

"And me?" he argued, his voice taking on an annoyed edge.

"At least for now," David stated, but his eyes held sympathy. "Do not leave your estate for two days, and then we will reassess the situation." His tone held no room for negotiation, and Luke didn't want to fight him. The only thing he cared about right now was Rachel.

❧ 17 ❧

Dʀᴇssᴇᴅ ɪɴ ᴀ ᴡʀᴀᴘᴘᴇʀ, Rᴀᴄʜᴇʟ ʀᴇsᴛᴇᴅ ᴛʜᴇ sɪᴅᴇ ᴏꜰ ʜᴇʀ ʜᴇᴀᴅ against the bedchamber window pane as she absentmindedly stared out. Other than taking her meals in the dining room, she had not ventured out of her chamber for the past two days. Due to her impulsiveness, John was beaten and almost murdered in an alleyway. Thank goodness that David had seen John being dragged into the alley, or else...

Shuddering, Rachel couldn't continue thinking about what happened. Tightening her wrapper around her, a lone tear dropped from her eye and rolled down her cheek. She was aware her spontaneity wasn't always well received, but never had someone else suffered so cruelly because of her actions. If only she had listened to John and David rather than antagonizing Lord Melville. Even though Lord Melville was a despicable rogue, she had naïvely believed he was not a horse thief or a murderer.

"If only I had listened," she mumbled to herself.

The worst part was that she had lost John's friendship. After Rachel rode off, she had hoped that John would race after her or throw rocks at her windows, intentionally seeking her out and providing her with much-needed comfort. But that had not happened. He had every right to hate her, although it broke her heart to admit that.

The door opened, and Savannah walked in with a blossom-colored dress draped over her arm. Laying the dress on the bed, she opened the window, allowing a breeze to cool the room. Smiling a little too cheerfully, she announced, "Your aunt and uncle have requested that you join them in the drawing room."

"No, thank you," Rachel responded. "Please inform them that I have a headache."

Not deterred by her lack of enthusiasm, Savannah replied, "Your aunt anticipated you might say that and informed me that you have twenty minutes, or they will join you in your bedchamber."

Not bothering to lift her head off the window, Rachel decided to ignore her lady's maid, who was walking around the room, preparing for the day. After Savannah pulled out the chair at her dressing table, she patted the top, inviting Rachel to sit down. Shaking her head, Rachel admitted, "I don't want to leave my room."

Sighing, Savannah brought a chair closer to her and sat down. "For two days, you have done nothing but stare out that window." Leaning forward, she asked softly, "What happened to make you so melancholy?"

Finally, lifting her head, Rachel murmured, "I did something horrible."

"Which was?" Savannah prodded.

Rachel's mouth opened, but she couldn't seem to find the words to share how she'd killed a man. Instead, she lowered her gaze and chose to ignore Savannah's worried gaze.

Savannah leaned back and jested, "Well, that was informative." Walking over to the dressing table, she retrieved a brush and brought it back. Savannah unbraided her hair and started brushing.

Like a whirlwind, Savannah brushed and pinned her hair

back into a low chignon, grabbed the dress from the bed, and helped her into it. Urging her towards the door, Savannah continued to fasten the buttons on the back of her dress as she walked.

After fastening the last button, Savannah opened the door and gave her a slight push out the door. Rachel was greeted in the hallway by the sight of David leaning against the wall, obviously waiting for her to make an appearance. When he saw her, he smiled his relief and offered his arm.

As he escorted her to the drawing room, he said, "I have been worried about you." He snuck a peek at her. "How are you faring?"

Rachel shrugged. "About as well as you, I suppose."

Stopping suddenly in the hall, David turned to face her, and his eyes shone with compassion. "I am a trained agent. I have killed men with bullets, with my dagger, and with my bare hands, but it never gets easier." He attempted a smile but failed miserably. "You saved John's life and mine as well. I haven't had a chance to thank you for that."

Taking a deep, shaky breath, Rachel closed her eyes, and the image of all the dead men in the alley came back to her. Forcing her eyes open, she stated, "If it weren't for me, John would never have been in that alley to begin with."

A look of confusion came to David's face. "You had nothing to do with Lord Melville's attempt to recruit John, or his thugs' effort to kill him."

With a resigned look, Rachel glanced over David's shoulder. She couldn't bear to see his disapproval. "I forced John to go into Mrs. Felix's estate and draw Lord Melville's ire. If I hadn't, then..." Her voice trailed off because they both knew what happened next. "And now John hates me."

Before David could reply, her aunt stepped out of the drawing room and saw them in the hall. Hurrying over to them, Aunt Jessamine put her arm around Rachel's shoulder and began leading her towards the drawing room. "We have been waiting, child." Turning back around, she asked David, "Are you coming?"

"Yes, ma'am," came his reply as he followed close behind.

Stepping into the room, Rachel saw Emmett standing near the mantle of the fireplace, and her uncle was at the drink tray. Both watched her enter, and their expressions seemed to mirror her mournful soul.

Pushing her gently down on the sofa, Aunt Jessamine sat next to her and reached for her hands. It appeared as if the inhabitants of the room feared that she would bolt. Once they were both situated, Emmett walked over, unbuttoned his coat, and sat down in the chair adjacent to the sofa. Watching her carefully, he shared, "There is quite a tale going around Rockcliffe right now. Apparently, two days ago, three men were killed in an alley and witnesses have claimed a blonde-haired lady fled the scene moments after the last shot was fired."

Panicking, Rachel's eyes sought out David, who gave her a reassuring nod, as she tried to regain control of her racing heart.

Leaning forward in his seat, her cousin's next words were spoken with tenderness. "When I spoke to the magistrate earlier this morning, I assured him that my cousin was not in the village at the time, and the matter has been dropped, partly because of who your father is."

Aunt Jessamine's hands tightened around hers. "Were you there, Rachel?"

Again, her eyes sought out David for permission. Instead of granting it, he answered, "We were both there."

"Blazes, Rachel," Emmett exclaimed as he jumped up. "What were you thinking?"

"Emmett," her aunt admonished. "Stop this at once." She focused on David. "Can you tell us what happened?"

Nodding his consent, David took a few minutes to explain what had transpired in the alley and why they were forced to flee the scene. He finished with, "If it weren't for Lady Rachel, then both John and I would be dead."

To Rachel's surprise, Emmett reached down and pulled her into an embrace. "I am sorry, cousin. I wish I had known."

Her arms went around him, and she returned the embrace wholeheartedly. After he released her, Rachel's aunt and uncle came over and embraced her with no less enthusiasm. Emmett stepped up to David and shook his hand, thanking him for helping his cousin.

Aunt Jessamine sighed. "You poor dear. I can't believe you have been suffering all this time and we had no idea."

"I bet John is grateful that you became such an expert marksman," Uncle Edwin remarked.

Walking towards the window, Rachel placed her hands on her arms. "John hates me."

Silence filled the room, and Rachel glanced back to see if anyone was still there. She was met with stunned faces. Her aunt walked closer to her, asking, "Why would you think that?"

"It doesn't matter," she answered softly. "He hasn't come to visit since that day, and I doubt he will come again."

David spoke up, "John hasn't come to visit because I ordered him to stay home."

"Why would you do that?" Rachel questioned, dropping her arms.

He frowned. "John's face and clothes were bloodied, and he wanted to come and comfort you. However, I knew the magistrate would come around and ask questions. I asked, rather ordered, John to stay on his estate so your aunt and uncle and their staff would not have to lie to the magistrate or Lord Melville."

Emmett clenched his jaw. "What does Lord Melville have to do with this?"

Sighing, David put his head back and looked at the ceiling. "I assure you, the less you know, the better."

Her uncle humphed. "It is a little too late for that. Rachel killed a man in an alley while under my protection. I want to know what is going on, or I will put her on one of my whaling ships bound for the Arctic. If that is the only way to keep my niece safe, then so be it."

Shivering at the thought of the freezing weather, she rushed to explain, "Lord Melville is the one stealing horses from Downshire Farms. He tried to kill John and most likely has killed his own aunt."

Muttering expletives, Emmett paced back and forth. He stopped and said, "We need to alert the constable."

"Lord Melville has admitted to killing the constable, and either killing or bribing four other constables. He has no qualms about killing anyone who turns him down," David informed them. "Letters have gone out to request help from the Crown, and the best option will be to wait for their assistance."

Frowning, Aunt Jessamine asked, "For how long?"

"It should be any day now," David admitted. "Until then, we must be cautious in our movements. Lord Melville has no reason to suspect your family, but under no circumstances should he ever be left alone with Lady Rachel."

Uncle Edwin turned and pointed at her. "You, young lady, are not allowed to leave this estate for any reason."

David cleared his throat, drawing her uncle's attention to him. "I had planned to escort Lady Rachel to Downshire Farms today. I need to speak to John."

With a swipe of his hand, her uncle declared, "I forbid it. My brother tasked me with Rachel's safety, and I intend to keep her safe. I must admit I have done a wretched job up to this point. I had assumed there was no danger around the sleepy, coastal village of Rockcliffe, but I was wrong."

At the thought of seeing John, even for a moment, Rachel felt a twinge of happiness. Knowing that he had stayed away, not because of her, but because David ordered him to, gave her hope that perhaps he didn't hate her.

Rachel put her hand over her heart and pleaded with her uncle. "Please, Uncle Edwin. We will just ride there and back."

"No," Uncle Edwin argued. "It is not safe."

Throwing a desperate glance at her aunt, Aunt Jessamine nodded knowingly. Placing her hand on her husband's sleeve, her aunt said, "Let her go, Edwin. If not, then Rachel will be forced to sneak out to see John, without David's protection."

Throwing up his hands, her uncle exclaimed, "Fine!" He pointed his finger at David. "It is your head if Rachel does not come back safely."

"Understood, sir," David acknowledged, bowing stiffly.

Aunt Jessamine pulled Rachel into an embrace and whispered in her ear, "Don't forget to tell John how you feel about him."

"I... uh..." Rachel stuttered as her cheeks grew warm.

Her aunt dropped her arms and smiled. "I highly recommend you practice your speech before you see him again."

RESTING HIS ARMS ON THE FENCE, LUKE LEANED IN, WATCHING the foals interact with their mothers. It had been two long days, and he was tired of waiting to see Lady Rachel. Last night, he had almost ridden over and thrown rocks at her window. However, he had no doubt that David would have shot him if he had disobeyed his direct order.

Two days ago, his life had flashed before his eyes, and Luke knew he'd been given a second chance. Previously, he had lived, but with no purpose, no direction. He would change that. But first, he had to reveal the truth to Rachel and beg for her forgiveness. With her by his side, Luke knew he could change, become a better man. He had agreed to wait to see Rachel for two days and that time was up!

Pushing off the fence, Luke shouted, "Hugh! Saddle my horse!" Turning towards the stable, he was surprised to see his stablemaster leading Magnus out, already saddled.

Hugh smiled. "I assumed correctly, I see."

"You did," Luke said. "Thank you."

As he started to mount his horse, he heard one of the stable hands shout, "Lady Rachel is approaching."

A collective cheer went around the stable yard, and Luke found himself smiling as his eyes greedily roamed the hillside waiting for a glimpse of her. Admiring Rachel as she rode in was a pleasure. She rode with grace and expertise. Her eyes latched onto his, and she smiled. Although it seemed forced, almost as if she wasn't happy to see him.

As she stopped next to him, Luke held his arms out to help Rachel off her horse. Once she was on the ground, he didn't release his hold on her, but looked deep into her eyes. "I've missed you," he confessed.

Rachel's eyes softened, and a genuine smile formed on her lips. "And I've missed you."

Tearing his gaze away from her lovely blue eyes, Luke nodded a greeting to David, who was dismounting. Dropping his arms from her waist, he offered his arm and led her towards a field that overlooked his estate.

Walking along a small footpath that meandered through the long grass, Luke kept glancing at Rachel. He would have given his entire fortune to know what she was thinking, or feeling, at this moment. He decided the silence had gone on long enough. "How are you faring?"

With a quick glance at him, Rachel answered vaguely, "As

well as can be expected, I suppose." She turned her gaze back towards the path. "And you? How are you faring?"

"I'm well," Luke replied somewhat enthusiastically. When Rachel glanced at him with a furrowed brow, he smiled. "I'm alive."

Rachel smiled, but it didn't reach her eyes. "I can see that," she said before turning away.

Luke stopped, and Rachel turned to look at him, a look of confusion on her face. The wind blew strands of her hair over her face, and he reached out and tucked it behind her right ear. Instead of removing his hand, Luke allowed his fingers to tenderly trace down the slope of her neck.

She kept her gaze on him, and Luke saw sadness in her countenance. Lowering his hand towards her shoulder, he asked, "Why are you hurting?"

Blinking rapidly, she lowered her eyes and turned to look away, but he moved his finger under her chin and forced her to look at him. "Rachel," he whispered, "let me help you."

Her lower lip trembled slightly as her lips parted. "I wanted to tell you how sorry I am for the pain I caused you."

He didn't respond, partially because he was confused. What did she mean? What pain had she caused?

She continued, "I should have listened to you about Lord Melville, and because of me…" Her voice hitched, and her breathing grew shaky.

Keeping his finger under her chin, Luke leaned closer, repeating, "Because of you… what?"

Closing her eyes, Luke almost smiled as he felt Rachel's chin tilt determinedly. Opening her eyes, she took a shallow breath. "If I hadn't impulsively ridden towards Mrs. Felix's estate, then Lord Melville wouldn't have hated you as much. He wouldn't have sought you out in the village and ordered men to kill you."

Her words shocked him, not because they were accurate, but because Rachel believed them. Dropping his hand from her chin, he raked it through his hair as he tried to think of something to say. Her notion was ludicrous. His first reaction was to laugh, but Rachel's whimpering eyes met his, silencing all his thoughts. Instinctively, he pulled her into an embrace.

Her arms circled around him, and she laid her cheek over his beating heart. As they held each other, Luke could feel his heart starting to heal. Finally, here was a woman he could trust. Leaning back far enough to look in her eyes, he acknowledged, "You were extremely reckless to approach Mrs. Felix's estate and agree to tea with Lord Melville. However," he paused, "you did nothing wrong."

A small crease appeared between her two eyes, and Luke wanted to kiss it away. Instead, he waited until Rachel began, "Because of me..."

He cut her off before she could finish. "You determined that Mrs. Felix is most likely dead."

"Well, there is that," Rachel admitted, "but, also..."

"You found out Lord Melville was aware of the horse thieves using the stable to stash the horses."

"If I hadn't..."

Luke put a finger on her mouth to silence her and smiled when the small crease appeared again. Slowly, he said, "Lord Melville hated me from the moment he saw me at your uncle's estate, and he tried to recruit me to work for him. Either way, he would have killed me, but I was lucky enough to be saved by a hoyden and her protector."

Rachel's eyes were unconvinced, but she remained silent.

"Now it is my turn to apologize," Luke spoke deliberately. "I am sorry that you were forced to kill that man in the alley. I wish I could take that pain away from you."

Bringing her hand up, Rachel removed his finger from her mouth. "I was so scared, John. I thought I was going to lose David," she hesitated, "and you."

With a crooked grin, Luke teased, "I take it that you find me tolerable."

He was rewarded to see Rachel's eyes twinkle in response. "Some of the time. Other times I still find you boorish."

Realizing that she was still holding his hand, Luke tightened his hold as he continued the banter between them. "Perhaps you could give me lessons on how to be less boorish."

"I could, but I am starting to become fond of your moods," Rachel admitted as a slight pink hue came to her cheeks.

"You are?"

Nibbling on her lower lip, Rachel stopped and gave him a brave smile. "I... uh... have money, lots of money and..." Her voice trailed off as she averted her eyes.

Amused by her wording, Luke prodded, "You have money..."

Rachel's eyes returned to his, and she surprised him by saying, "What if I bought you a stud farm?"

"Can you repeat that?"

"A stud farm," she repeated. "I would like to buy you a stud farm."

He lifted his brow in confusion. "Why?"

Rachel smiled up at him. "I want to give you your dream."

What Luke should have done was throw his arms around her and tell her the truth. Instead, he frowned. "You can't offer to buy people stud farms."

Taken aback by his words, Rachel's words became determined. "I'm not offering to buy just anyone a stud farm. I'm offering to buy *you* a stud farm."

Attempting to understand her logic, he pressed again, "Why?"

Tightening her fingers around his, Rachel gazed up at him, her eyes reflecting vulnerability. "I was hoping we could be... uh... partners."

Luke frowned. "Partners?" That was not the arrangement he had in mind. "I don't want a partner," he stated gruffly.

Removing her hand from his, Rachel took a few steps back, her eyes saddened by his harsh words. "I understand," she said sadly. Those two words were like daggers to his heart.

Throwing his hands over his face, Luke grunted loudly. "No, you don't understand." He lowered his hands and tried again. "You don't need to buy me a stud farm or be my partner, because…"

Speaking over him, Rachel pleaded, "Please stop. I understand." She turned back towards Downshire Farms.

Closing the distance between them, Luke turned her to face him and his hands cupped her cheeks. "I will not stop until I make you understand how much you mean to me. I am making a mess of this. I am not just a horse trainer, I am…"

Lifting on her toes, Rachel pressed her lips into his for a moment, effectively silencing him. As she lowered herself back down, she said, "I don't care what your profession is. You could be a chimney sweeper for all I care." She brought her own hand up to cup his cheek. "In my opinion, most lords are not honorable men, but are men who cheat and lie for their own amusement." Smiling, she added, "I would take an honorable horse trainer any day."

He was unable to think rationally as Rachel brought her hand around his neck and pulled him down to initiate a kiss. As his hands started to wrap around her waist, a distinctive clearing of a throat could be heard nearby, and he had no doubt about who was issuing the warning. Instead of Rachel stepping back, or blushing into his chest, she turned her head and exclaimed, "Not now, David!"

Tilting her head, she smiled coyly, whispering above his lips, "Now, where were we?" just before she kissed him again.

This time when David cleared his throat, Rachel broke off the kiss and cast him an intense glare. "I will give you £5,000 if you leave us alone for five minutes." Her words were more of a demand than a request.

He chuckled as he heard David reply, "You have five minutes."

As her lips met his, Luke knew he should savor every moment he had with her before she cast him off when he revealed the truth. Her lips parted, and he deepened the kiss, relishing the fact that she chose him. Not his title... him.

After many blissful moments, Rachel leaned back and smiled up at him, her eyes radiating happiness. "That was worth every pound," she whispered as her other hand remained on his chest.

The sound of a carriage approaching on the gravel pathway could be heard in the distance. They turned to see who was visiting Downshire Farms. As far as Luke was aware, no potential buyers were scheduled to visit the new set of foals.

Suddenly, Rachel stepped out of his arms, and he immediately felt an emptiness at the loss of contact. With a wide smile on her face, she announced, "Lady Lansdowne is here." Grabbing his hand, she started pulling him towards his estate. "I can't wait to introduce you to Lord Downshire's sister, Eliza. She will love you." She pointed towards two riders that were trailing the carriage. "Lord Jonathon and Mr. Larson made the journey as well."

Luke dug in his heels and pulled back on her hand. "Wait, I really need to tell you something."

Rachel stopped pulling and faced him. "What is so urgent?"

"I haven't been completely honest with you," Luke started with hesitancy. "What I'm trying to say is that I am..."

His words were covered up by his sister, Eliza, who had her head sticking out of the carriage window, shouting, "Rachel!" The carriage came to a halt, and Luke knew he had run out of time.

❦ 18 ❦

Luke watched the scene unfold, anxiety building within him. This was a disaster!

Rachel ran towards the carriage while Eliza, the Marchioness of Lansdowne, opened the door and raced to meet her. They embraced warmly, removing any doubt that the two were as close as Rachel had claimed.

Suddenly, Eliza put a hand to her mouth as she ran a few steps, then bent down behind some tall grass. Without hesitation, his new brother-in-law, Benedict, rushed to his wife's side.

Inexplicably, Rachel was smiling widely at his sister, who was wiping her mouth with a handkerchief. Clapping with glee, she proclaimed, "You are with child!"

Eliza smiled and placed her hand on her stomach. "I am."

Shrieking, Rachel ran to embrace her again. Luke shook his head as his brother, Jonathon, approached him. "I would complain about the piercing noise, but it tends to die down after a few moments."

Smiling at Jonathon, Rachel stepped back from Eliza and embraced him. "It is good to see you, too. I hope your arrival means that England is safe from those French spies who infiltrated Parliament."

Before Jonathon could reply, Benedict interjected, "If you recall, Jonathon was on his wedding tour with Hannah when the French spies swept through Parliament." As he embraced Rachel, he lifted his brow at Jonathon. "He only made an appearance at the end."

Jonathon smiled smugly. "True, and during that time, I managed to discover Eliza's and Kate's whereabouts, whereas you took days to find out where they were being held."

Confused, Luke turned towards Eliza, and asked incredulously, "You and Kate were abducted?" He turned towards Jonathon. "Spies infiltrated Parliament?"

Chuckling, Jonathon placed his hand on his brother's shoulder. "We have a lot to catch you up on." Just then, Jonathon spotted David. He took a step forward, extending his hand. "David, is that you?"

With a smile, David replied, "Jonathon," then turned to Benedict, "Benedict."

Mr. Larson interjected, "Mr. Pearson, you should address them as Lord Jonathon and Lord Lansdowne."

Both men laughed as they shook hands with David. While shaking his hand, Jonathon stated, "As far as I am concerned, David can call me whatever he wants." Stepping back, Jonathon glanced at Luke and Rachel, informing them, "He was one of the agents on the *Brazen Hine* when we fought Camden and rescued Hannah, who is now my wife."

David smirked. "No surprise there. You fought as if you were two men that day."

"Camden? Our brother-in-law?" Luke asked Jonathon.

Benedict chuckled. "We have a lot to catch Luke up on, but can we adjourn to your estate first?" Putting his arm around Eliza's shoulder, he said, "My wife needs to rest."

Eliza grunted her disapproval. "I have been resting for three days. I want to go riding."

"No," Benedict argued, shaking his head. "The doctor said it is not safe in your condition."

"My condition?" Eliza repeated in annoyance.

Turning towards Luke, Jonathon tilted his head towards Mr. Larson and smiled. "Do you see why Mr. Larson and I rode outside the carriage?"

Luke caught Rachel's perplexed expression as she watched their exchange, but her eyes brightened as she saw Mr. Larson approach.

"It is good to see you, Lady Rachel," Mr. Larson said, bowing respectfully.

In response, Rachel curtsied. "It is good to see you as well. How long were you in London before you started back to Scotland?"

Mr. Larson offered a minute smile. "About a week." Any trace of humor disappeared from his face as he focused his attention on Luke. With a nod of his head, he muttered, "Lord Downshire."

Dreading Rachel's response, Luke turned his gaze towards her and was met with a shocked expression which turned into an icy stare. "Rachel, I can explain..." His voice trailed off as she put her hand up to stop him.

"You... are Lord Downshire?" Rachel's words were deliberate, as if trying to comprehend what she'd just heard.

"I am," Luke confessed quickly. As he was met with silence, he added, "but I have attempted to tell you multiple times." He heard Jonathon and Benedict both mumble 'blockhead' under their breaths. Ignoring their unhelpful chatter, he took a step towards her, but she took several steps back, shaking her head. It was apparent she did not want him near her. "Rachel, please, let me explain," he pleaded.

Blinking back tears, Rachel's lips formed a tight, white line as her eyes tracked him, the pain of his betrayal evident in her features. With a stubborn tilt of her chin, she answered, "Everything out of your mouth has been a lie. There is nothing left for us to discuss."

Luke watched as Rachel's bottom lip started to tremble, a sure sign that she was trying to hold back tears. He caused that pain, and it was killing him. With pleading eyes, he asked, "May I please escort you home?"

Wrapping her arms around her waist, Rachel shook her head firmly. "No, I believe we have nothing more to say to each other, Lord Downshire." She emphasized his title, making it clear what she thought of him. She was not a lady who was impressed with titles or honors, and she hated liars.

Mr. Larson took a step forward, offering his arm. "Would you allow me to escort you home, Lady Rachel?"

Without a word, Rachel slid her hand into the crook of his elbow.

As Luke watched them walk off, he felt despair swoop into his heart. He felt lost.

Jonathon clasped his shoulder. "Give her time. We will devise a plan to get her back."

Chuckling, Benedict escorted Eliza towards his estate while saying, "I would be hesitant to accept Jonathon's help. Hannah didn't even realize he was proposing on his first attempt."

Urging Luke forward, Jonathon replied good-naturedly, "True, but Benedict managed to soundly insult Eliza the first time they met."

As Luke half-listened to Jonathon and Benedict banter back and forth, his attention was on what Rachel must be thinking. He would call on her tomorrow, and they would work through this. They had to work through this.

When they reached his estate, Luke slammed open the door and shouted, "Mr. Kelly! Where the blazes are you?"

His young maid, Angelica, walked into the entryway carrying a bucket. She smiled up at him. "Good morning, John."

Ignoring his family's presence, Luke roared, "Do not call me that ever again! It is Lord Downshire." His words echoed throughout the main floor. The maid began to tremble and fled from his presence.

Stepping up next to him, Eliza gave him a look of censure. "That was a little harsh, don't you think?"

Luke held back his retort. He didn't have to be told that he was out of line, but he didn't feel like being nice, or accommodating, at this moment.

Entering the room, Mr. Kelly's smile seemed forced as he addressed Luke. "Ye bellowed, m'lord?"

He ignored Jonathon's cough behind him, which suspiciously sounded like a laugh. "Please ready the guest rooms and inform the staff that I no longer wish to be addressed as John."

"As ye wish," Mr. Kelly said, with a tilt of his head. He turned to leave, but then he hesitated. "Did ye tell her th' truth or did th' truth come out?"

Clenching his jaw, he admitted, "I didn't tell her in time."

Mr. Kelly sighed and shook his head. Apparently, his butler was disappointed in his behavior as well. He didn't care. He had never cared what people thought about him until Rachel came into his life. She made him care about others and about her. She did this to him!

Storming towards his drawing room, Luke didn't bother to see who followed him. As far as he was concerned, he wanted to be alone.

LEANING ON MR. LARSON FOR SUPPORT, RACHEL KEPT replaying the past events in her head and chiding herself for not seeing it earlier. How could she have missed that John... no, Luke, was Lord Downshire? The signs were all there, and she was a fool. It was one elaborate lie, and Lord Downshire's entire staff was in on the ruse.

Keeping her head down, Rachel couldn't face the men at the stable. She had smiled at them and chatted with them on previous occasions, but they probably were laughing at her behind her back. How could they not? She wasn't so clever after all.

Her gaze came up as she saw Hugh rushing towards her, concern evident on his brow. "Miss Rachel, what is wrong?" He stopped and frowned deeply. "Ye know."

Watching her horse being led towards her, Rachel withdrew her hand from Mr. Larson's arm and in a surprisingly steady voice questioned, "Did everyone know?"

Hugh averted his eyes as he nodded. "We are all truly sorry." His voice sounded remorseful, but she wasn't ready to hear an apology.

Allowing Mr. Larson to help her mount, Rachel thanked him before she urged her horse into a run. Eventually, David would catch up with her, but she wasn't in the mood to talk to him. She had a suspicion that he knew and had helped Lord Downshire with his deceit.

As she rode back to her uncle's estate, the anger boiled hotter and seethed deeper until she felt like she was going to burst with rage. Veering her horse towards the cliff that led down to the shoreline, Rachel dismounted and stared out at the water. Smelling the salt in the air, she tried to calm her beating heart.

She heard David dismount and approach, but not in his usual stealthy manner. After a few moments, his voice was hesitant as he spoke. "Are you all right?"

Spinning around, Rachel demanded, "Did you know?"

With a pained expression, David nodded in response.

Frowning, she followed up with another question. "When did you discover the truth?"

David kicked the dirt with his boot before answering, "I knew from the very beginning."

"And you didn't think of telling me the truth?" She pursed her lips. Was there no one in the world who could be open and honest?

"I was planning to," he started, but then his voice trailed off. He took a deep breath and continued, "However, I overheard him speaking to Mrs. Maddix the day he came calling and I decided to keep his secret."

She put her hands on her hips. "So, my aunt knows as well?"

"She does," he confirmed, glancing over her shoulder.

Rachel couldn't believe it. Advancing on David, she exclaimed, "I thought we were friends! How could you do this to me?" She shoved him in the chest, which didn't seem to affect him, nor did he try to stop her. "You lied to me. I trusted you!"

"Lady Rachel…" David began, but his voice fell flat. "I am sorry."

Glaring up at him, Rachel's eyes welled with tears at her friend's betrayal. "I want you to leave. I don't want your protection anymore."

"Please don't say that," David pleaded.

Clenching her fists together, Rachel shouted, "Did you and Lord Downshire have a good laugh at my expense? Did I amuse you because I didn't figure it out?"

David shook his head, his eyes downcast. "It wasn't like that."

A tear fell down her cheek. "Just leave me be," she demanded. She couldn't stand the sight of her protector anymore, and she turned towards the path leading down to the water.

"It is not safe for you on the shoreline," David warned.

She turned back to face him, anger lacing her words. "I don't care."

A short while later, Rachel stood at the water's edge and finally let out a sob. Eventually, she would have to walk back up that path and deal with what life had just thrown at her, but for now, she wanted to rest. Everyone around her had been in on the ruse. She felt humiliated.

Without warning, a man with foul-smelling breath and a thick French accent whispered next to her ear, "It looks like we have been given a gift."

Opening her mouth to scream for help, a filthy, calloused hand covered it, and Rachel felt herself being dragged back towards the cave behind her. Fighting with all her might, she tried to resist, but that did little to stop her from being pulled into the cave.

Once inside, he threw her against the cold, stone wall and placed a knife blade to her throat. She stopped resisting as the man's body pressed against her, pushing her back tightly against the uneven boulders. There was enough light at the entrance to identify six rough-looking men, dressed in French military uniforms, and they were all lewdly watching her as if she was dessert.

Knives and pistols were tucked into their waistbands, and muskets rested against the cave walls. A dinghy was pushed against the opposite wall.

After a moment, the man lifted the knife off her throat, but he didn't step back. With a wicked smile, he said, "If you are a good girl, then we mean to show you a right fine time." Slowly, the man ran his other hand up and down her arm, appearing amused when she trembled with fear.

When his hand hovered over her chest, Rachel started squirming against the wall and didn't stop until he again shoved the knife against her neck, causing blood to trickle down her throat. Two other men came over and grabbed her arms, wrenching them to the side.

The leader laughed roughly as he lowered the knife and stepped back. "There is no one to help you." He tucked the knife into his belt. "If you play nice, we might let you live."

Fear overtaking her senses, Rachel screamed as loud as she could, her voice echoing repeatedly in the dark, dreary cave. Flashes of light appeared before her eyes as a fist slammed into her face. Despite the pain, she did not stop fighting. She continued to struggle against her captors. She would rather die than willingly participate in what the man alluded to.

Breaking an arm free from one of the men, Rachel slammed her elbow into his face, but was subdued quickly by another man. She couldn't fight six of them. Regardless, she was not going to stop fighting till her last breath. The leader slapped her left cheek hard. As he raised his hand to hit her again, Rachel heard the roar of a pistol and saw the man drop.

Before she could blink, David ran into the cave and shot one of the men holding her arm back before he punched the other man, setting her free from their clutches. "Run," he ordered. "Run and don't look back."

When she didn't move fast enough, David shoved her out of the cave, and shouted, "RUN!"

Running as fast as she could towards the pathway that led up the cliff, she took her first step onto the rocky path as she heard the roar of multiple pistols being discharged. Racing up the path, she scrambled to keep her footing and small rocks cascaded over the side of the cliff.

As she neared the top, she climbed over a large boulder and was about to step up onto the level ground when a hand grabbed her skirt, yanking her back. Throwing herself forward, she gripped the rock to balance herself as her assailant tugged relentlessly on her dress. Looking back, she saw the sneering man trying to climb up the boulder. Instinctively, she slammed her boot into his face, causing him to release her dress and fall back.

Clawing her way to the top, Rachel sprinted towards her horse, and with a burst of adrenaline, she mounted and immediately kicked him into a run. The sound of a pistol roared behind her as pain exploded in her left arm. Ignoring the pounding in her arm, she kept her body down and didn't look back. Another bullet whizzed past the side of her head, and she urged her horse to run faster.

She had to get help! She raced through the fields, knowing she had to reach Eliza, Jonathon, Benedict, and Mr. Larson. They were the only ones that could save David now. "Hang on, David," Rachel pleaded under her breath. "Help is coming."

❦ 19 ❦

Luke stormed into his drawing room and strode straight to his drink tray. Pulling the top off the decanter, he poured himself a drink and gulped it down before his family even made an appearance. Filling his glass again, he downed it just as fast and slammed it down on the tray.

Escorting Eliza to the sofa, Benedict sat down next to her and reached for her hand. Luke groaned inwardly at the open affection these two displayed towards each other. He had witnessed the love they had for each other at the wedding, but now it was purely vexing.

Walking towards the fireplace, he put his hands on the mantle and leaned into it. In every scenario he had acted out in his head, not one involved his family showing up and revealing his identity. Slamming his hand against the mantle, he straightened and turned his body to acknowledge his family.

Glaring at Jonathon, Luke was surprised to see that his brother was obnoxiously grinning at him. "What?" he growled. "Why are you smiling like a bloody fool?"

As Jonathon chuckled, Benedict jested, "Don't mind Jonathon. He always looks like that."

His life was crashing around him, and his family thought it was amusing. With rage in his voice, he exploded, "What is wrong with all of you?"

"Nothing is wrong with us," Jonathon replied, lifting his brow. "You are just upset that Lady Rachel caught you in your lie."

Feeling his shoulders droop, Luke dropped onto a floral chair. "I am," he admitted painfully. Silence descended over the group, and he had no desire to talk about Rachel anymore. Instead, he asked, "Now can someone explain to me what happened with Eliza and Kate?"

Jonathon leaned forward from his seat on the sofa, suddenly attentive. "We have kept a lot of secrets from you, but we need to get you caught up. We believe the French are landing in Rockcliffe and are planning to invade England."

"Did you receive my letter?" he asked his brother.

"That is why we are here," Jonathon confirmed with a bob of his head. "The Crown has evidence that suggests a French frigate, loaded with infantry soldiers, slipped past the blockade at the channel and targeted Scotland as an ideal landing place."

"That is preposterous," Luke stated. "London is at least a two-week journey from Rockcliffe on foot. Despite that, the French soldiers would be easy targets as soon as they landed, because everyone would surely notice a French ship in our harbor."

"We don't know all the specifics, but the information was credible," Benedict shared.

Skeptical, Luke asked, "And who gave you the information?"

With an amused smile, Eliza replied, "Kate discovered the information just before she shot her step-brother, saving Lord Camden in the process."

"Her husband?" Luke questioned confused.

Eliza laughed. "Her second husband."

Jumping out of his seat in outrage, Luke yelled, "Kate has a *second* husband?" After a moment, he composed himself and returned to his chair. "Start from the beginning," he ordered.

Giving him a pointed look, Jonathon asked, "How much do you want to know?"

"Everything," Luke said firmly.

Promptly standing up, Jonathon removed his tailcoat and draped it over the camelback sofa. "I hate dressing like a bloody gentleman, and this could take a while."

Benedict chuckled at Jonathon. "Would you prefer the clothes you wear when you go into the rookery?"

Jonathon smirked. "At least *those* people leave me alone." Turning back towards Luke, he started, "We discovered that Mother was committing treason. She was going through Father's correspondences and consorting with a known French spy." He glanced over at Eliza before adding, "Our brother-in-law, Lord Camden, was that French spy, but we discovered later that he was actually an imposter."

"An imposter?" Luke questioned with a furrowed brow.

Eliza spoke up, "Kate really married Michel, a French spy, who had recently murdered the real Lord Camden and his family and assumed the role. When he married Kate, no one questioned Lord Camden's sudden appearance in his family's seat in Parliament."

"Then how was this imposter exposed?" Luke asked.

Rising, Jonathon walked over to the drink tray while explaining, "My father-in-law, Lord Pembrooke, was an agent before he inherited his title. He provided us with that information."

Pouring two glasses of brandy, Jonathon handed one to Benedict before he continued. "Adrien Stanton was Lord Camden's cousin, and he was working undercover in France, but broke cover when he came across a document that proved his cousin planned an assassination attempt on our prince regent."

Benedict took a sip of his drink and lowered the glass. "When Michel came to retrieve Kate, who had run away the night before, Adrien realized he was not his cousin. Thus, we discovered his deceit and killed him before he could flee back to France."

Rubbing his eyes, Luke wanted to clarify one thing. "Did Mother really die in a carriage accident?"

Eliza shook her head. "No. She was killed a few days prior."

"And Kate's imposter husband?" he prodded.

Jonathon took a sip of his drink before saying, "He was killed on his ship."

Tilting his head back to look at the ceiling, Luke tried to make sense of what was being shared. Lowering his head, he asked the group, "Is that how you learned about the French's plans to land in Rockcliffe?"

Placing his glass on the table in front of him, Benedict responded, "No, that came later. Before Michel was disposed of, he told us of a scheme that involved French spies infiltrating Parliament to collapse the English government from within. We then discovered it was in hopes of swaying the vote to end the war against France, thus sending our military into disarray as they were forced to retreat from Europe."

He huffed, "What lords were foolish enough to vote to end the war?"

Turning his loving gaze towards Eliza, Benedict admitted, "The French spies were very persuasive. They abducted the wives and children of the lords to force their hand. Luckily, Eliza and the other women escaped, due to Kate's quick thinking."

"Kate? My shy, reserved sister?" Luke questioned in an incredulous tone. "Do you expect me to believe that Kate tricked French spies?"

Smiling, Eliza nodded. "She was magnificent. She stood up to her father…"

Cutting his sister off, Luke clarified, "Our father?"

Eliza shook her head. "No, Kate and I are not truly twins.

Anne was pregnant with me when Diana was pregnant with Kate, and Father decided to raise us as twins to avoid scandal."

Leaning back in his chair, Luke was stunned. He looked at Jonathon for confirmation of Eliza's words.

His brother said simply, "A lot has transpired these past few months."

"Apparently," Luke mumbled.

Smiling, Eliza continued with her story. "As I was saying, Adrien," she paused to clarify, "now the real Lord Camden, tried to save Kate, but she ended up saving him."

"Of course, she did," Luke replied sarcastically. "And naturally she thanked him by marrying him."

Arching an eyebrow at his sarcastic tone, Eliza revealed, "Kate and Adrien are a love match. Prinny himself endorsed the marriage and St. George's was filled with members of the ton rejoicing in their union."

"My apologies," Luke grumbled. "I am taken aback by this entire story. My younger sister has remarried the true Lord Camden after her French spy husband was killed aboard his ship. Unbelievable."

Ignoring Luke's sarcasm, Jonathon stated, "Kate's real father, Phillipe, escaped, but we believe he is coming to Scotland to meet up with the French troops."

Benedict reached for his glass on the table. "We have been assigned by your uncle, Lord Beckett, to determine the threat of a French invasion and attempt to stop it, or slow it down, while the Royal Army and the Army Reserve marches towards the England-Scotland border."

"I see," Luke responded even though he didn't see at all. Glancing between Jonathon and Benedict, he asked, "How are two agents going to stop a French invasion?"

Even though Luke wasn't speaking to Eliza, she answered, "Very carefully."

Just then, Mr. Larson stormed into the room with a

murderous expression on his face. He closed the distance between them in mere moments, grabbing Luke's lapels on his coat, and pulling his arm back. Without hesitation, he punched Luke in the face.

Dropping his hold on Luke's tailcoat, Mr. Larson stood over him with rage sparking in his eyes. In a steely voice, he declared, "You were supposed to help Lady Rachel, not make her a laughing-stock."

Jumping up from his seat, Luke returned Mr. Larson's ire with his own. "I did no such thing."

"No?" Mr. Larson scoffed. "Did you not order your entire staff to lie to Lady Rachel about who you really were?"

"I did, but…" Luke confirmed but stopped when he heard Eliza gasp. Stepping around Mr. Larson, he tried to explain himself to his sister. "At first, I thought Rachel was stealing one of my horses, and she assumed incorrectly that I worked at Downshire Farms."

"And you didn't think to clarify who you truly were?" Mr. Larson asked in contempt.

Raking his hand through his hair, Luke revealed, "When she identified herself as Miss Rachel, I knew she was disguising her identity, and I wanted to see…" His voice drifted off, and he lowered his gaze to avoid Mr. Larson's disapproving look.

Eliza rose and prodded, "You wanted to see what?"

He winced. "At first, I wanted to prove her duplicity, her hidden agenda, because no one could be as kindhearted as she pretended to be. However, I learned that she is full of life and joy. She helps people for no reason other than being kind. She is unlike any woman I have ever known. And…" He stopped and closed his eyes, hesitant to admit his next words. "I find her intriguing, her outlook refreshing. Furthermore, I saw that titles do not impress her, and I wanted to get to know her as a man, not a marquess."

Walking towards the window, Luke put his hand on the

window sill and stared out over his lands. For so long, he had worked hard to make Downshire Farms profitable, but now he would give it all up to be able to speak to Rachel again. A touch on his sleeve broke him out of his thoughts. He tilted his head to look at his sister and was surprised to see compassion in her eyes. "Did it work?" she asked.

Luke lowered his head in defeat. "I don't know," he admitted. "I think so, but…" He turned around and met Mr. Larson's gaze, which didn't appear as frightening anymore. "I did order my staff to lie to Rachel, but they genuinely care for her… as do I. At no time was anyone laughing at her." He smiled sadly. "Rachel managed to work her way into our hearts, just by being herself."

Silence descended upon the room, and Luke dropped onto a nearby chair. No one had to remind him that he was responsible for his own failure. He should have told her the truth when he had the chance. No, he should never have lied to her in the first place.

He rubbed his sore jaw where Mr. Larson hit him before he turned towards Jonathon. "I can't believe you let him hit me."

Shrugging, Jonathon appeared unconcerned. "Mr. Larson tends to do as he wishes." He smirked. "To be honest, we all wanted to hit you for lying to Rachel."

As Luke opened his mouth to reply, he heard a loud crash in the main hall before he heard Rachel's piercing scream. "John!"

ARRIVING AT LORD DOWNSHIRE'S ESTATE, RACHEL JUMPED OFF her horse and ran towards the door, throwing it open. Running into the main hall, she screamed, "John!" Correcting herself, she shouted, "Lord Downshire!"

When he didn't immediately appear, she became frantic at the prospect of Luke not being at his estate. Where could he be? A moment later, Luke ran out of the drawing room towards her. She met him halfway, demanding, "Where is Eliza? Jonathon? Benedict? Where are they?"

Not stopping till he gripped her lower arms, a worried brow marked Luke's forehead, and there was a look of intense anxiety in his eyes. "What happened to you?"

Rachel didn't have time for questions, she had to save David. Shaking off Luke's hands, she screamed, "Eliza!"

"What's wrong?" Eliza asked as she rushed out of the drawing room followed by Benedict, Jonathon, and Mr. Larson.

Running up to Eliza, Rachel grabbed her arm and pleaded with her. "You have to save David. They are going to kill him!"

Outwardly calm, Eliza's eyes turned calculating and burned with purpose as she met Rachel's imploring gaze. "Tell me exactly what happened."

Taking a short, shaky breath, Rachel couldn't seem to control her shivering, but that was the least of her worries right now. "I went down to the shoreline to think, but I was dragged into a cave by six men wearing French uniforms. They wanted…" Her voice trailed off because she couldn't say the words aloud. "David shot the leader, but I heard many pistols firing as I ran up the hill…" Her voice broke as she trembled at the memory.

With a determined brow, Jonathon stepped closer, his voice firm. "Where is the cave?"

Focusing on Jonathon, Rachel saw his mouth move as he asked her a question, but her mind was filled with the memory of David fighting for her life. A hand on her shoulder caused her to jump, jolting her back into the present, and she heard Benedict's voice. "Tell us where the cave is."

Forcing her mind to clear, Rachel tilted her head towards

Luke. "It was the cave where you first kissed me. You have to go show them," she pleaded with urgency.

Luke huffed, "I am not leaving you."

Knowing that David did not have much time, Rachel countered, "Fine. I will take them." Ignoring Eliza's plea, she turned to rush towards the door.

"Like bloody hell you are," Luke said as he jumped in front of her. "You are injured."

As she glared at him, a voice behind her caught her attention. "I will take them, Lady Rachel." Spinning around, Rachel saw Hugh standing back with a determined stance. "Is it th' cave directly below th' Maddix's estate?" When she nodded in the affirmative, he responded, "I know where that is."

Rachel was relieved to see Jonathon, Benedict, and Mr. Larson rushing towards the door, but she didn't see Eliza. Turning around, she saw her standing behind her with concern in her eyes. Rachel pointed at the door and ordered, "You have to go with them!"

Eliza's eyes roamed her torn dress and arm. "You have been shot. I can't leave you."

"You have to go save David," Rachel pleaded as she saw the indecision on Eliza's face. "He is my friend."

"You are acting irrationally, Rachel," Luke declared from behind her, "the men will go help David."

Ignoring Luke's comment, she pressed, "You must go now!"

With a final anxious glance at Rachel, Eliza took off after the men, despite Luke ordering her to stop. Rachel knew David would need all the help he could get to fight against those French soldiers, and Eliza was *Shadow*, England's top spy.

Once Eliza and the men left, Rachel suddenly felt drained. She put her hand on the wall to steady herself and took a moment to regain her strength. Her eyes were heavy, and she felt her shoulders drooping. She needed to get back to her uncle's estate and rest.

After a few deep breaths, she started towards the main door but was stopped by Luke's hand on her right elbow. Not having the strength to resist, Luke gently turned her to face him. "Where do you think you're going?" he asked directly, but there was a softness to his words.

She brought her hand to her forehead. "I need to go home. My aunt will be worried."

His eyes grew wide in disbelief. "You have been shot. We need to send for a doctor."

Rachel twisted her left arm to look at her wound but only saw layers of dried blood. "It is merely a flesh wound. I am fine," she assured him.

Luke frowned. "You have blood all over your arm." His eyes roamed her face and clothes as he reminded her, "Your dress is ripped, there is a nasty gash on your neck, and I saw deep scratches on your back."

Her hand flew to her throat as she remembered the devilish glint in the man's eyes as he pressed the knife against her throat. A sob escaped her lips as she tried to shake away the image in her head. Luke's voice seemed far away as he said, "You are shaking, Rachel. Let me help you."

Focusing on his voice, Rachel opened her eyes, but her lower lip began to tremble as she reluctantly nodded. Gently, Luke put his hand on the small of her back and urged her towards the drawing room. Over his shoulder, he shouted, "Mr. Kelly!"

Immediately, the butler appeared, and his compassionate gaze watched her as he asked, "What can I do?"

Luke barked, "Send out every available man to find Rachel's cousin, Dr. Emmett Maddix, and inform him that she has been shot. Bring him back posthaste."

"As ye wish," Mr. Kelly stated. "I have also requested boiling water and towels."

"Thank you," Luke responded before turning back towards her. Reaching for her, he hesitated. "May I look at your arm?"

Nodding, Rachel felt him gently touch her arm and slowly tilt it as he examined her injury. When he touched the wound, pain radiated down her arm, and she jerked it back. As she looked at Luke's hand, she saw bright red blood smeared on his fingers, and her vision started to blur. Without warning, everything went black.

20

Luke saw Rachel sway and reached for her just as she fainted. Cradling her in his arms, he laid her on the sofa in the drawing room. Placing a pillow under her head, he knelt next to her as his eyes took in her dirt-encrusted face and hands, and her filthy, torn dress.

Even though Rachel hadn't shared many details of her attack, it was apparent that something horrible had happened in that cave. Her ripped dress, the deep scratches visible at the top of her back, and the bruising along her forearms, all testified that she must have been in a fight of horrific proportions.

Two maids walked into the room, one carrying a large bowl filled with water. Snapping his fingers, he demanded, "Bring the towels and water to me." Even before the bowl touched the table, Luke reached for a towel and dunked it into the water. Wringing out the excess water, Luke tenderly wiped Rachel's face, removing the dirt on her cheeks and forehead.

Once her face was clean, Luke moved to her neck, being careful of her gash, and cleaned off the dried blood. As he started to bathe her arm, he heard loud shouting in the main entry, growing louder by the minute. Rachel's cousin, Emmett, stormed into the room with a bag under his arm. He raced over and shoved Luke to the side.

Kneeling next to his cousin, Emmett methodically examined her neck and then her arm, before turning back to Luke. "What did you do to Rachel?" he demanded in a low growl.

Looking perplexed, Luke responded adamantly, "I did nothing to her. A group of French soldiers ambushed her near the shore."

Laughing dryly, Emmett's eyes held nothing but contempt for him. "You expect me to believe that Rachel was accosted by French soldiers on the shores of Scotland? Are you mad?"

"It is true," Luke contended. "From what I gather, David rescued her, but she was shot during the ordeal."

Frowning, Emmett clearly didn't believe what Luke was telling him. "Rachel was shot from behind," he pointed out. "Pray tell, how did she manage to travel all the way here if she was shot on the shoreline?"

Even knowing the truth didn't sound plausible, Luke replied honestly, "She rode."

Emmett scoffed, "My injured cousin rode all the way here, bypassing my parent's estate, for what purpose?"

He glanced at Rachel's pale face. "She came to get help for David."

"From you?" Emmett asked in disbelief.

He shook his head. "No, my brother is an agent of the Crown and Rachel sought him out."

Reaching into his bag, Emmett pulled out a pistol and pointed it at Luke's heart. "Pardon me if I don't believe you, Lord Downshire," he said mockingly, "but I find your story to be a little too far-fetched."

"It is the truth," he responded, returning Emmett's ire with his own. Luke didn't understand how Emmett knew about his ruse, but there wasn't time to discuss that now. "Please, I will tell you everything you want to know later. Rachel needs your help!"

Looking back towards Rachel, Emmett's eyes softened for a moment before he blinked it away. He turned to Luke and huffed, "And I'm supposed to believe the man that claimed to be a lowly horse trainer, but apparently is the Marquess of Downshire."

"Dr. Maddix," Luke started as he tried to appeal to the only man that could save the woman he loved. "It is true that I lied to Rachel, and that was wrong. I admit it. However, I would never hurt her."

"Perhaps not physically," Emmett accused.

Lowering his gaze, Luke knew that Emmett's words were accurate and justified. "You have to help Rachel."

"Do not fear, my lord," he drawled, "I will do as you command."

"I am not asking as a lord, I am asking you as a man," Luke stated with vulnerability in his plea. "Please help Rachel."

Emmett lowered his pistol slightly, but hostility still filled his eyes. "I will help my cousin, but you need to leave," he ordered firmly.

Luke shook his head. "No, I want to stay with her."

"I can't allow that," Emmett said with no regret. "I don't trust you, and I need to focus all my attention on Rachel."

Mr. Kelly walked into the room with another bowl of water and more towels. Standing near Emmett, the butler didn't seem concerned that the doctor was aiming a pistol at him. Addressing Emmett, Mr. Kelly asked, "What else do ye need, Dr. Maddix?"

Tilting the pistol towards the door, Emmett glared at Luke. "I need Lord Downshire to leave this room. Then send in a maid to help me examine Lady Rachel."

Luke took a step towards Rachel, and Emmett cocked the pistol in response. Neither man was willing to back down, so they stared defiantly at each other until Mr. Kelly calmly spoke. "Dr. Maddix, I was here when Lady Rachel rode up tae seek out

Lord Jonathon. Lord Downshire was th' one who sent for yer help. He is telling th' truth."

Narrowing his eyes, Emmett nodded and lowered his pistol. "Thank you for that, Mr. Kelly. Regardless, Lord Downshire needs to leave, now."

Feeling as if his feet were made of iron, Luke couldn't seem to move from his position. He didn't want to leave Rachel. He couldn't leave her. He decided to plea once more. "I want to help."

Turning his back on Luke, Emmett knelt beside Rachel and started examining her injured arm. She let out a pain-induced moan. A moment later, Emmett finally replied, "I believe you have done enough."

A FEW HOURS LATER, LUKE WATCHED THE RISE AND FALL OF Rachel's chest, assuring himself that she still lived. Since he had not been allowed in the room during her examination, he'd sat outside the door until Dr. Maddix had finished removing the bullet from her arm.

Now, Rachel was lying in a four-poster bed in one of his guest chambers. Her face was pale, and her blonde hair had fallen out of her chignon. Leaning forward in his seat, Luke touched her silky, smooth hair and prayed that she would not die.

Emmett's voice came from behind him. "I gave her a small dose of laudanum for the pain. Most likely, she won't wake till tomorrow."

Sitting back in his seat, Luke asked the one question he had been dreading, "Will she live?"

"Aye," Emmett assured him, "assuming infection doesn't set in."

Nodding his understanding, Luke continued to watch her breathing and was surprised when Dr. Maddix said, "I believe I owe you an apology."

He shifted in his seat to gauge Emmett's sincerity. "For what?"

Emmett sat on the edge of the bed. "I assumed the worst of you when I heard Rachel was shot, and for that I am sorry."

"You had every right to be suspicious," he admitted. "I am just grateful you came so quickly."

With a half-hearted grin, Emmett replied, "I happened to be traveling back from the village when four of your footmen descended upon me and were frantic to have me ride back with them. On the way, they explained to me what little they knew about Rachel being attacked. Furthermore, they explained how their master had lied to Rachel and why."

Taking his hand, Luke rubbed the back of his sore neck. "I never meant for my lie to get so out of control," he confessed. "I was wrong, and I hope Rachel will forgive me."

Glancing at his cousin, Emmett's eyes softened. "I have no doubt that she will forgive you. She has always had a kind, loving heart." He turned back to look at Luke. "Fortunately, David got to Rachel in time, and she was not taken advantage of by those men."

Luke sighed gratefully. He'd been worried about that very thing. "That is a huge relief," he replied.

With haunted eyes, Emmett's face grew solemn, and he turned his focus towards his cousin. After a moment, he spoke softly, "I knew a girl that was not so lucky."

"What happened?" Luke asked after a brief silence.

"I was serving as the surgeon aboard the HMS Regulus, and we were sent to fight against the colonists." He scoffed. "We had just chased down a Yankee privateer ship and had boarded it, intending to look for deserters from the Royal Navy. Instead, my captain, Lord Allister, impressed six men," he hesitated, his voice becoming strained, "and a young boy into service with no hesitation or regard for their welfare."

"Did Lord Allister state a reason for taking the boy?"

"Yes, he said he needed a cabin boy." Emmett shook his head. "However, the captain of the privateer ship begged to be taken instead of the boy, but Lord Allister disregarded his request. When the captain refused to let the boy go, Lord Allister shot him dead, in front of his crew, for mutiny." His voice grew pensive.

Luke shook his head, frowning. "That is horrible."

A matching frown formed on Emmett's lips. "That is not even the worst part." He paused before saying, "One of my duties was to perform a physical exam of all crew members. That is when I discovered the lad we impressed was actually a young woman. She had bound her chest with bandages and cut her hair in hopes of disguising her gender from the Royal Navy."

"Why would she do that? Surely, she would not have been taken if Lord Allister knew she was a woman," Luke said.

With a clenched jaw, Emmett revealed, "If they discovered she was a woman, she would have been taken for the captain's enjoyment, with no other pretenses."

"Did Lord Allister have no honor?"

"Honor is a shifty business when you are at sea. The rules of decency don't seem to apply." Picking up Rachel's wrist, Emmett grew quiet as he felt her pulse. Replacing her hand beside her, he shared, "I did my best to hide Eleanora. I even convinced the captain to let the lad work alongside me, but eventually, the captain discovered the truth."

Emmett leaned back against the bed frame, his eyes shone with sadness. "A few nights later, I was called to the captain's quarters. His cabin was in shambles. Eleanora was in the middle of the room, dead, with a pool of blood under her head. Her shirt was ripped open, she had scratches all over her body, and her face had visible bruising." He sighed. "As I rushed to her, Lord Allister ordered me to examine him first. He dared to imply the girl was mad and had attacked him."

"Did he have any wounds?"

"Only scratches from Eleanora's nails." Emmett lowered his head. "I became unhinged. I grabbed the pistol from the captain's table, and I shot him in the leg. I wanted him to feel a small fraction of the pain that he had caused Eleanora."

"What happened next?"

Emmett huffed, "Lord Allister wanted me to hang, but my uncle is Lord Exeter, and I am second in line to inherit his estate. That prevented them from executing me. After being court-marshaled for 'conduct unbecoming an officer and a gentleman', I was discharged from my commission, but not before Lord Allister shot me in the leg. He cited 'an eye for an eye' and left me rotting in a cell for weeks."

"Is that why you loathe the nobility?" he asked. When Emmett gave him a surprised look, he clarified, "Rachel told me that you seemed jaded by titles and English theatrics."

Emmett nodded. "I suppose I am. When I signed up to serve our King and country, I wanted to help drive back Napoleon and preserve our freedom. But instead, I discovered that our navy plucks people from their country and impresses them into service, depriving them of the same rights that we claim to value. Furthermore, the revered captain, Lord Allister, was just a man, with no honor or respect. A man who killed a young woman because she would not submit to his carnal desires."

"My condolences," Luke said with genuine sorrow. "I can't imagine the torment that you have had to endure."

Surprise flickered in Emmett's eyes at his words. After a moment, he remarked, "And I am sorry I thought about shooting you. I was wrong about you."

Lifting his brow, Luke jested, "You actually thought about shooting me? I thought you were bluffing."

Emmett chuckled. "You should know that your staff favors you when Rachel is around. Apparently, you have become a pleasant person since my cousin's arrival."

Shrugging one shoulder, Luke saw no reason to deny the truth of the statement. "Rachel has helped me see things differently. She is unlike any woman I have ever known. She is inquisitive, full of life, and is a compassionate person that acts on her heart's desires." His eyes drifted towards her still form. "I daresay that she has made me a better man."

"Good, because my cousin can have a vicious tongue when she's provoked," Emmett teased.

Luke laughed. "I have been on the receiving end of Rachel's tongue lashings several times. It is quite vexing... and humbling."

Emmett leaned forward as he shared, "One time, Rachel and I were..."

"Luke," Jonathon interrupted from the doorway. "May I speak to you for a moment?"

Glancing at Rachel, Luke debated about leaving her, but Emmett spoke up. "I will stay with her," he reassured him.

"Thank you," Luke responded as he stood and walked towards the door.

🥀 21 🥀

Wᴵᴛʜᴏᴜᴛ sᴀʏɪɴɢ ᴀ ᴡᴏʀᴅ, Lᴜᴋᴇ ғᴏʟʟᴏᴡᴇᴅ Jᴏɴᴀᴛʜᴏɴ ᴜɴᴛɪʟ they reached his library. Walking further into the room, he saw Eliza and Benedict solemnly sitting on a settee with a book opened between them, but the book had been long-forgotten, based upon the direction of their downcast eyes.

Jonathon cleared his throat to alert Eliza and Benedict to his presence. Eliza brought her gaze up and asked, "How is Rachel?"

He winced, attempting to keep the emotion out of his voice. "Alive."

Eliza closed the book and placed it on the table in front of her. "I spoke to Rachel's cousin, Dr. Maddix, and he informed me that he removed the bullet. He also indicated that all the other wounds were superficial."

"Let's hope infection doesn't set in," Luke said.

"Being shot is not necessarily a death sentence," she stated reassuringly. "Rachel will pull through."

He gave his sister an exasperated look. "And you would know this how?" he asked sarcastically.

"Eliza has been shot twice," Benedict reported calmly. He smiled lovingly at her. "Haven't you, dear?"

With no patience for these games, Luke shook his head, annoyed. "Did you find David?" He watched as their faces became carefully expressionless, confirming what he already suspected. "He is dead, isn't he?" His words were soft. He didn't want it to be true.

Jonathon touched his shoulder, his eyes holding compassion. "I am sorry. When we arrived at the cave, we only saw five dead bodies. Four were stripped of their coats and all identifying articles of clothing. Furthermore, something had been dragged through the sand into the water. We concluded that the two surviving soldiers fled in a small boat."

"And David?" Luke asked.

Benedict lowered his gaze, his voice hitching. "David had been shot multiple times and had been run through. He fought valiantly and killed four of Rachel's assailants."

Closing his eyes, Luke lowered himself onto a chair, still partly in shock from the news. "What about his body?"

"Hugh is taking care of the details," Jonathon replied, pulling up a chair next to him. "David will have a proper burial."

Nodding, Luke had no idea what to say, but managed to murmur, "I will pay for it." Poor Rachel would be devastated when she found out. He was devastated.

Eliza was the first to break the silence. "We are sorry about David, but we need to ask you a few questions."

He didn't respond but glanced her way.

"Besides seeing the French soldiers in the boat, have you noticed anything suspicious around Rockcliffe?" Her tone was gentle but firm. "Anything at all?"

Trying hard to focus on her question, Luke nodded. "Um… David, Rachel, and I went to a meeting at a pub called The Fat Whaler." He paused, reigning his emotions in. "Once there, a man named Thorne informed us that the French were preparing to invade and would soon overthrow King George." He glanced worriedly at Jonathon. "He was trying to build a militia."

"Were any of you recognized?" Benedict asked.

"No," Luke confirmed, shaking his head. "None of my workers attended the meeting, and Rachel was dressed in boy's clothing."

Eliza grinned at his admission about Rachel's clothing. "When is the next meeting?" she inquired.

"Tomorrow night. We need to get word to the magistrate. The man implied that they are rallying members of other villages. There is a lot of disdain for mad King George and our prince regent."

"Have you spoken to the constable yet? He could round up some of the dissenters," Jonathon suggested.

"Unfortunately, I can't," Luke acknowledged. "Just before he tried to have me killed, Lord Melville admitted to killing him."

"What?" the group shouted in unison.

Jonathon's steely gaze landed on him. Luke knew that when he had that look, Jonathon was not a man to be trifled with.

"Start from the beginning," Jonathon ordered.

Luke started tapping his fingers on the chair's arm as he shared the events leading up to Lord Melville attempting to kill him and the encounter in the alleyway. He finished with, "Luckily, David saved me, and Rachel shot one of the men to save us."

"And the five constables?" Benedict pressed. He shifted in his seat and now sat on the edge of the settee.

Luke sighed despairingly. "Our first constable disappeared about six months ago, and three more disappeared in the middle of the night. The fifth constable arrived over a week ago, but Lord Melville admitted killing him because his loyalties couldn't be bought."

"Do you think Lord Melville's aunt knows about his villainous actions?" Eliza questioned.

"No," Luke said. "Supposedly, she has been in a coma for

almost seven months. Rachel offered to read to her, but Lord Melville refused."

Benedict furrowed his brow. "How long has Lord Melville been living with his aunt?"

"I don't know," Luke admitted.

Dr. Maddix's voice came from the doorway, answering the question. "Lord Melville showed up around the same time Mrs. Felix went into a coma." He walked further into the room. "I apologize for the intrusion, but I was walking by when I heard the name Lord Melville." He shook his head. "I loathe that man."

Luke shot up from his seat and demanded, "Why aren't you with Rachel?"

Turning his gaze towards him, Dr. Maddix replied calmly, "No need to worry. I left a maid to attend to her."

Eliza pointed towards a chair, inviting Emmett to join them. "Why do you hate Lord Melville?"

Sitting down, Emmett revealed, "I was at sea seven months ago, but during that time, Lord Melville showed up to care for his ailing aunt. However, by all accounts, Mrs. Felix was a healthy widow that simply disappeared from Society one day. He claims that she is in a coma, but I wouldn't be surprised if he just killed her."

"Why would Lord Melville kill his own aunt?" Benedict asked.

Emmett shrugged. "Greed or money are the standard culprits. Mrs. Felix is extremely wealthy, and it was no secret that her only living relatives were her estranged nephew and niece. I'm sure Lord Melville came to ensure he got his hands on his aunt's fortune, one way or another."

"I think we need to visit Mrs. Felix's estate and see what we can learn," Eliza concluded.

Jonathon nodded. "That is a splendid idea. Right now, there are too many variables to be simple coincidences. We need to determine if Lord Melville is involved with the French, or if he is just a murderer."

Frowning, Luke spoke up, "When we tracked the horse thief to Mrs. Felix's estate, we saw multiple guards posted around the perimeter, but we only saw one young serving maid inside. It did not go well for us when we approached the main door."

Eliza arched an eyebrow. "Who said anything about going through the main door?" She turned towards her husband. "Are you ready for another break-in?"

"Are you mad?" Luke exclaimed. "You can't break into an estate!"

Ignoring Luke's outburst, Eliza focused on Jonathon. "I believe it would be best if we sent for Adrien. If someone is creating militias to fight with the French, we need all the agents we can get to slow them down until the Royal Army comes."

"I agree," Jonathon said. "Rockcliffe is only seven hours' ride from his estate in Northumberland."

Turning to stare down Jonathon now, Luke asked in disbelief, "You are sending for Adrien, the new Lord Camden. Isn't he on his wedding tour?"

"Luke," Eliza stated sternly, causing him to look at her. "If the French land in Scotland and march towards London, they could do terrible damage to the countryside before the Royal Army intercepts them." She frowned, her eyes reflecting worry. "Also, if the French have a large enough force, they could over-power the limited number of British ground troops and Army Reserve. If we can assemble enough militia to fight them, we could diminish their numbers, or at least keep them busy until our troops arrive."

Rising, Jonathon walked towards the library door and shouted, "Larson!" Turning back to face the group, he recapped, "There were four French spies on English soil, and we eliminated two of them. Sadly, two are still at large. One is Kate's father, Phillipe, and another is a spy with the code name, *Rogue*."

Leaning back in his seat, Benedict added, "We have every reason to believe that *Rogue* is here in Rockcliffe leading the invasion, assuming we are correct in our assessment that this is where the French plan to land."

Mr. Larson walked into the room. "Yes, Lord Jonathon?"

Glancing at Eliza, Jonathon said, "We are going to break into the Felix's estate tonight. Luke informed us that there are guards posted around the perimeter. We will all need to go."

"Agreed," Mr. Larson confirmed. "I will take care of the arrangements."

"Wait," Luke shouted. "This is lunacy. If what you are suggesting is true, how can three agents take on the French army and a militia?"

With tight lips, Eliza grabbed the book from the table and rose. "Very easily, assuming you don't stand in our way." She offered him a haughty smile. "Besides, we are breaking into an estate at night. I highly doubt the whole French army is sitting around having tea in Mrs. Felix's drawing room." Clutching the book to her chest, she walked out of the room without looking back.

After a few moments, Emmett chuckled. "I like her."

Jonathon put his hand on Luke's shoulder and leaned in. "You miscounted. There are four agents here."

"You have to be bloody kidding me," Luke mumbled under his breath. His sister was an agent? What was next? *Shadow* was a woman as well? He shook his head. That was impossible.

LATER THAT EVENING, LUKE STORMED INTO HIS DRAWING ROOM wearing a black shirt, dark trousers, and his black Hessian boots.

He was about to open his mouth to complain about the dark clothing when he noticed Eliza, Jonathon, and Benedict were dressed in a similar fashion. The only exception was Eliza, who also wore a dark cap low on her head.

Striding towards Eliza, Luke kept his voice firm as he addressed her. "You will stay behind and rest. I forbid you to go."

Benedict's eyes grew hard, but as he began to step forward, Eliza put a hand on his chest to stop him. She repeated Luke's words slowly, "You 'forbid' me?"

"Yes. It appears you have been given too much liberty by your husband and Jonathon. It is in all our best interest if you let the men handle this assignment," Luke stated, trying to ignore the anger coursing through Benedict's eyes. Maybe he had gone too far. Tilting his head to see Jonathon's reaction, he was surprised to see his brother wore an amused grin.

"How dare..." Benedict started to growl but was cut off by Eliza's glance.

With a swipe of her hand, Eliza's cap was off her head, and she tossed it onto the table. Walking up to Luke, her eyes narrowed, seeming to take his measure and finding him lacking. Eliza's confident presence caused his resolve to shrink, especially when she said, "You are not in a position to dictate my actions." Her eyes narrowed even further. "Next time you say something so half-witted, I will not be as generous."

Staring at his younger sister, who had just threatened him, Luke asked quietly, "When did you get to be so frightening?" He was supposed to be the one in charge of the family, but at some point, his sister had taken over without him knowing. Taking a step back, Luke asked Jonathon, "Why am I dressed like this?"

Rolling her eyes, Eliza answered for Jonathon, "We wear black at night because it is easier to blend into the shadows."

Hearing Eliza say 'shadows' reminded Luke of the letter Rachel wrote. Walking over to the drink tray, he took the lid off the decanter, and informed the group, "I failed to mention that Rachel wrote *Shadow* about the French spies. Hopefully, he will arrive soon." He poured himself a drink, then noticed there was silence in the room and turned back around.

With a sideways glance towards Eliza, Jonathon revealed, "*Shadow* is already here."

As soon as the words were out of his mouth, Luke had no doubt who *Shadow* was. Gulping back his drink, he slammed the glass onto the tray. "Can someone explain to me how the daughter of a duke managed to become a notorious assassin without attracting attention to herself?"

Benedict took a step towards him, his jaw clenched, and his eyes narrowed. "Explain to me why I shouldn't kill you for disrespecting my wife in such a horrendous fashion?" His words were filled with controlled fury. "My wife is not an assassin!"

Luke gulped, swallowing his sudden trepidation. He nervously glanced at the pistol tucked in the waistband of Benedict's trousers. Perhaps he had gone too far... again.

Turning to face him, Eliza again placed her palm on Benedict's chest. She smiled up at her husband and said, a little too sweetly, "Rachel seems to be fond of Luke, so there must be some redeeming qualities about him. If none emerge soon, then you can kill him."

Benedict backed down but continued to glare at him. Eliza turned and shook her head at her brother. "We'll talk about this later, Luke. We have more important things to do now."

Mr. Larson walked into the room. "The horses are ready," he announced.

After a quick ride through his property, Luke showed them the woodlands that formed the property line on the south side. Dismounting their horses, they secured them and ran towards the safety of the trees. Benedict pointed north towards the stable, and Jonathon and Mr. Larson moved out.

It was decided that Luke would stay with Benedict and Eliza

as they navigated their way towards Mrs. Felix's estate. Using the trees as cover, Eliza carried a black longbow in her hand and had a quiver full of arrows at her shoulder. The moon was high in the sky and illuminated the large field and surrounding trees.

A twig snapped in the distance, and in a blink of an eye, Eliza was kneeling on the ground with an arrow nocked and pulled back. A shadowy figure walked through the trees towards them. Before Luke could react, he felt the rush of air as an arrow whizzed past his head, which was almost immediately followed by a thud.

With wide eyes, he turned to face Eliza, but she was already moving, keeping low, as she approached the dead man. Yanking her arrow out of the man's chest, she calmly placed it back into her quiver. With a tilt of her head, she indicated they should keep moving.

After about thirty yards, Benedict put his fist up in the air, and everyone stopped. Luke scanned the area to see what had caught his brother-in-law's attention. Suddenly, someone jumped out from the cover of the trees, aiming a pistol at Benedict.

Without hesitation, Benedict grabbed the man's wrist, twisting it back until the man dropped the pistol. The man swung at him with his free arm, but Benedict ducked and punched his assailant in the stomach. Releasing the man's hand, Benedict placed his hands on both sides of the man's head, and with a quick jerk, he dropped the man onto the leaf-coated ground.

Frozen in place, Luke could not seem to decide who he was more afraid of… his arrow-wielding sister or his even more violent brother-in-law. Reminding himself not to make either of them angry ever again, he trailed behind them.

Moving closer to him, Eliza whispered, "Have you been inside before?"

"I have, but I have never been upstairs," Luke admitted.

On the other side of him, Benedict pulled a pistol from his

right boot and extended it towards him. "Do you know how to use this?"

Luke nodded. "I do, but I have never shot a person."

"Good," Benedict replied quickly. "Stay here and cover us. With any luck, you won't have to."

Staying low, Eliza and Benedict weaved in and out of the trees until they arrived at Mrs. Felix's brick estate. Amazed, he watched as they expertly scaled the wall. They reached an upper window, and Eliza attempted to pull it open. When it failed to budge, they moved on to the next window, which was unlocked. Eliza allowed Benedict to go first, and then he assisted her through the window.

Luke jumped in alarm when an owl hooted in the distance. How could Eliza and Benedict stay so calm as they met their assailants?

A brief time later, Benedict and Eliza reappeared and scaled back down the wall. Crouching, they ran back to the cover of the trees. Together, they made their way back to the meeting point, encountering no resistance. However, Jonathon and Mr. Larson were not so lucky. The sound of a pistol discharging came from their direction.

They heard shouting in the distance as two shadowy figures ran through the trees directly towards them. Nocking her longbow, Eliza kept the bow taut as she peered into the night. Releasing her arrow, it sailed past the two men. It must have hit its intended target, because a deep groan was heard through the darkness.

In the moonlight, Luke could make out the shadowy figures of Jonathon and Mr. Larson. They all ran to their horses and kicked them into a run.

The roar of another pistol came from behind, and Luke saw Jonathon jerk forward. His brother had been shot!

❦ 22 ❦

TRYING NOT TO SNICKER, LUKE SAT BACK IN A CHAIR AND listened to Jonathon grumble incessantly about the pain as Dr. Maddix bandaged the wound on his right shoulder. Taking a sip of his drink, he was grateful that Emmett had lingered at his estate watching over Rachel. Even though Jonathon initially refused to be seen by the doctor, he finally bowed under pressure. Dr. Maddix confirmed that the bullet merely grazed his skin and did not require stitches.

Cutting the excess bandage, Emmett announced, "You will live, Lord Jonathon."

Reaching for his shirt, Jonathon replied dryly, "Delightful." He grunted as he put his shirt on. "I can't believe you have been shot twice, Eliza. This is bloody awful."

Eliza smiled at Jonathon. "I believe I said those exact words the last time I was shot."

With a chuckle, Mr. Larson teased, "I seem to recall Eliza complaining less than Jonathon."

Observing his sister, Luke realized Eliza, now dressed in a dark yellow gown, had grown into a beautiful woman with auburn hair, high cheekbones, and olive skin. The thought of her being shot seemed inconceivable, and it petrified him. "Why wasn't I notified that my sister was shot? Twice, may I add?" His voice didn't reflect anger but resigned curiosity.

Jonathon finished tucking in his shirt. "There is a lot that we kept from you."

Taking a sip of his drink, Luke stared into the amber liquid. It was his fault that he knew so little about his family. Except for attending his sisters' weddings, he hadn't left his estate. He thought he was protecting himself, but it turns out he was the one that suffered alienation from his family. He placed his glass on the table. "That ends now. I want to know everything."

Eliza beamed in approval. "Welcome back, brother."

Cleaning up his supplies, Emmett placed them into his bag, before saying, "If you will excuse me, I believe I will go check on Rachel."

"Stay," Benedict ordered, his tone commanding. "We are going to need all the help we can get."

Emmett nodded and returned to his seat.

Removing the pistol from his trousers, Mr. Larson rested it on his thigh as he stared bleakly at Rachel's cousin. "Dr. Maddix, I would caution you to use discretion when speaking of the Beckett family." His deceivingly conversational tone sent chills up Luke's spine as he recognized the words for what they truly were... a threat.

Mr. Larson's words did not seem to intimidate Emmett. He appeared amused as he rested his elbows on the velvet chair's arms. "It is clear to me that the men," his eyes twinkled as he glanced at Eliza, "and lady, in this room, are assets to the Crown and are loyal to the King. I would like to offer my support as a former navy surgeon, in whatever capacity I am needed." His words were bold, and no doubt sincere.

Mr. Larson nodded his approval and returned the pistol to his trousers.

Putting his glass on the table next to him, Luke directed his question at Eliza. "Did you learn anything while you were in Mrs. Felix's house?"

Eliza sighed. "Yes, we did." Glancing with pity at Emmett, she confirmed, "Mrs. Felix is dead. We were able to sneak into her room because the window was slightly ajar, probably to lessen the smell of death."

"Thick layers of dust covered everything, but except for missing linens and an overturned chair, the contents seemed to be intact," Benedict added. "We didn't spend too much time looking for the body, because we suspect she is buried somewhere on the property. We did, however, find letters addressed to Lord Melville and his sister on her desk."

Lifting his brow in confusion, Luke asked, "Why would Mrs. Felix write letters to her nephew if he was living in her house?"

"Our thoughts exactly," Eliza said. "Unfortunately, that is not all we found."

Taking a sip from his glass, Benedict grew pensive. "We barely stepped into the hall when we heard people speaking French. Glancing over the stair rail, we saw a large group of men loitering on the main level." His voice grew serious. "Some of them were wearing French uniforms."

"There is more," Eliza informed the group as her eyes grew guarded. "We found maps of Portsmouth, Chatham, and other major southern British shipyards."

Confused, Luke inquired, "Why would the French have maps of our shipyards?"

Benedict's keen eyes bored into his. "They are targeting the shipyards to cripple our Royal Navy."

Mr. Larson's expression was angry and determined. "We need to warn them."

"Agreed," Benedict concurred.

Emmett huffed furiously. "I knew Lord Melville was evil. I'd heard he fashions himself a rogue and sleeps with every maiden he can get in his clutches. Now it seems he is also consorting with the enemy and plotting to destroy our navy."

Jonathon shifted to focus on Emmett. "What did you say?"

"I knew Lord Melville…"

With a swiping motion, Jonathon cut him off. "No, after that."

Frowning, Emmett said slowly, "He fashions himself a rogue…"

Turning back towards Eliza and Benedict, Jonathon asked, "Do you think Lord Melville could be the French spy, *Rogue*?"

Mr. Larson did not seem as convinced. "Not every lord that sleeps with loads of women is a French spy. If that were the case, then our own Prinny would be suspect."

With a less-than-amused look at Mr. Larson, Eliza stated, "Lord Melville is in an ideal position if he was *Rogue*. He has a large enough estate to house French soldiers, the financial backing to support them, and no one would expect an attack from the seaside village of Rockcliffe."

"There are plenty of estates that offer seclusion," Benedict speculated. "Why would Lord Melville target Mrs. Felix's estate?"

Jonathon frowned. "I suspect they aren't even related."

Rising, Luke walked over to the drink cart. "How would Lord Melville gain access to Mrs. Felix's estate if they weren't related?"

Sighing, Jonathon replied, "By force."

Benedict shrugged. "Coercion."

"Death," Eliza said, frowning.

Pouring himself a drink, Luke mumbled under his breath, "It seems that you have been doing this for a long time."

Ignoring his comment, Jonathon ran his hand through his hair. "Larson and I snuck into the stable, and we discovered eleven thoroughbred horses."

Luke's face brightened at the mention of his horses. "All eleven were there? That's great news."

Jonathon shook his head. "Not so great. We also found chickens, pigs, and piles of men's clothing in various stalls."

Returning to his seat, Luke nodded. "There has been a rash of robberies around the village, and it appears that Lord Melville is the culprit."

"If it would help, I would be happy to shoot him," Emmett offered as he stretched his legs out in front of him.

Eliza smiled in approval at Emmett. "Even though I appreciate your offer, we have to keep Lord Melville alive for now."

"Pity," Emmett mumbled under his breath.

Benedict chuckled. "Eliza is right. We don't know when or where the French are going to land, and we haven't discovered who is leading the charge for the militia. Until we discover those things, we can't approach Lord Melville and lose our advantage."

Luke couldn't believe what he was hearing. He was in a room with four agents, and this was their solution? He huffed disapprovingly. "Are you suggesting that we just wait? Wait for what?"

With a fleeting glance at Jonathon, Eliza offered him a sympathetic look. "Sometimes the best course of action is to sit back and prepare for the battle."

Nodding, Benedict added, "We will keep Lord Melville under watch and attend the militia meeting."

"We also need to send out a ship, one that won't arouse suspicion, to look for the French frigate," Jonathon stated. "Somehow the French are sending troops to shore without coming into the harbor."

"Do you suppose they are sending six soldiers at a time on a dinghy?" Luke asked.

"Could be," Jonathon mused. "But that doesn't seem the most effective way to dispatch troops."

"My father has a fleet of whaling ships, and many of them have already returned from this season's hunt," Emmett informed them. "It wouldn't be suspicious if he sent out one or two on a training exercise."

"If your father needs persuasion, we could send Mr. Larson over to say a few words," Luke jested, chuckling.

With a stony glare, Mr. Larson slowly shook his head, and Luke wiped the smile off his face.

"All right, this is a working plan," Eliza announced as she rose. As all the men stood as well, she focused on Emmett. "Your assignment is to have your father send out as many whalers as he can to look for the French ship. Let us know if you need assistance."

Placing a hand on the small of Eliza's back, Benedict announced, "Gentlemen, it is time for me to get my wife to bed. If you will excuse us."

Watching Eliza lean into Benedict as they left the room, Luke felt a twinge of envy at the love that was evident between them. Previously, he would have criticized their blatant show of affection, but now, he wanted that. He wanted that with Rachel.

WALKING PAST RACHEL'S ROOM, LUKE HEARD FRANTIC shouting coming from within. Throwing open the door, he was prepared to face an assailant but instead saw Rachel tossing and turning on the bed, moaning.

Rushing in, Luke sat on the bed and placed his hands on her shoulders, attempting to ignore the fact that she was only wearing a nightgown. "Wake up, Rachel. You are having a nightmare."

When she stopped thrashing about, he dropped his hands and leaned back. Her eyes opened slowly, blinking a few times before asking, "What are you doing in my bedchamber?"

"Technically, you are in my room," he replied, unable to resist the urge to tease her.

With wide eyes, she shot up, keeping the blanket clutched to her chest, and glanced around the room. "This is your bedchamber?"

Luke chuckled, feeling pleased that Rachel was finally awake. "No, this is one of my guest rooms." The small crease between her eyebrows appeared. He decided to stop teasing. "Do you remember getting shot?"

Glancing down at her bandaged left arm, Rachel kept her gaze lowered as she asked the one question he had been dreading. "Did they get to David in time?"

Waiting till Rachel brought her hopeful gaze up to meet his, Luke felt horrible knowing that he was about to dash those hopes. "No," he revealed softly. "They did not."

Her sob was full of grief. Reaching for her hand, Luke's heart broke when she pulled her hand back. "Get out," she ordered between sobs. When he didn't move, she shouted, "Get out!"

"Rachel..." Luke stopped when Rachel put her feet over the side of the bed and stood up. Walking over to the open door, she placed her hand on it and tapped her foot impatiently on the carpet.

Sighing, Luke rose and walked towards her. Instead of exiting the room as she expected, he reached for the door and closed it. "No, I am not leaving you," he said, his eyes urging her to understand. "You are hurting, and I want to help you."

Rachel's mouth gaped, and her eyes grew wide with fury. "You want to help me?" Sarcastically, she accused, "No, you just want to lie to me." She shifted her gaze away from him. "This is just a game to you, isn't it?"

"No, it was not like that," Luke insisted. "When you mistook me for a horse trainer, I grasped the opportunity to be someone different; not a marquess, or the future Duke of Remington, just a regular man."

"You could have a career in theatre, my lord," Rachel responded dryly.

Taking two bold steps towards her, he exclaimed, "No 'my lord' for you." He waited for her to meet his gaze. "I care for you, Rachel."

Rachel humphed. "You will have to excuse me, but I am having difficulty believing the words that are coming out of your mouth."

Lifting his brow knowingly, Luke reminded her, "If you recall, I am not the only one that lied about my title."

"That is different," she contested.

"How so?"

Glaring up at him, she replied, "I may have left off my title, but everything else was truthful." Her blue eyes grew reflective, but the hurt in them was no less palpable. "I was friends with John, but Lord Downshire is someone I do not know."

"I am the same man," he said, attempting to reassure her.

She shook her head. "No, you are not. And frankly, I do not care to know Lord Downshire."

Dropping her gaze, Rachel started to turn, but he placed his hands on her shoulders. "Wait. What are you saying?"

Averting her eyes, Rachel's words were soft at first. "I tire of the games that bored lords play. They place bets at Whites over the silliest details." Her eyes sparked with annoyance. "Now, these same infuriating lords are placing bets on who can make me fall in love with them first."

She attempted to shake off his hands, but Luke didn't release his hold. "That is wrong of them."

"You are just like them."

"No, I am not," Luke claimed, shaking his head. "I left for

Scotland because I also tired of the ton's games of entrapment. Also, my mother was a despicable person," he paused, "and apparently a French spy."

Rachel's expression grew guarded, but he detected a hint of sympathy in her tone. "I had limited interaction with the duchess, but Eliza confided in me about some of the horrible things that her mother did. However, I didn't believe she would stoop so low as to betray her own country."

Dropping his hands, Luke admitted, "Neither did I."

Taking a step back, her lips formed a tight line. "You need to leave my room before anyone sees you."

"Not until you tell me where this leaves us?"

"Us?" she repeated, her eyes wide. "There is no us."

Lifting his brow, he countered, "I disagree. The way you kissed me proved to me that you have feelings for me."

She rolled her eyes dramatically. "I kissed John, not Lord Downshire. And that was before I discovered you lied to me."

Luke smirked. "You even offered David £5,000, so you could keep kissing me."

Instead of the rebuttal he expected, Rachel's eyes filled with tears. She brought her white sleeve up to wipe them away. "Because of me, David is dead," she said, her voice shaky.

Luke moved to embrace her, but she stepped out of his grasp. "No, David was killed by French soldiers," he insisted. "They killed him, not you."

Tears streamed down her bruised and swollen cheeks. "He died protecting me, even though I said horrible things to him."

"You were upset," Luke murmured, attempting to reassure her. "He knew you cared for him."

A sob left her lips as her body trembled. "I had just fired him and told him to leave me alone. I refused to listen to him even when he said the shoreline wasn't safe." She dropped her tear-streaked face into her hands, sobbing uncontrollably.

Hearing the pain in her voice, Luke wanted nothing more

than to comfort her, but would she allow it? He ventured, "I know you are angry with me, and you have every right to be, but can we put our differences aside and mourn the loss of our friend together?" He opened his arms and hoped Rachel would accept.

Lifting her head, she nodded and walked into his waiting arms. Luke embraced her tightly as she wept. When her sobs lessened, he carefully led her over to the settee and sat next to her. Placing his arm around her shoulder, he pulled her close as they comforted each other.

Eventually, Rachel's breathing deepened, and she slept while Luke held her close. Kissing the top of her head, he realized his feelings for her were stronger than he thought. He loved her. At some point, Rachel had stolen his heart.

How was he going to convince Rachel to forgive him, let alone court her? Sadly, he remembered David had always given him great advice when it came to Rachel. Tears welled up in his eyes as he took the time to grieve the loss of his friend.

Walking over to the door, Savannah held it open. "It will all work out."

Rachel took a deep breath, walked out, and headed for the dining room. Her steps faltered, however, when she realized she didn't know where the dining room was. Before she could retreat to the safety of her bedchamber, Angelica came out of a room with a tray in her hand.

When the young maid saw her, she smiled. "You are alive."

Feeling herself relax, Rachel returned her smile. "Yes, a simple bullet isn't going to stop me." Glancing around the hall, she asked, "Can you point me in the direction of the dining room?"

"I will take you," Angelica said, promptly putting her tray down.

As she was led towards the dining room, Rachel inquired, "How is your mother faring?"

"Very well. In fact, she is coming back to work tomorrow."

"Are you going to continue working?"

Angelica glanced over, her eyes radiating happiness. "I am; especially since Lord Downshire gave the entire staff raises."

"Why did he do that?"

Angelica smiled. "Because of you."

Puzzled, Rachel shook her head. "I didn't ask him to give anyone raises."

"Oh, you didn't have to," Angelica remarked. "From the moment Lord Downshire first met you, he began changing for the better." She stopped at an open door. "The dining room, my lady."

Rachel frowned at the use of her title. "You know?"

Putting her hand up to the side of her mouth, Angelica whispered, "From the very beginning. Lord Downshire threatened to fire anyone that called you Lady Rachel or him Lord Downshire."

Amused that the maid acted as if she were sharing a great state secret, Rachel chuckled. "He did not."

"Oh, yes," Angelica shared, still whispering. "He started yelling at…" She stopped speaking, and her eyes grew wide as saucers.

A deep male voice came from behind Rachel. "Angelica." She did not have to turn around to recognize that voice, because she would never forget Luke's rich baritone. With a slight curtsy, Angelica started to leave when he continued, "Thank you for escorting Lady Rachel to the dining room."

"You are welcome, my lord," Angelica replied before she spun around.

Turning to face Luke, Rachel's treacherous heart leaped at the sight of him. His square jaw was clean-shaven, drawing her eyes to his handsome face. How had she ever mistaken him for a simple horse trainer? Even though she was still angry at him, staring deep into his brown eyes was affecting her resolve. Reaching for her hand, Luke brought it up to his lips, lingering on her skin.

"Morning," he said hoarsely, keeping his gaze on her. "I was on my way to check on you."

"There is no need, since I am here now. I apologize that I overslept, but I had a late night last night. Well, you remember…" Rachel stopped speaking as she felt her cheeks grow exceedingly warm. Good heavens, why was she rambling?

Giving her a private smile, Luke took her hand and placed it in the crook of his arm as he led her into the dining room. Believing she was still mad at him, she tried to yank back her hand, but he held tight. As she started to express her displeasure, he winked playfully at her. How dare he wink at her!

"Rachel!" Eliza exclaimed. She pushed back her chair and rushed over to greet her. Dropping her arm, Luke stepped to the side as Eliza pulled her into an embrace. "I was so worried about you."

"I am all right," Rachel confirmed, dropping her arms.

Looping Rachel's arm through hers, Eliza escorted her to a chair next to hers at the table. Before she could protest, Luke placed a plate of food in front of her. Looking up at him, she murmured, "Thank you."

Pulling his chair closer, Luke claimed the seat on her other side. "Would you like to go on a carriage ride this afternoon?"

"No, thank you," Rachel answered, reaching for her fork.

Not deterred by her rejection, he asked, "How about going for a ride on Chester?"

That was not fair. Luke knew her weakness for Chester and was using it against her. Before she could do something crazy like accept Luke's invitation, Benedict replied for her, "I highly doubt Dr. Maddix will allow Rachel to go riding, since she was shot only yesterday."

"Good point," Luke remarked. "A walk, perhaps?"

Rachel wiped her mouth with her white linen napkin then placed it back in her lap. As she reached for her teacup, she admonished in a hushed voice, "I am still mad at you."

Leaning closer, Luke smirked and kept his voice low. "I know. You can't hide your emotions very well."

"That is not true," Rachel argued over the rim of her teacup.

Smiling, Jonathon placed his cup back on the saucer. "It is true," he confirmed. "Everyone knows you are mad at Luke and it provides us with ample entertainment."

"Ignore Jonathon," Benedict said, smiling. "We all try to, anyway."

Rachel chuckled, but her smile was wiped away when she saw Luke was watching her with a twinkle in his eyes.

In a chastising tone, she asked, "Do you mind?"

In response, he smiled, a lopsided one that had her heart fluttering in response.

Changing tactics, Rachel decided to ignore him while she ate but quickly realized she'd lost her appetite. As she pushed her plate away, she offered the group a weak smile. "Thank you for trying to save David."

Eliza reached for her teacup. "When were you informed about David?" she inquired, appearing quite innocent.

With a panicked glance at Luke, he seemed eager to hear her answer as well. "I... uh... heard this morning," Rachel stammered.

"Interesting," Eliza murmured. After taking a sip, she asked, "You didn't hear it by chance when Luke went into your room last night?"

Jonathon had just taken a sip of tea when Eliza asked her question, and he choked on his drink. After wiping his mouth, he glared at his brother. "You were in her room?" His tone was accusing.

"Rachel was having a nightmare, and I heard her shouting from the hall," Luke informed the group, completely ignoring his brother's ire.

Benedict chuckled at Jonathon. "If I recall, you were constantly sneaking into Hannah's room."

"And she is now my wife," Jonathon pointed out.

Luke smiled mischievously. "Then I will just marry Rachel." Outraged, she started to jump out of her seat but stopped when he chuckled. "Please, don't leave. I was only teasing."

"Thank goodness," Rachel replied.

Tilting his head, Luke whispered in her ear, "Don't sound so relieved. Many women consider me quite a catch."

Trying not to be too distracted by Luke's nearness, she muttered under her breath, "I am not one of them."

"We shall see," he challenged, his warm breath on her ear.

Attempting to calm her racing heart, Rachel tried to regain her thoughts. Luke had never flirted with her so boldly, and she found she liked this fun, playful side of him. No, she was still mad at him. He had lied to her.

As she opened her mouth to remind Luke, once again, that

she was mad at him, Emmett stormed into the dining room. Once his blazing eyes landed on her, he shouted, "You are engaged to Lord Melville?"

Luke stood so fast that he knocked down his chair as he glared down at Rachel. "When did this happen?"

Rachel stared incredulously at him. "Of course I am not engaged to Lord Melville. I don't even like the man."

Walking closer to his cousin, Emmett demanded, "Then explain why Lord Melville showed up and asked my father's permission to marry you."

Standing up, Rachel threw her hands in the air. "I don't know why. Maybe he is mad?"

Reaching out, Luke placed his hand on Rachel's elbow and turned her towards him. "You can't marry Lord Melville. We suspect he is a French spy."

"Are you daft?" she asked, jerking her arm away. "I have no intention of marrying Lord Melville. Not even if he was the last man on Earth."

"Why do you suppose Lord Melville is under the impression you two are engaged?" Eliza questioned.

"I don't know," Rachel responded, shaking her head. "The last time I saw Lord Melville was when we were at his aunt's estate."

Shifting in his seat, Benedict placed his arm on the back of Eliza's chair. "Did you say anything that could have given him the impression you favored him?"

Rachel put a hand up to the side of her head. "He offered for me over a week ago, but…"

"What?" Luke roared. "He offered for you?"

Turning to face Luke, she glared as she poked him in the chest, hard. "It was the same day that you were spying on me."

Luke grabbed her finger and held it in place. "If I had known he was proposing to you, then…"

She yanked her finger free. "Then what?" Rachel pressed, stepping closer to him. "You have no claim on me. If I did want to marry Lord Melville, then you would have no say in the matter."

Watching the emotions flitter across her face would have normally distracted him, but Luke was angry. He groaned inwardly, knowing he was doing a poor job of controlling his emotions. He was trying to prove to Rachel that he was more than just a brooding lord. Calmly, he placed his hands on her shoulders and decided to change tactics. "You are young, and you don't have to marry the first man that offers for you." He smiled.

Luke ignored Eliza's slight gasp and kept his eyes on Rachel. His smile faded when she narrowed her eyes. Apparently, she was not pleased.

Shaking out of his hold, she took a few steps back. "How dare you! You think of me as so weak-minded that I would accept an offer of marriage without love being the first criteria."

Reaching his arms out, Luke rushed to clarify. "No, I wasn't implying…"

"Enough," Rachel declared, her eyes reflecting pain; pain that he had caused. "Just so you are aware, I have been offered for, numerous times, and I turned them all down."

With an apologetic smile at Eliza and Benedict, Rachel stormed out of the room, completely ignoring her cousin.

Silence descended on the group until Benedict said, "I was wrong. Luke is a bigger ignoramus than Jonathon when it comes to love."

"That was painful," Jonathon stated as he placed his fork on his plate.

Fingering the napkin on her lap, Eliza asked Luke, "Were you trying to offer Rachel a compliment or insult her? Because I have deciphered thousands of enemy codes, and I still couldn't tell."

"At least he called Rachel young," Benedict offered, chuckling.

"I didn't handle that very well," Luke admitted. Yanking back his chair, he dropped down and placed his elbow on the table. "Whenever I am around Rachel, I can't seem to think clearly. She twists my words around and infuriates me."

Emmett leaned up against the wall. "I should have known my cousin wouldn't have accepted Lord Melville's proposal. If she hadn't accepted any of the others, then why his?"

"She really has been offered for?" Luke asked.

Chuckling, Jonathon rested his arms on the table and leaned forward. "I have heard rumors that Rachel has been offered for at least a hundred times."

Looking towards Emmett for confirmation, Luke was surprised to see him nod as well. "Rachel is beautiful, titled, and witty, but a hundred proposals? That seems a bit unbelievable," he remarked.

Jonathon's face broke out into a broad smile. "You don't know, do you?"

"Know what?" Luke grumbled.

"Rachel's father is Lord Exeter," Jonathon shared, "but, her maternal grandmother was the Duchess of Rutland." Luke just stared at him expectedly, so he continued. "When she died, she left her entire fortune to her only granddaughter, Rachel. Thus, making her one of the most eligible women in England."

Eliza nodded. "Our own cousin, the Duke of Whitmore, attempted a suit with Rachel."

Dropping his arm onto the table, Luke sighed. He had

nothing to offer Rachel. She already had a title and wealth. Why would she ever accept him as her husband? He was a recluse that lived in Scotland.

"It would appear Rachel has decided to make a hasty retreat," Eliza announced, peering out the window.

"Confounded woman!" Luke shouted as he shoved back his chair. Turning towards the window, he saw Rachel riding Chester towards her uncle's estate. "Mr. Kelly!"

Appearing immediately, Mr. Kelly said, "Ye bellowed, m'lord?"

He pointed out the window. "Did you let Lady Rachel leave the estate?" he growled.

"I didn't stop th' lass if that is what ye'r asking," Mr. Kelly replied. "Was I wrong tae assume she wasn't our prisoner?"

Jonathon started laughing but turned it into a cough when Luke glared at him. Turning back towards Mr. Kelly, he ordered, "Get my horse ready. I am bringing her back."

Benedict smirked. "Are you planning to compliment her again? That worked so well last time."

As he prepared to run out the door to bring back the most obnoxious female he'd ever met, Luke stopped and said, "No, but I have an idea."

❦ 24 ❦

Dismounting, Rachel hoped that Luke didn't accuse her of stealing his horse again. She only planned to borrow him until she could convince him to sell Chester to her.

The main door opened, and Aunt Jessamine rushed down the steps. "My dear child, I am so happy to see you."

As she started to hug her aunt, Rachel faltered.

Aunt Jessamine pulled back and asked, "What is wrong?"

Tilting her arm to look at her wound, Rachel saw red blood saturating the bandages. Maybe riding so soon after her injury was not her best idea. Not realizing she'd begun swaying, she was surprised when her aunt helped prop her up.

Within moments, her uncle appeared and scooped her up in his arms. Carrying Rachel up to her bedchamber, he gently placed her on the bed. "I am worried about you," he said with a frown. "A few days ago, I sent a messenger to your father and told him you were in danger. Most likely, he will arrive within the week to take you home."

As much as she wanted to contradict her uncle, Rachel knew he was right. She had wished for adventure, but it had become too much. David's death had made it more than she could bear. "I think that is for the best," she agreed.

Putting his hand to her forehead, Uncle Edwin appeared to be checking to see if she had a fever. Removing his hand, he studied her eyes before saying, "Now, I am petrified."

"Why?" Rachel asked, confused.

"I don't believe you have ever agreed with me before," her uncle teased with a faint smile.

Her aunt bustled in with a basin of water and placed it on the side table. She sat down on the chair next to the bed. "Emmett told us how you were shot." Her words sounded pained. "Lord Downshire also arrived this morning and shared the details."

Uncle Edwin reached for his wife's hand. "We are saddened by David's death as well. However, we are grateful that he saved you."

A tear fell from her eye as Rachel remembered her friend and his final sacrifice to keep her safe. "It was my fault. If I hadn't gone down to the shore, then David would still be alive."

Shaking her head, Aunt Jessamine responded, "You don't know that. Life is a peculiar thing with its twists and turns, but one thing we know for sure, life is predictably unpredictable."

"Now, what is this nonsense about Lord Melville?" Uncle Edwin asked.

Rubbing her hand on her blanket, Rachel replied honestly. "I do not want to marry that man."

"Good," Aunt Jessamine stated firmly. "There is no way we would have allowed that union anyway." Leaning forward, she brushed a strand of hair off Rachel's face. "I think you should rest."

Before she could agree, sharp clinks could be heard on her bedroom window, and Rachel turned her head to see small pebbles hitting the glass.

Her uncle chuckled. "It appears your suitor is trying to get your attention."

"He is not my suitor," came her swift reply. "I find Lord Downshire to be irritating."

Aunt Jessamine cast an amused glance at her husband before saying, "Is that so?"

Rachel nodded. "It doesn't matter anyway. He lied to me, and I can't trust him."

The sound of pebbles hitting the glass increased and her uncle frowned. Turning towards the window, he said, "I don't condone that Lord Downshire lied to you, but I want you to try to understand why he did it."

She huffed, "Isn't it obvious? He is just another bored lord who has nothing else to do with his time except toy with other's emotions."

Her aunt gave her a pointed look. "Do you truly believe that?" When Rachel didn't respond, she shared, "Except for visiting Lord Downshire when he first arrived, I have not seen him in almost seven years. He established Downshire Farms, remodeled his estate, and never socializes with the nobility in the area. You can say whatever you want about Lord Downshire, but being a bored lord is the furthest thing from the truth."

Feeling chastised, she looked back towards the window. Her uncle rose from the bed, declaring, "If you don't talk to Lord Downshire, then I will."

Putting her feet over the edge of the bed, Rachel stood up, walked over to the window, unlatched it, pushed it open, and leaned out far enough to see Luke standing below.

When Luke saw her, he quickly dropped the remaining pebbles from his hand. He smiled, but it seemed forced. "Good morning, my lady," he said while he executed a short bow.

Even though his movements seemed stiff, Rachel responded in kind, "Good morning."

Reaching down to the ground, Luke picked up a bouquet of flowers and extended it towards her. "I brought you flowers."

Dropping his gaze towards the ground, he muttered in a hushed tone, "Absolutely not. There is no way I can climb that wall."

Rachel could hear someone whisper a response, but she couldn't make out the words. Returning his gaze back to her, Luke smiled. "I would like to apologize for my behavior earlier. I did not mean to imply that no one wanted to marry you…" His words dropped as she heard urgent whispering coming from beneath her.

When the whispering stopped, Luke's smile was strained. "The fault is not in ourselves, but in the stars."

Trying not to laugh at Luke's botched attempt to quote Shakespeare, Rachel started to correct him when she heard two different hushed voices chastising him. He frowned, and responded to the whispering, "I didn't mess it up. Why am I quoting Shakespeare anyway?"

Aunt Jessamine placed her hand on Rachel's shoulder. "Poor Lord Downshire. Maybe you should invite him to join us in the drawing room?" She smiled knowingly. "And include his council advising him from the side."

She sighed. She did feel some pity towards Luke. He had made such a grand gesture. "Would you like to join us in the drawing room for some tea?"

"I would be honored," he replied.

Before she closed the window, Rachel had a hunch who was speaking to Luke, so she added, "Jonathon and Benedict, please join us as well." Latching the window, she descended the stairs as the sound of knocking echoed throughout the main entry. The door was opened immediately, and Luke strode in with Jonathon and Benedict in tow.

Upon seeing her, Luke's eyes lit up, and a pleased smile graced his lips as he approached her. Stopping in front of her, he reached out and handed her the bouquet of flowers.

"Thank you," she murmured as she placed them down on the table next to her.

He reached out again, then hesitated and lowered his hand. "I am sorry for upsetting you earlier. It was not my intention to insult you, but whenever I am around you, I seem to say the wrong things."

Being familiar with that sentiment, she responded, "I understand. I have the same problem."

"You do?" Luke asked, surprised.

Rachel nodded. "You seem to make me angry and happy at the same time. It is very perplexing."

Luke smiled playfully. "More happy than angry?"

Lifting her eyebrow, she admitted truthfully, "Perhaps, but I am still mad at you for lying to me."

"Ah, yes." His eyes twinkled with amusement. "What if I offer you Chester in exchange for your forgiveness?"

Reigning in her emotion, Rachel didn't want to appear too eager to accept his offer. Clasping her hands, she demurely tipped her head. "I accept your conditions." Without warning, her arm started throbbing, and she winced in pain.

"What is it?" Luke asked, his concern evident on his brow.

Tilting her arm, Rachel looked down at the blood-soaked bandage, realizing her aunt hadn't had time to change it. She looked up and saw Luke clenching his jaw. She expected him to shout at her for reinjuring herself, but instead, he scooped her up and walked her into the drawing room.

After requesting water and a fresh bandage from a maid, Luke gently sat her down on the settee, removed the cloth bandage and inspected the wound. Once a basin of water was placed next to him, he cleaned the wound and wrapped a clean cloth around it.

When he finished, Luke gave her a crooked smile. "You are a much better patient than my horses when I have to doctor them."

Rachel stifled a laugh when she heard Benedict mumble, "Imbecile," under his breath.

Instead of being offended, she answered, "Thank you."

Walking into the room, Emmett noticed the discarded bandages and rushed to his cousin's side. "Are you all right?"

"I am," Rachel reassured him. "Lord Downshire just reapplied the bandage."

Nodding his approval, Emmett sat down next to Jonathon.

Tilting his head to address her aunt and uncle, Luke surprised Rachel by saying, "As we discussed earlier, I will be taking Lady Rachel back to my estate now."

"I beg your pardon," Rachel said, glaring at Luke. "I am not going anywhere."

"You must. It is not safe for you here," Luke replied in a strangely urgent voice.

Sitting across from her, Uncle Edwin seemed pained as he admitted, "I have failed to keep you safe this past week, even with a full-time protector around you, and it ends now. Lord Downshire's estate not only has footmen but almost fifty men that work for Downshire Farms. Furthermore, he informed us that four agents of the Crown are residing at his estate, and one is a woman who can be with you day and night."

Rachel's eyes scanned the room, and everyone appeared to agree, except her. "Are you all mad?" she questioned. "I am perfectly safe here."

Uncle Edwin shook his head. "You're not. It is either reside at Lord Downshire's estate until your father arrives, or I will place you on one of my whaling ships for a month."

"Pray tell, what harm could possibly fall upon me here?" Rachel asked sarcastically.

Emmett's eyes were directed towards the window when he announced, "Well, to begin with, your betrothed just showed up."

Turning towards the window, Rachel saw Lord Melville set the brake on his carriage before he hopped out. He straightened his grey tailcoat and adjusted his white gloves before moving towards the main door.

Grabbing Rachel's hand, Luke said, "We will go out the back."

"Wait," Benedict ordered. "We have an opportunity here that we don't want to waste."

"What opportunity?" Luke growled.

"I highly doubt Lord Melville suspects Rachel is aware of his treachery," Jonathon stated, rising from his seat. He turned his focus to her. "Do you think you can meet with Lord Melville and try to get him to talk?"

"About what?" Rachel asked, unsure what he was asking of her.

"Anything," Benedict replied. "We will be listening from the next room over. Just keep him talking."

"Rachel is not a spy," Luke reminded the group. "It is too dangerous for her."

A loud knock broke up their conversation, but Rachel had already made her decision. Turning towards Jonathon and Benedict, she confirmed, "Both of you will be listening nearby?" In response, they nodded.

Gripping her hand tighter, Luke leaned in. "This is lunacy. You don't have to do this."

Rachel dropped his hand. "I know, but I have to face him. I don't want people to think I am truly betrothed to Lord Melville."

Jonathon grabbed Luke's arm, and the men quickly exited, leaving her aunt and Rachel sitting on the settees. A few moments later, Lord Melville was announced, and he walked into the room. When his predatory eyes landed on her, a shiver traveled down her spine.

"Mrs. Maddix, perhaps you would allow me to speak to Lady Rachel... alone," he said with a smile that lacked any warmth.

Pursing her lips thoughtfully, her aunt finally responded. "Your request is highly inappropriate, Lord Melville. However, I will grant you five minutes."

As soon as her aunt left the room, Lord Melville sat down next to her. Angling his body on the settee to face her, he reached for Rachel's hands and brought them up to his lips. This time she did not have gloves on, and she felt his lips on her skin. He lowered her hands but did not release them. As his gaze wandered over hers, he announced, "I have spoken with your uncle, and he has granted us permission to be wed."

Keeping her voice civil, Rachel asked a question of her own. "But you haven't spoken with my father?"

"Of course not," Lord Melville stated. "He is in London." He smiled as if she was a simpleton.

Slowly, she tried to remove her hands from his. "I am afraid I require my father's blessing before I can even consider an offer of marriage."

Lord Melville tightened his hold on her hands, refusing to let her go. "A father's blessing is merely a formality, my pet. In Scotland, we can marry just by saying the words in front of witnesses."

"I'm sorry," Rachel replied with a shake of her head. "I must refuse your offer of marriage."

Any pretense of being charming was stripped away, and Lord Melville's face grew cruel. "I apologize if I made it seem as if you had a choice in the matter."

"I beg your pardon?"

Holding both of her hands with one of his large ones, Lord Melville trailed his free fingers down her cheek. "I know you were in that cave, and you saw the French soldiers. Unfortunately, your guard killed four of my men before he was taken down." He roughly grabbed her chin and tilted it towards him. "And you somehow escaped the debacle."

"I don't know what you are referring to," she lied.

Lord Melville appeared amused by her denial and moved his hand towards the cut on her throat. "One of the men informed me that you were a scrappy one and had to be held down at knifepoint." Pressing his finger on the cut, Rachel tried not to wince in pain. "I was also told that the young blonde-haired woman was shot in the arm while she tried to flee." His hand moved towards her left arm, and he squeezed her wound, causing her to cry out in agony.

For an instant, she saw Luke's enraged face in the doorway, but it quickly disappeared behind the wall again.

With a cruel smile, Lord Melville leaned closer. "It is simple, really. If you marry me, I will offer you my protection."

"And if I don't want your protection?" she asked, attempting to keep the fear out of her voice.

He laughed as if her words were meant as a joke. "Then I will be forced to kill you." His words were said plainly without a hint of remorse. "But I will let my men have you first." He smirked. "Then I will take joy in killing your family, one by one."

"Why would you do such a thing?" She had to keep reminding herself that trained agents were nearby, and she was not in any real danger, even though her heart was racing.

Lord Melville brought his hand back up and traced her bottom lip. "From the moment I saw you, I knew I had to have you." His finger stopped, and he pulled her lip forward. "Then I discovered you were a wealthy heiress, and I vowed to make you mine."

Rachel leaned back, freeing her lip from his grasp. "But I don't want to marry you."

He chuckled cruelly. "It doesn't matter what you want."

Rachel frowned. "It sounds as if you are more interested in my money than marriage to me."

Lewdly, Lord Melville's gaze dropped to her square neckline, making her regret not wearing a shawl. "You mistake me, my pet. Your money will keep me in the lifestyle that I have become accustomed to, but I will equally delight in sharing a bed with you."

He leaned in for a kiss, but Rachel turned her head, causing him to kiss her cheek. Not deterred, he said, "I look forward to taming your willful streak."

While she attempted to yank back her hands, Lord Melville used the momentum to pull her towards his chest. Placing his hand on the back of her neck, he whispered into her ear, "If you do not behave, I will discard you just as easily as I killed your horse-trainer friend."

At his words, Rachel stopped struggling, and she glanced helplessly towards the door. She once again saw Luke's concerned eyes on her just before an arm snaked out and pulled him back behind the wall.

Lord Melville must have taken her silence for acceptance, because he removed his hand from her neck. "I will be back in two days' time, and we will be wed. After that, I will be gone on an errand for a fortnight."

Feeling emboldened after seeing Luke, she inquired, "Where is your errand?"

Without warning, he grabbed her cheeks with his hand and squeezed them as his eyes grew colder. "Life will be easier for you if you don't bother me with your useless chatter."

"Lord Melville," her aunt admonished from the doorway. "I believe it is time for you to go."

Dropping his hand, Lord Melville leaned back and rose in one motion. Before he turned to leave, he snarled, "There is no one to protect you now."

Shrinking back, Rachel saw Lord Melville smile in approval

as he left the drawing room. As soon as the main door was closed, Luke rushed into the room and sat down next to her. With compassion in his eyes, he asked, "Are you all right?"

Rachel shuddered and did not struggle when Luke put his arms around her, pulling her close. "Did you hear that?" she said into his chest.

"We did," Jonathon confirmed as he walked into the room. "Thank you for doing that."

Rachel started to move out of Luke's embrace, but he wasn't ready to let her go. Instead of fighting it, she relaxed back into the comfortable feeling of being in his arms. "He threatened to kill me and my family if I didn't marry him," she stated softly.

"I know," Luke murmured, kissing the top of her head. "We won't let that happen."

Benedict came into the room, announcing, "Your family will be joining us at Luke's estate until we sort this all out."

Knowing she was breaking all the rules of propriety, Rachel didn't care as she sat with Luke's arms around her. She never wanted to let him go.

❧ 25 ❧

CROUCHING DOWN NEXT TO RACHEL ON THE SETTEE IN HER bedchamber, Emmett had just finished rebandaging her arm when he said, "I believe the risk of infection has passed, but try not to do anything foolish." He smiled knowingly at his cousin.

Swatting her hand at him, Rachel laughed. "I think my time in Scotland has cured me of my impulsive behavior."

"Why is that?" Emmett asked curiously as he placed his instruments into his doctoring bag.

Smoothing out the net overlay on her floral high-waisted dress, Rachel admitted, "Because of me, Luke was almost killed, I was attacked, and David died protecting me." She paused, then remembered something else. "Oh, and I shot a man in an alleyway."

Emmett put his bag onto a chair and sat down next to her. "None of those things were your fault. You did not cause any of those things to happen."

Fingering the net, Rachel diverted her gaze from her cousin. "I don't feel that way."

"Ah, you feel guilt," Emmett responded, wiping his face with his hands. "I know that feeling well." He waited till she looked at him before he continued. "The captain on my ship impressed a young lad from an American privateer ship into service. As it turns out, the young lad was a young woman named Eleanora. She was in disguise, but we were unable to hide it for long. The young woman spurned the captain's advances, and he bashed her head in, leaving her to die on his cabin floor."

Rachel's hand flew to her mouth. "Oh, cousin. That is horrible."

"Every day, I see her dead face, with her eyes wide open, knowing that I failed her," Emmett sighed.

Scooting closer to her cousin, Rachel put her hand on his arm to comfort him. "It was not your fault."

"It was," he argued. "I tried to hide her, to help her, but my captain was no fool."

"It sounds to me like you did the honorable thing and tried to save her," Rachel asserted.

He rose quickly, reaching for his doctoring bag. His tone was resigned. "Either way, I failed Eleanora."

Standing up as well, Rachel placed her hand on his sleeve as he looked at her forlornly. "I see it differently. Without you, she would have been alone on that ship, but you were her friend and tried to help her."

Emmett's eyes grew reflective. "Ever since you were little, you have viewed life as an adventure, and you always look on the bright side of things. Don't let the past few days change you. Don't let these events define you."

Dropping her arm, Rachel gave him a sad smile as she quoted him from the village, "I am not a girl anymore, and it is time I grow up."

"I was wrong," he replied, wincing apologetically. "Just as you are wrong about feeling guilt. David's death was not your fault."

Rachel wrapped her arms around her waist. "If only…"

"Stop," her cousin's voice rose. "Don't go down that path, because it will not bode well for you."

A knock on the door interrupted them, and they turned towards the noise. Luke walked into the room, appearing concerned as he said, "I heard yelling."

Emmett nodded his head in approval. "I was telling Rachel about Eleanora."

Rachel frowned. "Emmett told *you* about Eleanora. When?"

With a boyish grin, Luke tugged at the sleeves of his black dinner dress coat. "It was right after he tried to shoot me."

Emmett chuckled. "This is true."

Perusing her evening dress, Luke's eyes shone with approval, making her feel beautiful. He stepped closer and offered his arm. "May I escort you to the drawing room?"

"You may," Rachel replied coyly, placing her hand on his arm.

As they walked towards the drawing room, Rachel found herself sneaking glances at Luke. For the first time, she couldn't think of anything to say. She decided to approach a safe topic. "The weather has been nice."

Luke threw his head back and laughed. Stopping, he turned his amused gaze towards her. "You did not just speak to me about the weather."

"There is nothing wrong with talking about the weather." She hesitantly lowered her gaze. "It is a safe topic."

Placing a gentle finger under her chin, Luke compelled her to meet his gaze. "I don't want to talk about safe topics with you. I want to know everything about you; your opinions, good and bad."

Her eyes twinkled with merriment. "I thought my opinions made you angry."

Luke chuckled under his breath. "Have no doubt, they do." He smiled. "But they also give me a glimpse into your soul."

"Do they now?" Rachel bantered playfully.

Placing his hands on her hips, Luke's eyes kept flickering to her lips. "I find you to be a beautiful woman, one that I would gladly go to war over." His voice became hoarse. "However, it is not just your beauty that distracts me, but your playful mind."

Not sure of his meaning, Rachel repeated, "Playful mind?"

He stepped closer, so no distance was between them. "Your mind is what makes you so incredibly unique, and your adventurous view on life fascinates me." His smoldering gaze pierced deep into her soul. "*You* fascinate me."

Lowering his head slowly, her breath hitched in anticipation of Luke's kiss. When his lips brushed against hers, a loud clearing of a throat could be heard in the hall, causing them both to jump back in alarm.

Bringing her fingers to her mouth, Rachel looked over and saw Jonathon leaning against the wall. He appeared entirely too pleased with himself. After smiling at them for a few moments, he finally said, "I came to find Luke because I thought he might like to meet his new brother-in-law."

Pushing off the wall, Jonathon headed down the stairs while Luke mumbled, "Sometimes I really hate my brother."

Together, they made their way towards the drawing room, and Rachel heard laughter coming from within. At the door, Luke stood aside and waited for her to enter before he followed.

As Rachel entered, she saw a handsome, brown-haired man with broad shoulders, sitting down next to Eliza. They seemed to be chatting about something highly amusing based on the laughter they shared. When the man spotted her, he stood and bowed.

Turning towards them, Eliza provided the introductions. "Lord Camden, I would like to introduce you to my good friend, Lady Rachel, and my brother, Lord Downshire."

Bowing, Lord Camden smiled at her. "Call me Adrien."

Before she could respond, Luke put his hand on the small of

her back and growled, "So you are the blackguard who married my sister after the death of her first husband."

Rachel was afraid of Adrien's reaction, but she was surprised to see him smile in response. "You are exactly how Kate described you."

Feeling Luke's hand tense on her back, Rachel stepped forward and smiled. "It is a pleasure to meet you, Adrien. Eliza told me that you just came from your wedding and how happy you have made Kate."

Adrien's eyes softened at the mention of his wife, just as she thought they would. "I am a lucky man," he stated.

Walking towards an available settee, Rachel sat down and was pleased when Luke sat next to her. Jonathon and Mr. Larson sat in chairs next to Eliza and Adrien. Benedict strolled into the room, wearing dark dress clothes. "Sorry I am late," he said. "I had to search through Luke's clothes before I found something that was somewhat adequate."

With a raised brow, Adrien glanced around the room. "Now, can someone please explain to me what is so urgent that I was summoned away from my wedding tour to help?"

Grabbing a chair and positioning it near Eliza, Benedict spoke first. "A French ship is somewhere off this coast, and a group of French soldiers are staying at an estate about twenty minutes north of here."

Looking confused, Adrien replied, "And you couldn't have taken care of this yourself?"

Rachel smiled but hid it behind her gloved hand. Jonathon leaned forward and stated, "We think we discovered the identity of the French spy, *Rogue*. A Lord Melville showed up about seven months ago, and suddenly his estranged aunt is in a coma."

"Again, there are four agents in this room," Adrien responded, expectantly. "And I was on my *wedding tour*."

"The French are trying to build a militia to fight alongside their army when they land. The constables keep turning up dead in Rockcliffe, and I suspect that constables in other villages are being murdered as well," Eliza added.

Benedict leaned forward in his seat, his lips tight. "We also found maps with the locations of the navy's shipyards circled. Most alarming was Portsmouth and Chatham." He pulled out a few pieces of paper from his jacket, extending them to Adrien. "Eliza recreated the maps and shipyards that were circled."

"Portsmouth has the world's oldest dry dock and has been a significant naval port for centuries. Surely, the port is well guarded," Luke said.

"It is, but the dastardly French are planning to use England's civil unrest against us. I was afraid of this based on the ill timing of the bill." Adrien groaned as he looked at the papers. "They are raising up a militia to fight alongside their well-trained soldiers and are planning on taking possession of our shipyards." He frowned. "And this time, it could work."

Everyone was nodding except for Luke and Rachel, so she asked, "This time?"

Jonathon shared, "Back in 1805, Prince Frederick, our commander-in-chief of the Forces, knew that an invasion by Napoleon was imminent. In response, Britain relied on the patriotism of the people to volunteer in guerrilla-type warfare against the French troops."

Mr. Larson huffed, "But this time, patriotism is at an all-time low, and many will side with the French rather than fight for king and country."

Eliza nodded at Mr. Larson. "Luckily, last time the Royal Navy defended our channel, making it impenetrable and forcing Napoleon to abandon his plans." Eliza placed her hands on her lap. "However, if France can build up a large enough army with British deserters, then they can sweep through the English countryside, leaving death and destruction in their wake."

Benedict rose and poured himself a drink. "In response,

England would have to withdraw troops from Europe, weakening our allies, and ensuring a victory for Napoleon."

"Surely there are enough men loyal to the King to fight them back, aren't there?" Luke voiced in disbelief.

Shaking his head, Adrien said, "I believe the urban areas will put up a fight, but the countryside will be left defenseless. The Whigs are rallying support to end the war because of the financial and emotional toll it is taking on the impoverished. The men are leaving their families alone and penniless to fight in a war they don't believe in. I hardly believe the men in the rookery will stand and defend our country."

Now understanding the severity of the situation, Rachel observed, "Which is why the bill to end the war was being pushed through Parliament. Not only did it rally more support to end the war, but if the bill had passed, then the chaos of withdrawing troops in Europe would have further delayed their arrival on English soil, thus giving the French more time to turn the people against the monarchy."

Walking over with a glass of water, Benedict handed it to Eliza, saying, "Invading England has always been France's main objective. They want to gain access to our trade routes, and they are doing it at a time when support for the war is at an all-time low."

"This explains why the bill did not mention the Royal Navy," Adrien confirmed. "The French wanted as many ships and their crews out of the shipyards as possible. If they succeed in disabling or destroying the British shipyards, it will cripple our naval production for decades." He winced. "Furthermore, if the French take over the shipyards, it will force our English ships to seek out distant harbors. Our navy would become weak and vulnerable."

Eliza took a sip of water and lowered the glass to her lap. "Ideally, we need to stop the growing militia, and prevent the French from landing." She smiled apologetically at Adrien. "We need all the help we can get until the Royal Army and the Army Reserves arrive."

"When will that be?" Adrien asked.

"I would imagine a few days from now," Mr. Larson commented. "However, if the French are successful in building up militias in other villages, then our limited army will be outnumbered. They would be able to march to London uncontested. Hopefully, the troops in London would be able to stop the invasion."

"Why did the military leave England with such a small number of troops to defend our isle?" Rachel inquired.

Jonathon ran his hand through his hair. "The majority of the military is fighting with our allies in Europe and along the peninsula. There are also ground troops and warships fighting the skirmish in America."

"What is the plan?" Adrien questioned.

Eliza placed her glass on the table. "First, we need to attend the meeting at the pub and hope we can discover more information about this French conspiracy. With luck, we will know when the French are landing and the ruse they are using to enlist men for their militia."

Rachel watched Emmett and her Uncle Edwin burst into the room, wearing matching blank expressions. Her uncle frowned, deeply. "I sent out two of my fastest whaling ships this morning, and they already discovered the location of two French frigates."

"Two French ships?" Luke repeated, surprised. "How did they locate them so quickly?"

Her uncle's jaw tightened. "It wasn't difficult, since they both are docked in a cove at Hestan Island."

"Where is Hestan Island?" Benedict inquired.

"Hestan Island is two miles out to sea but can be reached on foot during low tide," Emmett explained. "Smugglers have been using that island as a refuge for decades. The coves are deep and keep ships hidden from prying eyes."

Eliza frowned. "You don't think the French plan to walk their troops to shore?"

"That is what I would do," Rachel's uncle stated. "Anyone who marched from Hestan Island to our shore would only be visible to people near the causeway or from Mrs. Felix's estate. Whereas a French frigate coming into our harbor would attract considerable attention, especially since they would have to unload their troops in small boats."

"All right," Eliza said with a tight smile. "We have five agents, a doctor, a horse trainer, and whalers at our disposal. Let's figure out a way to keep the French from invading England."

❧ 26 ❧

As they walked towards The Fat Whaler, Luke kept his nose covered with his white sleeve. He took a moment to breathe in the familiar scent of lavender soap that lingered on his shirt. He knew the moment he removed his arm the pungent smell of Jonathon's clothes would assault him. Lowering his sleeve, he asked, "Why do your clothes reek of..." His voice trailed off because he couldn't pinpoint the specific revolting odor.

Jonathon laughed, utterly unaffected by Luke's complaint. "This is what the rookery smells like."

"I disagree," Benedict argued. "While the smell of waste, unwashed bodies, and rotting animal corpses are incredibly strong on the east side, I highly suspect that your valet dips your clothes in urine to maintain that horrible stench."

"Kate smells like vanilla," Adrien murmured softly, with a dreamy look on his face.

Benedict chuckled. "And that is how to focus on what is important."

As the four men neared the pub, Luke hoped that Rachel was safe. Eliza and Mr. Larson stayed behind to guard her, but he still had an uneasy feeling about leaving her. Remembering the last time Rachel came with them, Luke knew she would be safest tucked away at his estate, especially since *Shadow* was protecting her.

Chuckling under his breath, he still found it nearly impossible to comprehend that his younger sister could be *Shadow*. With her perfect memory, Eliza had always had a gift for languages and would often tutor him when he saw her on holidays. He recalled a letter where she'd told him about trying to make perfume and how Uncle Charles's estate had to be evacuated. He sighed. At some point, his sister had grown up and turned into a remarkable woman.

A massive guard stood at the door of the pub with a large, curved fishing knife shoved into his belt. His eyes tracked them as he opened the door and stood aside. The hall was filled with men drinking and laughing loudly with one another. A young barmaid, with a provocatively rounded neckline, sashayed up to Adrien, fluttering her eyes at him. When Adrien didn't respond, a small pout formed on her lips as she asked, "Can I get you a drink?"

"No. Leave us," Adrien replied as he extended her some coins.

Making their way towards the back of the square room, their boots kicked up the straw strewn along the floor. Taking a seat at a long rectangular table, Luke listened to the jovial mood of the room. He felt sick knowing these men were about to commit treason.

A hush fell over the room as Thorne hopped onto a table in the front, dressed as an English gentleman. "Tomorrow is the day that you will have your revenge against a blood-thirsty monarch; tomorrow is the day you will march towards your freedom."

Cheers filled the room, and he waited for them to die down before continuing. "Your king abandoned you long ago, and his pompous son has drained England's coffers for his own enjoyment. Your landlords and employers have cast you aside as worthless, believing textile workers are expendable. Now it is your turn to take back what is rightfully yours."

The boisterous group of men began banging their glasses on the tables as the room erupted in cheers. Thorne called for silence and announced, "We have the man who helped orchestrate this alliance between Napoleon and the people of Britain. I would like to introduce Mr. Phillipe Durant."

Luke heard his brother and brother-in-law mutter expletives under their breaths. Turning his head, he saw that all three of them had the collars of their coats pulled up, trying to conceal their faces. That was most unusual.

Turning back towards the front of the room, Luke saw Phillipe smiling as he stood next to Thorne on top of the table. In a thick French accent, he said, "I received a letter from Napoleon just the other day, and he praises you for your bravery and insight. You will all be justly rewarded when England is under Napoleon's rule. You will be free from the injustices that King George has placed upon you! You will be free from a monarchy that doesn't care if you have food in your children's bellies. Your taxes will not go to a prince regent who spends it on his mistresses and other frivolous things. You will be your own kings!"

The cheering increased to a roar around the room, going on for some time before Phillipe put his hand up. The din died down, and he informed them, "We have organized militia groups in surrounding villages, and they are preparing to join us as we march to victory. Even now, riders are rushing towards London to rally support for our cause."

Smiling widely, Phillipe reached into his pocket, pulled out a handful of gold coins, and showed them to the crowd. "You will all be paid ten shillings tonight and will each receive twenty gold pieces once we conquer London. Most importantly, you will be allowed to keep anything you find in the palaces of King George."

Luke watched as the men's eyes lit up at the sight of the gold coins and the promise of great wealth. To these men, Phillipe offered a life-changing fortune, but at what cost? To betray their country? He scoffed. Suddenly, he thought about what Rachel had taught him. Maybe greed didn't motivate these men. Perhaps their motivation was need.

Taking a closer look at the men in the room, he saw most of their clothes were tattered and faded. Their faces were thin and dirty. These men appeared more desperate than blood-thirsty.

Phillipe's voice interrupted his thoughts. "… and you will be allowed to keep your muskets."

The clamor died down again, and Phillipe exclaimed, "If you want to engage in a fight to change your own destiny, then come up and enlist. You will be given your shillings and the location of the rendezvous point. If you do not, then you are free to go." His words became clipped as he added, "But if you dare speak of what was said tonight, then you and your families will be killed."

As Phillipe stepped off the table, the men jumped up in anticipation and began pushing their way towards the front. Leaning forward, but keeping his face shielded, Adrien spoke to Luke in a hushed voice, "You need to go enlist and find out where the rendezvous location is."

"Why me?" Luke asked.

Adrien winced as he admitted, "Phillipe is my father-in-law."

"Ah," Luke nodded as he rose. "He is Kate's father, the French spy."

The three men bobbed their heads in confirmation, and Luke shoved his way towards the front. Thorne sat at a table recording the recruit's names and handing out coins. When it was his turn, Luke identified himself as John. Waiting for the man to reveal the rendezvous location, Phillipe approached him, asking, "Are you ready to take back what is yours?"

Dropping eye contact, he mumbled, "Yes, I am."

Phillipe's eyes wandered over his face and clothes. "You seem familiar. Have we met before?"

Luke shook his head. "No, sir."

Trying to appear unconcerned by Phillipe's scrutiny, or the pistol tucked into his breeches, Luke kept his posture relaxed but his eyes downcast. After a moment, Phillipe took a step back. "My apologies, you just reminded me of someone I used to know."

"Perhaps you bought a horse from my master?" Luke asked submissively.

"No, that is not it," Phillipe said sharply. "Meet tomorrow at the causeway during low-tide." He took another long, puzzled look before turning towards another recruit.

Making his way towards the back, Luke realized his relations were nowhere to be found. He walked out the door, surprised that the guard hadn't stopped him, and cast his eyes up and down the street. A moment later, he saw Benedict walking out of the alley a few yards ahead of him with Adrien and Jonathon following close behind. He lengthened his stride to catch up to them, but he glanced into the alley as he passed and saw the guard lying on the ground, unmoving.

When he caught up to the group, Luke inquired, "What happened with the guard?"

"Nothing," Benedict said, keeping his head straight. "He just wanted to know why we didn't enlist."

"Did you kill him?" Luke pressed.

Benedict replied cryptically, "No, we just talked to him."

"I see," Luke mumbled as he reminded himself, again, that he did not want to make Benedict angry.

LOUNGING ON THE SETTEE IN LUKE'S LIBRARY, RACHEL realized she'd been reading the same sentence over and over. Finally, she placed the book down on the table and tucked her feet under her dress. The hour was late, but she had hoped to see Luke one more time before she retired for the night.

Rachel had to admit that she loved staying at Luke's estate, and not just because of his extensive library. His entire staff had been accommodating, and the cook frequently sent up delicious confections for her to enjoy.

The clock struck eleven, and Rachel knew it was futile to stay up any later. As she stood to snuff out the light, the sound of breaking glass echoed throughout the two-story library as a large rock rolled near her foot. Before she could react, a gloved hand reached through the broken pane and unlatched the lock. Pulling the window out, Lord Melville stepped into the room with a pistol aimed at her chest. The sight of him sent a chill of cold recognition coursing through her body, and she felt fear closing in on her.

Smirking, he said, "Don't look so surprised. You didn't think I wouldn't have you followed?" He stepped closer to her. "I told you that you would be mine, and I meant it."

Glancing towards the door, Rachel thought about running for help when the sound of a pistol being cocked caused her to return her gaze to Lord Melville.

He stepped closer to her and lowered the pistol. "If you behave, then no one will have to die tonight." Lord Melville brought his hand up to touch her cheek. "I am impressed that you were able to become friends with Lord Downshire so quickly. It is widely rumored that he is a recluse."

The library door swung open, and Luke stormed into the room with Benedict and Jonathon. Lord Melville grabbed Rachel's arm, yanking her against him. As he kept the pistol aimed at her, Lord Melville shouted at Luke, "You were supposed to be dead!"

"Your thugs failed," Luke stated, clenching his jaw. "As will you."

Lord Melville laughed disdainfully. "As if you, a mere horse trainer, could stop me."

Benedict cleared his throat and shook his head. When Lord Melville glared at him, he explained, "He is not just a horse trainer…"

"Right. He is technically the *lead* horse trainer," Jonathon interrupted.

"True," Benedict conceded. "But, this *lead* horse trainer is also the Marquess of Downshire."

Turning his pistol towards Luke, Lord Melville hissed, "No, that cannot be."

"It is true," Luke admitted, keeping his eyes trained on Rachel.

Rachel felt Lord Melville bob his head up and down. "That does make sense. Why else would a lady sniff around a horse trainer?"

Tensing, she was outraged that Lord Melville said such a horrible thing. However, her anger melted into fear when the cold metal of the pistol returned and tapped against her head.

Slowly, Lord Melville began backing towards the opened window, forcing her to go with him. "I am going to take my betrothed, and no one had better try to stop us," he ordered.

"Wait," Luke urged, stepping forward. "Take me instead."

Lord Melville scoffed. "And why would I do that?"

With pleading eyes, Luke said, "If you won't take me, then release Rachel, and I will sign over everything I have to you, including Downshire Farms."

The pressure of the pistol eased slightly as Lord Melville asked in disbelief, "You would trade your entire fortune for a woman?"

"For Rachel, I would," Luke responded, his eyes conveying the truthfulness of his words.

Tears welled in her eyes as she gazed at Luke, her eyes pleading for him to understand how much he meant to her. Luke stood erect, his body rigid and immovable, but his eyes raged with emotion.

Lord Melville dismissed Luke's words and continued dragging her to the window. "Rachel is mine. I knew it from the moment I saw her."

Jonathon spoke up, drawing Lord Melville's ire, "You can't just claim a woman because you saw her. Typically, women like to be wooed."

Benedict nodded. "It is true. Jonathon tried this same tactic to claim his wife, and it was a disaster."

With a raised brow, Jonathon asked, "Have you considered finding a willing wife rather than abducting one?"

"Once Rachel and I are married, then I will have her fortune," Lord Melville declared. He leaned forward and kissed her cheek. "And I will ensure my wife is satisfied."

She felt like gagging as his warm breath hovered against her cheek. Jerking away from him, she stomped her slippered foot on his Hessian boots, but he didn't even seem to register her vague attempt to free herself.

"Do you not have Mrs. Felix's fortune?" she asked him, defiantly. "Why force me into marriage?"

Rachel could hear him sneer behind her. "As I said before, I have developed a taste for extravagance, and I refuse to return to the need to earn my income."

"Did you work as a leech collector?" Benedict asked intently. "Or a gong farmer?"

Jonathon nodded at Benedict. "I could see him working as a gong farmer. He does strike me as someone who would remove human excrement from privies."

"Shut up!" Lord Melville demanded, waving the pistol at them.

As he started to step out of the window, Eliza glided into the room wearing a maroon, high-waisted gown with a provocative neckline and a small, feathered reticule hanging around her wrist. Her auburn hair had been let down, and it flowed down her back. She gasped when she saw Lord Melville pointing a pistol at Rachel's head.

Confused, Rachel frowned at her friend's behavior. Her frown deepened when Eliza smiled coyly at Lord Melville before walking over to Benedict. It appeared that Eliza was boldly flirting with him. But that was preposterous! Wasn't it?

"Who do we have here?" Lord Melville asked in a seductive tone.

Possessively placing his arm around Eliza's waist, Benedict pulled her tight against him. "She is my wife."

"Come to me," Lord Melville ordered Eliza. When Eliza didn't move, he pressed the pistol against Rachel's temple. "I will kill her if you don't do as I say."

Tentatively, Eliza walked over to Lord Melville, and his eyes lewdly roamed her body. Tilting his head at the window, he demanded, "Go through the window and wait for me on the other side."

"No, she is my wife!" Benedict exclaimed. "Do you have no honor?"

Rachel felt Lord Melville shrug behind her. "Apparently not."

With a final glance at Rachel, Eliza stepped through the window and waited as Lord Melville dragged Rachel through. Once they were outside, he dropped his painful grip from her arm and shoved her towards the awaiting carriage. "Get inside, now!"

Stepping into the carriage first, Eliza slid over so Rachel could sit next to her. When Lord Melville sat across from them, he tucked the pistol into his trousers as the carriage sped away. "You are a pretty thing," he said, staring lustfully at Eliza.

Rachel swore she saw Eliza blush at Lord Melville's

comment. Not understanding what her friend was doing, she was shocked when Eliza traced her finger along her neckline, causing Lord Melville's eyes to be drawn to her chest. Leaning forward, Eliza slowly started lifting the right side of her skirt up until it hit her knee. With an alluring glance at Lord Melville, she raised it higher until it reached mid-thigh.

Lord Melville was so entranced by the sight of Eliza's leg that he failed to recognize the threat. In a blink of an eye, Eliza pulled her dagger out of its sheath and plunged it deep into his thigh. Leaning forward as he screamed, she retrieved his pistol from his trousers and handed it to Rachel. Reaching into her reticule, she pulled out a small overcoat pistol, opened the window, and discharged her weapon.

The carriage came to a clamoring stop as Eliza yanked out her dagger from Lord Melville's leg. Howling in pain, his hand covered the wound as blood stained his trousers. The door was wrenched open, and Adrien stood there with a pistol pointed at Lord Melville. Stepping aside, he used his other hand to assist Rachel and Eliza out of the carriage.

Ducking his head, Adrien stepped into the carriage and hit Lord Melville in the back of his head with his pistol, rendering him unconscious.

"How did you catch up to us so fast?" Rachel asked, confused.

"I didn't have to catch up," he explained. "I convinced the driver to let me take his place." He waved his pistol, waggled an eyebrow, and grinned. He quickly jumped out and climbed up to the driver's bench, retrieving a green shawl.

Handing it to Eliza, Adrien explained with a smile, "Benedict insisted that you put this on the moment we subdued Lord Melville."

"How kind of him," Eliza replied as she immediately draped it around her shoulders, covering her chest.

The sound of pounding hooves alerted them to approaching

riders. Rachel turned to look and saw three men, but her eyes focused only on Luke.

Reining in his horse, Luke dismounted and cautiously approached her. His eyes roamed over her as if searching for injuries. "Are you all right?" he asked.

"I am now," Rachel confirmed, just before she stepped into his embrace and wrapped her arms around his waist. This was madness. When did she start turning to Luke for comfort, knowing only he could offer her the peace she so desired? This had to stop. Never had she depended on another the way she now relied on Luke. But at this moment, she was tired and weak. Tomorrow, she would be strong.

27

Sitting on the settee opposite Rachel, Luke kept his eyes focused on the low-burning fire in the hearth. Neither spoke as Lord Melville's screams echoed throughout his estate.

Ironically, Lord Melville's gut-wrenching howls mirrored what he was feeling inside. When Rachel was abducted, the feeling of panic had overwhelmed him, and he'd been prepared to kill Lord Melville, if necessary, to get her back.

He turned his gaze towards Rachel. Her feet were tucked under her dress, and she was reading a book by the fire's light.

No matter how hard he tried to convince himself that he deserved her, Luke knew in his heart that he did not. She was everything he was not; she was kind, loving, and compassionate, whereas he was cynical, had a short temper, and was selfish. He ran a stud farm in Scotland, of all places. He knew when he inherited the title of duke, he would have to return to England, but until then, he was content to remain here.

He craved his solitude, his isolation. Rachel would tire of him and grow to resent him. She craved adventure, and he could not offer her that. Furthermore, what kind of life could he give her? Not one that she deserved.

Rachel placed her book on a side table and broke the silence. "Thank you for offering to take my place."

"You would have done the same."

"Regardless," Rachel paused, her blue eyes unguarded, "it was very brave of you."

Knowing he must tell her of his feelings, Luke stood and moved to sit next to Rachel. Her eyes glistened with pleasure as he sat down. He thought for just a moment about forgetting his conscience and following his heart. However, he could not do that to her. She deserved every goodness, and his cynical thinking would eventually corrupt her.

Staring deep into her eyes, he said, "Rachel, I have grown to care for you…" His words drifted off as he tried to collect his thoughts.

Her eyes lit up with anticipation. "And I care for you as well."

Reaching for her hands, Luke stared at their joined hands and sighed. "Being around you has made me immensely happy. These have undoubtedly been the best days of my life."

Rachel smiled up at him, joy radiating in her features.

Trying to ignore her smile, Luke continued, "But we can't go on as we are. We would never suit."

"I don't understand," she murmured, her smile dimming, her brow furrowing.

Rubbing his thumb over her hands, Luke tried to explain. "You burst into my life and helped me to see past myself and my burdens. You are exceptional in every way, and it is time I accept that." He frowned. "I don't deserve you, and we both know it."

Slipping her hands out of his, Rachel's voice reflected pain. "I don't feel that way. I find you more than tolerable." She gave him a shaky smile.

"I can't give you the life you deserve," Luke admitted reluctantly. "I am a reclusive lord who owns a stud farm in the small, sleepy town of Rockcliffe. I don't mingle with the ton, nor do I call on my neighbors and have tea. I like my solitude, and you…" His voice grew emotional as he expressed, "Your soul craves adventure and excitement. If we married, you would eventually grow to despise me."

Rachel shook her head adamantly. "I could never despise you."

"We were thrust upon each other during unusual circumstances," Luke stated. "You are only in Scotland because your father sent you here to be safe. Soon, you will go back home to your friends where you belong."

Hurt flashed in her eyes as she ventured, hesitantly, "We are friends, aren't we?"

"Yes, for now," Luke confirmed, "but over time you will forget about me."

A tear dropped from her eye and rolled down her cheek. "I could never forget you."

Reaching over, he wiped the tear away and allowed his finger to linger on her soft skin. "You will with time. I do not intend to spend time in London until my father dies. And even then, it will only be during the Season."

"What if," she hesitated, "I visited my aunt for holidays?"

He lowered his hand. "I don't believe that is a wise idea." He knew his heart couldn't take seeing Rachel for short periods of time, knowing she could never be his. "It will only delay the inevitable."

"Which is?"

"My life is not conducive to having a wife," he painfully acknowledged.

"Don't you need an heir?"

He shook his head, glancing over her shoulder. "Jonathon will sire children."

"You have it all figured out, don't you, Lord Downshire," she huffed. He looked up to meet her gaze and saw that her eyes held censure. "You just plan to run your stud farm… alone."

"I don't expect you to understand, but I choose what I do with my life." He frowned. Why didn't she see that he was doing this for her?

She pursed her lips, silent for a moment, then said softly, "Well, I will always consider you a friend, Luke Beckett. You may think so little of me that you can cast me aside, but I care enough for you to let you know the truth."

Expecting her to rail at him, Luke was surprised when she gripped his hand and leaned closer. "You have built walls around your heart, convincing yourself that you are not good enough to love another or be loved in return. I believe you came to Scotland with the intention of discovering who you truly are, the man behind your title." She smiled, her eyes crinkling in the corners. "And you succeeded."

She reached her free hand up to cup his cheek, and her quiet, sincere words seem to penetrate his hardened heart. "You can do better, be better. Behind your gruff exterior, you have a tender, loving heart. I have seen it, so don't try to deny it," she asserted. "If you choose to send me away, I will go, but that is *your* choice. I will not force myself upon you, because like you, I believe you would grow to resent me."

Raising his hand up, he placed it over hers on his cheek. "I could never resent you, Rachel. I doubt I will ever care for another as much as I care for you."

Another tear fell from her eye as she kept her gaze on him. "And I never could resent you, but I think you are confused." She leaned forward and kissed him softly. Pulling back too soon, her lips hovered over his as she whispered, "I will always love you."

Stunned, Luke could only watch as Rachel lowered her hands, rose, and slowly walked out of the room. He stared at the door for what seemed like an eternity, willing her to return. Dropping his head into his hands, he breathed a heavy sigh.

He was startled to hear Eliza's voice. "Why aren't you running after her?"

"Leave it, Eliza," Luke growled. Looking up he saw her lift an eyebrow at him. He should have known that his growl wouldn't work on his sister, either.

Placing her hand on her hip, Eliza returned his glare with one that had just as much viciousness. "I would leave it alone, except you have just made the biggest mistake of your life."

Jumping up, Luke challenged, "How would you know?"

"I know because I have been where you are," Eliza admonished. "The feelings of inadequacy are not unique to you." She stepped closer to him, her voice softening. "I almost didn't trust my heart. I refused to love Benedict because I was scared."

"I am not scared!" he roared. "I did the honorable thing. I let Rachel go so she can have a better life."

Eliza scoffed. "A better life?" She shook her head. "You mean a better man."

Luke walked over to the fireplace mantle and gripped the edges. "That is precisely what I mean. I don't deserve her. Rachel deserves to love someone and be loved wholeheartedly in return. I can't be that man."

Eliza regarded him for a moment, then conceded dryly, "You are right. If you will not fight for Rachel's love, then you don't deserve her."

Spinning around to leave, Eliza stopped when Luke asked, "Are you finished torturing Melville?"

"We haven't started," she revealed, her hand resting on the door handle. "Emmett was just stitching up the wounds on his head and leg."

"Oh," Luke replied, turning back towards the fire.

"Luke," his sister said.

"Yes."

"You are a fool to pass on Rachel."

"I know," he said. "Trust me, I know."

THE NEXT MORNING, AS THEY RODE THEIR HORSES TOWARDS HER uncle's estate, Rachel listened as Eliza shared details about Lord Melville's interrogation. Apparently, he was in so much pain from having the back of his head and his leg stitched up that he begged for brandy to help ease his pain. Laughing, Eliza revealed, "He became so inebriated that he mistook me for his sister and informed me that he was impersonating Lord Melville." She put a finger loosely to her lips, imitating Lord Melville. "He kept shushing me as he told us how he killed Mrs. Felix to gain access to her estate and buried her near the stable."

Adrien piped in, "My favorite part was how he insisted he was in love with Lady Rachel."

Rachel laughed. "He did not."

Jonathon rode up beside them, saying, "It is all true. He spent a good hour describing all the reasons he adored you."

"He claimed he loved me?" she asked, astonished.

"He did," Eliza confirmed, smiling. "He loved how you smelled like rosewater, how your eyes twinkled in the sunlight and how your voice rivaled the songbirds in beauty."

"As much as he claimed to love you, he really was more interested in your fortune," Emmett shared.

Jonathon's eyes were alert as he kept his gaze straight ahead, sparing her only a glance. "He was in the *Grande Armée* when he was selected to impersonate Lord Melville. He went from poverty to high Society and did not want to go back to his old station."

Benedict offered a sympathetic smile. "He viewed you as the solution to his problems."

"Did he kill the real Lord Melville?" she inquired hesitantly.

Adrien shook his head. "No, the real Lord Melville is one of the owners of the East India Company and has been living overseas for the past few years."

"He did confirm he was *Rogue* and shared the general area where the muskets are hidden. Sadly, he passed out shortly after, and we were unable to continue asking him questions," Jonathon said disappointedly.

Adjusting the reins in his hand, Benedict chuckled. "It was the easiest interrogation I have ever witnessed, and we have Emmett to thank for that."

"Oh, what did Emmett do?" Rachel asked, turning to face her cousin.

Smiling slyly, Emmett informed her, "I may have stitched up Lord Melville with the largest needle that I had in my bag." He winked at her. "It is the needle I typically reserve for livestock."

Rachel saw the amusement in her cousin's eyes, and it pleased her immensely. Slowly, he was becoming the person that she recognized from her youth. She smiled at him. "Is that why Lord Melville was screaming so much?"

Waggling his brow at her, Emmett revealed, "I was not as gentle as I might have been, but I was very thorough."

Adrien laughed. "If you ever want to stop working as a doctor, you can work for the home office. There are a group of agents specifically assigned to extract information from traitors and spies. They could use your skills."

Amused, Emmett shook his head. "No, my uncle has requested my presence in London to begin learning about his estates and holdings."

Hoping that her cousin would join her in London, Rachel asked, "Are you going to go?"

"I think I will. It is time," Emmett stated, looking straight ahead.

They dismounted in front of her uncle's estate and walked

along the path that led down towards the estuary. It had been decided that it would be best to walk along the rocky coast towards the causeway, rather than approach Mrs. Felix's estate from the shoreline and be exposed to the French soldiers.

Walking next to her, Adrien said, "*Rogue* did confirm there is an outcropping of rocks near the footpath from the Felix property to the shoreline. Supposedly, there is a small cave that has almost a hundred muskets stored, along with ammunition."

Emmett frowned. "I don't mean to alarm everyone, but the waves have carved out a multitude of caves over the years. It might take time to find the right one."

Wearing tan trousers and a white shirt, Eliza had her longbow and quiver stuffed with arrows hanging on her right shoulder. She nodded in agreement. "We assumed as much, and low tide is only five hours away."

Adrien smirked and jested, "So, we have five hours to find a cave full of muskets, hide those muskets, stop the militia from joining the fight with the French, and push the French back toward Hestan Island. Sounds simple enough."

"We have been in worse situations," Jonathon joked.

Glancing around the group, Rachel realized that Luke was not keeping pace with them. Looking over her shoulder, she saw him trailing behind them with the same gruff look that she remembered from the first few times she'd spoken with him. It is not my problem, she thought to herself. He doesn't want you.

"I wonder if..." Rachel's voice trailed off as she tilted her head towards Emmett. "Do you remember that sea cave we used to explore in the u-shaped cove?"

Frowning, Emmett clarified, "You mean the one where we waded through waist-high water?"

"That was when we were children, and it's only that deep when it is high tide," Rachel reminded him.

Remembering the cave's layout from their childhood, she was relieved that she had taken Eliza's advice about wearing men's clothing today. She would most definitely be getting dirty. "I believe there was a raised platform along the back wall that could easily fit one hundred muskets, and they would stay dry."

Luke's disgruntled voice came from behind her. "That does not seem very safe."

Turning her head so she could smile smugly at him, Rachel countered, "I disagree. It is perfectly safe."

Mumbling something under his breath, Luke stormed past them and started down the pathway. With every step, Rachel remembered the circumstances that surrounded David's death. She suddenly felt very melancholy.

Jumping down the last few feet to land in the sand, Rachel ignored Luke's outstretched hand as he offered to assist her. Brushing past his hand, she knew she was acting childishly, but she was not in the mood to be nice to him. In a moment of weakness, she had confessed her love, but he still rejected her.

Quickening her steps, Rachel walked alongside Eliza and Benedict as they prepared to explore the caves near the causeway. Jonathon, Emmett, and Adrien trailed behind with Luke, and no one seemed to be in the mood to talk.

As they approached the causeway, the shoreline shifted from large, imposing cliffs to rolling hills and soft sand that stretched down into the calm water lapping lazily onto the shore. About fifty yards past the causeway, the shoreline again changed dramatically to large, sharp rocks dominating the beach, which slowed their forward progression.

The Felix's property was a little over a hundred yards from the causeway. A footpath led from the estate to the shore, its entrance originating from a U-shaped cove with high rock outcrops. They proceeded cautiously, keeping watch for any guards that might be posted on the shoreline.

Two imposing rock outcrops framed the path at the shoreline, then it opened into a broad, sandy cove, surrounded by large boulders which led to rolling hills, and eventually, the Felix's property. Rachel walked towards the cave that she suspected held the muskets, but a hand grabbed her arm from behind, followed by the words, "Would you like me to help you search the cave?"

Swiftly turning around, Rachel shook her head. "No, thank you."

Not releasing her arm, Luke leaned closer. "I know dark places frighten you. Let me help you," he urged in a hushed voice.

Defiantly, she stated, "I don't want your help."

"You are going to take my help whether you like it or not," Luke said annoyingly as he gestured for her to lead the way.

Huffing, Rachel marched towards the cave's entrance that sat deep in the rock outcroppings. To access the cave, she had to wade through foot-high water, but she barely registered the cold as she mumbled something about Luke's stubbornness. She was so preoccupied with her thoughts that she wasn't prepared for the overwhelming panic that gripped her heart and mind when she stepped fully into the cave.

Breathing in the moist, salty air, her feet couldn't seem to move on their own, and her breathing became fast and shallow. Panicking, her hand flew to her throat. She couldn't seem to catch her breath. Luke's calm voice whispered next to her ear, "Breathe, Rachel. Just breathe."

Opening her eyes, Rachel tried to concentrate on Luke's voice, but it wasn't working. Leaning back, his eyes betrayed his concern, but his lips curled into a playful smile. "Are you looking for an excuse to kiss me?"

"No," she said in between breaths.

Lifting his brow, Luke's smile widened. "Are you sure? Because if I recall, you tried this before and kissed me in another cave."

She took a deeper breath as she denied, "I did no such thing."

Leaning back, Luke patted her shoulder, looking relieved. "You are going to be fine. Just breathe."

Resting the back of her head against the cold stones, Rachel greedily breathed air into her lungs. After a moment, she muttered, "I can't do this."

"Don't worry, I can get the muskets…"

"No, I can't do this," Rachel insisted firmly, her voice echoing off the water and rocks.

Leaning forward, Luke frowned. "Are you referring to us? Because…"

"No," she asserted, rushing to clarify. "I am tired of acting brave when I am so scared."

Luke glanced outside the cave before saying, "If you are concerned about the French, I can put you in my fastest coach and send you wherever you want to go."

Wrapping her arms around her waist, Rachel shook her head. "Two months ago, I was abducted and thrown into a cargo hold of a brig to be sold to a brothel. Since then, I have been attacked twice, shot in the arm, killed a man, and now the French want to kill us. I can't close my eyes without seeing those dead bodies in the alley, and during the day, I am haunted by memories of David."

"What are you saying?" Luke asked with concern in his eyes.

"I want to go home," Rachel admitted regretfully.

Placing a hand on the back of her neck, Luke lowered his forehead until it rested against hers. "Once this is over, I will make sure you get home. I promise you that." The deliberate way he spoke those words reassured her that he was in earnest.

"Thank you," she breathed, her voice hitching with emotion. She was not strong, and it was time for her to stop pretending. She was just a hoyden. She wasn't brave, she was just rebellious.

Leaning back just enough to gaze into her eyes, Luke's eyes held warmth and compassion. "I don't care what you say, but to me, you are the bravest person I know." A small smile grew on his lips. "You were attacked and shot, yet you still rode to find help for your friend. I have never met someone as tenacious as you when it comes to helping others." His other hand sought out her hand, making her feel cherished and protected. "People cannot help but become better when they associate with you."

Peering deep into his eyes, Rachel found herself wondering what she was going to do without Luke to support her. Never had someone accepted her for who she truly was, and she longed to stay in his company. In his arms, she felt like she was home.

"Not to intrude," Benedict said from the outside of the cave, "but we are trying to stop a French invasion."

Dropping his hand, Luke stepped back but maintained eye contact with her. "You are stronger than you realize."

Together, Rachel and Luke fully entered the cave. They heard trickling water along the rock walls. Wading through water up to their knees, they noticed the color of the water grew lighter as they moved towards the back.

"How is this possible?" Luke asked in awe as he put his hand in the light blue water.

Admiring the beauty of the water, Rachel explained, "There is light passing through underwater openings, causing the water in the cave to become illuminated." Holes in the rocks above streamed additional sunlight into the cave.

The muskets were standing in rows along the rock walls, alongside small crates of ammunition. Grabbing three muskets, Rachel approached the front of the cave and handed them off to Benedict. While she went back for more, Luke walked by carrying a large armful. They continued removing the guns and ammunition until they were all out of the cave.

Walking back to shore, Rachel hurried in front of Luke, so she didn't have to walk beside him. It was hard enough being around him, but when he said wonderful things to her, it became overwhelmingly difficult to resist pleading with him to take a chance on her.

The muskets were relocated closer to the causeway, hidden behind a small outcropping of rocks, backed by a rocky hill with gorse bushes hanging over the sides. As she placed the muskets behind the boulders, she noticed that the location had a perfect line of sight to the causeway.

Benedict approached her, carrying two muskets. "Are you familiar with these .75 caliber flintlock muskets?"

"I am," Rachel acknowledged, admiring the muskets known as Brown Besses.

He handed her a musket. "Are you as accurate with a musket as you are with a pistol?"

"I am." Running her hand along the iron barrel, Rachel took a moment to get a feel for the weight of the gun. "My father kept Brown Besses around our country estate, and on occasion, I used them on fox hunts."

Turning towards the causeway, Benedict kept his gaze on the horizon, his eyes alert, but pained. "How would you feel about being a sharpshooter when the French get within a hundred yards of the beach?"

Lowering the musket, Rachel felt a sense of dread come over her as she thought about taking another person's life. "I don't know…" Her voice trailed off.

Benedict turned his gaze back towards her, and his eyes held compassion. "I know it is a lot to ask, but your country needs you. We need you."

A low whistle drew their attention, and they turned to see Emmett waving them closer. Rachel and Benedict ran as fast as they could over the rocky coast until they stopped in front of her cousin. He pointed towards the Felix estate. "French soldiers are training at the Mote of Mark hill," he informed them before he turned around and started running towards the hill.

"What is the Mote of Mark?" Benedict asked in a hushed voice as they trailed behind Emmett.

She kept her eyes on the rocky path as she explained, "It was a hill fort in the dark ages, and the summit of the knoll is still partially enclosed by a massive stone and timber barrier."

They followed Emmett until they saw Eliza, Luke, Jonathon, and Adrien huddled behind birch trees and juniper shrubs. Their eyes were trained on the French-uniformed soldiers, who held their weapons out front and marched in double file. An order was shouted, and the soldiers moved into a defensive position, with their muskets aimed right at them.

28

DUCKING LOW BEHIND THE SCRUB BRUSH, LUKE'S HEART BEGAN to race. Did the soldiers see them? Another order was given, and the French soldiers returned to their line formation. He let out a breath of relief.

Crouching next to Jonathon, Adrien pulled his pistol from the back of his trousers. "I count fifteen soldiers, including the officer in front."

Luke turned towards them. "We can't attack them," he argued in a hushed voice.

Jonathon's eyes grew determined as they tracked the soldiers. "We have to," he asserted. "We need to eliminate as many enemy soldiers as possible before low tide."

Eliza reached for her longbow and held it in her right hand. "We will need to surround them if we want to have a chance of defeating them."

"The north side has masses of boulders from the ruins of the wall," Rachel informed them. "It is the easiest way to approach the hill undetected."

"Good," Eliza said as she kept low and moved towards the north side without waiting for Benedict.

With a huff of irritation, Benedict grabbed a musket and followed his wife.

Gripping a musket, Emmett stated, "I will head towards the west side of the knoll. I know of a tree where I can perch and stay hidden." He crouched low and disappeared through the shrubs.

Luke counted three muskets remaining. As Rachel reached down and picked one up, he attempted to snatch it out of her hands. She looked at him, determination in her eyes. "Trust me. I am a good shot." He lowered his hand and nodded.

Out of the corner of his eye, he saw Eliza and Benedict scaling clusters of large boulders as they hurried up the knoll.

In a hushed voice, Luke asked, "Does Eliza have a death wish?"

"She is getting into position," Jonathon revealed as he kept his eyes trained on his sister.

Turning his gaze towards Rachel and Adrien, Luke saw they were both in position to fire on the French soldiers. Jonathon pulled a pistol out of his right boot and shoved it at him. "Are you ready to play hero?"

"Do I have a choice?" he huffed.

Time seemed to slow as they watched the French soldiers perform the training exercises. An officer pulled off his hat and wiped his brow. Adrien groaned. "Phillipe is the officer in front."

Luke cast a confused glance at Adrien. "Your point being?"

He lowered his pistol and sat back. "I can't kill my father-in-law. Kate might not forgive me."

"I thought Phillipe threw Kate in front of a carriage?" Luke questioned in disbelief.

"He did," Adrien confirmed, glancing over at him, "but he is still Kate's father. It might upset her if she found out I was responsible for his death."

Nodding, Jonathon appeared to accept Adrien's flawed logic.

"With any luck, Phillipe will lay down his arms when we attack."

Adrien scoffed, "I doubt it."

Pulling a dagger from his left boot, Jonathon tucked it in the front of his trousers. "Make your shot count," he advised Luke. "Every soldier we kill outright, we don't have to engage in person." He winced. "Forget that. I want you to stay concealed in the shrubs with Rachel." He put his hand out for his pistol.

Frowning, Luke responded, "I will be fine."

With a clearly disbelieving look, Jonathon dropped his hand. "Fine, but don't die on me." He half-smiled. "I have no desire to be the next Duke of Remington. It is too much responsibility for me."

Luke smiled genuinely at his brother. "I don't plan to die."

"Good." Jonathon crouched down into position and aimed his pistol.

Standing above him, Adrien's eyes narrowed, and he pointed his pistol towards the soldiers now less than twenty yards away.

As Luke aimed his pistol, he whispered, "When do we fire?"

"When Eliza gives the signal," Jonathon replied, his eyes never leaving the soldiers.

The sound of Phillipe barking orders at the men in French was the only noise that could be heard in the wind. Without warning, a lone arrow hit a soldier in the chest, and he dropped out of formation. Shouting in confusion, the French soldiers pointed their muskets towards the north side of the knoll.

Taking advantage of the panic, Jonathon, Adrien, and Rachel fired their weapons, and three French soldiers dropped to the ground. Discharging his pistol last, Luke was pleased to see he hit the enemy, albeit in the leg. The sound of a lone musket roared from Benedict and Eliza's direction.

In a flash, Jonathon and Adrien charged out of the shrubs and began to engage the enemy, somehow avoiding the bullets fired in their direction. Rushing a soldier, Jonathon punched and then stabbed him before the soldier could recover. Pulling out the dagger, he moved on to the next French soldier, then another.

Keeping low, Luke followed behind and reached for a knife he found attached to a dead soldier's uniform. Peering through the acrid smoke, he saw a soldier pointing a musket at Adrien's back. Instinctively, he tackled the man. Kneeling over him, Luke punched the man in the face, knocking him unconscious.

Lifting his eyes, Luke was relieved to see Adrien, Jonathon, and Benedict were still alive, each battling an assailant.

When the last soldier dropped, Jonathon glanced over, looking relieved when he saw Luke.

Luke turned his head towards the shrubs where Rachel was hiding, and terror filled his entire body. Phillipe held Rachel in front of him, with a pistol in his right hand aimed at her head. "Rachel!" Luke shouted at the top of his lungs.

Keeping Rachel in front of him, Phillipe angled her body to ensure that Eliza did not have a good shot from her location. He snarled, "Put your weapons down, or I will kill the girl." Complying, Luke slowly lowered his knife and was thankful to see Adrien and Jonathon doing the same.

Straightening up, Adrien replied nonchalantly, "You won't make it out alive this time. If you surrender now, I will put in a good word for you with the executioner. I will even ensure you have pleasant lodgings in Newgate."

Phillipe's eyes grew hard. "If you follow me, I will kill her."

"You are a coward. You hide behind women," Jonathon shouted in disgust. "Just kill her and get it over with so we can kill you."

Whipping his head towards Jonathon, Luke growled under his breath, "What are you doing?" To his horror, he saw Adrien lean down and pull out a small pistol from his right boot.

Shoving Rachel forward, Phillipe ordered, "Put that pistol down!"

"No," Adrien shouted back. "I don't take orders from you."

Phillipe scoffed, "You will." His eyes scanned the horizon before they snapped back to Adrien. "Soon, England will fall, and Napoleon will ride victorious through the streets of London."

An arrow whizzed past Phillipe's head, narrowly missing him. Repositioning himself behind Rachel, he continued moving. With one hand around Rachel's waist, the other kept the pistol firmly against her head, he backed slowly towards the cover of the trees.

"I married your daughter over a week ago," Adrien informed Phillipe, who stopped moving and appeared to be listening. "It was a lavish affair. Even Prinny attended."

"How nice," Phillipe said dryly before he continued his backward trek.

Tucking the knife into his trousers, Jonathon appeared calm as he stated, "I am surprised you are taking the girl hostage when you could take *Hawk* instead."

Those words had the desired effect. Phillipe stopped in his tracks, and his eyes roamed the group of men hungrily. "Which one of you is *Hawk*?"

Stepping forward, Adrien bowed as if he was in a ballroom. "I am, dear Father."

"You?" Phillipe scoffed, scornfully. "I don't believe *you* are the spy responsible for so many French soldiers' deaths." He shook his head skeptically.

Adrien shrugged. "It is true. I worked as Admiral Garnier's under-secretary for years and stole valuable documents right from under his nose." He smiled smugly. "It was quite easy, actually."

Phillipe stepped backward again, pulling Rachel with him. "It doesn't matter. Soon you will be captured and killed for your treasonous acts."

With a dry laugh, Jonathon jested, "The same argument could be said about you."

Ignoring Jonathon's comment, Phillipe continued moving. This time, Luke stepped forward. "Take me instead."

Stopping, Phillipe looked at him quizzically, as if noticing him for the first time. "And why would I take you?"

Luke took another step closer. "I am the Marquess of Downshire and the eldest son of the Duke of Remington." He took another step. "I am worth far more than some silly girl." He paused before adding, "And I will come willingly."

"Luke?" Phillipe asked, his face softening as he looked at him. "Do you remember me?"

"I don't," Luke answered honestly.

A faint smile formed on Phillipe's lips. "I used to take you on walks around the abbey when you were young." Then the smile left his face. "But your father kicked me out when Diana got pregnant. She was forced to raise his bastard. Diana accepted that burden with grace and…"

Jonathon's bark of laughter silenced Phillipe's words. "Mother hated Eliza and cast her off at age ten. She did not accept anything with grace," he shared.

Turning the pistol towards Jonathon, Phillipe shouted, "Don't talk about Diana that way. She was a good mother."

"No, she wasn't," Eliza proclaimed, stepping out from the safety of the boulders. Immediately, she nocked an arrow, pulled it back, and aimed it at Phillipe. "Diana was cruel and vindictive. She was never a mother to me." Her words were filled with pain.

"Eliza?" Phillipe asked. He kept Rachel between them, but the pistol was now pointed towards Eliza. "You are *Shadow*?"

Without hesitation, Eliza answered, "I am." She took a step to the left, causing Phillipe to shift his body. "I was in the room when Diana was killed." She took another step. "I even tossed a dagger into her shoulder before my uncle sent in agents to slash her throat."

Phillipe waved the pistol as he declared, "How could you do that? She loved you!"

"No," Eliza denied vehemently. "Diana loved herself." She took another step, and each time, Phillipe positioned Rachel between them. Standing confident, her next words held a warning. "Put the pistol down, or you will die."

"I tire of your game…"

Just as Phillipe turned the pistol back to point at Rachel's head, Eliza released her arrow, hitting the center of his hand. Dropping his weapon, he roared with pain as he cradled his injured hand. As Rachel attempted to run, Phillipe reached out and grabbed her arm, refusing to let her go.

Rachel kicked him in the shins, but he maintained his hold on her arm. Suddenly, a musket was fired, hitting Phillipe in the back, throwing him forward.

Without hesitation, Rachel ran, leaping into Luke's open arms. Closing his arms tightly around her, he kissed the top of her head, relieved beyond words that she was alive.

Striding out of the trees, Emmett held the musket in his hand and walked over to Phillipe's body. He crouched down and took his pulse. With a satisfied nod, he confirmed, "He is dead."

"At least I wasn't the one who had to kill him," Adrien remarked as he reached down to pick up his knife.

Emmett arose and addressed Eliza. "Thank you for placing Phillipe in my line of sight." He smirked. "That man sure loved to talk."

Eliza tipped her head graciously. "My pleasure."

Trembling, Rachel tightened her hold around Luke's waist, and he kept murmuring that everything was all right. Benedict rushed over to Eliza and kissed her soundly on the lips, whispering something in her ear. She blushed.

"We have taken out two French spies in the past twenty-four hours, but in three more hours, we will have the French army and a militia to contend with," Jonathon recapped as his gaze wandered towards the estuary.

Placing his arm around Eliza's shoulders, Benedict asked the group, "Any ideas how we are going to stop a militia and an invading army?"

Tucking his knife into his left boot, Adrien said, "Well, we have three hours to come up with a plan." He grinned. "Normally, I have all the brilliant ideas, but I am fresh out."

Thinking about what he saw at the militia meeting, Luke declared, "I have an idea."

✺ 29 ✺

Two hours later, Luke marched determinedly onto the Maddix's property with more than thirty workers from Downshire Farms, plus thirty footmen, a combination of his and the Maddix's staff. Rachel walked beside him, still dressed in men's clothing. Moving steadily, they approached the path that would lead them down to the shoreline.

Stopping at the top of the cliff, Luke turned and placed his hands onto Rachel's shoulders. "I implore you to go back to your uncle's estate and wait for us."

Rachel pursed her lips, and a look of sheer determination came to her eyes. "I can't stay back and do nothing while you put yourself in harm's way."

Luke stifled a groan, because as much as he loved her hoydenish ways, he wanted to shake some sense into her. "You don't have to do this." Glancing at the others, he said, "No one would think less of you if you went back."

Shaking his hands off her shoulders, Rachel tilted her chin. "I would think less of myself."

As much as Luke admired Rachel for her grit, he wanted to

strangle her. Changing tactics, he growled, "Woman, go home and wait for us."

Ignoring the snickering from the group, Rachel took a step closer to him and looked up at him with resolve. "I am not your concern, Lord Downshire. Please refrain from being such a boor around me." Turning towards the group, she smiled. "Is everyone ready?"

Knowing that he was fighting a losing battle, Luke tried to grab Rachel's arm to escort her down the hill, but she moved closer towards Eliza. He dropped his hands in defeat. As much as he hated to admit it, Rachel was right. He had no right to tell her what she could or couldn't do, especially since he had spurned her the night before.

But he cared about her. The thought of her in danger, or hurt, or worse, caused his heart to mourn.

Shaking off his thoughts, Luke knew he would have to deal with his emotions later, if he stayed alive. Leading his men, they walked along the shore and spotted the militia group of roughly eighty men waiting at the causeway. Some of the men appeared anxious as they watched the horizon, whereas others watched them approach on the sand with trepidation on their faces.

With a quick glance back at his sister, he saw Benedict and Eliza, carrying her longbow and quiver of arrows, make their way towards a cluster of birch trees that had a vantage point overlooking the causeway.

The ragged militia men's eyes grew wide as they neared, and they drew their swords and daggers. A few of them held pistols, but their hands were shaking. Most of these men were dressed in threadbare shirts and kilts, with worn stockings and boots. They did not appear to be well-trained fighters.

Luke put his hands up to stop his group and turned to face the militia. He pulled the pistol from his waistband and slowly crouched down to place it on the sand. As he was rising, he said,

"I am here to speak to you as countrymen. I am not here to fight you."

A few of the men lowered their weapons, but their eyes were wary. "My name is Lord Downshire, and I am here to urge you to reconsider your treasonous actions."

Stepping out of the group, Thorne stated, "You are not welcome here, Lord Downshire. These men are here to set themselves free and will be rewarded as kings."

Luke shook his head. "No, you are using them because they are expendable."

"No!" Thorne shouted. "These men deserve to be free from the clutches of your mad King George and his frivolous son, Prinny."

Casting aside Thorne's words, he addressed the militia with a determined voice. "Like many of you, I abhor high Society, which is why I fled to Scotland. I wanted nothing to do with the pompous lords and ladies in England. I even convinced myself that I was better off alone." He frowned. "I have been living in a prison of my own making, but when a hoyden came into my life, I began thinking differently."

Glancing at Rachel, Luke smiled and was rewarded to see her smile in return. "I believe in my heart that you are fighting not because you want freedom from King George, but rather to earn wages to feed and clothe your families." A few of the men in the militia lowered their gaze which encouraged him to continue. "I will pay each one of you that puts down your arms twenty gold pieces and an honest job on my stud farm, if you so desire."

A murmur went through the militia, and many of them looked at Luke in amazement as he put his hands up. "That is not all. I have become aware of the struggles that many of you face because there is no doctor in the village. Last week, I sent for a doctor to reside in Rockcliffe, and I am creating an endowment to pay for a hospital to be built."

As excited chatter rose from the militia, Thorne started slowly clapping as he walked closer towards Luke. Dropping his hands, he sneered, "And why should we believe you, an over-privileged, pompous lord that has never worked a day in his life?"

Stepping forward, Emmett proclaimed, "Then believe me." His eyes roamed the makeshift militia. "I have grown up in Rockcliffe, doctoring many of your family members over the years, and some of you work for my father during whaling season. I served in the Royal Navy, and I was dishonorably discharged because I shot a lord in the leg. I have no loyalty towards nobility, but Lord Downshire is not like any of the lords I have ever met. His words are true, and if he doesn't act on his promise, then I will."

"As will I," Rachel said, stepping forward. "I am Lady Rachel, daughter of Lord Exeter, and I promise you a hospital will be built in Rockcliffe."

Walking closer to Rachel, Thorne scoffed loudly. "Lord Downshire brought a lady to fight alongside him." Spinning to face the group, he shouted, "What honorable man would bring a woman to fight his battles?"

Thorne's words convinced some of the militia, but Luke's next words wiped Thorne's smile off his face. "Lady Rachel is not here to fight my battles, but to defend England from a French invasion. More importantly, *Shadow* and *Hawk* are both here to fight as well."

Most of the militiamen tucked in their weapons as they looked with fear at Luke and his group of men. Many of their eyes gravitated towards Adrien and Jonathon.

Thorne swiveled around with a pistol in his hand, pointing it at Luke. "You are a liar! Everyone knows *Hawk* is in France, and why would *Shadow* be on the shores of Rockcliffe?"

"*Shadow!*" Luke shouted. "A sign, if you will."

An arrow whizzed past Luke and landed in the sand near

Thorne's feet. Luke saw the fear enter Thorne's eyes, but he blinked it away as he kept his pistol aimed at Luke. "It does not matter. Lord Melville will deal with *Shadow* and *Hawk*. Both are cowards that hide behind code names."

Jonathon stepped forward. "I hate to be the bearer of ill tidings, but Lord Melville is delayed at Lord Downshire's estate."

"Does 'delayed' mean waiting to be executed?" Emmett asked, smirking.

Thorne's eyes narrowed and spewed hate as he said, "We have another leader that will be here soon."

Adrien spoke up, announcing in a jesting tone, "If you are referring to Phillipe, he won't be coming. His body lies right over there." He pointed towards the cliff's edge. "He wasn't pleased when I informed him that I married his daughter."

Glaring at Adrien, Thorne shifted his body, so he could see the militia out of the corner of his eye. "These men are lying to you. They are only trying to protect their own interests. Kill them." When none of the militia moved, he shouted in a shrill voice, "I said, kill them!"

"Do not be fooled by this man's trickery," Luke urged. "The French are using you to increase their numbers. They want you to fight against your own countrymen, while they take over England's shipyards. I have no agenda except to stop this French invasion and help the villagers of Rockcliffe." His eyes pleaded with them. "Let me help you."

"No," Thorne shouted as he aimed the pistol at Luke's heart. "You will not ruin what took years of planning by playing a compassionate lord. You will not win!"

As Thorne cocked the pistol, Luke braced himself to be shot, but an arrow hit Thorne in the chest, knocking him back. It did not kill him, however. Thorne regained his balance and aimed the pistol again at Luke, but another arrow hit him, this time in the heart. Dropping to his knees, the pistol slid from his hand as he fell into the sand.

Any resistance the militia still had vanished at the death of Thorne. The men looked at him expectedly. "I am bound by my word," Luke stated, keeping his voice firm. "You will all be paid not to fight for the French, but I am asking you... nay, pleading with you, to band with us and fight *against* the French."

Walking towards the cluster of rocks, Luke reached down and grabbed a Brown Bess, holding it up. "We have enough muskets for everyone, and you will be allowed to keep the weapon as promised. We are hoping you will use these muskets to keep the French from reaching our shore."

Jonathon addressed the group, "We will not fault any of you that choose not to fight, but you need to make your decision in haste." He pointed towards the causeway, where French infantry soldiers, dressed in white and blue military uniforms, could be seen in the distance. Each soldier carried a musket in front of them as they slowly marched in formation from Hestan Island.

The French were coming!

A FEW OF THE MILITIA RAN FOR COVER, BUT MOST OF THE MEN stood, staring at the imminent threat on the horizon. Fortunately, the low tide, the deep mud, and a few feet of water on the causeway ensured the French would have to endure a grueling two-mile march towards the shore. Unfortunately, the French wore knee-high boots which helped them navigate the mud.

Snapping into action, Rachel started grabbing the muskets, shouting, "Who can shoot a Brown Bess?" When hands went up, she started handing out the guns alongside Luke and Emmett.

Once all the muskets were distributed, she ensured everyone had adequate ammunition.

As she walked back to retrieve her own Brown Bess, Luke's hand reached out, pulling her into a tight embrace. She didn't fight it, because she needed his strength.

Leaning back, he looked at her with pleading and tearful eyes. Tenderly, his hands came up to cup her cheeks. "I am sorry for being a cad. Please forgive me."

Reaching up to touch his hands, Rachel smiled at him with intense longing. Regardless of his feelings, she knew in her heart that she could never stay mad at Luke. She loved him, and he was too dear to her to push him away, even if it meant they would only remain friends.

"You are forgiven." She took a quick glance towards the horizon and knew they didn't have much time. "Be careful."

Nodding, Luke lowered his hands. "You are the bravest hoyden I know," he said, his dark eyes, full of concern, searching her face.

Jonathon was barking orders to the men with muskets, organizing them into groups of five. After inspecting each group, he informed them, "Do not shoot your muskets until they are in range. Then step aside and reload while the next group gets into position."

"*Shadow's* accuracy with the longbow far surpasses the muskets, as does the speed of nocking the arrows," Adrien yelled to the men. "I will give the signal for the first group to raise your muskets once *Shadow* is out of arrows."

Closing one eye, Jonathon aimed a musket towards the approaching French ground troops. He lowered the gun and advised, "Everyone will most likely have two, possibly three shots, depending on how quickly you can reload before we are forced to engage in close combat."

Standing in line formation, the men with the muskets positioned themselves closest to the causeway, waiting anxiously.

Tilting her head, Rachel acknowledged Hugh and Mr. Kelly, who were both in the first group with her.

Looking up at the causeway where the French were approaching in lines of five across, she could not see an end to their numbers. Turning her head towards the group of men, she knew they had less than two hundred men to defend the coast.

Luke's voice whispered in her ear, "If this turns into a massacre, I want you to run to my estate, grab Chester, and ride to safety." His hand reached out and grabbed hers. "Promise me, Rachel. I can't fight if I know you aren't safe."

Gripping his hand, Rachel vowed, "I promise."

A lone French musket fired at their line formation, causing sand to puff into the air but not close enough to make a hit. A moment later, arrows began to hit the French soldiers in their chests, one after another, but the soldiers kept marching towards them, stepping onto the backs of their dead comrades to advance through the mud.

Rachel had lost count of how many soldiers Eliza had killed when Adrien shouted, "Ready!" He paused while they raised their muskets. "Aim!" Rachel waited with dread for the next word. "Fire!"

Anticipating the kick back, Rachel planted her foot and aimed for a French soldier. She was relieved to see him drop. Stepping aside, she loaded her Brown Bess as another round of muskets discharged at the advancing enemy. Repeatedly, one group fired while the other groups reloaded. Dead French soldiers were spread across the estuary, some floating face up, the water lapping over their bodies.

The sound of cannons roaring could be heard in the distance and Rachel feared the French frigates were getting into position, so they could shoot at the shore. She took a deep breath and pushed down her worries. She had enough to fear. The French were only a few yards offshore, and now they were running towards them.

Shoving her back, Luke exclaimed, "Run, Rachel!"

Holding onto her musket, Rachel ran towards the outcropping of rocks where they had previously hidden the weapons. Reloading her Brown Bess, she carefully aimed and fired at a French soldier, who was charging out of the water. Before she had a chance to load again, Eliza and Benedict dropped down next to her and took cover.

Benedict cupped Eliza's cheek as he pleaded, "Stay alive and protect our baby." Pulling her forward, he pressed his lips to hers as a tear fell from Eliza's eye. He leaned back and stared deep into her eyes, the love between them was undeniable. "Promise me, Eliza," he ordered, his voice firm, unyielding.

In a soft but pained voice, Eliza replied, "I promise."

"I love you."

"I love you, too," she answered back.

With a final glance at his wife, Benedict pulled out his pistol and dagger and ran towards the fighting. Holding up her own pistol, Eliza turned towards Rachel, and with fiery intensity in her eyes, said, "Are you ready to keep our men alive?"

Not bothering to nod, Rachel aimed her musket and fired on the soldiers as Eliza shot with her pistol. Between them, they killed many soldiers, but it wasn't enough. The French were still advancing, although they were met with incredible resistance. These Scots were not giving up their lives without a fight.

Rachel's eyes tracked Luke, who was sword-fighting with a French soldier. Tripping over a dead body, Luke fell onto his back as the soldier loomed over him, lifting his sword to run him through. Aiming her musket at the man, she shot him in the heart before he even started lowering his sword.

Jumping up and turning his head, Luke gave her a nod to acknowledge her act but grabbed his sword to engage in another battle. As she reached for more ammunition, a feeling of dread washed over her. Staying hidden behind the rocks, Rachel turned her back to the fighting and informed Eliza of their precarious situation. "We are out of ammunition."

Eliza's face grew grim as she continued to watch the battle unfold. "I believe it is time for us to run for our lives," she said, her voice hitching with emotion.

"And leave the men?" Rachel asked frantically. Panic surged through her, knowing there was nothing else they could do to help the men they loved.

Regretful tears welled in Eliza's eyes as she turned her head to face Rachel. "It won't be much longer before the French troops vastly outnumber our men." She let out a stifled sob. "I doubt they will survive, and my heart can't take watching my husband, brothers, and friends be slaughtered."

Turning around, Rachel watched her friends and family battle courageously, but more French troops advanced to shore every moment, joining the fight. Benedict, Jonathon, and Adrien were all fighting more than one opponent at a time, and Emmett was right alongside them.

Her eyes strayed towards Luke just as he ran his sword through a French soldier. Without hesitation, he turned to battle another who came rushing at him. Even though the men were fighting hard, bodies of her friends and enemies coated the sand. The distinctive clang of sword-fighting could be heard alongside the wailing of the injured.

Reaching over, Eliza grabbed her hand. "We need to leave before it is too late."

With one final glance at Luke, Rachel followed her dear friend as they started to run up towards the path that would lead them to safety. As they took their first step onto the path, they stopped and stood aside as Mr. Larson came charging past them with his sword raised. Right behind him was what seemed to be an endless number of red-coated soldiers, all with their swords drawn and prepared to join the battle.

Gripping Eliza's hand, Rachel watched as the British ground

troops continued running past them with no sign of hesitation. At last, the final soldier ran past, and a group of officers rode their horses towards the sand.

Running back to the cover of the rocks, Eliza and Rachel watched their brave men fight alongside the British troops. Vastly outnumbered, the French forces quickly laid down their weapons and surrendered.

The distant roar of cannons could still be heard, and the billowing of smoke could be seen on the horizon. At first, Rachel thought the French frigates were firing at them, but looking closer, it appeared the frigates were battling with another warship.

In a hushed voice, Eliza urged, "We need to depart before we are seen. It would be difficult to explain why two ladies are dressed in men's clothing and shooting muskets at the enemy."

"Where is your longbow?" she asked.

"I hid it."

Nodding her understanding, they quickly retreated towards the path and ran towards their waiting horses. Racing back to Luke's estate, Rachel could not believe that their plan had worked.

They were safe!

🜺 30 🜺

A FEW HOURS LATER, RACHEL WAS DRESSED IN A PUCE-COLORED gown with puffy sleeves, her hair piled high on her head. She felt rested after a long soak and was now heading towards Luke's drawing room just as the sun was setting.

Walking into the room, Rachel saw everyone was assembled. Well, almost everyone. "Where is Adrien?" she asked, glancing around the room. Eliza and Benedict shared the settee as Mr. Larson, Jonathon, Emmett, and Luke sat in chairs creating a semi-circle.

Eliza smiled up at her. "The moment the fighting was over, Adrien left to be with Kate."

"That is sweet," Rachel admitted as she sat on a chair near Jonathon.

Luke turned his gaze towards her. His face was severely bruised, swollen, and altogether painful-looking. "How are you faring?"

Feeling relieved that the fighting was over, Rachel sighed. "I am well." She smiled at him. "How are you?"

"Better, now that I've seen you," Luke said, his eyes reflecting vulnerability.

Blushing, Rachel lowered her eyes. As much as she tried to pretend that Luke didn't affect her, she knew she was lying to herself. He was undeniably handsome, but it was the way he accepted her as she was that caused her heart to ache. Why did he not love her in return?

Reaching for her teacup, Eliza took a sip before she turned towards Mr. Larson. "I have never been more relieved to see you than I was this afternoon."

Mr. Larson chuckled his understanding. "I am impressed by the speed of Lord Downshire's thoroughbred horses. After I commandeered one, I rode for hours in the dark till I found the troops resting for the evening. I explained the situation to the major, and they marched through the night."

Jonathon rose and walked towards the drink tray, drawing her attention to him. He had a black eye, swollen nose, and a small cut on his right cheek. "Before you arrived, we had the French cowering in fear," he jested.

With a lifted eyebrow, Eliza looked knowingly at her brother. "Is that so?"

Handing a drink to Benedict, Jonathon winked at his sister. "We have been in worse scrapes. Isn't that right, Benedict?"

"Far worse," Benedict confirmed, giving him a lopsided grin as his swollen lip refused to move with the rest of his face.

As she accepted a cup of tea from Eliza, Rachel asked, "Was it my imagination, or did I hear cannons firing in the distance when we were near the causeway?"

Refusing a drink from Jonathon, Emmett, who looked equally battered, answered, "After my father's whaling ships located the French frigates in a cove near Hestan Island, he sent them back out to try to intercept a British ship to assist in the fighting." He smiled, or rather he attempted one with his cut lip. "As luck would have it, one of the ships chased down a British warship sailing up the Irish sea."

Benedict took a sip of his drink and placed the glass down on the table. "Originally, when we discovered that the French were preparing to land in Scotland, Lord Beckett sent word to Admiral Snodgers, who deployed the HMS Garnock up the Irish sea, in hopes of intercepting the French frigate. Luckily, the two French ships were no match for the Garnock's speed and size."

"It worked out splendidly." Rachel was impressed until she saw Luke's crestfallen expression. Placing her cup down, she asked, "What is wrong, Luke?"

His jaw tensed as he brought his gaze up to hers. "About twenty-five of my men were killed, and that does not include the number of men from the militia that died."

Tears sprang to her eyes as she thought about all the men that had died today to protect England from the French invasion. "I am sorry," Rachel offered, not knowing what else to say.

Luke smiled faintly as he nodded his head. Standing, he walked to the drink tray and poured himself a drink. While he stood there motionless with the glass up to his lips, Rachel rose and walked towards him. When he saw her, he lowered his glass and smiled sadly.

"Did Hugh or Mr. Kelly die?" Rachel asked.

He shook his head. "No, they were spared."

Rachel stepped closer and placed her hand on the sleeve of his black dress coat. "It is not your fault that your men died."

"Isn't it?" Luke huffed, his eyes reflecting pain. "I asked them to fight."

She took a step closer, hoping her next words would provide him with comfort. "You asked them to defend their country. You gave them a choice. Sadly, some of them died to keep the French from invading England." She waited till he looked at her. "It was their choice to offer up their lives, not yours."

Peering deep into her eyes, Luke replied, "That same argument could be made about how David fought to save your life."

Knowing Luke's words were true, Rachel felt a great weight lift from her shoulders. "You are right," she expressed with emotion. "We both need to move forward but retain their memories in our hearts."

Covering her hand with his, Luke gazed at her face. When he focused on her broken nose, Rachel put her hand up to hide it, but he stopped her. "You are exquisite, imperfections and all," he said softly.

As they stared at each other, a loud commotion erupted in the main hall. The shouting increased, and Rachel heard her father's voice. Turning towards the door, she was rewarded to see her parents rush into the room with her aunt and uncle trailing behind. "Mother! Father!" Rachel shouted joyously as she ran to embrace them.

Her parents met her halfway and pulled her into a tight embrace. After a few moments, they stepped back, but her mother kept a firm hold on her hand. "Your uncle sent word that you had shot a man in an alley, and we rushed to retrieve you."

Rachel's father frowned as he directed his comments to Eliza. "Lady Lansdowne, you ensured me that my daughter would be protected if I sent her to Scotland, but apparently I sent her into the middle of a French invasion."

With an iron gaze, Benedict rose, shielding his wife from Lord Exeter's ire. His bruised face hid most of his emotions, but his eyes narrowed dangerously. "My wife just helped stop that French invasion, at the risk of her own life, and I would think carefully about the next few words that come out of your mouth, for they could be your last." Benedict's jaw clenched so tightly that a muscle under his ear pulsated.

To Rachel's surprise, her father's face broke into a broad smile. "I see why you are one of Lord Beckett's favorite agents. Your threats are quite good, very believable."

Benedict eyed Lord Exeter suspiciously for a few moments before his jaw relaxed. "I am actually retired," he admitted, returning to his seat.

"Is Lord Beckett aware of this?" her father asked, amused.

"He keeps rejecting my resignation." Benedict's words were clipped.

"That is good," Lord Exeter responded before he shifted his focus back to Eliza. "As I was saying before your husband threatened to kill me, somehow my daughter has survived being attacked, shot in the arm, and two attempted abductions." Turning to Rachel, he inquired, "Did I miss anything?"

Giving her father an apologetic smile, she informed him, "Well, I was one of the sharpshooters when the French stormed the beach."

Opening his mouth to protest, her father hesitated, then closed it, but she did not miss the ticking of his eye. Clearing his throat, Lord Exeter turned back towards Eliza. "Even though my daughter seems intent on killing herself, you managed to keep her safe, and I thank you with all my heart."

"We thank you," Lady Exeter rushed to add, smiling gratefully at Eliza.

Her father put an arm around Rachel's shoulder. "It is time to take you home," he declared.

"No… you can't leave," Luke sputtered.

Turning his gaze towards Luke, her father asked, "And you are?"

Placing his glass on the drink tray, Luke walked closer as Rachel provided the introduction. "Father, I would like to introduce you to Lord Downshire."

"I see." Lord Exeter frowned, his eyes roaming over Lord Downshire with displeasure. "And why should you have a say whether or not I depart with my daughter?"

Rachel kept her gaze on Luke, hoping that he would trust his heart and reveal that he still cared for her, at least enough to ask her to stay longer. However, he replied, "I just wanted a chance to say good-bye."

"Proceed, then," her father said, granting permission.

Reaching down slowly, Luke tenderly took her hand into his

own and raised it to his lips. "Thank you for everything, Lady Rachel." His lips kissed her gloved hand, and she had to blink back tears. She loved this man so dearly, and she desperately wanted to give him her heart, but he didn't want it.

As she reigned in her emotions, Rachel spoke softly, "You are welcome, Lord Downshire." Her eyes pleaded for him to say something else, anything that would delay her departure. Instead, he released her hand and stepped back. And with that one step backward, Luke shattered her heart.

Her father placed his arm around her shoulder. "Are you ready to go home?"

With a final glance at Luke, she admitted sadly, "I am. There is nothing to keep me here."

LYING IN BED, LUKE MUTTERED CURSE WORDS AT THE SUN AS IT dared to peek its way between the drapes. He had no desire to leave his bed or see the pity in his staff's eyes when he informed them that Lady Rachel had left Rockcliffe.

A few times last night, he had decided he would throw caution to the wind and chase after Rachel, begging her to never leave him. He even went as far as having his horse saddled, but he couldn't do it. He wouldn't do that to Rachel.

For the first time, he had gotten to know a woman, her true character and strength, without the burdens of his title. And she was brilliant and a hoyden... his hoyden. Tossing a pillow across the room, he groaned loudly. No, Rachel was not his. He had sent her away for her own good. After all, she was witty, kind, compassionate, and he was just a lord who owned a stud farm.

He was a recluse and wasn't good enough for her. Everyone knew it!

Rachel was his love match. Luke knew in his heart that he could never love someone as much as he loved her. How could he?

His door was thrown open, and Eliza strode into the room. Walking straight for the drapes, she pulled them open. "Good morning, Luke," she announced in an annoyingly cheerful voice.

"Are you mad, Eliza?" Luke growled. "I could have been sleeping nude."

Jonathon laughed as he walked into the room. "You are too stuffy to ever do something like that."

Sitting up in bed, Luke put a pillow behind his back before leaning against the wall. "What are you doing in my bedchamber? Do any of you have any sense of decorum?"

Walking into his room as well, Benedict had just taken a bite of an apple as he mumbled around a mouthful, "None whatsoever."

Luke huffed, "Is there anyone else in the hall that wants to come into my room?"

"Not by choice, mind you, but you gave us no other option," Emmett answered, striding into his room with a handful of papers.

"What is that supposed to mean?" Luke asked gruffly.

Placing her hands on her hips, his sister said, "Just what it sounds like. You have slept almost the entire day away."

With a wave of his hand, Luke dismissed her words. "Leave me. I never asked for your help."

Opening her mouth, Eliza was stopped by Benedict's hand on her shoulder. "We agreed that Jonathon would speak for us," he said, grinning. "Do you remember why?"

Crossing her arms over her chest, Eliza sighed, "Because we all voted and some of the group thought I *might* toss a dagger at Luke."

"Some?" Jonathon laughed. "Everyone."

Curious, Luke asked, "Who was in this group?"

"Eliza, Benedict, Emmett, and I," Jonathon listed. "Although, after we chose the spokesman, we decided to seek out your servants' opinions on the matter." He smirked. "I assume you are aware of this, but everyone under your employ believes you and Lady Rachel are a perfect match for each other."

"I do not care what they think," Luke insisted, glaring, "or what you think."

Leaning against the wall, Jonathon appeared completely unaffected by his glare. "We," he paused, glancing at Eliza, Benedict, and Emmett, "have come to help you find a way to win Rachel back."

Frowning, Luke shouted, "Are you daft? I don't want your help." His words were slow and deliberate.

"Stop being such a..." Eliza started but was stopped by Benedict's head shaking. She mouthed, *Sorry*, to Jonathon.

Turning his head back towards Luke, Jonathon continued, "We disagree." He offered a polite smile. "Now explain to us what went wrong."

He bunched up the sheets in his hand. "Nothing went wrong," he grunted, admitting nothing.

"I see," Jonathon muttered, crossing his legs at his ankles. "You are going to make us work for it. Well, you do recall that three of us in this room are agents of the Crown, and we are trained in the art of interrogation." Leaning over, Emmett said something to Jonathon in a hushed voice. In a serious tone, Jonathon added, "And we have a doctor that can diagnose a broken heart."

Benedict chuckled. "I heard that is a class at Oxford now."

Not remotely amused, Luke pointed towards the door. "Leave."

Jonathon shook his head. "We can't do that. If you don't

convince Rachel to marry you, then you are destined to spend the rest of your life alone."

The sound of Benedict chewing on the apple grated on Luke's last nerve. He was tired of this pointless conversation. It was none of their business if he chose to live alone. Since they weren't leaving, Luke decided to tell them the truth. Maybe then they'd leave him alone. "I will not ask Rachel to marry me, because I am not worthy of her."

"And?" Jonathon pressed with an expectant brow.

"And what?" Luke huffed. "I will not be responsible for forcing Rachel to live in Scotland. She is too adventurous and full of life to come live on a stud farm in Rockcliffe. Eventually, she would grow to resent me for forcing her to lead such a dull life."

In a hushed, but concerned voice, Benedict asked, "Is this about marital relations? Because we can help you with that."

"That is not what I am talking about at all," Luke snapped. "Bloody fool."

Stifling a smile, Eliza sat down on a chair. "Did you even ask Rachel what she wanted?"

"In a way," Luke maintained. "I listened to her. She was constantly talking about doing more, being more."

Eliza sat back in the chair and pursed her lips. "And you truly believe that if you married Rachel, you would stifle her?"

Leaning forward in his bed, Luke winced as he admitted, "Eventually, she would despise me. I will not have a marriage like father's and mother's."

"Ah," Jonathon exulted. "At last, we have the truth. You are afraid that your marriage will mimic our parents'."

Luke frowned. "Not just our parents, but almost every marriage among the ton."

Pulling up a chair, Emmett sat down next to him. "To clarify, you sent Rachel away, not because you don't love her, but because you love her enough to save her from an inevitably loveless marriage."

"Yes," Luke stated. Finally, everyone understood his dilemma.

Emmett turned in his chair to face Jonathon. "That is an idiotic premise."

Jonathon nodded. "I concur."

"I beg your pardon!" Luke bellowed, his eyes blazing.

"Allow me," Benedict requested, glancing at Jonathon before facing Luke. "Your mother was a villainess traitor that fell in love with a French spy. Your parents' marriage was doomed from the very beginning, and it had nothing to do with leading a dull life." He smiled lovingly at Eliza before adding, "You and Rachel love each other, and like any relationship of value, you can foster the love to grow, to expand. As your love becomes deeper, you learn to grow together, not apart."

"And if Rachel starts despising me?" Luke asked.

Watching him with compassion in her eyes, Eliza replied, "How could a woman ever despise a man who loves her above all else?"

"I do," Luke confirmed, his voice hitching. "I love her, and I would do anything to make her happy."

Eliza smiled warmly. "Trusting another with your heart is scary, but it can be vastly rewarding if you trust the right person." Walking over, Benedict took her hand and smiled back at her. The look they shared was undeniably full of love.

Jonathon pushed off the wall. "You are not asking Rachel to marry you for convenience. You are asking her to marry you for love."

Standing, Emmett handed him a stack of papers and smiled smugly as he stepped back.

"What's this?" Luke asked. But as soon as he read the first paragraph, he shouted, "Mr. Kelly!"

Immediately, his butler stuck his head through the door. "Ye bellowed, m'lord."

Putting the pages aside, Luke put his feet over the bed. "Ready my coach. I am departing for London immediately."

"It has bin waiting for ye all mornin'," Mr. Kelly reported with a bright smile.

"Excellent," Luke exclaimed, standing up. "I'm going to bring Rachel home."

31

RACHEL SAT IN HER FATHER'S STUDY ATTEMPTING TO REMEMBER the words she had previously written in the privacy of her bedchamber in Scotland. Tapping the quill's feather against her lips, the words seemed to be jumbled inside her head. She sighed. Maybe she should send a messenger to collect her pages from her aunt's house in Rockcliffe?

After Luke had said his final goodbye, she had fled to her bedchamber and stayed up all night writing the first draft of her book. It was loosely based on her adventures over the past two weeks. In her heart, Luke was the dashing hero of her story, and she wrote with him in mind. It was also a way to capture his memory forever because her words would be a testament of how much she truly cared for him. Unfortunately, they had departed so early the next morning that she had left the pages on her dressing table.

Crumpling the paper in front of her, Rachel tossed it across the room to join the rest of the discarded balls of paper. She couldn't think. To be honest, she didn't want to think too hard. Whenever she started to remember Luke, her heart ached, and she longed to see him again. What was wrong with her? Luke had broken her heart, and she didn't really know why.

He had given her a vague excuse of how they didn't suit, but she knew there was more to it. There had to be! Rachel knew he cared for her, more than he admitted. But it didn't matter. She had confessed her love to him, and he still sent her away. The message was clear... he didn't love her.

Glancing out the window, Rachel saw the carriages drive by her father's townhouse, oblivious to the inner turmoil she was feeling. Rising, she'd started towards her room when their butler, Mr. Parker, stopped her and announced, "Lord Downshire is here to see you, Lady Rachel."

Impossible. She must have misheard him. "Would you mind repeating who has come calling?"

"The man claims to be Lord Luke Downshire," Mr. Parker said, with a curious glance. "Would you like me to send him away?"

"No, no," Rachel rushed to say. "Is my mother home?"

"Lady Exeter is out calling," he informed her. "Would you like me to send a maid in to chaperone?"

She shook her head. "That won't be necessary. Please inform Lord Downshire that I will be there shortly."

Mr. Parker bowed. "As you wish."

Picking up her skirts, Rachel ran towards her bedchamber and was relieved to see Savannah still in her room. "Lord Downshire is here."

Shifting the bundle of linens in her arms, Savannah repeated, "He is here?" She beamed at her. "Why are you up here? Go to him."

Rachel dropped onto her bed. "What would I even say?"

Her lady's maid dropped the linens and walked over to her. Reaching for her hands, she pulled her up. "Just follow your heart," she advised.

Frowning, Rachel admitted, "My heart wants me to hit him."

Rolling her eyes playfully, Savannah pushed her towards the door. "Behave, Lady Rachel."

Slowly making her way towards the drawing room, Rachel took a deep breath before she entered. Lord Downshire was standing near the mantle with a bouquet of roses in his hand, looking at her mother's portrait above the fireplace. Wearing a black tailcoat, a white cravat, and grey, striped trousers, Luke was dashingly handsome. Curse that man!

Walking further into the room, Rachel placed her hands on the back of a blue camelback sofa and waited till Luke turned around. When he saw her, he smiled broadly and started advancing towards her. Two steps later, he looked at the sofa between them and stopped. With concern in his eyes, he asked, "How have you been?"

"I have been well," she replied vaguely. "And you, Lord Downshire? Are you well?"

He held up the bouquet. "I brought you roses. I was informed they are your favorite."

Coming around the sofa, Rachel reached her hand out to accept the bouquet. Their fingers touched, and she attempted to ignore the tingles she felt in her arm. "Thank you." She took a deep breath, enjoying the aroma of the roses. Curiously, she asked, "Who told you that roses were my favorite?"

Amusement flashed in his eyes. "The lady at the flower shop on the corner. Apparently, there are many gentlemen who buy you flowers."

Walking over to an empty vase on a table, Rachel placed the roses inside before sitting down on the sofa. Expecting Luke to sit across from her, she was surprised when he claimed the seat next to her while maintaining proper distance. She couldn't decide if that infuriated or pleased her.

Keeping her back rigid, Rachel lowered her gaze as she started tracing the floral print on her dress. What did one say to a man that she loved but who did not love her in return?

Luke cleared his throat, and she brought her eyes up. He smiled. "I brought Chester with me. I was surprised when Hugh informed me that you returned him before you left for London."

"It wasn't fair of me to take Chester away from his home."

Placing a hand on his thigh, Luke started tapping his finger. "But I gave you Chester in exchange for your forgiveness."

"That was wrong of me. I know why you lied to me, and honestly, I am glad you did," Rachel maintained, looking deep into his eyes.

"You are?"

"I am." Rachel offered him an apologetic smile. "If you had introduced yourself as Lord Downshire, I daresay I might not have given you a fair chance."

"It was still wrong for me to deceive you." He paused, and she held her breath in the wake of his long silence, waiting for his reply. "I was wrong about a lot of things."

"Can you be more specific?" she asked, her heart hopeful.

"I will, but first," Luke said as he reached into the pocket of his waistcoat. He pulled out folded pages. Opening the papers, he started reading.

"As Ruth gazed upon John, she knew that her life had changed in a moment. Never had a man spoken to her heart in such a fashion before, his words intoxicating, his voice penetrating deep into her soul. He was her future…"

Placing that sheet of paper behind another, Luke continued reading.

Ruth had always wanted more adventure in her life, more excitement, but the way her heart and soul ached at the mere sight of John was exhilarating, yet terrifying. She fully understood what she had been searching for was not adventure per se, but a partner that would love her unconditionally."

Hearing enough, Rachel reached to grab the papers, but Luke pulled them back. "Where did you find those?" she asked, her cheeks growing very warm.

"Emmett brought them to me after you left," Luke informed her.

Biting her lower lip, Rachel couldn't believe her cousin had betrayed her like this. "How grand," she mumbled. "If you will excuse me…"

Luke reached to take her hand, but Rachel jumped up, anxious to put distance between them. Looking up at her, he inquired, "Did you mean these words?"

"I did," Rachel admitted, but rushed to clarify, "but those are just characters in my book."

"Ah," Luke said, folding the pages. "And the brooding lord?"

She took a step back, attempting to collect her thoughts. "If you recall, he owns a sheep farm, not a stud farm."

"I see," he teased with a twinkle in his eye. "What about when he accuses Ruth of trying to steal a sheep?"

Rachel smiled, albeit a small one. "There may be some truth mingled with fiction." Placing her hand out, she demanded, "I would like my papers back."

He placed the pages back into his waistcoat. "I will make you a deal. If you come to my ball tonight, I will give your papers back."

In surprise, Rachel dropped her hand and blinked at him, unsure she'd heard him correctly. "You are hosting a ball?"

He quirked an eyebrow. "I want truth between us, Rachel."

"I expect nothing less."

"Did you mean what you wrote?"

Keeping her gaze fixed at his lapels, she started to say, "My book is fiction…"

Her words were stopped when he stepped forward, gently cupping her cheek with his hand. "Do you want to know what I think?" When she didn't respond, he continued, "I think you wrote this story with us in mind."

The intensity in his eyes caused her to suck in a quick breath. If she were brave, she would tell him the truth. She would say that she meant every word and confess her love again! However, she was not that brave, and the fear of being rejected again was too great.

Instead of pressing her for an answer, his thumb started caressing her cheekbone. Leaning in, he whispered in her ear, "You are so beautiful, my hoyden."

Allowing herself to bask in his nearness, Rachel's heart lurched when he lowered his hand and stepped back. "Please say that you will come." He spoke softly, but she could hear the intense, wistful plea in his voice.

His eyes were filled with a yearning, yielding desire which held her transfixed. She found she could not formulate any words, so she nodded in response.

"Rachel, I…" He stumbled for a moment, his eyes roaming her face. He looked at her as if he had more to say but then bowed. "Until tonight." He retreated quickly from the room without so much as a backward glance. It appeared that he was fleeing from her.

Taking a moment to recover, Rachel rushed towards the main door just as Luke was about to depart. "Where is your ball?" she asked, attempting to appear unaffected by his charms.

With an achingly tender smile, his eyes lit up in anticipation. "I will send a carriage."

STANDING IN HIS FATHER'S SPACIOUS, RECTANGULAR BALLROOM, Luke could not fathom how many people were crammed into this room. The cream-papered walls, which highlighted the alcoves that housed paintings, sculptures, and artifacts from around the world, many gifted to the Duke of Remington, were barely visible behind the influx of the guests present.

Most of the guests were clustered around the edges of the ballroom as not to disturb the elaborate floral chalk designs that were drawn on the center of the floor. A full orchestra sat in a corner and the musicians were warming up their instruments. Everything was staged perfectly. The only thing missing was the guest of honor.

Taking a sip of his drink, Luke's eyes darted towards the open door of the ballroom. Why hadn't Rachel been announced yet? Where was she? Panic set in as he thought about the possibility that Rachel wouldn't come after all. He gulped back his drink and placed the empty glass on the tray of a servant passing by.

Taking a deep breath, he focused his attention on his sister. Eliza was laughing at something Benedict had just said and placed her hand on his chest. They were utterly enraptured with each other, oblivious to the anxiousness that he felt. "Why did I agree to this nonsense?" he mumbled under his breath.

Dropping her hand, Eliza smiled knowingly at him. "What nonsense are you referring to?"

"This!" Luke exclaimed, tossing his hands up. "There are entirely too many people in this room, making it more blazing hot than usual." Glancing up at the crystal chandelier, he wiped the sweat from his brow as he frowned at the hundreds of burning candles radiating off the crystal pendants. "How did Anne find so many blasted people to attend this ball with only two days' notice?"

Benedict chuckled. "You will find that the ton will drop anything to attend a ball hosted by your step-mother, the Duchess of Remington."

"And yet, you have failed to notice that Rachel has not arrived," Luke pointed out with nervous irritation. "What if she doesn't come?"

"She will come," his sister assured him.

Pulling at his cravat, Luke was not as convinced. "I should have just proposed earlier."

He anxiously glanced at the door again. What if Rachel said no, and he had to return to Scotland without her as his bride?

Placing a hand on his shoulder, Benedict smirked. "It does not work that way. Women liked to be wooed, and each wants their own unique fairytale ending."

A servant passed by with more champagne, and Luke reached out and grabbed two glasses. Why didn't he just obtain a special license, he thought, as he downed one drink. As he went to gulp down the other, the announcement finally came. "The right honorable Earl of Exeter and his wife, the Countess of Exeter, and their daughter, the Lady Rachel Croft."

Handing both glasses to Benedict, Luke turned to watch Lady Rachel walk into the room. She wore a white dress, embroidered with rosebuds, and a square neckline, which high-lighted her exquisite, comely figure perfectly. Her hair was piled high on her head and woven with flowers and ribbons.

He swallowed nervously as he grabbed the glass of cham-pagne back from Benedict and gulped it down, ignoring his brother-in-law's chuckling.

Shoving the glass back at Benedict, Luke started walking towards Rachel. He found himself hampered, however, by the many gentlemen who had flocked to speak to her. As he fought his way through her admirers, he was rewarded to see her looking directly at him.

Politely postponing the other gentlemen's requests for dances, Rachel smiled expectantly at him as he found his voice. "Lady Rachel, may I have a moment of your time?"

"You may," she replied, offering her white-gloved hand.

Smiling nervously, Luke placed her hand into the crook of his arm as he escorted her towards the dance floor. With a glance over his shoulder at her rejected suitors, he remarked, "You have a lot of admirers."

"They admire my inheritance more than me," Rachel admitted, frowning.

He placed his hand over hers. "Any man who doesn't value you more than money is a fool."

She smiled up at him mischievously. "My grandmother also left me estates and valuable farmland."

"Did she now?" He smiled, and teased, "Well, that changes everything."

He led her towards the middle of the dance floor and turned to face her, preparing to wear his heart on his sleeve. "I don't care what your grandmother left you, Rachel. I recognize you for who you truly are."

"And who am I?"

He stepped closer. "My heart's desire." His words were spoken deliberately. He infused them with all his love and willed her to believe.

Before she could respond, he placed his hand around her waist and felt her stiffen. "What are you doing?"

The sound of music filled the ballroom as Luke reached for her hand and brought it up. He started swaying with the rhythm of the music. "What do you think I'm doing? I am dancing with you."

"Did you get permission to dance the waltz?" she asked, eyeing him warily.

Luke shrugged. "I'm not sure why, but people generally do what I ask."

She laughed, her eyes twinkling with merriment. "I think it is because you are the Marquess of Downshire. But if that isn't enough, you just give them that intense, piercing glare that causes people to shake in fear."

Luke chuckled. "I am glad that you said that. Lately, my glare has not been as effective."

After dancing for a few moments, Rachel inquired, "I thought you didn't dance?"

"My dance teachers would be furious at you for saying so. I have been told I dance splendidly," he huffed, feigning disappointment.

She shook her head. "No, you misunderstood me. I thought…"

"I know what you meant," he said, deciding to take pity on her. "Normally, I do not dance, but I find I make exceptions when it comes to seeing you smile."

As they danced, he marveled that Rachel was finally in his arms, molding perfectly, as if she was meant to be there. He slowly veered her towards the double doors, and once the music stopped, he led her outside onto the veranda. The cool night air was a welcome relief from the stuffy ballroom.

The veranda overlooked a small lake. The trees along the shore held brightly-lit lanterns, which sent sparkles dancing merrily across the water's surface. Luke escorted her down the short path towards a bench near the lake's edge and waited till she sat down before claiming the seat next to her.

He glanced back at the house and noticed Eliza and Benedict standing arm-in-arm on the veranda. He smiled. Trust Eliza to stay the perfect distance away, close enough to chaperone, but far enough to give them some privacy.

Luke took a deep breath, looking for the courage to give his rehearsed speech, but Rachel spoke first. "What a beautiful view."

In a rush to say something, he declared, "This will all be mine one day." Why did he just blurt that out?

Looking at him with curiosity, Rachel asked, "Is that what you desire?"

Sighing, Luke shook his head. "No, I prefer my estate in Rockcliffe."

"I assumed as much." She turned her gaze back towards the lake.

He shifted towards her. "But I will stay in London if that is what you desire."

Furrowing her brow, the line between her eyes appeared, and he found himself distracted. "Why would it matter what I desire?"

Reaching for her hand, Luke felt relieved when she didn't pull away. "I lied to you before when I said we wouldn't suit. I was frightened…" He paused, his voice hitching. "I was afraid that all marriages were destined to be like my parents', but I was wrong."

"Is that why you sent me away?"

His eyes roamed her beautiful face and he reached for her other hand. "It was. My greatest fear is that you would grow to resent me, and I would lose you. Not just your friendship, but your heart, as well."

"I could never resent you," Rachel insisted, her eyes imploring him.

Glancing down at their entwined hands, his heart was full, content. Bringing his gaze up, he began, "I was a reclusive lord, happy to live out my days alone. I never wanted for more until I met you." His eyes pleaded for her to understand what he was trying to convey. "You made me laugh again. You brought joy into my life and taught me to look past myself towards others."

Rachel's eyes were filled with tears, and she remained silent, smiling.

"You saved me, and for that, I am yours, always and forever," he stated, hesitating as he took courage to say his next words, "… and I love you with all my heart."

"You do?" she asked, surprised.

He chuckled. "How could I not?"

Her eyes lit up at his words.

Drawing courage from that light, he continued, "I have

learned that my heart craves you, and I will do anything to be with you, stay with you. I will change for you, I will live in London and go to soirées…"

His words were cut off when Rachel interrupted him. "I never asked you to change, nor do I want you to." She tightened her grips on his hands. "You may be a brooding lord, but you are *my* brooding lord."

He chuckled in response as her eyes filled with tears. Taking a shaky breath, she said, "My whole life I have pursued adventure and excitement, but now I understand, my heart was searching for you. You have accepted me for who I am." She smiled. "I don't care where I live, as long as I am with you."

He leaned forward and kissed her soundly on the lips. "You, my hoyden, are my new dream."

Sliding off the bench, Luke dropped to one knee, keeping her hands in his own. "I am torn. I want to order you to marry me," he started, offering her a one-sided grin, "but I have learned that is not effective with you."

Rachel chuckled. "No, it is not."

He grew serious. "I am not a perfect man, nor am I an eloquent man." His fingers gripped hers tightly. "But," he swallowed, reigning in his emotions, "when I am with you, I am a better man. And that is who I want to be." He felt his heart pounding as he prepared to ask his next question, even though he felt more confident in her answer than he had moments ago. "Will you marry me?"

Pulling back her hands to cover her squeal, Rachel jumped into his arms, saying, "Yes, yes, yes."

Laughing, he embraced her and murmured into her hair, "I love you." Not waiting for her response, he leaned back and gazed longingly into her eyes. "I love you," he repeated with heartfelt sincerity.

"I love you, too." Leaning into him, Rachel hovered over his lips with a smile on her face. "Does this mean I get to keep Chester?"

He laughed. "Yes," he assured her, "but to clarify, I am offering you my heart as well."

She brushed her lips against his. "I gave you my heart a long time ago."

His heart soared at her words and he placed his hand on the back of her neck, initiating a slow, thorough kiss, claiming her for his own. As he deepened the kiss, all the barriers around his heart were broken down and replaced by emotions that he'd thought existed only in fairytales.

Reluctantly, he broke off the kiss and leaned his forehead against hers. "I have a confession to make."

"Another one?" she teased.

"I did have an ulterior motive when I invited you to this ball." Confusion was evident on Rachel's brow, so he explained, "After you left Rockcliffe, I realized what a horrible mistake I made letting you go, so I rushed after you. When I arrived, the Duchess of Remington offered to take care of all the arrangements for the ball, and I may have let her assume it was to celebrate our engagement."

Rachel's eyes grew wide as she turned her gaze towards the ballroom. "Why would the duchess believe this was to be our engagement ball?"

He swallowed, nervously, as her eyes came back to his. "I may have already posted the banns."

"May have?"

Bringing his hand up to cup her right cheek, his eyes were filled with love for her. "You may recall, I never collected my prize for our wager."

She raised an eyebrow. "Are you referring to when we raced across the field near my uncle's estate?"

"I am." He offered her an impish grin. "And I decided your

hand in marriage was a fair prize, so I posted the banns as soon as I arrived in London."

Rachel smiled broadly, allowing the small dimple on the right side of her mouth to appear. "Even though I question your logic, I am pleased."

"You are?"

"How could I not be?" Leaning in, she kissed him firmly on the mouth. After a few moments, she broke the kiss and offered him an amused smile. "Just so you know, I would have married you by special license."

His mouth dropped open in surprise. Before he could respond, her lips molded into his and his words of protest melted away.

Eventually, they would need to go inside and make a formal announcement. But for now, it was between them; just a man and a woman, who loved each other dearly.

EPILOGUE

Sitting in a closed carriage, Rachel fingered the corners of the large sheets of paper in her lap. "I can't believe I just met with Mr. John Murray about publishing my manuscript. Pray tell, how were you able to arrange a meeting with him so quickly?" she asked, awe filling her voice.

Luke's arm was draped over her shoulder, pulling her closer. "Well, I have thoroughly enjoyed reading your writings, and I wanted to support your dream." He shrugged. "I simply contacted Mr. Murray, informed him of your superb intellect, and encouraged him to read your manuscript."

She chuckled knowingly. "Did you give the publisher your intense, piercing glare?"

"I did, and it worked on *him*." His eyes reflected concern as he gazed at her. "Are you sure you don't mind using a false author name on the book as Mr. Murray recommended?"

"The world is not ready for another lady to write a book. Besides, I think the name we selected was perfect," she said wholeheartedly. "David Pearson sounds like a wise man."

"But not as wise as the hero of your story," he insisted, his eyes twinkling with humor. "After all, John was brave, charming, witty, smart, defied convention…" He winked. "Did I miss anything?"

"You forgot handsome," she murmured coyly before she kissed him on the lips.

Luke shifted in the carriage, and she took a moment to thank her husband, again, for making it possible for her book to be published.

Leaning back, she laughed merrily as he tugged her closer, deepening the kiss, feeling the surrender of her body. After all, she was more than happy to comply. Kissing her husband of only a week had become her new favorite pastime. They had been married three weeks after the banns were posted and were currently traveling back to their estate in Scotland.

The carriage jerked to a stop, and Luke leaned back, breaking their kiss. He pulled back the curtain and looked out the window. His face lit up with anticipation, and he opened the carriage door, hopping out quickly. As Rachel put her hand into his, she peered out to see a quaint cottage with a thatched roof. Stepping onto the dirt path, she looked quizzically at her husband. "Where are we?"

The cottage sat at the edge of a village and was surrounded by tall grass mingled with red poppy flowers gently blowing in the wind. Luke smiled indulgently down at her. "Trust me."

"Always," she replied, looping her arm through his.

He led her towards the door and knocked. After a few moments, he pounded on the door and was met with the same lack of response. No one was home. He sighed. "It would appear we traveled all this way for nothing."

"Who are we…"

Her words were cut off by a young lady's voice. "May I help you?"

Turning towards the girl, Rachel was surprised to see a beautiful young lady with dark brown hair, and wide, expressive green eyes. She was dressed in a simple black frock, with a lavender ribbon tied around her waist, and a wide-brimmed blue bonnet shading her face.

"Is this the home of Constable Pearson?" Luke asked.

The girl's countenance dimmed which drew attention to her tear-stained face, whose paleness contrasted with the vivid crimson of her lips. "I am sorry to be the bearer of sad tidings, but my father passed away over a week ago." She glanced mournfully over her shoulder. "I have just come from visiting my parents' graves."

"Are you Emma, by chance?" Luke pressed.

"I am," she replied. "Were you friends of my father's?"

He shook his head. "No, we were friends of your brother, David."

A genuine but weak smile graced her face. "Please, do come in." She brushed past them and opened the door, leaving it wide open. "May I offer you some refreshment? I know we have tea, but I am not sure where it was left."

"Why is that?" Rachel asked, following her into the kitchen.

"After my father died, our housekeeper left because I didn't know how I was going to pay her wages," she admitted shyly as she searched through nearly-empty drawers.

"She left you," Luke said, a little too forcefully.

Emma froze, and her eyes grew wide at his tone. After a moment, her gaze transferred to Rachel and she explained, "I do have some money, but she urged me to keep it since she already found suitable work in the village."

"My apologies for my tone," Luke expressed. "My wife has stated, on more than one occasion, that I can come across as boorish."

Emma relaxed as she continued her search. "I'm afraid I did not catch your names."

"I am Luke, and this is my wife, Rachel," he informed her, smiling, as he sat down on a wobbly, wooden chair.

"And what of your family? Do you plan to live with them?" Rachel inquired, her concerned eyes roaming the dirty kitchen.

Turning around with a jar in her hand, Emma shook her head, sadly. "I am afraid I have no other relations to speak of." She placed the jar on the table, her voice becoming strained. "I am very much alone in this world, and I must accept my fate." Blinking away her emotions, she removed her bonnet and placed it on the table. "How did you know my brother?"

As Emma put the water on the stove to heat, Rachel sat down near Luke as she explained, "David was assigned to protect me…"

Her words were stilled as the kitchen door was thrown open and a middle-aged man walked into the room, oblivious to their presence. He was reasonably good-looking and was impeccably dressed in a blue tailcoat, white waistcoat, and matching cravat. His brown hair was brushed forward, and he looked the part of an English gentleman, but something didn't seem right about him.

"Emma, there you are…" His voice trailed off when he noticed she was not alone. "And who are your guests?"

Emma shook her head and pressed her lips together. "Really, Peter," she admonished, "you can't just barge into my home."

He huffed indignantly. "I can if you are my betrothed."

"I never consented to marry you," she responded, frowning.

"We shall see," was all he said.

Luke rose, his commanding presence dominating the small room. "Are you engaged to this man?" His tone held censure.

The man advanced closer to Luke but stopped. He was wise enough not to engage her husband, but his eyes sparked with annoyance. His mouth tightened, and his words were clipped. "You do not need to concern yourself with Miss Pearson's welfare."

Luke scoffed, and turned his attention back to Emma, dismissing the man. "We were hoping to speak to you privately."

"You may speak freely in front of Peter. He was my father's solicitor," Emma stated as she walked over to a chair, her youthful innocence demonstrated by her misplaced trust of this man.

Peter grabbed a chair and repositioned it close to Emma... inappropriately close. "I am now your solicitor, dearest." His gaze was piercing, possessive.

Luke adjusted his waistcoat as he slowly sat down. "As we stated before, we were friends with David, and we owed him money, in addition to a great personal debt."

"How much money?" Peter asked, suddenly interested in the conversation.

Ignoring his question, Rachel smiled at Emma. "David was assigned to protect me when I was in Scotland..."

Emma cut her off. "You are Lady Rachel," she blurted out. She turned towards Luke, her eyes wide in amazement. "And you are Lord Downshire, or John, as my brother informed me." At their puzzled expressions, she revealed, "David always wrote me letters when he was on assignment, and he predicted you would eventually marry." She grew sad, pensive. "He considered both of you his friends."

Tears welled up in Rachel's eyes as she shared, "I also considered him a friend, but it was my fault he was killed." She swiped at the tears streaming down her face. "David tried to warn me about going down to the shoreline that night, but I was stubborn and refused to listen. I was attacked and he..." Her words hitched as a sob escaped her lips.

Leaning forward in her chair, Emma reached for her hand, her voice full of compassion. "You must not blame yourself for David's death. He had a tendency to help damsels in distress." She smiled, her eyes growing reflective. "He always looked after people, even if you ordered him not to."

Luke grinned knowingly. "It sounds as if you have firsthand experience."

Emma laughed. "Heavens, yes. My older brother was relentless in his protection of me, but over time, I grew to understand that was how he showed he loved me." Her lips tightened, and tears welled in her eyes. "Excuse me," she whimpered, "I just miss him so much."

Peter reached over and patted Emma's leg. "There, there," he said, solicitously. "You must remember, it is not proper for a lady to show emotion in public."

Rachel frowned with displeasure at Peter's inappropriate display of affection and correcting comment. She glanced over and saw Luke's eyes were narrowed and his jaw was clenched tightly. Clearly, her husband was not amused, either.

"Now about the money you owe Miss Emma," Peter prodded, eagerly.

"We do owe you £5,000, or…" Luke stopped and turned to look at his wife. His eyes implored hers, silently seeking permission. Trusting her husband, she nodded her head, and his eyes filled with love. He turned his focus back towards Emma. "Or, you can become my ward."

Huffing, Peter shook his head. "Miss Emma is sixteen years old and does not need a guardian. She is old enough to marry and begin having children."

Luke's eyes grew hard in response to Peter's words, but determination laced his features as his gaze returned to Emma. "If you become my ward, Rachel and I will grant you every luxury that we can bestow upon you. We will continue your education, clothe you in the finest gowns and prepare you for a life in high Society, if you so desire," he informed her, his voice kind, encouraging. "You will not lack for anything, including love and family."

Peter turned towards Emma. "You are a constable's daughter. The ton will never accept you. It will only lead to more heartache."

In response, Luke's firm voice drew Emma's attention. "As

my ward, you will be entitled to a dowry of £25,000, and I give you my word that you *will* be embraced by the ton, whole-heartedly."

Emma's eyes grew wide, her mouth gaped open. "I would be an heiress."

"You would be far more than just an heiress," Rachel assured her. "You would be free to make your own choices, to fall in love, and choose your own husband."

Leaning even closer to Emma, Peter's voice grew hushed, urgent. "Do not be fooled by them. He wants you for his mistress."

"How dare you make such an offensive accusation!" Luke shouted, jumping up so fast that he knocked his chair over.

Rachel put her hand on her husband's sleeve, stilling his outrage. "Emma, you must believe that we only have your best interest at heart, nothing more."

Her wide, expressive eyes showed hope as she asked, "Why would you be so generous?"

Luke picked up his chair and sat down. He reached for Rachel's hand, his eyes lingering on her face before turning back towards Emma. "Because David was my friend. He taught me how to speak to Rachel and kept my secret, which allowed me more time to woo her." He gave a half-hearted smile as his voice hitched. "He also saved my life, but more importantly, he saved my wife's life. He gave his life to give me mine. Without Rachel…" His voice trailed off as a tear rolled down his face. "To repay my debt, I vow to protect you as he would have, to ensure you are happy and cared for."

Emma's face softened, and her lips turned up into a smile. "Thank you. I would like to accept your offer and become your ward."

"No, Emma!" Peter shouted. "We are to be wed."

She shook her head in response. "No, Peter. I already told you, you are like a brother to me. I could never marry you."

"Don't do this," he urged. "I love you."

Emma shifted in her seat, her eyes guarded. "And I love you, too… as a brother."

"You will regret this, make no mistake of that," Peter assured her as he stood up. He tugged down on his waistcoat before he stormed out of the room.

Emma turned her apologetic gaze back to them. "He means well," she said, but her tone was hesitant.

Luke rose from his seat and assisted Rachel. "We are traveling back to our estate in Scotland. Would you like to accompany us, or we can send back our coach, giving you time to pack up your home?"

Emma's eyes roamed wistfully around the room. "If you are not opposed, I would like to accompany you now. I find that my loneliness makes my heart ache."

Rachel reached out and embraced Emma. Leaning back, she reminded her, "You will never be alone again. You are now a part of our family."

Emma offered a brilliant smile that lit up her face, and her eyes sparkled with renewed happiness. "Thank you," she responded appreciatively.

"It is I who should be thanking you," Luke maintained, stepping closer. "If you had refused my offer to become my ward, we would have been forced to abduct you." He shrugged, his eyes full of merriment. "It makes life easier when my ward comes along willingly."

Emma laughed as she started walking towards the door. "If you will give me a few moments, I will pack my trunks. It won't be long."

When Emma left the room, Rachel turned to face her husband. Her heart was full because she was so immensely proud of him. "Just when I thought I couldn't love you more…" Her voice trailed off as she tried to reign in her emotions.

Luke's hand cupped her right cheek. "David would have

wanted us to care for his sister and get her far away from that man."

Rachel rose on her tiptoes and kissed him. His arms came around her, and she relaxed in his embrace. "You now have a wife *and* a ward. What will your staff think of you?" she teased.

Luke's eyes turned smoldering as he gazed upon her. "I don't care what my staff thinks of me," he said, "but if I did, then they would recognize that I am a man in love."

"Are you now?" she bantered back.

He lowered his lips till they hovered over hers. "I am a man who is madly, deliriously in love with his wife."

Smiling against his lips, Rachel realized what she felt for Luke was greater than any story she could have written or told. They were both imperfect, inevitably flawed, but they had found one another, against all odds.

As Luke pressed his lips to hers, she sighed in contentment. Their love story was predictably unpredictable and had only just begun.

COMING SOON

A Deceptive
Bargain

"She had nothing left to live for... except him."

by

Laura Beers

ABOUT THE AUTHOR

Laura Beers spent most of her childhood with a nose stuck in a book, dreaming of becoming an author. She attended Brigham Young University, eventually earning a Bachelor of Science degree in Construction Management.

Many years later, and with loving encouragement from her family, Laura decided to start writing again. Besides being a full-time homemaker to her three kids, she loves waterskiing, hiking, and drinking Dr. Pepper. Currently, Laura Beers resides in South Carolina.